Ab

Being an author has
dream. It was only
during her final year
soon she wanted th
got serious about her writing, and now writes books
she wants to see in the world featuring people who look
like her. When she's not writing, she's spending time
with her husband and dogs in Cape Town, South Africa.
She admits this is a perfect life and is grateful for it.

New Zealander **Alison Roberts** has written more than
eighty romance novels for Mills & Boon. She has also
worked as a primary school teacher, a cardiology
research technician and a paramedic. Currently, she is
living her dream of living - and writing - in a gorgeous
village in the south of France.

As an Air Force officer, **Merline Lovelace** served at
bases all over the world. When she hung up her uniform
for the last time, she combined her love of adventure
with a flare for storytelling. She's now produced more
than ninety-five action-packed novels. Over twelve
million copies of her works are in print in thirty
countries. Named Oklahoma's Writer of the Year and
Female Veteran of the Year, Merline is also a recipient
of Romance Writers of America's prestigious RITA™
Award.

With Love at Christmas

THERESE BEHARRIE

ALISON ROBERTS

MERLINE LOVELACE

MILLS & BOON

First Published in Great Britain 2020
By Mills & Boon, an imprint of HarperCollins*Publishers*
1 London Bridge Street, London, SE1 9GF

WITH LOVE AT CHRISTMAS © 2020 Harlequin Books S.A.

Her Festive Flirtation © 2018 Therese Beharrie
From Venice with Love © 2013 Alison Roberts
Callie's Christmas Wish © 2016 Merline Lovelace

ISBN: 978-0-263-29825-3

MIX
Paper from
responsible sources
FSC™ C007454

This book is produced from independently certified FSC™ paper to ensure responsible forest management.

For more information visit: www.harpercollins.co.uk/green

Printed and bound in Spain
by CPI, Barcelona

HER FESTIVE FLIRTATION

THERESE BEHARRIE

For Grant, who makes every Christmas
the best day of the year.

And for my family. I love you.

CHAPTER ONE

'MA'AM, I CAN'T LET you go in there.'

'But—'

'No "buts".' The man turned back to where smoke obscured the eco-estate where Ava Keller's home was. 'There's no way you're going into that.'

Ava gritted her teeth. She hated him. Though she'd never met the man before, she hated him.

The rational voice in her head told her she was projecting. That coming home from work to find her home covered in smoke had upset her. That being upset had manifested itself in her short tone and strong emotions. Like hatred.

Yes, the rational voice said. She was definitely projecting. But then, she'd never prized rationality in stressful situations. That was why, when she'd been left at the altar a year before, she'd attended the wedding reception. She'd eaten the cake. She'd gone on her honeymoon.

Rationality wouldn't make her feel less stressed. Nor would it make her less emotional. And rationality wasn't going to save one of the only things in her life that was still important to her.

So when an idea occurred to her and the rational voice warned against it, she knew she was going to do it. And though it was a bad idea—a *terrible* one—she would do it anyway.

Heaven help her.

She turned, walked a few steps away from the wall of

men blocking the path to her house, and let out a blood-curdling scream.

They hurried towards her, and later she would think that they must have made quite a picture. Those huge, muscular men in their official uniforms—some firefighters, some police—hurrying over to her as if they were lions and she were fresh meat.

She would also later think that at least ten men hurrying over to her had been overkill. But right now she was pretending to be a damsel in distress, and she was certain that merely the *idea* of that caused men to flock.

Really, her duping them was their own fault.

And that of her excellent acting skills.

Unfortunately, being a copywriter for a cybersecurity company didn't often allow her to illustrate how dramatic she could be.

'I think… I think I just saw a *person*.' She gripped the shirt of the man closest to her. 'Right there—down the path at that bush.' Now she injected a layer of panic into her voice. 'It's so close to the fire, Sergeant. And it looked like my neighbour. An old man with no teeth.'

There was a beat when she wondered whether she'd gone too far. She *had* laid it on a little thick. Mr Kinney was barely fifty. He had all his teeth and he wasn't in danger.

To make it more believable, she let out another tiny little screech. And when the man who'd blocked her from getting near her house moved forward to comfort her she cried, 'No, no, not me. Help *him*. Help him!'

If the fire didn't do the job first, Ava knew she was going to burn in hell.

But it worked, and three of the men ran down the path-way while the others moved forward, bodies tensed, ready to help if necessary.

It was all she needed. Without a second thought for how irrational she was acting, Ava bolted up the incline of the road she'd been blocked from earlier, and didn't stop until

she was so far from the men she'd left behind she could barely see them.

Nor could she see in front of her.

When panic crept up her throat, she ignored it. Told herself to remember all those nights she'd spent unable to sleep and Zorro had comforted her. To remember that it was only when she was looking after him that she felt capable. Able. And not as if some of her personality traits—her honesty, her bluntness—meant she somehow couldn't be a partner. A *wife*.

But all thought fled from her mind as her body adjusted to its new environment. The smoke seemed to be stuck in her mouth. Clogging her lungs. Burning her eyes. She pulled off her shirt and tied it around her nose and mouth, trying to keep her eyes open.

It didn't make much difference. The smoke was so thick she could barely see her hands in front of her. And the more she tried, the more her eyes burned.

So she wasn't entirely surprised when she walked right into a wall.

The force of it stunned her. But after a moment she realised it wasn't a wall. Not unless this wall had suddenly grown hands and gripped her arms to keep her from falling.

She was pretty sure she'd walked into a human. A human *man*.

As opposed to an alien man?

Clearly the smoke was doing more damage than she'd thought.

She heard a muffled sound coming from the man. He was obviously trying to tell her something, but he was wearing a firefighter's mask and she couldn't make out a single word. She shook her head and then, deciding that this interaction was taking precious time from her rescue mission, she pushed past him.

But she'd forgotten he had his hands on her arms, and they tightened on her before she could move.

'What are you *doing*?' the man asked now, wrenching off his mask.

She still couldn't see him. Which, she thought, was probably a good thing, since his voice didn't indicate that he felt any positive emotion towards her.

'I have to get to my house.'

'Ma'am, this area has been evacuated. The fire could reach us at any moment.'

'So why aren't you out there, making sure that it doesn't?'

'Are you serious?' The disbelief in his tone made his voice sound familiar. 'You *have* to leave, ma'am. Your property is not as important as your life. Or mine.'

'It isn't about my *property*,' she said, her voice hoarse from smoke and desperation. 'My cat is in there. I have to… I have to save him.'

Something pulsed in the air after she'd finished talking, and she could have sworn she'd heard him curse.

'Where's your house?'

Stunned, she took a moment to respond. 'It's not far from here. I can show you.'

'No. Just tell me the number and I'll make sure I find the damn cat.'

'Seventeen.' She hesitated when he handed her his mask and turned away. 'Wait! Don't *you* need this?'

'Yes,' he ground out. 'But you're going to need it more. Just put it on and go back to where you came from. I'll find you.'

It was a few seconds before she realised he wasn't there any more.

'Check under the bed!' she shouted at her loudest, and then she put the mask on and retraced her steps back towards the men—no easy feat with the smoke even thicker now.

She was immediately swarmed, but she ignored them—ignored the complaints and chastisement—and kept her eyes on the clouds of smoke in front of her.

She only realised she hadn't taken off the mask when someone gently removed it from her. A paramedic, she

thought, as it was replaced by an oxygen mask and she was asked to breathe in and out as the woman listened to her heartbeat before gently checking her body for burns.

Rationality won out now. It reminded Ava that she'd put her life in danger. That she'd put someone else's life in danger, too. And, even though the thought of losing Zorro sent pangs of pain through her body, she couldn't justify that.

So when the paramedic told her she needed to sit down, to drink some water, to get her heart-rate down, she obeyed, not voicing any of the protests screaming through her head.

A cat. *A freaking cat.*

That was what he was risking his life for. That was what he was abandoning all the rules of his training for. He could see the headlines now: *Volunteer firefighter Noah Giles dies trying to save a cat.* Smoke blurred his eyes, grated in his throat, his lungs, but somehow he made it to number seventeen. Smoke shrouded it, much as it did the other houses on the estate. When he'd been making his final rounds, checking that humans and pets had been evacuated, he hadn't expected to find anyone.

They'd had the entire day to evacuate the area, and it had been erring on the side of caution, really, just in case the veld fire should spread.

Except now he wasn't being cautious, he thought, coughing as he pushed open the door—in any other circumstance, he'd probably be annoyed that it had been left unlocked— and leaned against the wall. His head felt light, and it was pure determination that pushed him forward.

Determination spurred on by the emotion in the woman's voice when she'd told him about the cat. It had been familiar, somehow, and had hit him in a place he hadn't known existed. As if he cared that someone loved a cat as much as this woman loved hers.

And since he was risking his life for this cat, clearly he *did* care.

The damn cat had better be the most intelligent cat in the

entire world, he thought. He'd be pretty annoyed if he died for any other kind. Just before Christmas, too, when he was planning to tell his father that after seven years of restlessness he was finally ready to put down some roots.

But only in terms of where you live.

He grunted. Then chose to ignore the unhelpful voice in his head and focused on checking the entire house systematically. Being inside protected him from the smoke somewhat, but he knew he couldn't stick around for long.

When he got to the bedroom, something told him to look under the bed. Beady eyes stared back at him when he did so, and air gushed from his lungs. How could he be this relieved at finding a pet that wasn't even his own? He shook his head, refusing to think about it, and then belly-crawled under the bed and gently pulled the cat into his arms.

It gave a low *meow*—a warning, he thought—but he didn't pay much attention to it. His goal now was to get back to safety.

He was already back at the front door before he realised he couldn't let the cat go out into the smoke. And shortly afterwards he realised the same thing about himself.

He knew that the cat—which was already wriggling in his arms—would run away the second he put him down. And so, taking a deep breath—and once again rethinking all his decisions in life—Noah stuffed the cat inside his open jacket before buttoning it up.

There was some struggling—and a sharp pain as the cat's claws stuck into his belly—but eventually the cat stilled. He looked around for something he could use to cover his face before he braved the smoke again, but instead his eyes rested on a picture that stood on the mantelpiece. A picture of all the people he'd cared about growing up.

And among all their faces, his own.

If she'd ever wanted to discover how to upset a paramedic, she'd found out that evening.

'You *have* to go to the hospital.'

'No.'

'Ma'am—' The woman cut herself off and hissed out a breath. 'Look, your heart rate is still high, and one of the things that can happen with smoke inhalation is—'

'Cardiac arrest. Yeah, I know. I watched that TV show, too.'

'It's not from a *show*.' The paramedic wasn't even trying to hide her annoyance now. 'I'm a medical professional and I know that—'

Ava didn't hear the rest of the woman's speech. She'd stopped listening the moment she saw a man emerge from the smoke. Ignoring the now protesting woman, she stood and pushed forward.

And then stopped when she saw who the man was.

'Noah?'

She watched as he tossed aside a cloth—no, not a cloth; the throw that had once been over her couch—and then bend over and brace himself on his knees.

'Hey, paramedic lady!' Ava said, turning around in panic. But the woman was way ahead of her, and brushed past Ava with the oxygen mask and tank Ava had been using minutes before.

Just as they had with her, the men rallied around Noah. Though this time, of course, it was because Noah was their colleague, and not some foolish woman who'd run into the line of fire—literally—to save a cat.

She watched helplessly as they guided Noah towards the ambulance, and then, when they were there, tried to get him out of his suit. But he shook his head and made eye contact with her.

It jolted her heart. Had the poor thing sprinting as if it were in a life-and-death race it *had* to win.

So, nothing's changed in the seven years since you've seen him, then?

Clearing her throat—her mind—she took a step forward, her legs shaking though her strides were steady.

When she reached him, he pulled the oxygen mask from

his face, coughed, and then said, 'Are we going to have to talk about why you decided to run into a fire to rescue a cat, Avalanche?'

His words were said with a crooked half-smile, and then he began to unbutton the jacket she'd only just noticed was moving to reveal a squirming Zorro.

There had been a pause before she'd even realised it was her cat. And that pause came because she'd been distracted by the muscular chest under the white vest Noah had just uncovered.

No, she thought. It had been *years* since she'd seen Noah. *Years* since she'd even thought about the silly crush she'd had on her brother's best friend. Or about the kisses they'd once shared.

There was no way any remnants of that crush were still there. She'd been in a five-year relationship since then. She'd almost got married.

But you didn't *get married*, a voice in her head said enticingly.

So clearly, there *was* a way.

CHAPTER TWO

AVA REACHED OVER and pulled the cat into her arms. Noah noted the squirming stopped immediately. *Go figure.*

'No one calls me Avalanche any more.'

It was exactly the kind of thing he'd expected her to say. And even though he didn't know what to do about the nostalgia surging in his chest, he smiled.

'You used to love it.'

'I *never* loved it.'

'Why would I keep calling you that if you didn't love it?'

'I've asked myself that question for most of my life.'

He smirked. Then heard the next words come out of his mouth before he could stop them. 'I've missed you, Avalanche.'

Her eyes softened, and she reached out and placed the oxygen mask back over his nose and mouth. 'It's nice to see you, too, Noah—'

Her voice broke and he frowned, pulling the mask away again.

'Has someone checked you out?'

'I'm fine.'

'I told her she needed to go to the hospital,' said the paramedic he hadn't even realised was still there. 'But she doesn't believe me.'

'Why? What's wrong?'

'Nothing,' Ava said with a roll of her eyes. 'I'm fine.'

'Elevated heart rate,' the paramedic told him.

'She's at risk for cardiac arrest?'

'I am a healthy twenty-five-year-old,' Ava interrupted as the paramedic was about to give an answer. 'I have a healthy heart. In fact, I had a check-up at the doctor's last week and she confirmed it.'

Twenty-five. The last time he'd seen her she'd been eighteen. A kid, really. *Not that that stopped you from treating her like a woman.*

He clenched his jaw. Told himself to ignore the unwelcome voice in his head. But when his eyes moved over her—when they told him she was very much a woman now—the memories that voice evoked became a hell of a lot harder to ignore.

He shook his head. 'Smoke inhalation is dangerous.'

'Which is why *you* should be going to the hospital and not me. I was in there a fraction of the time you were.'

'But my heart rate is okay.' The paramedic nodded when he looked over, and he gave Ava a winning smile. 'See?'

'Smoke inhalation is dangerous,' she replied thinly, with a smile of her own, though hers was remarkably more fake than his.

It made nostalgia pulse again, but memories of the way things had been before he'd left made him wonder if nostalgia was really what he was feeling.

But she was right about the smoke inhalation, and because of it—and because he knew his team wouldn't let him work unless he got checked out—he agreed.

'Fine. But if I'm going, you're going, too.'

She opened her mouth, but he shot her a look and she nodded.

'Okay. But we're stopping at the veterinary hospital first. I need to make sure Zorro's okay.'

The fierceness of her voice softened as she said the cat's name, and he watched as she pressed a kiss into its fur. It stumped him—one, that she could show more affection to a cat than she could to a man she'd basically grown up with and, two, that she could show affection to *that* cat.

It was the ugliest cat he'd ever seen.

He assumed Ava had named him Zorro because of the black, almost mask-like patches on his face. And he supposed in some way those patches *were* cute. But he couldn't say the same for the rest of the cat's body. The orange, brown and white splotches looked as if the cat was the result of a scientific experiment gone wrong.

He'd never really been one for cats, and perhaps he was just biased against them. But, he thought, eyeing the cat again, he didn't think so.

He would never have said the cat was ugly as he looked at Ava, though. Her brown eyes were filled with emotion— love, affection, he couldn't quite tell—and her tall frame had relaxed.

And he realised that if he wanted her to get checked out he was going to have to agree to take the ugly cat to the veterinary hospital.

'He's sitting in the back.'

Five hours later they'd both been checked out. Noah had been put on oxygen for a portion of that time, while they ran tests, and when he'd met Ava in the waiting room later she'd told him the same thing had happened with her.

Though the test results had shown nothing alarming, they'd been given strict instructions to rest, and to return if any potentially dangerous symptoms emerged.

'You didn't have to wait for me,' Noah told her as she got up and joined him.

'I know. But I… I wanted to know that you were okay.' She ran a hand over the curls at the top of her head. 'I'm pretty sure Jaden would kill me if I were responsible for the death of his best man.'

'That's all I am to you?' he teased, though it came out a little more seriously than he'd intended.

'No, of course not.' She paused. 'You're also my only way to call the vet and ask about Zorro. My phone's died.'

He laughed, and it turned into a cough.

'You're sure you're okay?'

'Fine.' He waved a hand. 'Just normal after-effects.'

She bit her lip. 'I really am sorry. I didn't mean for you to get dragged into this.'

'I'm glad I was the one who *did* get dragged into it,' he retorted. 'At least I have training.'

'Ah, yes—one of the thousands of things you can do when you have family money.'

He winced. 'How did you go from apologising to insulting me?'

She grinned, and his mind scrambled to figure out why his body was responding. He'd given himself a stern talking-to when he'd left all those years ago. Hadn't spoken to Ava since then. His body had no business reacting to her smile.

'It's one of my unique talents.'

What are the others?

Now his mind froze, and when Ava didn't say anything else, he wondered whether he'd said it out loud. But her expression didn't change, and he put down the strange thought to the after-effects of inhaling smoke. There could be no other explanation.

Sure, keep telling yourself that.

'So, can I call the vet?' she asked after a moment.

He blinked, then handed her his phone and took the seat she'd vacated as she made the call.

He watched as she spoke to the vet. Watched as she set a hand on her hip and then lifted it, toying with her curls again. She'd cut her hair into a tapered style that somehow made the oval shape of her face seem both classic and modern.

He supposed those terms would work to describe her entire appearance. He'd always thought her beautiful—with an innocent kind of beauty that was much too pure for him—but with the haircut, and the clothes she wore that suited that cut, she *was* an enticing mix of classic and modern that made him want—

He stopped himself. Frowned at the direction of his thoughts. He couldn't think of his best friend's kid sister as

enticing. He couldn't think about wanting anything when it came to her.

She was just Ava. Little Avalanche. The girl who'd run in circles around him just for the fun of it when she was six. Who'd snorted if she laughed hard enough up until she was fourteen. Who'd asked him to be her first kiss so she could practise, and who'd eagerly responded when he'd kissed her a second time—

Nope. *No.* That line of thinking was going to get him nowhere.

But when she turned and smiled at him—and his body yearned to get *somewhere*—he realised that Jaden's wedding was going to be more complicated than he'd expected.

CHAPTER THREE

HE HADN'T CHANGED one bit.

No, Ava thought as Noah stood, her eyes flitting over him. He *had* changed. Though she now remembered how greedily she'd taken in his muscles earlier, she'd forgotten about them between then and now.

Possibly because he was wearing one of his colleague's ill-fitting T-shirts.

Probably because she'd been too distracted by his face.

It had happened before, too many times to count. And Ava didn't even blame herself for it. How could she? Objectively, Noah had the prettiest face she'd ever seen. And though the word didn't seem to fit with the rest of him—not any more, since the strong, muscular body he had now was more rugged than the lithe one he'd had when they were younger—she couldn't deny the perfect lines and angles of his face *were* pretty.

But just because she couldn't blame herself for it didn't mean she didn't find it annoying. It was. Because if he hadn't been so pretty she might not have found herself *still* having this absurd crush. *Years* later.

And then he walked towards her, rubbed a hand down her arm, and said something in that deliciously deep voice of his. And the voice in her head that had called her a liar when she'd put her crush down to just his looks laughed and laughed.

Damn it.

'Avalanche?'

'Hmm?' She shook her head. 'Oh. You said something?'
If only she could remember what. 'Yes.'

'Yes?' His hand dropped. 'What do you mean, *yes*?'

Double damn it. Clearly her guess had been wrong.

'I mean, yes—' She exhaled sharply when she couldn't
think of an appropriate cover-up. 'Yes, I have no idea what
you said and my attempt at hiding it has failed miserably.'

He stared at her, and then he laughed. 'Clearly you're
the same old Ava. Honest even when it doesn't benefit you.'

*'Would it kill you to not be so blunt? No one needs you
to be this honest.'*

'Yes, that's me,' she said brightly, hoping it would ban-
ish the darkness of Milo's voice in her head. The memories
that voice inevitably evoked. The pretence of the rest of her
wedding day. The weeks after, when she'd looked in the mir-
ror and asked herself why she couldn't be different. Better.
Easier. 'Would you repeat what you said?'

'I asked where you'll be staying tonight?'

'Jaden's,' she said automatically. But then she shook her
head. 'No, Jaden isn't here. He and Leela are staying over
at the vineyard their wedding is going to be at. They want a
better idea of what their wedding will feel like.' She rolled
her eyes. 'As if it will change anything. The wedding's two
weeks away. What are they going to do if it doesn't "feel"
right?' She sighed. 'I guess I'll be staying at a hotel.'

'Why not your mom and dad's?'

'They're with Jaden and Leela at the wedding venue.'

'Sounds horrific.'

'Yes,' she agreed with a small smile. 'I can't imagine any-
thing worse than a wedding at Christmastime.'

She knew that because *her* wedding had been at
Christmastime. And not only had her day been spoiled, but
her entire festive season. She was still not prepared to spend
the first anniversary of her being jilted at another wedding.
With the same guests. And the same whispers.

But she had no choice. Her brother was getting married.

'Of course, the fact that this isn't exactly a romantic week-

end for Jaden and Leela sucks, too. My parents and Leela's parents are there, so Jaden and Leela probably had to get separate bedrooms.'

It hadn't occurred to her before, but it amused her now.

'Oh, no,' Noah said with a frown. 'Your parents can't think—?' He broke off when she gave him a look. 'Apparently they can.'

'Unfortunately, my parents can and will believe whatever they want of their children.'

Like the way they thought the collapse of Ava's wedding had been because of Milo's faults and not Ava's. And how they still didn't see anything wrong with how grumpy she was—or wonder how much easier she could have been—even after a broken engagement.

'Anyway,' she continued, 'no one's there. And my access to all those places are locked in the drawer next to my bed.' She closed her eyes briefly. 'So, yes, a hotel.'

'What about Zorro?'

She lifted a brow. 'Are you still looking out for him?'

'I'm looking out for *you*.'

She thought she saw him hesitate before he continued.

'You're my best friend's sister. There's an unspoken moral code that requires me to help you when your brother can't.'

'I'd like to think that moral code comes from the fact that you and I were friends once, too,' she said slowly. 'It doesn't matter anyway,' she added, when the thought had her stomach twisting. 'The vet wants to keep Zorro overnight. He wants to make sure he's okay.'

'Are you okay with that?'

'Of course I am.'

'Sure,' he said easily. 'So there's no part of you that's worried about him?'

When her spoken agreement got caught by the emotion in her throat, she sighed. 'There's a *big* part of me that's worried about him. But he's in the best place to make sure he's okay.'

He studied her. 'He'll be okay,' he said quietly, and then, as if he understood that she wouldn't be able to hold back

the tears if they kept on talking about it, he said, 'You should stay with me.'

She stared him. 'What?'

'You should stay with me,' he said again. 'At my place.'

'What place? Your dad's?'

'I'm a big boy, Ava,' he said dryly. 'I have a place of my own.'

'I meant,' she said deliberately, when his words sent thrills down her spine, 'that you've been away for seven years. How do you have a place of your own?'

'I invested in property.'

'Of course you did,' she muttered. 'No, thanks, Noah. I think I'll just get a hotel room.'

'You don't know how long it'll be before you'll be able to go home.' He paused. 'You might have to spend a couple of nights there.'

'I'll survive.'

'What about Zorro?'

She narrowed her eyes. 'I told you—'

'Yes, he's staying at the vet's tonight. But what happens tomorrow, when they call you to tell you he's fine? That he can come home?'

'I'm sure I'll be back in my own house by then.'

'But what if you're not?' He waited a beat. 'I have a pet-friendly home.'

'Noah—'

'Ava.'

Their gazes locked. Her brain said, *No, Ava*; her body said, *Yes, please*. The juxtaposition fluttered on her skin, and she blamed her gooseflesh on that and not on how sexy and serious Noah's eyes looked. Or on the memory of how that was exactly how they'd looked before he'd kissed her all those years ago...

'No, Noah.'

She said it with a sigh of regret. She hoped he wouldn't hear that, but her filter wasn't working properly. She was too tired. Her throat ached. Her lungs pained. Her body re-

minded her that she'd done a full day of work before she'd arrived home to find the place full of smoke. Not to mention the swirling in her head at the unwelcome feelings and memories being in Noah's presence evoked.

'I've already put you out way too much tonight. I'm the reason you're here. You should go home by yourself—' Had she *really* just said that? '—and get some rest. Besides, I have to call my family now, before they hear about the evacuation, freak out and start driving back here in the middle of the night. And I do *not* want to tell them—specifically, Jaden—that I'm staying at your place tonight.'

'Ava...' he said softly, and walked closer to her.

Something pressed into the backs of her legs, and she realised it was one of the seats in the waiting room. Because when he'd moved closer to her she'd moved back.

Stay.

She straightened. 'Noah—'

'Let me speak,' he interrupted, and the tone of his voice— seductive, commanding—silenced her. 'It's been a difficult night. We're both exhausted, and it's going to take more energy than either of us has to find you a hotel. I'm not leaving you alone to arrange all this,' he said when she opened her mouth. 'And I'm not even mentioning clean clothes, proper toiletries, a warm meal. Stay with me.'

'What do I tell my family?'

'Whatever you like. It's the easiest option,' he said with a smile, as if he knew she was already starting to formulate the lie she was going to tell them. 'You'd do the same thing for me, Ava. We're family, too.'

She nearly laughed. 'I haven't seen you in seven years, Noah.'

'Doesn't change anything.' He paused. 'I've only seen Jaden three times during those seven years. All three times it was because he'd come to see me. Because he considered me to be family.'

'You're his best friend.'

'Family,' he said firmly. 'Friends come and go. And I

went. If we weren't family I wouldn't be back here at Christmas, preparing to be best man at your brother's wedding.'

'You're…stubborn,' she said, when defeat washed over her.

'I like to think of it as persistent.'

'Well, you better hope persistence will help us if Jaden ever discovers the truth about the lie I'm about to tell him and our parents.'

'Noah, you know I appreciate you offering me a place to stay, but—' Ava broke off, wondering how to tell him. But then she remembered that he already knew she was honest. 'But it looks like Father Christmas and the elves threw up in here.'

Noah chuckled. 'That's not a bad description, actually.'

He stood next to her and she held her breath, as if somehow it would make her less aware of him.

'I had a company come in and decorate for Christmas before I got here. They got a bit…carried away.'

She took in the tinsel that hung on every flat surface, the Christmas stockings that accompanied it. The Christmas lights that were draped around pieces of furniture that should not have lights around them. And, of course, the gigantic Christmas tree next to the fireplace.

'I think that's an understatement.'

'Probably.'

He took the handbag and coat that been draped over her shoulder and arm respectively, and hung them on a coat rack she hadn't noticed.

'I've been meaning to do something to make it less… *this*—' he nodded his head at the decorations '—but I haven't had the time.'

'Christmas season is fire season in Cape Town.'

'Yeah. And this season's been particularly bad. Hence the fact that I—a mere volunteer—have been fighting fires for pretty much the entire two weeks since I've been here.'

She took a seat at the counter in his kitchen, accepting

the glass of water he offered her. 'Is that why I didn't even know you were back here?'

'I told Jaden. It must have slipped his mind.'

'Must have,' she said softly.

But she didn't think that was it. Jaden hadn't been entirely forthcoming with her since he and his fiancée had announced that their wedding would be at the same time of year hers had been, almost one year later to the day. In fact, he was avoiding her. More so since Leela had asked her to be a bridesmaid.

So she would put down Jaden's neglect in telling her Noah was back to that, and not to the fact that he hadn't wanted her to know. Things had moved on since Jaden had caught them kissing that one time. It probably had nothing to do with the anger he'd felt towards both of them back then.

Probably.

'You okay?'

She looked up to see Noah's eyes steady on her. 'Perfect. This place is amazing.'

She looked around at the light green walls, the large windows that offered an incredible view of the mountains and the hills, the stone-coloured furniture. She took in the marble countertops, the sleek, top-of-the-line appliances, the white and yellow palette that brightened the kitchen.

And then her eyes rested on the sexy man who looked so at home in all of it. And although her heart did unwanted cartwheels in her chest, she forced calm into her voice.

'I mean, what I can actually see underneath all this tinsel is amazing.'

'Oh, ha-ha.'

She grinned. 'So, how about you show me to the shower, Mr Festive?'

CHAPTER FOUR

WHEN HE'D STUDIED photography after school it had been because he'd had a passion for it. He'd enjoyed the challenge of seeing things in new ways. In ways others didn't. He'd created a website to show off his work, and when he'd received that first enquiry to use one of his pictures he'd realised he could use his passion to make money.

Soon his photos had garnered more attention. And then a photo editor for a popular nature magazine had reached out to him about a job in Namibia. And suddenly he'd realised he could use his passion to give in to his wanderlust.

He supposed his surname had given him a push that most twenty-year-olds didn't get. The Giles name was still synonymous with the media empire his great-great-uncle had created. The empire that had been passed down to his grandfather, when his great-great-uncle had died childless, and then down to his father.

Having an empire and money behind him had meant he could take only the jobs that interested him. That he'd been able to use his skill and passion for jobs that *meant* something to the world. That he'd been able to use the money he didn't need to invest in properties back home in South Africa and wherever else his heart desired.

All while avoiding the pitfalls of settling down. The trap he'd seen his father fall into over and over again since his mother had died. But he couldn't deny that it felt good to

have a place of his own. Not somewhere he just stayed, but somewhere he *lived*.

He'd only been back in Cape Town for a fortnight, but it was a source of pride for him. And never more than at this moment, as he showed Ava to his spare bedroom.

When she'd disappeared into the bathroom he went to his own room and put some of the spare clothing he had there in hers. And then he went back to the kitchen, to start on the meal he'd promised her. Which, he thought even before he reached the kitchen, was a stupid idea. On his best days he could manage to fry an egg. And it would usually end up deformed. Edible, but deformed.

It would definitely not be the kind of warm meal he'd promised Ava, so he called the twenty-four-hour deli up the road. He was almost out through the door to go and fetch the food, too, before he realised he looked like crap. He'd changed out of his firefighter's uniform before going to the hospital, but he was still sweaty and grimy. And fairly certain he would not have wanted to meet himself, let alone hand over food to someone looking like he did at that moment.

He went to his room, threw off his clothes and headed to the shower. He heaved a sigh when the water hit his body. It kneaded muscles he hadn't realised were tight and painful. It also reminded him that he'd stuffed a cat into his jacket and the cat had *not* appreciated it.

He washed his hair, his body and then, feeling faintly human again, put on clean clothes. But before he put on his top he realised he should probably put something on the scratches on his stomach. They were deeper than he'd first realised. So he grabbed his top, heading to the kitchen where he kept the first-aid kit.

'I thought they fixed everything at the hospital.'

He was halfway through putting salve on the scratches when she spoke. He glanced back, and his throat dried when he saw her in his clothes.

They were too big for her, but they looked better on her than they ever had on him.

'Uh...they did. But they also took me at my word when I told them I had no external injuries. I forgot about these.'

She walked around the counter and he got a whiff of the fruity scent of the shower gel he'd put in his spare bathroom. It smelled a hell of a lot sexier on her than it did in the bottle.

Oh, boy.

'Which external injuries?' she said, and then, though he tried to angle his body away from her, she sucked in her breath. 'Oh, crap,' she said on an exhale. 'Did Zorro do this to you?'

'No,' he said dryly, struggling for normality. 'It was some other cat I put next to my stomach.'

'I'm sorry,' she said, and then she took the salve from him and began to smear it gently on his scratches. He felt his torso tremble—saw it, too, though he tried to ignore it—and hoped Ava wouldn't notice.

'I'm sorry,' she said again. 'Is it painful? It's a lot more enthusiastic than I'd expect from Zorro.'

'It's fine.' He gritted his teeth as her hand moved lower, down to the scratches near the waistband of his pants.

'Clearly it isn't.'

Her touch was still light, still gentle, but when she moved lower still he grabbed her wrist.

'It's fine, Ava.'

The words were said in a harsher voice than he'd intended, and her eyes widened. But that was better than having her move any lower and having his body respond in an unpredictable way—or a very predictable way. He was only just clinging to his control as it was.

'I'm—I'm sorry.'

'Don't be.'

He was still holding on to her hand, but he softened his voice. And then she looked at him and his world tilted.

Uh-oh.

What the hell was she *doing*?

She'd acted without thinking. Or she *had* been thinking,

but not about how it would feel to be touching Noah's bare torso. No, she'd been thinking about how her cat had hurt him. How her cat had hurt him because of *her*. Because Noah had gone back to save Zorro so she wouldn't have to.

But she wasn't thinking about that now either.

In fact, she couldn't be sure that she was thinking at all. Because now she was caught in Noah's gaze when she was pretty sure she shouldn't be. He was so close she could see the grey flecks in his blue eyes. She could see the emotions there, too.

The caution. The interest. The *desire.*

It had her remembering that he still had her wrist in his hand. And that realisation sent a heady heat slithering from the contact, up and around her arm, settling much too close to her chest. To her heart.

Her other hand was still braced on the lower half of his body. Much too close to his—

'Um…' she said, pulling her hands from his body and stepping back. 'It's probably okay now.'

'Yeah,' he replied in a hoarse voice. He cleared his throat. 'It was fine before you came in.'

'Of course.'

There was an awkward beat of silence, but Ava took solace in the fact that it came from both of them. She hadn't been the only one acting stupidly. She hadn't been the only one affected.

But thinking about it like that didn't comfort her as much as she'd hoped.

'Could you pass me my top?' Noah asked after a few moments.

'Yeah, sure.' She paused. 'Where is it?'

'Behind you.'

When she turned back to hand it to him there was a slight smile on his face.

'What's so funny?'

'Nothing,' he said, pulling on his top.

Disappointment sailed through her as she said goodbye to his abs.

'I was just thinking it's going to be an interesting wedding.'

'That's one way to put it.'

'You don't think so?'

'I think that I need to get through it in any way that I can. Which,' she said, considering, 'might involve alcohol.'

'Ah. You're old enough to drink now, aren't you?'

She cocked an eyebrow. 'You say that as if *you* weren't the one who handed me my first beer.'

His smile widened. 'See—interesting.'

'You and I have *very* different definitions of that,' she replied, and walked back around the counter. Her breath came out a little more easily now that there was space between them.

'Probably. But I think it might have the same results.'

Which was precisely what she was worried about. Because after the short, but very eye-opening interaction they'd just had, she was beginning to think her crush was no longer a secret.

Or perhaps she was more concerned that this unexpected flare-up of her crush was no longer a secret. Because if she'd managed to keep it secret after she'd asked him to kiss her for the *first* time, she certainly hadn't after she'd thrown herself into their second kiss.

But in the seven years since they'd last seen one another—years during which she hadn't even *heard* from him—she had managed to hide her feelings. And if what had just happened between them meant that Noah shared those feelings—

Noah? Sharing her feelings?

She nearly laughed aloud at the ludicrousness of it. She'd always known the reason he'd kissed her the first time had been out of pity. And the second kiss had just happened because he'd been heartbroken and hadn't known *what* he was feeling.

Anything they'd shared was in her imagination. Back then

and now. No one wanted Ava. No one wanted someone who spoke before she thought. Who was prickly for most of the time and defensive for the rest.

Just because Milo said it doesn't make it true.

But it does, she corrected the voice in her head.

Milo hadn't wanted to marry her after being with her for five years. He was the best person to know the truth. And if he hadn't wanted her Noah sure as hell wouldn't either.

The sooner she realised that, the better.

He was back from the deli in less than fifteen minutes. Ava had graciously allowed him to leave without commenting on the fact that he was buying their food. But maybe it wasn't grace. Maybe she just needed space to deal with what had happened between them, just as he had.

It was a natural reaction to being around a beautiful woman, he'd told himself on the way to the deli. He hadn't dated in so long he couldn't remember. His body had just been reminding him that he had needs; his mind just responding as any person who had needs would.

But when he returned and saw Ava sitting on his balcony, staring out over the mountains visible to most residents of Somerset West, he faltered. Had she looked this forlorn before? This defenceless?

Now she seemed nothing like the spitfire who had tried to save her cat from a blaze and everything like that little girl he'd once saved from being bullied. And when his heart turned in his chest and his arms ached to pull her into his arms, Noah worried that his reaction to her earlier hadn't just been natural. That it had been...*more*.

It didn't help that when her eyes met his—brown and steady—he instinctively knew she *wasn't* that little girl who'd needed saving. Her gaze wasn't as innocent, as trusting, as that little girl's had been. It was weary, cautious—as if she were ready to defend herself at any moment.

'This place is just as beautiful on the outside as it is on the inside,' she said into the silence.

Grateful for the distraction—his thoughts bothered him more than he'd thought they should—he nodded. 'This particular view sealed the deal for me.'

'I can imagine.' She pushed out from the table she'd been sitting at. 'I'd love to enjoy it some more, but I'm hungry. Like, *really* hungry. What do you have in there?'

He swung the deli bags out of her reach when she tried to peek inside them, and thought about how similar this was to how they'd been before he'd left. How similar it was to how *she'd* been before. And how it didn't make him feel like he needed to protect her.

'You'll find out when I serve it.'

'Spoilsport.' She followed him to the kitchen. 'Can I help?'

'No.'

'Excuse me?'

He smiled at the disbelief in her voice, and then took his time removing the takeaway dishes from the plastic bag and placing them on the kitchen counter.

When he saw her hovering, he said, 'Have a seat.'

'You're really refusing my help?'

'Yes.' He opened his fridge, showing her different drinks one by one until she eventually nodded at the fruit juice he took out. 'I didn't ask you here so you could help me cook, Ava.'

'I think you're using the word *cook* wrong,' she commented dryly, and then took the glass he offered her and went to the couch.

He could almost see her body sag into its softness. He was glad he'd refused her help.

'You know, the last time I was at your house—and this was when you still lived with your father—you didn't know what "cook" meant then either. I think you gave me and Jaden leftovers from the night before.'

'How do you know I didn't cook the night before?'

'Because it was delicious.' She smiled brightly at the look he gave her. 'And because your father's made me a few more

of those pasta dishes since you left and it was definitely not *your* cooking.'

His hands paused. 'You've seen my father since I've been away?'

He saw her cheeks pinken. 'Yeah... I mean, occasionally...' She cleared her throat. 'I've been helping him with some stuff. We're...friends.'

The pink turned into a deep red, and if Noah hadn't been so perplexed by the whole thing—if his heart hadn't been racing in his chest—he'd have found it charming.

'So, just to check that I've heard you correctly,' he said slowly, when his brain refused to process what she'd told him, 'you say you're *friends* with my father?'

'Don't make it sound so outlandish, Noah,' she said with a roll of her eyes. Her embarrassment seemed to have worn off. 'Your father is incredibly interesting. And he's young for his age. I can barely tell he's in his sixties.' She sipped her juice. 'And, while we're at it, I might as well tell you that by "occasionally" I actually mean at least every two weeks. More often if my schedule—and his—can manage it.' She lifted her shoulders at the look on his face. 'We enjoy each other's company, Noah. There's nothing wrong with that.'

All the blood seemed to drain from his body.

'Ava,' he said, his voice strangled. 'Are you trying... Are you trying to tell me that you're in a relationship with my father?'

CHAPTER FIVE

AVA STARED AT him for what felt like for ever. And then she choked back a laugh and used the opportunity.

'I'm sorry, Noah,' she said solemnly. 'We didn't want you to find out this way.'

His jaw dropped, and it took every bit of her self-control not to show her enjoyment.

'But...but...how? *Why?*'

'I don't think I have to explain *how*,' she said matter-of-factly. Man, she was really getting to use her acting skills today. 'I mean, I know for a fact that *you* know how to kiss. And, sure, there's some other stuff which I'd be happy to—'

'Ava.'

His voice had taken on a quality Ava had never heard before.

'Please do *not* allude to your sex life with my father.'

She bit her lip so hard she was afraid she'd draw blood. 'We're all adults, Noah.'

'No, we're not. You're still a *kid*.'

He was angry now, and Ava tried not to let him thinking of her as a kid bother her.

'You've been gone for a long time, Noah. I'm not a kid any more.'

'My father,' he repeated in a daze. 'My *father*.'

'Yes.' She paused. 'You asked me why earlier. I've already told you some of it. He's interesting. And kind. And he's got such a sweet heart. And an impressive—'

'Do *not* finish that sentence.'

'Why not?' she asked innocently. 'I was only going to say he has an impressive...' she dragged out the pause for as long as she could '...personality.'

He stared at her. 'You've got to be kidding me.'

She contemplated whether she should just say yes, she *was* kidding him. But there was one more thing she wanted to say first...

'You know, Noah, you not being at home has been really hard on your father. And, as your possible stepmother, I wanted—'

'Ava!' he barked, his expression stricken.

And, because she'd done what she wanted to, she grinned at him. 'You are *such* a sucker, Giles.'

There was a long silence before his features relaxed. Only slightly though, she noted.

'You were joking.'

'I was.'

Another stretch of silence. 'What made you think that joke would be *funny*?'

She laughed. 'The entire time I kept it going?'

She laughed harder when he threw the empty juice bottle at her, and she caught it triumphantly.

'You're going to have to try better than that.'

'Yeah, well, let me first get over the heart attack I've just had.'

She chuckled to herself as he prepared their food, still muttering, but when he brought over her plate—chicken, a portion of lasagne, potato salad, coleslaw—she gaped.

'Who do you think you're feeding? The South African army?'

'You said you were hungry.'

'Yeah, but I meant for a normal human-sized person.' She dug into the meal anyway, almost hearing the food echo as it dropped into her empty stomach. 'Thank you,' she said gratefully.

'Yeah, no problem.'

A companionable silence fell over them as they ate, and for the first time Ava realised how tired—and hungry—Noah must be. She saw the dark tint under his eyes, the slight creases around them.

'You should go to bed,' she said softly. 'You look exhausted.'

'Thanks.'

He gave her a small smile that had her heart flipping over.

'You don't look too great yourself.'

'Ah, I've missed this insult-for-insult thing we've always had.'

'Hmm...' he said, non-committal, and took another bite of lasagne, watching her all the time.

She refused to shift in her seat. Refused to look away. Even though she desperately wanted to do both. Tension ticked up.

'You didn't say it before,' he said after he'd swallowed.

'What?'

'That you missed me.'

'What do you mean?' Now she *did* shift. 'It's not just something you say when you see someone after a long time.'

'It's *exactly* the kind of thing you say when you see someone after a long time.'

'Yes, well...'

She left it at that, unsure of what else to say. The conversation was wading into dangerous waters and she, for one, had no interest in swimming. She just wanted to stand safely in the sand and frolic on the beach. She just wanted to feel the sun on her skin and *maybe* put her toes in the water.

But swimming held no appeal to her.

'Is it because—'

'Noah,' she interrupted with a half-smile. 'We've been through enough today. I think we should probably leave this conversation for another time.'

He studied her, and again she refused to let him see how uncomfortable it made her.

'Sure,' he said, and then he nodded at her plate. 'Are you done with that?'

Noah woke to a house that was significantly less festive than the one he'd gone to sleep in. But, he thought, as he took in the tinsel that now hung only over his fireplace—along with the stockings and the lights—and the significantly fewer Christmas-related items around the house, it was perfect.

He didn't know what to say when he found Ava by his Christmas tree. She had tinsel over each shoulder, draped around her neck, too, and was taking some of the ornaments off the ridiculously overdone tree.

Just as he had the night before, he watched her. She was muttering to herself, occasionally bopping her head as if she were listening to music only she could hear. It was so homely it was almost enticing, and he had to step back, out of her range of view, to deal with how that made him feel.

He wasn't interested in *homely*. He'd thought he'd once *had* homely—until he'd been old enough to realise the man he'd seen in his parents' bedroom when he was younger hadn't been his mother's *friend*. It hadn't been his father either. But by the time he'd been old enough to realise that his mother had passed away and his anger had seemed pointless.

Not that that had stopped the anger from finding a home, he thought, as he remembered the women who had come in and out of his life—of his father's life—after his mother's death. The women who'd never stayed long but had always left his father with that sad look on his face.

The same look his father had had when he'd confirmed that Noah's mother *had* cheated on him the one time they'd spoken about it.

If that hadn't put Noah off *homely*, his own attempt at it had taught him a lesson. A lesson his heart and his mind still hadn't forgiven him for.

So what was wrong with him now? Why did he feel drawn to the image Ava was creating by that Christmas tree?

He'd been back all of two weeks. He'd been reunited with her all of twenty-four hours. *Barely* that. Maybe that was why he felt as if something were wrong. Because it *was*. There was no possible way he could want something he'd never wanted before after only two weeks. There was no possible way he could want it with a woman he'd only been back in touch with for barely twenty-four hours after seven years.

What about the eighteen years before that? And what about that kiss?

His spine stiffened. Ava had told him last night that she didn't want to talk about the kiss. Not explicitly, but he'd got the picture. And he couldn't blame her. The only reason he'd even brought it up was because he'd thought *she'd* want to talk about it.

But, no. It seemed they were going to pretend it hadn't happened.

He took a moment to compose himself—it took longer than he would have liked—and then strolled into the living room.

'Mrs Claus?' He forced a cheer he didn't feel into his voice. 'Is that you?'

'Why, yes, little elf, it is.'

She turned to him, eyes twinkling, and he was immediately drawn back into the memory he'd just tried to suppress...

'Jaden is taking for *ever*.'

'His speciality,' Noah replied. 'He and Monica are probably making out somewhere.'

Ava's face twisted in disgust. 'Why would you put that image in my head? I'm perfectly happy thinking about my brother as a monk.'

Noah snorted. 'Jaden is *not* a monk.'

'Stop it.'

'You're an adult now, Ava,' he said with a smirk. 'At least, almost.'

'I'm *eighteen*.'

'Like I said—*almost* an adult.'

She narrowed her eyes at him. 'Just because I don't want to hear about my brother's sex habits doesn't mean I'm not an adult.'

'You're *eighteen*.'

She rolled her eyes. 'Yeah, and you were *such* a kid when you were eighteen.'

He had been, he thought. He'd made all kinds of stupid decisions between the age of eighteen and now. Most notably falling hard and fast for a woman who had no intention of committing to him. Worse yet, a woman who had shown him he was at risk of following in his father's footsteps.

'We should probably head to the pools without him,' Noah said after a few more minutes. 'We don't want to get there and have them turn us away.'

Ava nodded and walked ahead of him along the path to the pools. It was going to be thirty-eight degrees Celsius that day, and they'd decided—Noah, Jaden, Monica and Ava—to survive the heat by going to the natural rock pools near Noah's house.

They weren't private pools, but because they were situated in an ecologically sensitive area that the government only allowed twelve people access to per day. There were already four of them, so they'd got up extra early to take the short hike to the rock pools.

Or at least that had been the plan before Jaden hadn't shown up.

'You'd have thought he'd have told you he'd be late,' Noah commented.

'He doesn't do things just because we think he should,' Ava said with a sigh. 'He told me last night that he'd meet us at the starting point. His excuse then was that he needed to fetch Monica.'

'Why didn't you go with him?'

'Because he was meant to be spending the night at *your* house.' She gave him a look. 'Even though my brother is two years older than me, he still isn't an adult.'

'That lie was more for your parents,' Noah said, automatically defending his friend, even though Jaden was the reason Ava had taken that jibe at him.

'Yeah, well, he could have at least had the decency to pitch up on time.'

They didn't speak for the rest of the trip. In fact the only communication they had with one another was when Ava missed a step on an incline and called out, and he pushed forward to help steady her.

His hands rested on her hips, just above her butt, and long after he'd let go his fingers could still feel the softness— the plumpness—of her there. It made him *want* her—which was ridiculous. She was Jaden's *sister*. And he'd just dodged a massive bullet with Tiff. The last thing on his mind was wanting anyone—let alone the girl he'd once seen smell her armpits to test whether she needed to start wearing deodorant.

It was ridiculous, he thought again. Except his eyes dipped to the rounded curve of her butt in her cotton shorts. To her thighs, which were thick and strong and made him think things he shouldn't be thinking about his best friend's little sister.

It put him in a mood, which kept him silent until they reached the entrance of the pools and were told they were the first there.

'Yes!'

They high-fived each other, and then Ava turned to the guard. 'Is it okay for us to keep places for my brother and his girlfriend? They're slower than us, so we went ahead to could get spots for all of us.'

She smiled widely at the man, and Noah watched as he blinked and then nodded. Sympathy pooled in his stomach. He didn't think *he'd* be able to resist that smile either. It was the kind that could make anyone feel blinded. Combined with Ava's naturally husky voice, its effect was potent.

But he *had* resisted that smile, he told himself. And he still did. All the time. In fact he barely noticed that it made her eyes crinkle. Or that it softened her features, making her look like some kind of mythical creature.

Man, what had Tiff *done* to him?

'Noah?'

He blinked, his gaze zooming in on her.

'You didn't hear a word I said, did you?'

'Er...yeah, of course I did.'

'Liar.'

His lips curved. 'You want to know whether this is a good spot to sit in.'

She narrowed her eyes. 'That's a logical deduction. It's not because you were listening to me.' She tossed her head back. 'So, is it?'

His smile widened. 'It's perfect.'

They set up the blankets and umbrellas they'd brought, but by the time they were done Jaden and Monica still hadn't arrived. Neither had anyone else.

'Screw this,' Ava said after a moment. 'I'm hot, I've walked further than I generally do most days, and I deserve a swim.'

She was pulling off her top and wriggling off her shorts before he could say anything to stop her. And by the time he could he found that his voice was gone. Stolen by how beautiful her body was.

She's off-limits...she's off-limits...she's off-limits.

He repeated the words inside his head, over and over again, hoping it would drown out the other voice in his head pointing out how beautiful the brown skin of her body was against the white of her bikini. How the rounding of her breasts, her hips, was the stuff of fantasies. How they would be the stuff of *his* fantasies in the future.

She's off-limits...she's off-limits...she's-off limits.

She gave him a smile he didn't understand, and then she threw her clothes at him. The pile landed against his chest, his hands barely lifting in time to keep everything from fall-

ing to the ground. And then she turned and his heart hammered, his body tightening as he got a better view of the butt he'd been admiring earlier.

With one sly look over her shoulder, Ava ran and dived into the water.

It took all the time she was under the water for him to realise that she'd been trying to seduce him. But his mind rejected that explanation even as it pointed out all the ways her actions had been an attempt at seduction.

Before he knew it he was pulling off his T-shirt and following her into the water. When he emerged, he found himself a short distance from her.

'Cooler now?' he asked, surprised at how steady his voice was.

'Never been cooler.'

Her eyes were twinkling, her expression teasing, but there was a seriousness there, too, somehow, and he wondered if that could be more seduction.

'This isn't in my head, is it?' she asked him softly.

'I don't know what you're talking about.'

She gave him a small smile. 'So maybe we should keep it like that, then. We'll pretend like you aren't looking at me the way you are now. That I didn't say anything about it—about us—at all.' She paused. 'We can pretend it didn't happen—just like after the first time we kissed.'

'You asked me—'

'You could have said no,' she interrupted him. 'In fact, you *should* have said no. I'm your best friend's sister. You had no business kissing me.'

'I know.' Somehow he found himself even closer to her.

'Why would you want to be my first kiss, Noah?'

'You asked me to be.'

'And now I'll always have the story of how my brother's best friend kissed me for the first time.'

'You were sixteen. Too old not to have been kissed.'

She laughed—low, husky—and it vibrated through his body. 'Is there a timeline for that I don't know about?'

'Yes.'

'Like the rules about who your first kiss should be with?'

'Honestly, I don't care.' And in that moment Noah thought he'd lost his mind. 'I don't care about the rules and the ages.'

'Because you *wanted* to kiss me.'

'Yes.'

'Just like you do now.'

He didn't answer her. Only slid a hand around her waist and pulled her against him as their lips met.

CHAPTER SIX

'WHAT?' AVA ASKED, when the silence extended much too long for her liking. When the expression on Noah's face went from easy to tight and the emotion rippling across his features made her stomach tremble.

'Nothing.' His voice was hoarse.

'Are you okay?' She dropped the ornament she held in her hands to the couch and moved forward. 'Should I take you to the doctor? Back to the hospital?'

'No.' His voice was stronger now. 'No,' he said again. 'I'm fine. I just got a little…distracted.'

The air moved more easily into her lungs. 'By what? I thought you were about to have a heart attack.'

'Sorry,' he said. Still, she heard the strain. 'This looks great, by the way. You didn't have to do it.'

'I know,' she said, and picked up the ornament she'd dropped, putting it with the others. 'But it was the least I could do after you took such great care of me and Zorro yesterday.'

He studied her, and as the seconds ticked by Ava tried not to wriggle under his gaze.

'You couldn't sleep, huh?'

She laughed, but the words jolted her. How had he known? 'I slept fine.'

He arched a brow.

She hissed out a breath. 'Fine. I slept okay for the first bit, and then I woke up and my mind started thinking about

everything that happened and everything that's going to happen and I couldn't go back to sleep.' She forced a smile. 'At least it's the weekend.'

'Hell of a time to have to think about your house burning down.'

She shrugged, though sadness wove through her. 'I haven't had the heart to check.'

'I'll call the station.'

Ava continued removing the ornaments from the Christmas tree while he went outside to make the call. As she did so, she wondered why she hadn't told him that her house had been at the bottom of the list of things she was worried about. At the top of the list was whether Noah was okay and whether Zorro was.

Because early that morning she'd realised again how much danger she'd put him in by having him go back for Zorro. The smoke could have had a worse effect than she'd imagined. Because, of course, as that thought had occurred to her she'd done an internet search on smoke inhalation and found out the most horrific things. Things even that TV show hadn't prepared her for.

Which had got her thinking about Zorro. And how, though she hated it that she'd put Noah in danger, she couldn't bring herself to regret it. She'd thought about all the times she'd cried and Zorro had curled up near her. Not anywhere close to her body—he was still a cat—but close enough that she'd understood he was offering her as much comfort as a cat could.

She'd thought about how he'd helped her stave off loneliness when it had threatened to overwhelm her. When thoughts of how much she needed to change had kept her up at night. When the hopelessness that she wouldn't be able to change had done the same. As had the fear that no one would ever love her. Zorro had kept her calm through it all.

And then, of course, she'd thought about the wedding. And the fact that she was being forced to participate in it

when it was the last thing—the *very* last thing—in the entire world she wanted to do.

She was fully aware of the resentment that had come along with that thought. Fully aware that it had spilled over too many times during the planning of Leela's bachelorette party, which—thankfully—was now behind her. She had worried that during these last two weeks her resentment would spill over in ways she wouldn't know how to clean up.

'Well, the fire is still ongoing,' Noah said as he walked back into the room. 'But the wind's shifted, which means the direction of the fire has changed.'

'Away from the estate?'

'Yes,' he said, and started helping her remove more decorations from the tree. 'They're waiting for the smoke to subside and then they'll check everything out. It might still be a while before you can move back in, though.'

'Oh. *Oh*...' she said again, on an exhale. 'That makes me feel better than I thought it would.'

He frowned. 'I thought you were worried about your house?'

'I was. I *am*.' She stood on her tiptoes to get to the higher parts of the tree. 'But there are other things, too.'

'Like what?'

'Oh, you know...' She didn't elaborate, and though the silence that fell between them felt expectant—as if it wanted Ava to elaborate too—they both let it extend.

'I know you were pulling my leg about you and my father yesterday,' Noah said after a while.

His tone was casual, but Ava knew he was fighting to achieve it.

'But before that conversation went so terribly wrong, I did get the impression you were friends with him.'

'I am.'

With most of the decorations off, she reached up for the angel at the top of the tree. It was higher than she could reach, but she managed to touch the bottom of it. Think-

ing she could tip it over, she jumped and tried again. Except
that did nothing except make the branches of the tree rustle.

'Here.'

It was the only warning she got before Noah's hands were
on her hips, lifting her.

Her breath whooshed from her lungs and heat spread
through her body. It felt intimate, this completely innocent
gesture of his, and it charged the air around her. Around
them, she thought, when she glanced down and saw the ex-
pression on his face.

She reached up for the angel quickly, thinking that as soon
as she got it down they'd go back to being easy around one
another. Except when he put her down and she turned to put
the angel with the other decorations she was faced with his
chest. And though it was covered by his T-shirt, she could
still see the muscles of it.

Which wasn't a surprise, since a picture of him without
his top on had been seared into her brain the day before. No,
she thought immediately. A *long* time ago. Specifically, the
day he'd followed her into that water and she'd had the op-
portunity to run her hands over every glorious inch of it...

Her fingers itched to do it again. His body was different
now. Bigger. Stronger. And she wanted new memories that
could replace the ones she visited on particularly hard days.
Which also made her think that she'd lied when she'd told
herself that her relationship with Milo had stopped her from
thinking about Noah.

'Excuse me,' she said softly as the thought shook her.

She put the angel on the couch and took another step
back, suddenly thankful Noah hadn't closed the door after
he'd made his call and a slight breeze was blowing through
the house.

'So,' she said very deliberately, 'I know putting a Christ-
mas tree up is a sacred thing, but—'

'It isn't.'

'What?'

'Sacred.'

She frowned. 'Of course it is. It's a pivotal part of mentally preparing for Christmas.'

'Okay,' he agreed. 'But it's not sacred.'

'Noah,' she said with forced patience. 'How many times have you helped us put up our tree? You know it's sacred. We do it and we have dessert and fruit after, along with whatever cold drink we desire.' She frowned. 'You *know* this.'

'I know that's how *you* celebrate it, Avalanche.'

He lowered himself to the couch, and something about the movement made her think he hadn't slept well either.

'But my dad usually did our tree on his own. I'd get home and it was already done.'

'So you came to celebrate with us?'

'No, I just visited.' She gave him a look and he smiled. 'So I came to celebrate it with you. So what?'

She thought about it for all of two seconds. 'Get dressed.'

'What?'

'Get dressed. We're going to the shop. First, to buy me something a bit more presentable for being out in public,' she said, frowning down at his clothes which she still wore. 'And as soon as we've done that we're going to buy something nice for breakfast. Chocolate croissants, eclairs…maybe a fruit platter so we don't feel entirely guilty about our life choices. And then, dear Noah, we're going to decorate your tree.'

'This wasn't such a bad idea after all,' Noah said an hour later, when they were back from the shops and were taking a pre-tree-decorating break on the balcony.

Ava shot him a look. 'Oh, please. You complained from the moment I suggested it. And now that we have this delicious spread—' she gestured to the breakfast they'd bought, consisting mostly, if not completely, of the kind of food she'd suggested earlier '—you're changing your mind.'

'I'm an adult,' he said mildly. 'I can change my mind as and when I see fit.'

She grunted and popped a piece of croissant into her mouth. He grinned at the inelegance of it. He might not be

prepared to think about the more uncomfortable moments or memories being around Ava brought, but he still enjoyed spending time with her.

'Okay, so,' she said after a moment, 'it might seem like I'm dodging your question about your father, but I'm not.'

'Hence you bringing it up now?'

'Exactly.' She gave him a winning smile. 'A couple of years ago Jaden asked me to drop off something you'd sent for your father after the last time the two of you had seen one another.'

'It was the magazine my pictures were in.'

'Yeah. A small magazine with, like, a ten-person readership.'

It had been an international magazine with thousands of readers. He smiled.

'Anyway, something came up, but Jaden had already promised your dad he'd bring it over. So I took it, and Kirk invited me in for a drink—completely platonically,' she added dryly, 'and we started talking. And became friends.'

Noah sat back, his coffee in his hand. 'Sounds simple.'

'Don't make it sound like there was some *thing* that had to happen for us to be friends.' She tilted her head. 'Or wait—maybe there was. He'd just finalised his divorce—'

'His fourth.'

'And he wanted some company,' she finished, as if he hadn't interrupted her.

'What do *you* get out of it?'

She sighed. 'I don't know. Like I told you yesterday, he's a lovely man. And he's wise.'

'Not wise enough to stay away from marriage.' Anger and resentment rippled through him.

'Noah,' she said in a low tone.

It sounded like disappointment. He wasn't sure why that stung. Or why it felt worse than anger.

'Besides, I guess that other than that it was a way for me to get away from wedding planning. It takes up your entire life

and makes you feel worse than you can imagine.' She rolled her eyes. 'And it's supposed to be the best day of your life.'

'What are you talking about? Leela and Jaden weren't even engaged two years ago.'

'Yeah, I know.' She stared at him. 'You don't remember, do you?'

He frowned. 'Don't remember what?'

'Or maybe you don't even know,' she said softly, almost to herself.

And then she laughed, but the sound of it was strangled and it had his stomach turning.

'I'm sorry, I hadn't realised.' Her eyes met his, and there was pain and a sick kind of amusement in them. 'I'm talking about *my* wedding, Noah.'

CHAPTER SEVEN

'YOUR WEDDING?' HE REPEATED.

'Yes,' she said calmly, but she broke off flakes of crust from her croissant, undermining the tone. 'I was supposed to be married now.'

The thought of it had his mind spinning. A sick feeling stumbled through his stomach. An ache echoed through his chest.

'Clearly I'm missing something here. Why don't you start at the beginning?'

'There's not much to tell,' she said, in a way that made him think there was. 'I started dating a guy about a year after you left.'

A light blush spread over her cheeks, though he wasn't sure why.

'We were together for four years before he proposed. And we were engaged for a year before he left me at the altar.'

'He—' If he'd thought his mind had been spinning earlier, it had nothing on what was happening inside of his head now. 'A guy you were in a serious relationship with for five years left you at the altar? What the—'

'I appreciate the sentiment,' she interjected, with a smile that was half amused, half sad. 'I shared it. Still do some days.'

She went quiet for a moment, and when her eyes met his there was pain there that illogically he wanted to fix.

'But I'm over it.'

She'd never been a good liar. 'I'm sorry, Avalanche.'

'Thank you.'

A beat of silence passed. He wanted to say something about how relationships weren't worth the pain. Or point out that this was the exact reason why he didn't want to get involved with anyone. But it didn't seem like the right thing to say, especially when part of it was a lie.

He didn't want to get involved with anyone because he was terrified that history would repeat itself. And Noah had no intention of living his life in the same way his father lived his.

'You were going to get married and you didn't invite me?' he said, deciding on a more innocuous route.

But as soon as he'd said it, and emotion tightened in his chest, he realised it wasn't so innocuous after all.

'I was going to get married and I *did* invite you. I just never got a response to my email. Just like with all the others I sent.'

He opened his mouth to ask what email, but froze as dread filled him. The night after they'd kissed—after he'd felt things he never should have for his best friend's younger sister…after he'd been *caught*—he'd blocked Ava's email address.

Pre-emptively, he'd thought back then, because he hadn't wanted her to ask him why he was leaving without saying goodbye. Why, after they'd kissed, he'd decided to take advantage of an opportunity he'd been avoiding deciding on for a month. He hadn't wanted her to ask him whether that decision had anything to do with her. In fact, he'd wanted her to think it had *nothing* to do with her and everything to do with how things had ended with Tiff.

A stupid hope, he knew.

Just like the stupid decision he'd made when he hadn't known any better. Because of it he'd missed out on seven years of Ava's life. He hadn't heard from her and hadn't wanted to contact her. Hadn't thought he'd had the right to in case she was avoiding him purposely.

'Ava, I'm so—'

'Nope. *No*,' she said, in a tone that was a little too bright, with a smile that was a little too bright. 'Don't apologise. You were travelling around the world. Photographing new and exciting things. You don't have to apologise for not replying to my emails.'

'I do.' He braced his wrists on the table. 'I blocked your email address.' Shame rose in his throat as he took in the expression on her face. 'After the...er...the kiss—' *real mature, Noah* '—I blocked it.'

'You *blocked* my email address?' she repeated. 'After you kissed me, you blocked my emails?'

Her voice had gone thin, and it felt like a warning. But he had to face the fact that he'd made a mistake. It was the only way he could redeem himself.

'It was a stupid thing to do. I was an immature kid, and—'

'After you kissed me.' She slammed a hand on the table. '*You* kissed *me*, Noah.'

'I know.'

And now his shame had nothing to do with how she was responding and everything to do with how he'd crossed a boundary with her—with Jaden—that he'd never be able to erase.

'I'm sorry.'

She tossed her head back and looked up. If he didn't know any better he'd wonder if she was crying. But Ava didn't cry. He hadn't seen her cry since that girl had bullied her. It had been a watershed moment for her, he thought. The girl had *wanted* to make her cry; Ava had refused to give her what she wanted. And since then Ava had refused to cry in front of people in general.

He knew because he'd asked her about it. Long before the day they'd kissed. Which was why he knew that the betrayal and hurt on her face after Jaden had caught them—and Noah had then ignored her—would be the worst she'd let him see. He'd respected her for it, even as disgust had pooled inside him.

Exactly like now.

But, unlike then, when her eyes met his now they were clear of emotion. 'It's okay. We were both kids. It was a mistake.'

Was it?

He didn't ask. It wouldn't have been fair.

'Besides,' she continued, 'I got the information I needed from Jaden. That you were safe.' She answered his silent question. 'And when I started hanging out with your father I got it from him.' She paused. 'Life goes on.'

He didn't reply to that. The morning had been an overload of information that he wasn't ready to dwell on. But even as he thought that questions sprang to his mind.

She'd been engaged? She'd invited him to the wedding? Why hadn't Jaden told him? Why hadn't his father? She was friends with his father? Why did he feel betrayed? Confused? Raw?

The thoughts were unwelcome, as were the emotions. Acknowledging either was bound to lead him down a path he had no intention of travelling. The path of examining his past. Of facing his mistakes. Doing it with Ava about blocking her emails was enough for that day.

Except the universe seemed to have another idea.

'Tiff's going to be there, you know. At the wedding.'

Immediately after she'd said it she regretted it. Partly because she knew Jaden had wanted to tell Noah that the woman who'd broken his heart would be part of the wedding. Mostly because the stunned, strained expression on Noah's face wreaked havoc on her heart.

You're hurt and now you're lashing out, hurting other people in the process.

She squeezed her eyes shut—trying to ignore the voice that confirmed she was a terrible person—and focused on the upside. She'd done the right thing. Jaden should have told Noah about Tiff coming ages ago. He should have given Noah the opportunity to opt out of being his best man as soon as he'd known Tiff was going to be a bridesmaid.

'I'm sorry, did you just say Tiff is going to be at this wedding?'

'*In* the wedding. She's the maid of honour.'

He swore and shook his head. 'How the hell did *that* happen?'

'Because the world is cruel and does things like this all the time.'

'Your ex isn't going to be there, too, is he?'

She laughed at the incredulity of his tone, and relief rippled through her when it broke some of the tension.

'No, thankfully not. But Jaden *is* getting married almost to the day when my wedding was supposed to happen last year, so I still think the world is cruel.'

'He's—' Noah broke off with a shake of his head. 'What the hell happened? It sounds like Jaden thought about what would hurt the people he loved the most, and then decided to do just that.'

'It's not entirely his fault,' she said in his defence, though she'd been blaming him for a while. 'He was outnumbered. Leela wanted to get married close to Christmas, and the venue only had this date available. Tiff is also one of Leela's friends,' she added. 'I hate to break it to you, but she's responsible for introducing Jaden and Leela.'

'How?'

'Jaden bumped into Tiff at a restaurant and was forced to greet her. She was with Leela, and there was enough of a spark between the two of them that they exchanged numbers. So…' She considered. 'Not entirely his fault.'

'He still should have told me.'

'Absolutely. Which I kept telling him. But he said he wanted to tell you in person.'

'A heads-up over the telephone—or even an email—would have been appreciated.'

'Maybe we should give him the benefit of the doubt.'

Noah made a low sound in his throat and, taking in the look on his face, Ava giggled.

'It's not funny.'

'Oh, absolutely not,' she said, and laughed some more. 'But I can't keep being mad about this, Noah. It's *exhausting. I'm* exhausted.' Her laugh turned into a hiccup of despair. 'See what I mean? I'm tired of this. And of feeling this way. So I'm going to laugh and try to get through this *stupid* wedding, where every member of my family is going to look at me with sympathy, or ask me why I haven't moved on yet, or how my year has been. *Urgh.*'

She tilted her head back and tried to gain some semblance of control over her emotions again.

'Tell them it's none of their business,' Noah said after a moment. 'And then ask them about the most inappropriate thing you've heard about them.'

'What?'

He was grinning when she looked at him. 'You know how we keep hearing things about our family members? Like my uncle has two kids no one talks about. *Two.* So, my suggestion is, if someone asks you about how you've been doing, or makes some reference to the wedding, you ask about the two kids no one's talking about.'

She stared at him, and then grinned. 'That is the most brilliant thing I've ever heard.'

CHAPTER EIGHT

'WELL, THEN,' HE SAID, on a roll now, 'prepare yourself for something even better.'

'Not possible.'

'Oh, but it is.' He waited a beat. 'I don't think I'm going to like this wedding any more than you're going to.'

She narrowed her eyes. 'Continue.'

'And since I don't have any family there to embarrass—except maybe my dad, and he's as open as they come about his mistakes—maybe you and I should make a little wager.'

'A wager?' Ava sat back and rested her legs on the chair in front of her. 'You intrigue me, Mr Giles. What are the terms of this wager?'

'If you're going to try and put your family members on the spot, you'll have to do it in front of me. I'll give you points for how well you do it.'

'And in return?'

'You entertain me.'

'Oh, no. No, no, no,' she said with a laugh. 'That's not a *wager.*'

'It is. I'll bet you that you can't get a thousand points.'

'How dare you? Of *course* I'll get to a thousand points.' She paused. 'We'll discuss the determination of points later. But first I have to point out that I'm not really getting anything out of this bet. And, no, entertaining you doesn't count.'

'Okay, fine,' he said with a grin. He was enjoying this process almost as much as he was enjoying seeing the light

back in her eyes. He hadn't realised until it was gone how much he cherished it. 'What do you want?'

'Hmm…let me see. Money would be too easy for you.'

'I'm fine with money.'

'No,' she said, with a smile that made his body ache. '*I'd* like to be entertained, too.'

The thought gave him visions of the two of them in that rock pool again. He shook his head. He was still recovering from his first memory. And from the feel of her waist under his hands. And from the way she'd looked at him afterwards, when she'd turned and he'd been so tempted to kiss her. And then from the reminder that he had no business being tempted by her, especially after what she'd just told him she'd gone through.

'I propose this,' she said, interrupting his thoughts. *Thank heaven.* 'We both try to entertain each other. It can come in the form of me saying inappropriate things to my family, or you doing something silly like…singing a song during the reception. Just an idea,' she said with a grin when he opened his mouth to protest. 'Whoever reaches a thousand points first, wins.'

'I'm *so* proud of how much you've grown into this,' he said with mock pride. 'I accept your proposal. I do, however, want to know how the scoring is going to work.'

'We have to witness the other person doing things in order to give points.'

'Fair.' He paused. 'The points are given in tens. From ten to one hundred.'

'One hundred is the maximum?'

'Unless there's a spectacular opportunity to take it all.'

'Take it all?' she repeated. 'As in win?'

'Yes.' A ripple of excitement went through him. 'Like doing a song during the reception.'

'I like it.' She bit her lip. 'Okay, but before we continue, this *can't* ruin Jaden and Leela's wedding. So, sadly, no singing. Unless, of course, we've received permission.'

'I completely agree.'

'So how are we going to score points?'

'Ah, that's harder.' Leaning in, he said, 'How about dealer decides? It'll be open for discussion, of course, but we each decide how much we want to give the other.'

'Fine, but there should be ranges. Ten to fifty points if we do something to defend ourselves. The two secret children thing, for example.'

He nodded.

'Sixty to a hundred points if we do something to defend the other person.' The side of her mouth curved. 'So, if Tiff says something about how you look, for instance, I'll just mention how much *she's* changed.'

'Into a decrepit old woman?'

She let out a sparkling laugh. 'Fifty points to you. But, no, just how much better she looks as a brunette than a redhead.'

'Sixty points. Seventy if the delivery was good.'

'Perfect,' she said, and leaned forward, stretching out her hand. 'Do we have a deal?'

'We do.' He started forward, but paused. 'Wait—when is the start, and when is the finish?'

Just as she opened her mouth her phone rang from where it was charging in the kitchen. She ran inside the house and a few minutes later reappeared.

'That was Jaden.' She blew out a breath. 'After I reassured him—again—that I'm fine, he wanted to know if I could meet him at the Stellenbosch Christmas Market. Apparently their visit to the venue has encouraged them to spend more time with the wedding party. They want us there.' She rolled her eyes. 'I expect you're going to get a phone call, too.'

Seconds later her prediction proved true. The conversation was quick, and when Noah hung up Ava said, 'I guess we're starting today.'

'And the winner will be declared at the end of the wedding. Deal?'

'Deal.'

They shook hands.

* * *

Ava knew how significant her deal—wager, bet—with Noah was. By agreeing to it she was making sure she wouldn't be alone during the wedding, or during the run-up to it. And, while it had started out as a way to distract them both from the wedding, having an ally would do more than just distract Ava.

It would help with the loneliness she'd felt during this process, since she was the only one who wasn't looking forward to the event. It would help her keep up the pretence that she was fine. Unhappy about the wedding, but completely fine within herself.

Which was a lie, but no one had to know that. Hell, at the best of times she managed to ignore it herself.

At the worst of times she tried to figure out how she could turn herself into someone more palatable. And then she'd wonder if being more palatable meant she'd find someone who would actually want her.

But now, with Noah at her side, the wedding would fall into one of the best times. She was sure of it.

She left Noah's house before he did, telling him they needed to arrive separately so that they could avoid any questions. In the car park she put on some make-up, and then looked down at the yellow floral dress she'd bought earlier that morning with Noah. She liked how bright it was against her skin. Liked that it made her feel like sunshine even when darkness still tumbled around inside her.

Taking a deep breath, she went to find her brother and future sister-in-law at the market. It was enthusiastically decorated for Christmas, and the prerequisite Father Christmas was in a cordoned-off area for kids to have their pictures taken with him. She smirked as 'Father Christmas' was handed a screaming child, before spotting Jaden and Leela at a large table.

'Ava.' Jaden got up and pulled her into a hug. 'Are you okay?'

'I'm fine,' she said brightly, before brushing a kiss on

Leela's cheek. 'Like I told Mom and Dad *and* you on the phone last night, I was evacuated in time.'

'We wanted to come as soon as you called.'

'I know. But it made no sense. Your wedding venue is over an hour away, and it was late. I didn't want any of you driving when I was fine and I'd booked myself into a hotel. Again, I *told* you all this last night.'

'We were worried.'

She softened. 'I know, but I really am okay.'

'I heard the fire's changed direction, though,' Jaden said. She nodded. 'Have they told you when you'll get to move back?'

'Probably this evening.'

She said it even though it wasn't the truth—or at least she didn't know if it was. But she'd managed to temper their worry—though not as much as she'd first thought, she considered, looking at her brother. Still, convincing them to stay at the vineyard the night before had been no mean feat. They'd hovered over her since her wedding day—although, true to the tradition of her family, none of them had actually *asked* her about it.

But that didn't mean their concern for Ava had disappeared. And if she'd told them she'd had to go to the hospital—that Zorro had had to, too, and that he was still there—they'd have overreacted. She wasn't in the mood for that. Less so since she'd probably have to tell them *more* lies to hide the fact that she'd stayed at Noah's the night before.

If she couldn't move back to her house this evening she'd figure something out. But for now she had to distract her brother, so he wouldn't pry any more than he already had and become suspicious. Insults were the quickest—and easiest—way to do so.

'You need to get a life, Jaden. You can't be this worried about me after I told you I was fine.'

'Forgive me for caring.'

'Is that how you apologise to someone you care about?'

He rolled his eyes. 'I'm sorry that you're the most annoying little sister in the world.'

'Are we handing out apologies?' Noah asked, joining their group.

Jaden's face split into a grin and they did a little handshake and back pat, before her brother introduced Noah to Leela. Noah forewent another handshake and pulled Leela into a hug, and then they all settled at the table.

'So, where is it?' Noah asked.

'What?' Jaden replied, with a wider smile than Ava had seen on him in a long time.

'My apology?' When Jaden frowned, Noah said, 'I've heard there are some things about this wedding you haven't told me.'

Jaden's expression immediately dimmed, and Ava caught Leela's eye and gestured that they should get up. 'We're going to get some drinks,' she said, putting an arm through Leela's. 'We'll give you two a chance to catch up.'

'He feels bad about it,' Leela said when they were far away from the table. 'About the Tiff thing. About *your* thing, too.'

Ava blinked, and then let go of Leela's arm. This was the first time either Leela or Jaden had referred to their wedding being so close to the anniversary of Ava being jilted.

Ava had always assumed that it was out of a desire for self-preservation. That neither of them wanted to face Ava's potential wrath. But Ava had no desire to engage over it now. There was nothing any of them could do to change what was happening.

'I'm sure everything will be fine,' she said soothingly. 'Why don't you tell me about your trip? How did everything go?'

As she'd known it would, talking about the wedding distracted Leela. She went from serious to animated in seconds, and for a moment Ava wondered where Leela got her excitement from.

Ava had never been excited about her own wedding. Nervous and anxious, yes, but not excited. In fact, those nerves,

that anxiety, had built and built until finally she'd been standing at the altar. She wondered now whether those emotions had been because she'd anticipated that Milo would leave her there.

Even now she couldn't figure it out. But she didn't think too hard about it. The memories of that day had gone on a shelf at the back of her mind—deep in her memory storage cupboard—along with the memories and emotions of Noah seven years ago. Memories and emotions that were best left alone.

She paid the bartender for their drinks, and then she and Leela made their way back to the table. Things didn't seem too tense, but that didn't keep Ava from asking as she settled in next to Noah.

'All sorted?' she said under her breath as Jaden said something to Leela.

'About as much as it can be.'

'You have the moral high ground now,' she told him. 'But the moment he finds out I stayed at your place last night—'

'Don't even say it,' Noah muttered. 'He might hear, and I'm still begging for forgiveness for the last time something happened between us.'

'From him or from me?' she asked, before she could stop herself, and then she shook her head. 'Forget that. I don't have the energy to go down that road. No!' she said when he opened his mouth. 'If you try to talk to me about this I'm going to deduct points from you.'

'Against the rules.'

'There *are* no rules.'

'There's one rule now.' His eyes didn't leave hers. 'No deductions.'

'Fine.'

They stared at each other. But when it turned into something more than just defiance they both looked away.

Directly into the eyes of her brother.

CHAPTER NINE

'I TOLD YOU,' Ava said after a moment.

But the look on Jaden's face didn't change. It was almost as if he hadn't heard his sister.

Noah swallowed, and wondered whether it was too late to back out of the wedding. He didn't *have* to deal with these looks, or the reminder that Jaden had once thought Noah had taken advantage of Ava. Or that he sometimes believed that himself.

Ava nudged him with her elbow under the table, and then repeated her words. 'I told you, Noah. He was going to tell you.'

'Er…yeah. Sure…'

'What are you two talking about?' Jaden asked.

'Well, I ran into Noah yesterday,' Ava said easily. 'He was part of the team dispatched to the estate to deal with the fires. Anyway, I asked him about Tiff by mistake, and he didn't know.' She tilted her head. 'Even though he's been here for over *two weeks*, Jaden.'

'He was fighting fires,' Jaden said defensively. 'And why would you mention it anyway, if you weren't sure I'd told him?'

'Oh, I don't know.' She leaned forward. 'Maybe it was the surprise of seeing him at all, since you didn't even tell me he was here already.'

Jaden opened his mouth, but just then two other people joined their group. One Noah didn't recognise, though Jaden

told him it was a colleague he'd grown close to. The other he recognised all too well.

He stood when the rest of them stood, and gave himself permission just to look at her. Ava was right; Tiff had dyed her hair. But other than that she looked the same as she had seven years before. Tall, smooth brown skin. Perfect features. One of the most beautiful women he'd ever seen.

But she'd changed the course of his life. He couldn't be drawn in by beauty any more.

'Noah,' she said, and surprised him with a hug. 'You look good.'

'Thank you.' He didn't bother telling her she looked good, too. She already knew. 'It's a…a surprise to see you.'

'But a *good* surprise?' she asked teasingly.

He opened his mouth to reply, but was interrupted by a snort coming from beside him. When he turned to look at Ava she widened her eyes in innocence. It immediately eased some of his tension.

'Ava,' Tiff said, in a tone that suggested she wasn't Ava's biggest fan. 'Such a treat to see you again.'

'Treat…inevitability…' Ava lifted her shoulders. 'To each his own, I guess.'

'Delightful, as always.'

Ava offered Tiff a smile, and he wondered if she thought the smile was sweet. It wasn't. It was terrifying. But it seemed to do the trick, because Tiff moved to sit at the opposite side of the table and not next to him, as he'd thought she'd initially intended to. Jaden's other groomsman—Ken—sat next to Ava.

'Sixty points,' Noah whispered as they took their seats again.

'Really?' Ava pulled her face. 'It hardly deserves that much. I was barely trying.'

'The rules are the rules.'

'Fair enough.' But her hand found his under the table and squeezed.

If someone had asked him how the afternoon would go

after that moment, he wouldn't have been able to answer. Not coherently anyway. He was much too aware of the two women at the table who represented such different things in his life.

He'd fallen so hard for Tiff that he wasn't surprised he still had the bruises to show for it. He'd met her during the second year of his photography course and had asked her out, considered getting his own place so that they could move in together, and had even been planning on proposing to her all in the space of a year. *One year.*

It hadn't seemed strange to him that their relationship had moved so fast. He'd only been thinking about that feeling in his chest when he was with her. How it made him feel invincible.

But he wasn't. Neither was their relationship. And when it had crashed and burned he'd seen nothing *but* how fast it had been. He'd seen that pace over his entire life, in his father's relationships—had witnessed it, had judged it—but he hadn't seen it in his own life. It was his biggest regret. And, though he'd never tell his father, his biggest failure.

His relationship with Tiff had changed him. Had changed the way he saw relationships. Changed the way he saw his father. How could he blame the man for falling so hard and fast when Noah had experienced it himself? So easily, too. It was worse because Noah knew his father's behaviour somehow linked back to what had happened with his mother.

But Noah's behaviour had come *before* he'd discovered Tiff cheating on him. He could only imagine what would have come after if he hadn't stopped himself.

He'd practised tight control in his dating life since then. He'd gone out occasionally, but he'd never invested too much of himself. He was too afraid of being sucked into that emotion again. Emotion that would lift him high enough that he'd *want* to experience it even after it had plunged him back to the ground.

That was how his father started his cycle; Noah refused to let it become his own.

And now, sitting opposite the woman who'd started it all...
It shook him more than he cared to admit.

As if sensing his thoughts, Ava bumped her shoulder against his. When he looked over she winked at him, and rolled her eyes in an exaggerated way before stifling a yawn. He smirked, and then full-out grinned when he felt a movement under the table and heard Ava hiss in response. Jaden sent her a pointed look—to go along with the kick under the table, Noah assumed—and again some of his tension faded.

Ava had always had the ability to do that. Which might have been why he'd ignored all his newly made resolutions the day he'd kissed her. There had been no control in that, and it had confused their relationship even more.

He'd had no idea what their relationship had been when they were growing up. He *still* didn't. He couldn't quite call them friends. Not in the way he'd call Jaden a friend. Nor was their relationship like that of family, no matter how much he'd tried to convince her—and himself—of that.

If it was, he was going to hell for all the improper thoughts he'd had about a family member. And so, just like he had before—before that kiss, at least—he would ignore the fact that those thoughts existed. Because although he couldn't define their relationship, he knew that it came with boundaries.

Unspoken ones at first, and then, after Jaden had caught them kissing, clearly outlined ones. In hard tones, loud volumes, and even louder disappointment.

He'd felt ashamed that he'd kissed her even as he'd done it. He hadn't needed Jaden to tell him he should have been. So when he'd moved away and hadn't said goodbye, he'd thought it for the best.

Except, he thought, remembering how Ava had looked when he'd told her he'd blocked her email address, maybe it hadn't been.

But it was in the past now. And that was where he needed to leave it all. His relationship with Tiff. The way he felt about relationships as a result. Whatever he'd once shared with Ava.

The way he was going to get through this wedding was to stay in the present. No matter how much the past called to him.

She'd sensed the change in him the moment her brother had joined them.

No, she thought. It had happened when her brother had caught them in that strangely intense look they'd shared. The easiness between them had slipped behind a barrier she only now realised had been there when they were younger, too. The kindness—the softness in his eyes when he'd look at her—had changed into something else. Something more... *polite.*

If she hadn't hated politeness before—the insincerity of it—Noah's reaction would have ensured it now.

And then Tiff had swooped in with her perfect beauty, and Ava had felt the Noah she'd been talking to—*engaging* with—since they'd reconciled slip even further away from her.

The tension had built inside her so much that at the first opportunity Leela gave them to leave the table, Ava jumped up and exited the tent that enclosed the market.

There was no one else in the field behind the tent, and it eased the weight that was on her chest. Until she heard the rustling of the grass behind her.

'Ava! Ava, wait!'

Her legs kept moving, though she wasn't completely sure why. Did they want distance from this stupid wedding and its stupid planning? Or were they running from the man who didn't have to do much to turn them into jelly?

'Hey,' Noah said, catching up to her.

She didn't stop.

'You okay?'

'Fine.'

'Ava? Ava, *stop.* Stop walking.'

She stopped—but not because he'd asked her to. They were far enough away from the market now that the live

band who'd been singing songs about the festive season was muted. Plus, they'd reached the side of the field where a row of trees provided shade.

'What's going on?'

'Nothing. I just needed a break from…everything. The wedding.'

He studied her. 'Okay, fine. Let's pretend like I believe you. Which I don't.'

She didn't respond.

'Why did you agree to be in this wedding when you clearly don't want to be?'

'Have you ever tried refusing when a bride asks you to be a bridesmaid?'

He gave her a look.

'Or a groom asks you to be best man. Whatever. You know what I mean.' She took a breath. 'Not only did Leela ask me without any warning—I'm still working on forgiving my brother for *that*—she did it at Sunday lunch in front of both my family *and* hers. As much as I wanted to, I couldn't say no.'

'Surely they would have understood?'

'Surely Leela should have known that having her wedding exactly a year after mine *and* asking me to be in her bridal party wasn't a good idea? And yet here we are.'

He shoved his hands in his pockets, but Ava could have sworn he'd wanted to reach out to her first.

'I'm sorry.'

She waved a hand. 'Why should you apologise? You're in as much of a mess as I am.' She forced the next words out of her mouth. 'How was it? Seeing Tiff again?'

'Strange.' He kicked at the grass in front of him, watched as the dry golden-brown blades flattened. 'But fine.'

She snorted. 'Yeah, *right.*'

'If you can lie about what's going on, I can, too.'

'Touché.'

They stood like that for a few moments, and then Ava sighed. 'We should probably get back.'

'Why? So Leela can talk us into finding things to add to the wedding favours at the market?'

'Technically, that's what we're supposed to be doing now.'

'There are other people in the bridal party.'

'Yeah. And they've been doing the majority of the work for the past year. You weren't here, and I've been about as helpful as this conversation has been in working out our frustrations.'

He smiled. 'You have such an elegant way of describing things.'

'Of course I do. I'm a copywriter. I have to find wonderful ways of describing boring things all the time.'

'Should I be offended that you're calling me boring?'

'Not you. Or this conversation, really.'

She angled her body and he began to walk next to her at the sign. But their pace was slow, giving them plenty of time to avoid their duties.

'It's easier not to talk about things.'

'About the wedding?'

'About all of it.' She sighed. 'But even though I haven't spoken about it people still—'

She cut herself off. Revealing it to him felt as if she was confiding. She didn't *confide*. Confiding meant making herself vulnerable. Exposing herself, flaws and all. And she wouldn't do that when she was determined to keep those flaws to herself.

But she'd already said too much.

'People still treat you differently?'

She nodded. 'They treat me differently, and then they try to cover it up—which, again, makes them treat me differently. It's annoying. I mean, they were annoying before, but now they're *super*-annoying.'

'I know what you mean. Not about the annoying part,' he said when she shot him a look. 'At least not *entirely* about the annoying part. But, no, I meant about my father.'

Ava stopped herself from sucking in her breath; holding

it in at the information he'd offered. Noah didn't ever speak about how his father's actions made him feel.

Or maybe he just didn't ever speak about it to you.

And why would he? she wondered in response to that inner voice. They'd never had the kind of relationship where they'd bare their souls to one another. Well, *she* had. But that was because she'd been young and foolish. Because she'd thought Noah was just as much her friend as he was Jaden's.

But their kisses had drawn lines in the sand. They'd managed to ignore the first line because they'd ignored the fact that the kiss had happened at all. And the second line...

Well, they'd never had to deal with that until now. She could feel that they were approaching it. But she wouldn't cross it.

If it was going to be crossed *he* would have to be the one who did it.

'It was worse when I was younger and didn't understand it. The only thing I knew was that whenever my father brought a new "friend" home, people would look at me in a certain way. The same way. When I was older I realised it was with sympathy.' He paused. 'They'd never say anything about it; they'd just give me sympathetic looks. And when he got married there were fake congratulations. When he divorced, fake consolation. It drove me mad.'

'I never realised.'

'Yeah, well... I became a pro at hiding it.' He gave her a slanted look. 'You, not so much.'

She laughed lightly, though it wasn't really funny. 'You'd be surprised.' But again, because that felt like confiding, she continued. 'It's never been my aim to hide it. Except maybe with my parents. They believe—' She cleared her throat when emotion stuck. 'They believe that I'm better than I am. I don't want to disappoint them. Not any more than I already have.'

Noah stopped, reaching out and grabbing her hand, forcing her to stop, too. 'You've *never* disappointed them.'

'You don't think their daughter being jilted in front of all

their friends and family was a disappointment?' The words spilled from her lips unfiltered. 'You don't think realising there's something wrong with their daughter disappointed them?'

'Ava!' He said her name in both warning and surprise. 'Where is this coming from?'

'It's always been there,' she said flatly. 'I'm pretty sure you've experienced it yourself.'

CHAPTER TEN

NOAH HAD NO idea what Ava was talking about. Or where her words were coming from. Had he missed this side of her? Or had she just changed since he'd last seen her?

The latter, he thought, when his mind reminded him of who she'd been back then. Confident in her decisions. Brazen in her efforts. Fearless in her mistakes. The insecurities she was showing him now had come after. And the thought of it had his blood boiling.

'Who *is* this man?'

She blinked. 'What?'

'The man who left you. Who is he?'

'Why?'

'Because I'm going to kill him for doing this to you.'

She stared at him, her hand slackening in his. 'I don't— I don't understand.'

'The last time I saw you, you weren't this person. *He* did this to you.' The venom in his voice surprised him.

She shook her head. 'Don't be an idiot, Noah.'

'He broke your heart and made you doubt yourself.'

'He didn't break my heart.'

But she didn't say he hadn't made her doubt herself. The absence of those words echoed loudly between them.

'I'm going to make it painful,' Noah said after a moment.

'Noah, stop it.' She let out a harsh breath. 'It doesn't matter. It's over.'

'And you're fine with being like this now?'

'I've always been like this.'

'This is *not* who you've always been.'

'How would you know?'

'Because I know you.'

'You *knew* me. Or you thought you did.'

'No.'

'Yes. Because *I* didn't really know myself then either.' She pulled her hand from his completely. 'It's been seven years, Noah. Seven years and things have happened and I've changed. I've got to know who I really am. It has nothing to do with him.'

She walked ahead now, leaving him staring at her back. He had no idea what had just happened. He didn't know where her fierce response had come from. Nor the fierce protectiveness in his chest.

He hoped what she'd said wasn't true. Knew that there was enough of the old Ava there to give that hope life. Because if there wasn't he'd have to wonder if he'd had anything to do with it. If his walking away—walking away after kissing her—had been part of what had caused her to change so drastically.

But that wasn't possible. It was too vain for him even to think that. And it told him he needed to re-evaluate the power he'd thought he had in a relationship he couldn't even define.

It bothered him for the rest of the afternoon. Bothered him more than having the woman who'd broken his heart sit across from him. More than having to listen to her make conversation as they went through the market, trying to find things to add to the favours to give the Keller wedding more of a festive feel.

He ignored Tiff for the most part, and breathed a sigh of relief when she seemed to get the picture. But there was no relief from the situation with Ava. And by the time Leela gave them updated information about the rehearsal dinner, happening in a few days' time, he still hadn't figured it out.

'Are you coming?' Jaden interrupted his thoughts.

'Where?'

'To my place for drinks.' Jaden frowned, making it clear that Noah had missed the invitation. 'To end the day.'

I can't think of anything I want to do less.

He didn't say it. Instead he looked at Ava, and she gave an imperceptible shake of the head. She wasn't going. And since she was still staying with him—he assumed—he'd pass, too.

'Nah. I'm still not feeling great after the fire yesterday. I should probably get some rest or I might be out for longer than I want to be.'

'What fire?' Tiff asked.

'It's a little too late to be concerned about my well-being,' he replied flatly. Being out of sorts with Ava had destroyed his filter. He felt bad almost immediately, and added a weak, 'But thanks for asking.'

'You sure you're okay?' Jaden asked as his frown deepened. 'Should I come over to your place for a catch-up?'

'No,' he said—a little too intensely, he thought, when he saw the surprise on Jaden's face. When he saw the smirk on Ava's. 'No, it's fine. We'll catch up another time. Go have fun.'

Giving him a suspicious look, Jaden nodded. 'Ava?'

'Oh, no. I can't imagine anything more terrible.'

She gave her brother a smile, and Noah saw Jaden's annoyance soften.

'But thanks for asking.'

She aimed a sweet, slightly mocking smile at Noah, and he couldn't help the way his lips curved in return. But when Jaden narrowed his eyes at them Noah sobered immediately. Thankfully Jaden didn't say anything about it, and then he and Ava were alone.

'I thought that would never end.'

'Me, too.' He paused, and was about to say something about what had happened between them earlier when she spoke.

'Forty points for that jibe against Tiff. You could have got fifty, but then you said thank you and it kind of spoilt it for me.'

'I felt bad.'

'You shouldn't have. She broke your heart.'

'Yeah, but we were kids.'

'You're defending her? After what she did?'

He quirked an eyebrow. 'How much do you know about that?'

'Nothing.' Her cheeks went pink.

'Jaden told you, didn't he?'

'No.' When he didn't reply, she sighed. 'I swear he didn't.' Then she mumbled something.

'What?'

She mumbled again.

'Ava,' he said exasperatedly.

'*You* told me, okay? Inadvertently. That night you and Jaden were sitting out on the balcony, talking about it.'

He remembered the night in question. It had been the day after he'd found Tiff half-naked with another man in the driveway of her house. He'd worked through most of his shock at that point. Mainly because Tiff had tried to explain it away—although why she'd even tried made no sense to him—and he'd accepted that things were over.

He'd been in the first stage of trying to figure out what that meant when he'd told Jaden.

'Where were you hiding?'

Though her cheeks darkened, she answered him. 'On the veranda underneath the balcony. Pretending to read a romance novel so my parents thought I was being productive. Which I *was* being. At first.' She wrinkled her nose. 'But you weren't really keeping your voices down.'

'It was a private conversation,' he said sternly.

'I know. I'm sorry.'

He waited a beat. 'No, you're not.'

'No, I'm not.' She lifted a shoulder. 'It's the reason we can have this conversation, isn't it?'

'You say that as if it's a *good* thing.'

'Well, I told you that my fiancé left me. Think of it as an equal exchange of information, if you like.'

'I'm not sure I do.' But then he shrugged. 'It was a long time ago. Much further back than what happened to you.' He paused. 'You'll get over it.'

'But it changes you. It changes you in general, I mean,' she added hastily when he frowned.

'It wasn't too bad in my case.'

She narrowed her eyes, but then her features relaxed. 'Sure.' She paused. 'Do you want to get out of here? I mean, it's pretty and all, but the live Christmas jingles are getting to me. And Father Christmas keeps looking at every pretty woman who passes in a way that's threatening to ruin my childhood memories.'

'Yeah, fine.'

But he didn't trust the change in her mood.

It was early evening as they headed for the car park, and the light was dim enough that the market's Christmas lights had been switched on. He couldn't deny it gave things a festive feel. The kind he'd only ever really felt in South Africa.

It was strange, considering he'd been all over the world. He'd spent Christmases in America, in the UK, in other African countries. He'd seen Thanksgiving and snow—things that made it clear Christmas was on its way.

Comparatively, there wasn't much in South Africa that did that. But there was a *feeling* here. When the Christmas carols started playing in stores late in November. When the decorations went up and Christmas trees could be found in the strangest public places around the country. When Christmas lights went on and families got together.

The feeling was so much more special now, since he'd been away for such a long time. And it made him realise how bad it must have been for his father to be away from South Africa at Christmas time.

Kirk loved Christmas. Once, when Noah had asked why, his father had told him he wanted to make sure Noah got the experiences he hadn't had growing up. But Noah knew that wasn't it. Not when his father's zeal for Christmas seemed to

have started the year after Noah's mother had died. And since then Noah and his father had never spent a Christmas apart.

So maybe it wasn't so much Christmas in South Africa that Kirk loved as it was spending time with *Noah* during Christmas. Which was the kind of long-term commitment that Noah hadn't seen in any of his father's other relationships.

Noah, a voice in his head said in warning. It sounded disappointed, and it reminded him of how Ava had said his name when he'd mentioned his father's disregard for marriage earlier. It stung now, as it had then, but almost immediately resistance surged inside him.

He couldn't just *forget* how Kirk's relationships had affected him. How they had caused him to have the mixed-up belief that because of his father's relationships he'd attract the same kind in his own life. How a part of him didn't believe it was all that bizarre, since his first serious relationship had ended with him being cheated on just as his father had been.

'It's not that bad.'

He blinked. 'What?'

'The lights.' She looked back at the market, at the trees that surrounded it, the lights that adorned them. 'It's quite festive.'

'I agree.'

'So why are you scowling?'

'I was thinking about my father.'

He heard her unspoken question and realised it was the second time he'd brought his father up with her that night.

'He loves Christmas.'

'Yes.'

He lifted his eyebrows. 'You know?'

'For as long as I've known you, I've known Kirk loves Christmas. And we're friends now, remember? I decorate his tree with him.'

He hid his surprise. 'Do you make him buy food, too?'

'Yes, actually.'

She smiled at him and he angled his body towards her, as if to catch that smile.

'But the whole thing is much more successful with him. We actually decorate the tree, for instance.'

'Isn't that what we're going to do at home now?'

She gave him a strange look, and he realised his body was now completely facing hers. He also realised he'd spoken about 'home' as if he had one. As if the years he'd been a vagrant, photographing anything from fauna to civil wars, hadn't been an attempt to figure out whether he *wanted* a home.

'I should probably find somewhere else to stay.'

'Or you could stop resisting my help and just come to my house until you can go back to your own,' he said. 'You can't stay with your family unless you want to explain to them where you stayed last night. And we've already been through why a hotel won't work.'

She turned to face him, the distance between their bodies minimal now, and suddenly his thoughts stepped into dangerous territory. *Forbidden* territory, only ventured into once before. No, twice, he thought as Ava's eyes met his.

He didn't give much thought to the first time they'd kissed. Ava had told him she'd wanted to know what it felt like; he'd agreed. Because if it hadn't been him it would have been someone else. That had been a given, but he'd known what kind of mood she'd been in that night. She wouldn't have cared about *who* she'd got to kiss her.

At least with him she'd been safe.

He'd brushed off the stirrings of his body back then. Told himself it was just hormones. Sexual frustration. And when she'd given him a bright smile, declaring it had never happened as she bounced off, he'd set it aside.

But now he remembered those stirrings. Because they were back, and more acute now than they'd been then. More acute now than they'd been when he'd kissed her the second time. The time that had nothing to do with familiarity

or safety. The time that had been about danger and unsafe territory.

Just like now.

'Fine. But only because I need to help you with your tree. Because I owe you.' Her voice was husky.

'You don't owe me anything, Avalanche.' He lifted a hand and brushed at the hair curling over her forehead. 'If you did, you've already repaid me.'

'No,' she denied.

She took a step closer to him, though he didn't think she was aware of it. At least not fully. Just as he wasn't fully aware of his other hand lifting and resting on her waist.

'How could I have?' Her voice was breathless now. 'I did nothing.'

'You saved me from Father Christmas and the elves throwing up in my house. You helped set up my tree. Or you will. And you saved me from the humiliation and emotion of seeing my cheating ex-girlfriend again.'

'I didn't save you from anything.'

'You did,' he said, and felt the mood shift from flirtatious to serious. To intense.

The air sizzled around them.

'Noah…'

She said his name on a sigh; half defeat, half frustration. But there was more in her tone, and he couldn't quite figure it out. Because he couldn't, he took a step back.

Before he could speak, her phone rang.

'The vet,' she said, her face tightening into an expression he almost felt in his stomach. But her voice was steady when she told him, 'I'll meet you at your place later.'

She'd answered the phone before he could reply.

'I'm *so* sorry, my sugar plum,' Ava murmured to Zorro as she snuggled him. She could feel his displeasure, but he didn't claw his way out of her embrace. Which he would have done if he hadn't missed her just a tiny bit.

Eventually she let go of him, setting him on her lap and

waiting to see what he wanted to do. He gave her a look that confirmed he wasn't happy, but settled into a sitting position. She supposed it was the lesser of two evils. He didn't want to go back into his carrier, and the rest of her car seemed equally unappealing. She had no doubt he'd run far away from her the moment they got home.

It took her a second to realise that she wasn't sure *when* they'd get home—she hadn't heard anything about the state of her house yet—and she dropped her head back against the headrest and evaluated her life choices.

She'd managed to call the vet that morning, but the receptionist had said the vet had been called in to an emergency operation and would return her call that afternoon. She'd completely forgotten about Zorro after that. She'd been too enamoured with her childhood crush. Too busy playing games with him that would have no winner. Not if she kept going the way that she was.

The moment they'd shared as they'd left the market had been a clear sign that going back to Noah's would be a mistake. But her options were limited—just as Noah had pointed out. No family, no hotel. And the fire *had* changed direction. Surely it wouldn't be long before she'd be able to go back home? It wouldn't kill her to stay at Noah's for one more night.

Maybe they could just focus on decorating the Christmas tree. And they could keep the conversation neutral, like talking about their jobs.

But then she remembered what had happened when she'd needed to take the angel off the top of the Christmas tree. And how talking about her writing career earlier had led to her almost confiding in him.

She let out a breath. She didn't have much choice, and she could hardly stay parked at the end of Noah's road for ever. So, like her cat, Ava chose the lesser evil and made the short trip back to the house of temptation.

CHAPTER ELEVEN

'EVERYTHING OKAY WITH ZORRO?'

'See for yourself.'

Ava lowered herself to her haunches, opened the door of the carrier, and out came the ugly cat. He immediately drew himself up as he looked around, realising he wasn't at his own house. Noah almost held his breath when the cat aimed its creepy, unblinking stare at him, but quickly realised that was ridiculous and let out the air in his lungs.

If only he'd been able to shake off the unsettled feeling he'd had since leaving the market as easily.

'I'm going to be honest with you. I'm not entirely sure what I should be looking for.'

She laughed softly, almost hesitantly. 'The vet said he's fine. He's on anti-inflammatories, but they didn't think it was serious enough for antibiotics. Which once again proves how much I owe you.'

'You don't owe me anything.'

Zorro gave a loud meow, and Ava quirked a brow. 'Humour me.'

'Fine,' he said, mostly because he was tired of arguing. 'What will it take for you to think we're even?'

'A flat hundred points?'

Not expecting that, he leaned forward. 'I'm not sure I can accept. This isn't a part of the bet.'

'So let's *make* it a part of the bet.'

'No,' he said after a moment. 'That blurs the lines too much.'

'It blurs the lines of the imaginary game you and I set up?'

He shrugged, and she let out a breath.

'How about supper, then?'

'I feel *so* appreciated.'

'Noah.'

He smirked. 'I have to eat.'

'Yes, you do.' She went to the kitchen, opened a cupboard door. And then did the same for each of the other cupboards. 'There's nothing here.'

'There are eggs.'

'Nothing,' she repeated. 'How do you feed yourself?'

'The deli. Plus, there are still croissants from this morning left over.'

'I'm not feeding you croissants for supper.' There was a beat before she continued. 'Watch Zorro. I'm going to the shop. I'll be back before you can get weird about babysitting a cat.'

True to her word, she left before he could protest.

'Your owner has a habit of leaving before I can argue with her,' he told the cat after a moment. 'Should I interpret that as a sign of her approach to life?'

The cat jumped onto his kitchen counter and gave him a level stare, as if to say, *You're on your own here, buddy. I'm not saying a word about her.*

'Loyalty,' he commented. 'I guess I can respect that.'

Not wanting to examine how he felt about calling a cat loyal, he got himself a beer. His body groaned when he lowered himself on the couch shortly after, and he realised it hadn't entirely been a lie when he'd told Jaden he needed rest.

His throat felt significantly better, though there was still the occasional cough. But he'd survive, he thought, and brought the beer to his lips.

He just wasn't sure he'd survive having Ava stay another night.

Things had become uncomfortable at the market. Probably

before that, he realised, remembering how she'd responded to his 'I blocked your emails' news. It annoyed him, but there wasn't much he could do about it. Talking about what had happened would only make things worse. And clearly ignoring it did, too. But he had no energy to try and figure out how to make things better. So he'd let things sort themselves out.

He set the beer on the table, kicked off his shoes and made himself comfortable on the couch, switching the TV on. With some undemanding Christmas movie playing, he settled back and told himself to relax.

Clearly he'd listened to himself, too, because when he opened his eyes again there were people on the TV screen he didn't recognise from before, and his house smelled of an enticing array of spices.

He shifted, and then frowned when he felt pressure on his chest. When he saw why, he wasn't sure how he'd missed that Zorro was sitting on his chest. The cat was giving him that blank, staring look, and this time it seemed to say, *Sit up. I dare you.*

Not appreciating being taunted by a cat, Noah shifted, and Zorro gave him a look of disgust—or disappointment—before gracefully leaping off his chest.

'Oh, you're awake,' Ava said as she moved a pot from the stove to the counter.

'I didn't realise I'd been asleep.'

'I figured. Your beer was only half-drunk when I got back from the shop.'

'How long ago was that?' he asked, standing before doing a quick stretch. He felt his body crack, heard it sigh, and then shook his arms out.

When he met Ava's eyes again, she blushed.

'Not too long,' she said, though it sounded forced. 'An hour? Hour and a half?'

'I must have been tired.'

'Clearly.' She paused. 'You didn't sleep well last night. Why?'

'Sometimes a fire sits with you.'

'Did this one sit because of me?'

He was going to deny it, but then figured he had no reason to lie. 'Partly. But it's never easy to think about the people who are going to lose their homes. And the damage to the area.' He shrugged. 'Part of the job.'

'I didn't realise.' Her expression twisted in sympathy. 'Why would you want to volunteer, then?'

'You're asking me that *now*?' he said with a smirk. 'I did the training when I was eighteen. You know that.'

'Yeah, I guess I'm just delayed in asking about it.' She took plates from his cupboard. 'Doesn't change the fact that I want to know.'

He grinned at her sass. 'Sure. My dad told me to find something I could do to help people. We used to make sandwiches and give them to the homeless every Tuesday. Every second Thursday we'd volunteer at the soup kitchen.'

She frowned. 'Really? Why didn't I know that?'

'It's not something we advertised. It wasn't about that for my dad. And he taught me that, too.'

'So even though you could afford to donate to charities who did things like that, you chose to do it yourselves?'

'We did both. It's part of the responsibility when you have more than others.'

He lifted a shoulder, though it felt as if he carried weight there. But he ignored it—just as he ignored the guilt he felt at the resentment he held for his father when Kirk had made such an effort raising him.

'In any case, after the fires in Kayamandi we were at the station, trying to figure out how we could help, and I heard one of the guys saying they wished they had more volunteers. I knew it was something I could do.'

'Sounds like a noble decision,' she noted quietly. 'Though you were so scrawny back then.'

He laughed, unoffended. 'I guess. Things started to change after I took the training. I tried to do more.'

'And then you left.'

Was that a hitch he heard in her voice? 'Yeah, but I trained

as much as I could while I was away. Found stations to volunteer at if I stayed anywhere long enough. When I got back, the station put me through the final test again and brought me in when I passed.'

He accepted the fresh beer she handed him before dishing up their food.

'They needed as many hands as they could get.'

'Volunteer firefighter, silent philanthropist, photojournalist…'

She gave him a plate and he realised why what she'd made smelled that good. Biriyani. *Biriyani.*

'That's quite the CV, Mr Giles.'

'Yeah, but it doesn't include the ability to make biriyani.' He inhaled appreciatively. 'How did you manage to make this so quickly?'

She laughed. 'I became a pro when I realised I didn't care for the commitment of more than two hours for cooking. It probably doesn't taste as good as those ones, but you'll survive.'

He took a mouthful and groaned. 'This is just as good as any other I've tasted.'

She reached over the counter and patted his cheek. 'Oh, poor, naïve Noah. I do appreciate your inexperience.'

He snorted, but didn't reply. Not only because the food was genuinely amazing, but because her touch had seared his skin. And he couldn't do anything about it. Couldn't say anything about it. He was sure that if he did the easiness they'd somehow got back would disappear.

'I'm sure your dad is looking forward to having you around for the next few weeks.'

'Yeah.' He frowned. 'But it isn't for a few weeks.'

'No? He told me—' She broke off when he gave her a look. Again, a pretty blush stained her cheeks. 'He likes talking about you.'

'Does he? How much?'

'Every time I visit.'

Needing time to digest that information, he ate more food, and then took his time drinking his beer.

'I know we've spoken about it, but this friendship you have with my dad is weird.'

She laughed softly and settled next to him with her own food. But she didn't start eating. Instead, she ran her fork over the rice, ruffling it as she did so, over and over.

'I used to think so, too. And so does Jaden. And my parents.'

'They're probably worried he's going to rob the cradle. What?' he asked when she gave him an unhappy look. 'It's happened before. It'll happen again.'

'He's *lonely*, Noah. Your mother died when you were four. Can you imagine the loneliness that follows losing the love of your life *and* having to raise a four-year-old by yourself?'

'That loneliness has nothing to do with my mother dying.'

'Of course it does. Your father's love for your mother—'

'Made him weak.' Bitterness controlled his tongue. 'She cheated on him and he forgave her, even though I know how much she hurt him. That's when the real loneliness started.'

He ran a hand over his mouth, then pressed it to the counter.

'And then she died, and he started jumping from one relationship to another. But that had nothing to do with loneliness. He was—*is*—just running from his weakness. From her. From the memory of her.'

When she didn't respond he looked over at her, and winced when he saw her face.

'You didn't know.'

She shook her head slowly.

'I'm sorry, I thought—'

'Don't,' she interrupted. 'You have nothing to apologise for.'

'I thought… You're friends with him… Or Jaden…' He didn't know what he was saying. Or why he still felt as if he needed to apologise.

'Jaden wouldn't have told me,' she said after a long pause. 'He wouldn't have broken your trust like that. And your fa-

ther…' She took another pause. 'My friendship with your father started because I didn't want to…to talk about things.'

She cleared her throat.

'About being left at the altar. About how it messed with—' She broke off, gave a quick shake of her shoulders. 'My point is that your father never asked me about any of it. And, yeah, neither did *my* family, but your father's silence about it didn't come with expectations. He didn't… He didn't *need* me to pretend that I was fine when I wasn't.'

'But your family did?'

'It was better for us all if I pretended. That way they could move on with their lives and I could…*deal* with things.' Her face tightened, but she continued. 'And even though your father didn't ask me anything, he let me ask *him* things. And he answered, even though some of my questions were inappropriate.'

His heart thudded. 'What did you ask him?'

'How he could deal with the failures. With the broken relationships. With the brokenness.' She lifted her hands and he knew she was referring to herself. As if *she* were broken. 'He told me I needed to move on. Move forward. And that was it. That was about as deep as we got. He wouldn't have told me about it either.'

He didn't reply. Tried to process what she was saying.

'I think,' she said slowly, 'that, for him, moving on—moving forward—meant pretending like your mother didn't cheat.' She hesitated on the last word. 'I'm sorry.'

'Don't be. It makes sense.'

And because it did, he couldn't find the words to break the silence that fell over them. He ate the rest of his dinner, but didn't taste it. And then he excused himself and went to do the dishes.

A part of him knew that his feelings about his father were irrational. And that somewhere in those feelings there was an anger he'd transferred to his father after his mother had died. After he'd realised the truth of what she'd done, of what he'd seen. After his father had confirmed it.

Because how could he have been upset with his mother? His life had gone on in the same way it had before he'd seen his mother with another man. Even when, as an adult, he'd thought back to the few memories he had of before she'd died, Noah couldn't remember his parents acting any differently because of what had happened. It had only been after her death that things had changed. And he couldn't blame her for that.

But he did blame his father.

All Noah had seen growing up had been a steady influx of women in his father's life. Some stayed longer than others. Some were kinder than others. And sure, those who'd been kinder *had* stayed for longer.

But as the father of a young child, shouldn't his father have protected him from witnessing that? From experiencing the instability? From the consequences Noah now saw in his own life because of it?

Or had he wanted his father to protect him from what his mother had done?

He paused as the thought stumped him. As it had him wondering if his father wasn't the only one running from the memory of his mother. Whether Noah's stance on relationships was just as much because of his mother's cheating as it was because of his father's behaviour.

Was *he* weak, too?

'Noah?' Ava said softly, and he started when he saw her standing in the kitchen with him. 'Are you okay?'

'Fine,' he lied, though he didn't think he did it particularly well. Not when the uneasiness in his chest was reflected in his tone.

Had he been judging his father too harshly?

There was a long silence as she studied him. As he dried his hands off to give them something to do because her looking at him made him restless. And then she stepped forward and slipped her hands around his waist, laying her head on his chest.

In that simple movement the war inside him settled. As if

her body against his—her body in his arms—had brokered some kind of peace treaty. Pieces mended that he hadn't known were broken before. And one particular piece—one he'd known about but had ignored—clicked into place.

He couldn't run from her. He'd never been able to.

He tightened his arms around her and then stepped back, afraid of what he might do now that he'd allowed himself to acknowledge that he felt something for her. Afraid of what it meant that he'd let himself acknowledge it *now,* after discovering that his relationship fears extended more deeply than he'd thought.

It had thrown everything he knew about himself, about their relationship, into a hurricane he could feel inside him. And facing it would bring that hurricane's destruction into his life. Into their lives.

He couldn't do it. He wouldn't.

She sensed the shift before she saw it. On his face. In his body. His eyes.

But then, what did she expect? He'd just told her his mother had cheated on his father. And *she'd* told him that maybe his father had chosen not to remember that fact so that he could move on with his life. So that he could move on from Noah's *mother.* So that he could move on *with other women.*

Milo was right; she *did* have a knack for saying the worst things at the worst times. It had been one of the many things he'd told her when he'd listed the faults which made her unsuitable for marriage. Faults that had had her remembering every single failure in her life and how they'd somehow been a result of those faults.

'You're too honest.'

'You say the wrong things all the time.'

'You make light of everything.'

'You're so prickly.'

It sickened her that she still heard his voice in her head. That the insecurity she'd felt since then was almost a daily

occurrence. But the doubt didn't leave her just because she was annoyed it had come courtesy of her ex. Though she wished it didn't have her regretting simple things, like offering someone she cared about a hug because she wanted to comfort him.

To avoid thinking about it, she walked back around the counter and forced herself to finish her meal. She handed Noah the dish once she was done, and as he washed it, she went over to the couch where Zorro had made himself comfortable.

But her thoughts still buzzed in her head, like a fly caught in a room looking for an escape.

Suddenly determined to quieten them, she stood and got her phone. She scrolled to the appropriate song, linked her phone to Noah's Bluetooth speakers, and a few seconds later Christmas carols filled the room.

Zorro looked up in confusion at the sound, and Ava's lips twitched when, seconds later, she saw the same expression mirrored on Noah's face.

'Care to explain?' he asked as he joined her in the living room.

'We are *not* going to get sucked into the drama of this wedding and this season and our pasts,' she told him fiercely. 'So we're going to decorate this tree and have fun doing it.'

CHAPTER TWELVE

IT *WAS* FUN.

He hadn't expected it to be. He'd expected tension after their conversation. After their hug. But it was almost as if Ava had closed the door on anything that might have prevented them from having a good time. And somehow he found himself following suit, refusing to let himself dwell on the darkness of his realisations.

She'd always had the ability to do that. To make things seem…lighter. And whether that was because she joked about them or because she put her unique brand of I-don't-care on it, she never failed to make him feel better.

Which, he supposed, was part of his problem.

'Do you remember that year Jaden went through his goth phase?' Ava handed him a twinkling ball and pointed to where she wanted him to hang it on the tree.

'I do. Fondly. Although, as soon as it was over he vehemently denied it had ever happened.'

'And we'd believe him,' she said, eyes twinkling, 'if it weren't for photographic evidence.'

'You have *photos*?'

'*So* many photos.' She handed him another ball, waving her hand to indicate that he could put it anywhere. 'The goth one is my favourite. Especially because it happened over Christmastime, and the contrast between our Christmas tree and Jaden's all-black clothing is hilarious. Well,

that and the fact that I get to use it for my slideshow at the rehearsal dinner.'

His eyes widened. 'They're letting you do a *slideshow*?'

'*Letting* is not quite the word. I'd say forcing.'

She stretched up to put the last of the ornaments at the top of the tree, revealing the smooth skin at her belly. Noah swallowed.

'Leela wanted to include me. Again, I couldn't exactly say no. The upside is neither could Jaden. Though he's begged me to keep it "appropriate".'

'Which, of course, you'll ignore.'

'Of course,' she agreed, smiling winningly at him.

His heart pattered. 'An unfair advantage for our game.'

Something tightened on her face, but then she relaxed. 'Perhaps. But you have your best man's speech, so—'

'Oh, no.' He groaned.

'Oh, no?' she repeated with a smile, and finished putting tinsel around the base of the tree. 'Did you forget? Please tell me you forgot. It would make my night.'

'I *did* forget.' He rubbed a hand over his face, and then sank down into a chair. When he felt it dip behind him, he realised he'd almost sat on the cat. 'Sorry,' he said absent-mindedly, and then shook his head. 'Jaden didn't tell me.'

'I'm sure he didn't think he had to. It's a well-known responsibility of the best man. Which you should have known, considering...' She trailed off with a wrinkled nose, but he couldn't tell if it was because of their earlier discussion or because she was making fun of him.

'Yeah, well, my dad didn't once ask me to make a speech. He must have known I might have said something...un-filtered.'

'Or maybe he just didn't care about tradition.'

She smiled, and he realised it was a peace offering. An apology of sorts in case she'd offended him. But other than the fact that he had to take a moment to figure out whether she was right—she *did* seem to understand his father bet-

ter than he did—he hadn't been offended. And she should have known that.

'Look, I don't want us to tiptoe around each other because of—' he waved a hand '—everything. My relationship with my father is complicated. More so, I think, because I've never told him how I feel. About what happened with my mother or about his relationships after.'

There was pulse in the air, and Noah's heart dropped.

'I thought you said you didn't talk about deep things,' he said.

'I also told you we speak about you a lot,' she replied sympathetically. 'I mean, I might be wrong, but he's always spoken as if he knows about your disapproval. At least about his relationships after your mother.' She paused. 'Again, I know this is probably really weird for you, and I'm sorry. In fact, if I'd known you'd be coming back and we'd be having this conversation, maybe I wouldn't have become his friend.'

'You didn't think I was coming back?'

'You didn't,' she pointed out. 'For seven years you didn't come back.'

He straightened in his seat. 'It bothered you?' When she shook her head, looked away, his heart ached. 'It *hurt* you.'

'It's not… I'm fine. I'm *fine*,' she said again as he stretched out and took her hand, pulling her towards him so that she could sit down next to him.

He put his arm around her waist—gently, loosely—so that if she wanted she could pull away from him.

'I didn't realise. I should have, but I didn't.'

'Why should you have known? We weren't friends.'

'But we were *something*.' Unable to resist, he lifted a hand and cupped her cheek. 'I don't have the words to describe it, so I'll settle for that. Something. We were something.'

'Something?' she repeated, and lifted a hand over his. 'It's describes this—us—perfectly.'

He smiled, and then felt it fade. 'I am sorry. I shouldn't have blocked you. I should have tried to contact you.'

'Why didn't you?'

His hand fell to her lap and her own followed quickly, tangling with his. As if she wanted to tell him that her question hadn't been an accusation. As if she wanted him to know that her hurt didn't matter.

And, because it did, he answered her truthfully. 'I was scared. I was scared that I'd messed it up with that kiss.'

'How could you have messed it up when it had been fine before? After the first kiss.'

'Because before—' He sucked in a breath. 'Before you were just sixteen. You didn't know any better, and I... I made excuses.'

Her eyes widened, and when he realised how deep a hole he'd dug himself he tossed the shovel aside and dived in.

'I told myself anything I had to to make sure things wouldn't change—just like we agreed.'

'And the second time?'

'The second time... Well, the second time, there wasn't an opportunity for excuses. There was just accusation. Just guilt.'

Her hand tightened, and it felt as if she were pulling away from him. But he held on.

'It was easier to feel that way than to feel something else, Ava. And I was scared of losing my friendship with Jaden.'

'But what about *me*?'

He couldn't answer that question. Didn't know if he could tell her that his guilt had been about more than just his friendship with Jaden. It had been about taking advantage of her. Taking his broken heart out on her.

'I made a mistake,' he said softly.

'It wasn't a mistake. It was a choice. You made a choice.'

When she lifted her eyes to his, what he saw there stole his breath.

'Just like you chose to cut all contact with me.' She blew out a breath. 'You chose Jaden. I don't blame you for that. At least, I try not to.'

'I couldn't stay in touch with you and keep believing it was a mistake.'

He'd surprised himself with that, and when silence followed his words, he didn't know how to break it. Eventually she nodded, and then patted his hand with hers.

'Come on,' she said, her voice sounding as if she were fighting for the easy tone. 'We still have to put the angel on top of the tree.'

'Sure,' he said, determination lighting inside him. 'But first, I need to make another decision. We both do, actually.'

'What are you talking about?'

'I want to kiss you, Ava,' he said softly. 'But because it's going to complicate our lives, without a doubt, I need you to make that decision with—'

She pressed her lips to his.

She'd heard nothing more after Noah had said he wanted to kiss her. Which was probably why she was still kissing him, even though somewhere vaguely in her mind she knew he'd been warning her about something.

But who cared when his lips were on hers? When this gorgeous, sexy, *beautiful* man was kissing her?

In that moment she forgot that she'd been left at the altar. She forgot that even on her best days the fact that she had been left at the altar took something from her.

But not now. Oh, no, not now.

Now she was thinking that she was whole again. That Milo had been a fool to leave her. That *he* had been in the wrong. That *he'd* been the reason things hadn't worked out.

Because it was hard to think of herself as anything less than perfect when Noah Giles was kissing her.

He was the kind of kisser who did everything intentionally. Every touch of his tongue, every movement of his lips—all intentional. And all with the intention of making her—Ava Keller, the woman he was kissing—feel as if she were the only woman in the entire world.

She let him sweep her away with it. Let herself enjoy the way he knew which plunge of his tongue would give her goosebumps. Let herself lean into the way his fingers

brushed over her body, the way his hands kneaded and squeezed.

She felt powerful when she heard him moan. Felt a healing warmth pool in her heart just as she felt it pool low in her stomach. She didn't complain when he pulled away from her mouth and pressed kisses on her jaw, on the slope of her neck. Heard herself moan when his mouth claimed hers again with a passion—a *need*—she didn't think she'd ever felt from a man before.

This kiss was nothing like the ones they'd shared before. It wasn't inquisitive, nor desperate, though there was both curiosity and desperation in the mating of their lips now. But the overriding emotion Ava felt as she kissed Noah was the sense that it was *right*. That this was where she *belonged*.

It was a terrible thing to feel. And it would no doubt keep her awake long after it had ended. But for now, in this moment, she let herself feel right. She let herself feel whole. And when he shifted and pressed his body over hers she let herself be seduced.

'We probably shouldn't—'

Ava cut him off by pulling his head back to hers, and Noah smiled against her mouth, letting her kiss him.

He didn't want to be the one who stopped them. Knew that if he did he'd regret it. But then, he thought, maybe he'd regret it anyway. More intensely once he realised that he *was* kissing her. That he was *enjoying* kissing her. That he wanted nothing more than to *keep* kissing her.

'Ava,' he said with a sigh, leaning his forehead against her. 'This is turning into something that—'

'Something that both of us want and one of us *desperately* needs to get out of her head?'

He chuckled lightly, and pressed a peck to her lips. 'Yes. Both of us for both of those things.'

'Then why are you stopping?'

'Because it's too fast.'

'Hmm…' she said, and shifted under him.

He got up, and for the first time noticed the cat watching them from the opposite coach. He wasn't even sure when Zorro had moved. He'd been too…involved.

'Fast used to be your pace.'

'And look where *that* got me.' *And my father.* 'So I suppose the more important question at this point it why you're so determined to go fast.'

'I'm not—'

'Ava,' he interrupted gently.

She sighed. 'Maybe I think that if we go fast we'll outrun the reasons this is a bad idea. Or forget how poorly it could turn out.'

He stared at her, and then laughed. 'Well, you *do* have a point.'

Her mouth curved. 'I generally seem to.'

'And yet you still doubt yourself,' he said. 'You shouldn't.'

She opened her mouth, but nothing came out. She closed it again and nodded. 'I suppose. So,' she continued after a moment, 'I guess I should go to bed. Alone,' she said on an exhalation of breath that was as much disappointment as air.

He laughed. 'Or you could stay here and we could put the angel on the tree. And then,' he said, taking her hand, 'we could kiss some more.'

'But I thought you said—'

'Not going fast doesn't mean we can't stay in the same spot, Ava.'

He took the angel from the chair and put it on the top of the tree before pulling Ava back into his arms.

It was fine. It would all be fine. Fine. *Fine.* All completely fine.

Ava groaned as she made her way down the path that led to Leela's parents' house. Their property was gorgeous: beautiful green hills, tall trees and an incredible view of the Helderberg Mountain. And that didn't even include the view of the house: the tall white building that looked more like a showpiece than somewhere people lived.

But she barely saw it with her mind whirling around the way it was. Because this was the first time she'd see Noah since they'd spent that entire night making out. It had been an immensely satisfying evening, the kind she hadn't experienced in ages. But they hadn't slept together, and now, with the benefit of hindsight, Ava took solace in that fact.

Though it didn't help her feel any less guilty. And she knew that seeing Noah now, a week later, would be strange.

Still, she kept telling herself that it was fine.

Noah had helped her clean her house of soot the day after their night of making out, when she'd been allowed back onto the estate, and that had been fine. Granted, there had been touches and kisses, and maybe a half an hour of making out before he'd left, but things had been *fine*. Just as her work week—which had been so busy she hadn't had time to talk with him—had been fine.

It was all fine. Fine, fine, *fine*.

Which is why you're acting like a complete fool right now.

Ava paused, blew out a breath. And then inhaled deeply and exhaled for the same length of time. She was freaking out because of Noah, yes. But she knew it was also because this was the first wedding event where she'd have to face *people*. People who'd seen her fiancé walk away from her at her own wedding. People who'd seen the shock and hurt on her face.

She couldn't be surly. It would only prove to them that she'd had as hard a time about it as they believed. Besides, the time to be surly was over. It had been fine when they'd been planning. But now, with the rehearsal dinner, Leela and Jaden were actually starting their journey to committing to one another. She couldn't be surly about that.

And, in truth, she wasn't surly about *them*. She *wanted* Jaden and Leela to marry. She wanted them to be excited about their future together. She just hoped that neither of them would ever find out how it felt when all of it came crashing down around them.

Yeah, you're going to be completely fine.

Grunting at the stubborn voice in her heard, she squared

her shoulders and walked into the house. It was beautifully decorated. Tables were decked with the wedding colours—blue and yellow—though not overly so, so that it looked like as much of a wedding celebration as a festive one. There was a Christmas tree in the corner; lights draped across the room. The sliding doors were open to the pool with the mountain view just beyond it.

Even Ava had to admit she was impressed.

'Are you ready?'

The voice sent a thrill down her spine, and gave her the opportunity to school her face before turning to face its owner.

'For what?'

Noah's eyes swept over her—she felt almost naked when she saw the greed there—but he only smiled. 'To lose.'

'To— Ha!' she said, though her heart was still thumping. 'Try again, Giles. I'm already leading in this game.'

'By twenty points. Don't think that's a head start you'll be able to keep.'

'I'm not worried. You're much too nice for your own good.'

His lips curved, and then he leaned over and brushed a kiss on her cheek. 'You look amazing.'

Again, his eyes swept over her. This time he kept the perusal slow, steady, as if he were actually undressing her. She shifted her weight between her feet, resisting the urge to brush a hand against the blue-and-white polka dot dress she'd worn for the event.

She'd made an effort with her looks—she'd even put a yellow ribbon in her hair, for heaven's sake—because she'd known that good behaviour wasn't a guarantee. The dress was long, but the neck plunged between her breasts, and she hadn't been able to wear a bra.

She regretted it immensely.

'I appreciate your compliments, but if you don't pull yourself together people are going to ask if we need a room.'

'Not a bad idea.'

'What isn't?'

Jaden joined them with a frown, and both she and Noah straightened.

'Doing my speech for Ava later tonight,' Noah said easily. 'So she can give me some pointers.'

Ava kept her eyes on Jaden, but she could feel her face warming. Noah's words had sounded dirtier than he'd intended. Or perhaps *as* dirty as he'd intended. She couldn't tell with him.

'I'm not sure that's a good idea,' Jaden replied, and Ava let out her breath. 'Ava's not the best public speaker.'

'Well, had I known that's what you think about me I wouldn't have agreed to this stupid slideshow.' Ava tilted her head. 'But now that I know what you think about me I suppose it gives me a certain freedom. Maybe I should talk about that holiday in Zanzibar when you—'

'Ava,' Jaden said with a wince. 'Would you please not talk about my past relationships at the rehearsal dinner of my wedding?'

'But it's part of the fun,' she teased.

'Just wait until you—' Jaden's eyes widened as he realised what he was about to say. 'Ava, I'm sorry. I didn't mean—'

'Oh, look, it's Uncle Cyril,' she interrupted him brightly. 'I think I'm going to talk to him about our cousins.'

She left before Jaden could apologise again.

Before she could see more sympathy in his eyes.

CHAPTER THIRTEEN

'SHE'S JUST SAID she's going to talk to our uncle about the children he's estranged from.' Jaden groaned. 'Barely ten minutes in and I've already freaked her out.'

'I think that happened a long time ago,' Noah commented quietly, watching as Ava greeted the older man and began talking. He watched as the man put a hand on Ava's shoulder, saw her face blanch before she forced a smile and then said something that made the man frown.

She was playing the game by herself, he thought with a smile, and tried to figure out how he could make his way over to her without arousing suspicion.

'I don't know if that's true,' Jaden said, watching Ava, too.

Which, Noah thought in hindsight, was probably a good thing. He didn't know if his face held any of the lust—or those other pesky emotions—their kissing had brought to the surface.

'She hadn't been herself long before my wedding came along.'

'Really? Or is that just what you're telling yourself so you feel better about doing this at *this* time of year? Not to mention asking her to be in your wedding party after what happened?'

Jaden turned to him, his eyes narrowed. 'When did you become my sister's defender?'

'Since you've seemed to have abdicated the position.' As anger lit inside him Noah took a deep breath. 'But you can't

even answer my questions, Jaden, which makes me think you *know* how hard this has been for her. And don't even try arguing with me. You know I'm right.'

Jaden lifted the side of his mouth, though it wasn't in a smile. 'I don't like it that you're taking her side over mine.'

'Man, are you *listening* to yourself?' Noah grabbed a glass of champagne from a waiter to distract himself from the annoyance that had taken his anger's place. 'This isn't about sides. This is about you supporting your little sister through a tough time.'

Jaden blew out a breath and then stole Noah's champagne, downing it before Noah could complain.

'Wait,' Jaden said. 'How do you even know about all this? How do you know this is tough for her?'

'She…er…she told me.'

'She *told* you?' Jaden repeated.

Realising he was losing the higher ground, Noah ran a hand over his hair. 'Yeah, but only because we were talking about the wedding after the fire on Friday—' He stopped too late.

'Exactly *when* after the fire did you speak with my sister?'

'Round about the same time she told me about Tiff being a bridesmaid.' He wasn't proud of it, but his ex had walked in and given him the perfect opportunity to regain control.

'Look, about that—'

'It's fine,' he interrupted when his guilt immediately flared. 'I mean, what could you have done? She introduced you to the woman you're going to spend your life with. Ava,' he answered Jaden's unspoken question.

'She really ran her mouth off with you,' Jaden said with a frown. Then he shook his head. 'I should have told you.'

'Yeah, you should have.'

'I'm sorry.' He paused. 'I've been caught up with this wedding. Maybe too caught up, since I've been ignoring what Ava needs from me.' He set his empty champagne glass on a passing waiter's tray, and then patted Noah's back. 'But that doesn't mean you have free rein with my sister.'

'Wh—' Noah stopped, wondering how the conversation had turned pear-shaped again.

And because he didn't understand how—and because Jaden seemed to be in a strange mood and so did he—he didn't say what he wanted. That Ava wasn't an inanimate object. That she was a person with feelings. With agency.

'I don't know what you're talking about.'

'Yeah, you do.' Jaden said it easily, but there was a warning in his eyes. 'You know now and you knew it seven years ago, when you kissed her. She deserves more than what you've given the women who've come after Tiff.'

Jaden slapped him on the back again and walked away. It took Noah a few moments before he could figure out what had happened, and another few to process how he felt about what his best friend seemed to think of him.

But Jaden was right. Hadn't Noah himself thought about the control he exercised in his dating life not too long ago? The relationships he'd had after Tiff couldn't even be defined as such. There had been no emotions involved, on either side, and so no potential for hurt.

Still, Jaden's reaction had stung. More so because it was fair. And because now, after his conversation with Ava about his father—his mother—Noah knew his stance on relationships was more complicated than simply not wanting to repeat his father's mistakes.

He didn't want to repeat his father's pain.

He'd known it since the day Ava had told him about his father's advice to her to move on. But the more Noah thought about it, the more he'd realised that Kirk hadn't chosen to move on by forgetting about his wife's cheating, like Ava had said. No, Noah had been right when he'd thought his father was running.

But had he really thought that made his father weak? Because, if so, Noah was weak, too. Because though he'd chosen a different way to deal with it than his father had— choosing few to no relationships over a constant flow of

them—Noah's motivations were the same. Except he didn't think he'd ever outrun the pain. His father's or his own.

It turned his stomach. And strengthened his resolve that he couldn't fall for Ava. Not any more than he already had. Not when he didn't know if his pain would allow him to give Ava what she needed.

Jaden was right: Ava deserved more than what Noah could give her. Especially while he figured out what exactly that was. But when his eyes settled on her, Noah felt everything inside him yearn. And he knew his resolve wouldn't be easy to follow.

'If it wasn't against the rules I'd deduct all your measly forty points for leaving me alone for half an hour. *Half an hour!*'

'I'm sorry.'

'You sound sincere, but I can't help but think that you did it on purpose. So that you wouldn't have to reward me handsomely for all my efforts.'

'That bad?'

Ava took a glass of champagne from a waiter and gave him a look. 'It's bad enough that I'm going to drink this glass of champagne instead of the sparkling water I'd intended on drinking tonight.'

She downed it and reached for another.

Noah put a hand on her free hand when she moved the glass to her lips again, and there was understanding in his eyes when he said, 'You don't want to get drunk tonight, Avalanche. You want to be here for your brother and future sister-in-law. You want to give a funny, yet charmingly embarrassing speech with your slideshow for all these guests. And then you want to go home and pretend it didn't happen.'

She gritted her teeth. Forced herself to relax when he squeezed her hand. And then told herself not to cry.

'This is…harder than I thought it was going to be.' She sipped from the champagne to hide the tears prickling in her eyes.

'I'm sorry.'

'Don't be.' She forced a smile. 'It's not your fault.'

'No. But maybe if I'd stayed you wouldn't be going through this.'

She gave him an even look, ignoring the thrill going up and down her spine. 'If you'd stayed, Noah, I think I would have been in a lot more trouble than I am now.'

Her eyes shifted to behind him, and something tightened inside her when she saw her parents. And then she saw Noah's father just behind them, and that something loosened slightly.

'Ava?' Noah said when she pulled her hand from his.

She nodded her head in the direction of the new guests, and felt him straighten beside her.

'Aunty Ruth… Uncle Sam,' Noah said, giving them both hugs before doing the same with his father.

It was so familiar that it sent a pang through her for all the years they'd missed. But, putting it aside, she kissed her parents and hugged Noah's father. Kirk gave her an extra pat on the back, signalling his support, and she smiled with a slight nod.

She hadn't had to tell Kirk how being in Jaden's wedding had made her feel. But when she'd made her way to Kirk's house after Leela had asked her to be a bridesmaid—eyes dry and heart aching—he'd patted her on the back just as he had now. And then he'd told her some innocuous story about work and she'd listened, refusing to think about real life for the rest of the day.

Somehow Kirk had known that being in the wedding would bring all the memories back. The memories of inadequacy. Of disgrace. Of failure. Somehow Kirk had known, and not even her own family had. But then, Kirk's experiences put him in a unique position to understand. And, since her family hadn't had those experiences, how could they know unless she'd told them?

You told Noah.

But Noah didn't know all of it. There was both a comfort and a despair in that.

Because she couldn't reconcile it, she sipped her cham-

pagne and chatted with her parents. And ignored the concerned looks both Noah and Kirk sent her.

Tonight wouldn't be one of those moments when she gave up her control. No matter how stressed she was, she would get through her slideshow. Even with her insides quivering at the weight of keeping it together, she would get through it.

She *would*.

Ava was suffering. It was in the slight shake of her hand when she brought the champagne flute to her lips. In the way she smiled at her parents but her eyes remained cautious. How the corners of her eyes were crinkled with strain. How her lips thinned whenever she wasn't fake smiling.

He didn't understand how the others couldn't see it. Or, if they could, how they didn't care. And, since he'd specifically told Jaden about it, Noah had to believe his friend was *choosing* not to care. It bothered him so much he didn't know what to do with the anger vibrating through his body.

When it was announced that Ava wanted to say something about the happy couple, he almost snorted. There was no *want* in this situation. She'd been forced to say something. And, as miserable as she was about all of it, the fact that she'd agreed reinforced that she was determined to make the rest of her family believe she was okay. And make them feel better about themselves as a result.

Even at the cost of her own happiness.

He positioned himself towards the front of the room, ready in case something happened, though he wasn't entirely sure what could happen. But he wanted to make sure Ava knew he was there for her. He hadn't been before, but he would be now.

He tried not to think about what that meant for his determination not to fall for her.

'Hello, ladies and gentlemen,' Ava said into the microphone they'd handed her. 'For those of you who don't know me, I'm Jaden's baby sister, Ava. And for those of you who

do know me, you must be wondering why in the world Jaden would allow me to say something at his rehearsal dinner.'

The crowd laughed as Jaden pulled a face, his expression then relaxing into an easy smile. Noah turned his attention back to Ava. To anyone who didn't know her she'd look poised and relaxed. To those who did she looked tense and unhappy.

Noah clenched his jaw.

'But I managed to convince him so that I could tell you all how wonderful it is that he's finally found the love of his life in Leela.' She paused and smiled at them, and it seemed almost genuine. 'Actually, I'm going to *show* you, because I've come prepared with pictures!'

Noah was caught by her as she spoke, as she laughed, as she made the crowd laugh. She was perfect as she told stories of the different phases Jaden had gone through—goth phase included—and alluded to the women who'd been a part of those phases.

When she said that Leela had never been a part of any phase the crowd sighed. When she said she'd never seen her brother happier the crowd applauded. And when she wished them both well and toasted them the crowd drank to the couple and cheered as Ava kissed them both.

And still he was caught only by her. By the strength she'd shown in getting through it. By the love and affection she'd shown to her brother. Even though it had killed her.

When she left the room immediately afterwards Noah followed, finding her sitting at the top of the steps that led to Leela's parents' tennis court, her head in her hands.

'Hey,' he said quietly, sitting beside her, though all he wanted to do was take her into his arms and comfort her.

'Hey.' Her voice was raspy, but when she lifted her head, there were no tears on her face.

'That was pretty good,' he said after a moment.

'Funny and charmingly embarrassing?'

He chuckled. 'Exactly.'

'Great. So you'll support me as I get really, *really* drunk now?'

'You don't want to do that.'

'I don't.' She sighed. 'I just want to stop hurting.'

CHAPTER FOURTEEN

THE WORDS SAT between them and Noah didn't know what to do with them. He didn't want to push, but he also didn't want her to ruminate on it.

Just ask, dummy.

Nearly rolling his eyes at his inner voice, he said, 'Do you want to talk about it?'

'I don't think anyone's ever asked me that,' she replied after a long moment. 'Everyone just assumes I *don't* want to talk about it. Which is fair. I don't. But nor do they.' She paused. 'The Kellers have a talent for pretending things didn't happen. Or hiding their feelings about it.'

'Can't say I've noticed,' he commented dryly.

She laughed. 'You're practically part of the family and yet it hasn't affected *you*.'

'I'm not sure that's true.'

'Isn't it?' she asked, but didn't wait for an answer. 'You've always seemed pretty self-aware to me.'

'I'm not. I've only just realised I've been angry with my father for trying to protect himself from hurt. And that I've been blaming him for—' He broke off, knowing he couldn't say any more. Instead he picked up a stone and threw it across the court, wincing when it hit the net. 'I'm probably going to have to pick that up.'

'Probably.'

Silence lingered between them.

'I think...' He started to speak without realising, and when

his mind caught up to his mouth he almost stopped. But then he thought that the words were already there, and that if he wanted *her* to talk he needed to talk, too. 'Maybe you think I'm self-aware because something about you makes me feel like I can share things with you.'

'Or maybe you just need to talk.'

'No, it's you.'

'That's not true.'

'It's definitely true. Why else would I be sitting outside with you after your brother warned me not to? I could—'

'Wait—what?' She frowned. 'My brother told you *not* to come outside and sit with me?'

'Your brother told me that I needed to stay away from you.' He shrugged, but his emotion didn't feel as careless as the gesture.

'What a—' She stopped, shook her head. 'He had no right to do that.'

'He's looking out for you.' He paused. 'I don't know why he's decided to do that now. When it's too late to keep you from hurting like this.'

'He can't protect me from life,' she said after a moment. 'I fell in love. Got my heart broken. And he was there for me all through it.'

'He should have sussed the guy out. Clearly he wasn't right for you.'

'You don't know that.'

'I *do* know that,' he said. 'You're here, in pain, and not with this man. He wasn't right for you. And I bet you knew that long before he left you at the altar.'

She didn't reply, and suddenly something occurred to him.

'I'm sorry. I'm crossing the line.' His heart ached as he said it. 'I just assumed—'

'What?'

'That you're over him. I shouldn't have said—'

'No.' She interrupted him quietly. 'I *am* over him.'

She took a deep breath and lifted a hand to her face, be-

fore clasping it with her other hand and lowering them both between her knees.

'I'm not over what he did to me, but I'm over *him*.' She turned to look at him. 'You're right. He wasn't the right man.'

When unspoken words—unspoken emotions—stirred the air between them, hijacking the silence, highlighting the tension, Noah cleared his throat.

'So why didn't Jaden *do* something? Why didn't he warn the guy like he did me?'

'Maybe his warning abilities only came after his engagement.'

He laughed. 'Oh, no, those abilities have been alive and well since that time he caught us kissing. I still remember our discussion.' He winced. 'That's probably too civil a word, but you get the idea.'

He felt her surprise before he saw it. Before she angled her body; before her features twisted into an expression he'd have thought cute if he hadn't seen her eyes. If he hadn't seen the confusion, the anger, the hurt there.

The hurt bothered him the most.

'Exactly what kind of discussion, if not civil?'

'I…er…we just spoke about how inappropriate my actions were.'

'Your actions?' she repeated, tilting her head as she shifted even further away from him. 'You mean when you kissed yourself? Or when you kissed me and there was no reciprocation?'

'Ava, it's not—'

'Because *your* actions were inappropriate that day?' She stood now. 'Me wrapping my legs around you, pressing my body against yours, asking you—both verbally and non-verbally—to take me back to your place and—'

'Ava, please.' He stood now, too, his legs shaky. He couldn't hear her say those words again. Not when he'd been successfully running from them for most of the last seven years. 'You're upset about everything that's happened today—'

'How would *you* know?' She put her hands on her hips. '*What* do you know other than what I've told you?'

'Ava—'

'*No*, Noah. I can't be the bigger person right now. I can't pretend you blocking my emails doesn't bother me. Or ignore the fact that you've talked about me with my brother like I'm some kind of possession and not a woman with the ability to make my own decisions. Or,' she said with a frown, 'how that talking with my brother probably *led* to you blocking me.'

He gave a curt nod—he was helpless not to when she'd just confirmed everything he'd already known—and she rolled her eyes.

'Why the hell do I even bother?' she asked.

And walked away.

Men were ridiculous. They were annoying. They were the *worst*.

If she had her way she'd never have to deal with them again. Or at the very least she wouldn't have to stay at a dinner during which she was forced to look into the faces of two men who reminded her how ridiculous—annoying, the *worst*—they really were.

She'd detoured the moment she'd re-entered the room after her chat with Noah and had seen Jaden heading for her. Had gone so far as to wait in the bathroom for twenty minutes—not fun—so that she wouldn't have to speak with him.

By the time she came out the dinner was starting and Jaden was preoccupied. Noah, on the other hand, seemed to have been waiting for her. He nodded his head to the empty seat next to him and she nearly laughed. He thought she was going to sit next to *him*? Maybe she *should* have laughed, just to show him how ridiculous he was being.

Instead she ignored him and took a seat next to her parents.

How she got through the rest of the stupid evening, she had no idea. But as soon as dinner had ended and she knew people would no longer care whether she was there or not, she tried to leave the party.

Tried.

'Ava—wait.'

Ava clenched her jaw, then relaxed it and turned to face her aunt. She'd been avoiding the woman since she'd seen her glide in as if she was the queen of the party. Taking in her jewels and overly formal dress, Ava thought her aunt might actually believe that she was.

'I've been trying to speak with you all evening.'

'Really?' Ava arranged an easy smile on her face. 'I didn't realise.'

'I wanted to know how you've been.'

'Just peachy. I mean, as peachy as I *can* be after my fiancé—whom I loved—left me at the altar in front of my friends and family.'

Her aunt blinked, and satisfaction rippled through Ava. This was what her aunt wanted, wasn't it? To revel in Ava's misery. To take pleasure from the fact that her niece was struggling.

'Yes, well, that *was* what I wanted to know.' Her aunt smiled sympathetically. 'I can't imagine what it's like to re-build your life after something like that happens.'

'Hard. I've had days when I didn't want to get out of bed. Nights when I couldn't stop thinking about what was wrong with me. And then, of course, there are the people. Those who—for some strange reason—want to know about *what* happened without really caring *who* it happened to.' She let out a little sigh. 'Honestly, celebrating another wedding this soon has made *everything* better.'

There was a beat between Ava's last word and the feeling of utter dread as she realised she'd taken it too far. Damn it, why did she always take it too far?

'You told me you weren't going to keep on pulling people's legs like this, Ava!'

Ava's spine stiffened at Noah's voice, before her mind processed his words.

'I can't help it.' She gave him a smile she hoped was teasing, but she honestly couldn't be sure. 'It's so easy.'

'I know. But you make them panic.' Noah handed her a glass of champagne that he took from a waitress nearby and smiled at Ava's aunt. 'It was a running joke between us until I realised that she was freaking out her family.'

'This…this is a *joke*?'

'Afraid so.' Noah's smile was effortlessly charming. 'You know Ava's sense of humour.'

'I—I don't think I do.'

If Ava hadn't already embarrassed herself, she would have enjoyed her usually self-assured aunt's stammering.

'Of *course* you do,' Noah said, his smile widening. 'It's from her mother's side of the family.'

Ava stifled her laugh, and there was a long pause before her aunt gave a polite excuse and walked away.

It was just the two of them then, and she handed him back the champagne flute.

'Seventy points. It would be higher, but you used my embarrassment to get your points.'

'Which, in my humble opinion, should be the reason I get at least ninety points. I saw an opportunity and I went for it.'

'Eighty. That's my final offer.'

She didn't wait to see if he accepted, instead turning to the front door so that she could leave as she'd wanted to in the first place.

She got as far as the steps that led to the pathway a few metres from the door.

'You don't want to know how many points I gave you?'

She turned. 'For embarrassing myself?'

'For embarrassing your aunt. The point of this game.'

'Fine,' she said after a beat. 'How many?'

'Twenty.'

'*Twenty?*' She rolled her eyes. 'Keep your points.'

'Well, you started with fifty, by calling your aunt out for asking about you but not really caring. Then you lost thirty for lying about how you feel. Ten for each lie.'

'I didn't lie.'

'You said that you've struggled to get out of bed—' he

lifted a finger '—that you've wondered what was wrong with you—' another finger '—and that you *want* to be in this wedding.' He lifted a third.

Tired now, she sighed. 'You only have to deduct ten points. There was only one lie.'

She walked down the stairs and didn't bother to look back or stop when he called to her.

CHAPTER FIFTEEN

HE COULDN'T LET her leave like that. Not when he knew which one the lie was. Not when, after the second time she'd told him something was wrong with her, the truth made his stomach turn.

He ran until he was next to her, and when she sighed he ignored it.

'Just leave me alone.'

'Not when you're in this mood.'

She grunted, but again he ignored it. Instead he kept walking beside her, as if somehow his presence would manage to convince her that she could talk to him. That she could trust him.

But by the time they reached the car park, she still hadn't said anything.

He considered what he'd do if she got into her car and left the party. Would he get into his and follow her? He hadn't said goodbye to anyone—not Jaden, not his father—but he supposed he could make something up to satisfy them. But then he remembered the look Jaden had given him earlier— when he'd returned to the party shortly after Ava had—and he wondered whether anything he made up would be believable.

In the end he didn't have to make the decision. Ava stalked past her car and took a path just beyond the car park that he hadn't seen before. He hung back when the path became too

narrow for him to walk next to her, and although he wanted
to ask where they were going he just looked around him.

The path was enclosed by vines that created an archway
the entire way down. Soft pink flowers clung to the vines
and, without thinking, he picked one, then awkwardly stared
at it in his hand. Before he could decide what to do with it
his attention was drawn to the fact that the path had ended,
opening up to a medium-sized dam hidden from the main
property.

'Have you been here before?' he asked in a breathless
voice, too amazed that something like this could actually
be on someone's property to care.

'Once. A long time ago.'

She kicked off her shoes, tossed her bag to the side, then
pulled her dress up to expose her legs to mid-thigh.

'It was during the day, at an extravagant party much like
the one at the house now.' She breathed in deeply, and as she
exhaled she looked at the sky. 'Personally, I prefer it like this.
With the stars reflecting in the water from the sky. And a
small ball of silver right over there for the moon.'

She nodded her head in its direction, and then walked to
the edge of the dam, the water lapping over her feet.

'I don't know if that's a good idea, Ava,' he said care-
fully, as memories of the two of them in a similar situation
taunted him.

'I don't care if it's a good idea.' She'd walked deeper into
the water now, and it reached to her knees. 'It's cool and re-
freshing and it's making me feel better so I don't care.'

After a few more minutes he realised he wasn't going
to convince her to sit on the grass with him. Sighing, he
kicked off his own shoes, removed his socks and rolled up
his black trousers.

He put his phone and wallet on top of the rest of their be-
longings and walked to the water. He hissed when the water
touched his feet. But when she looked over lazily, and he was
drawn by the seduction of it, he no longer cared that *cool
and refreshing* wasn't quite how he'd describe the water.

'What are you doing, Noah?'

Even her words were seductive, he thought. But he didn't know if she'd intended them to be. Which made it even worse.

'You need someone to talk to,' he answered, instead of saying what he wanted to say. *I need to get you out of that dress and into my arms.* 'I'm here.'

She arched an eyebrow and his heart kicked.

'Something tells me that's not the only thing you're here for.'

Of *course* she'd be able to see through him.

'It's the only thing I'm asking for.'

Their eyes held for a moment, and then she shook her head. 'Why is it so important to you that I talk?'

'Because you've kept it all in for too long.' He paused. 'And you haven't told anyone what you're really feeling.'

'How do you know that?'

'I spoke with Jaden earlier. His reaction made me think that you haven't told *him* what you're feeling. The fact that your parents aren't rallying around makes me believe that you haven't told them either. And the way my father kept checking on you tonight tells me he suspects something, but doesn't know. And then, of course, there's the fact that you're standing here, almost waist-deep in a dam, which makes me think there are things you haven't figured out. Probably because you haven't said them out loud.'

She blew out a breath, and when her eyes met his they glistened slightly.

He took a step forward, but she shook her head, and he stopped. And then she sighed.

'Well, Noah, you're not wrong. Though I wish you were.'

Ava drew her dress up higher, so that the material of its skirt bunched just below her breasts. Then she moved deeper into the water.

'I wish it were as simple as this wedding reminding me of

the one I didn't have,' she continued. 'Or a Christmas wedding being a special reminder of my failure.'

'You didn't fail.'

'Of course I did.'

She spun, enjoying the way it sent ripples out across the rest of the water. Enjoying how it seemed so simple, uncomplicated. It inspired her to get through the rest of the conversation in the same way, even if what she was talking about *wasn't* simple and uncomplicated.

'I loved Christmas,' she said, just twisting gently now. It kept the ripples going, but didn't threaten her dress. 'You know how much I loved it.'

'Based on your opinion of my house, I thought you still did.'

Her lips curved at the dryness in his tone. 'I guess I still have some of that love inside me. But most of it's gone.' She sighed. 'The festivities I used to love just feel contrived now. The family time feels forced. Complicated and heavy. The things I used to love feel like they were a lifetime ago. Putting the tree up. Drinking and eating and laughing.'

'*We* just did that.'

'We did,' she said, surprise fluttering through her. 'But it was easier with you. You didn't keep looking at me to check if I was okay.'

'No,' he agreed. 'My reasons were different.'

She laughed softly. 'You're flirting with me even now?'

'Is it flirting if I'm being earnest?'

Not knowing how to answer him, she continued with the rest of her story. 'You weren't here. You didn't have to see how I looked when Milo left me in front of everyone I knew and loved. You didn't have to see me put on a brave smile as I followed him down the aisle, running after him as soon as I got out of that church.'

She tightened her grip on her dress.

'You didn't have to see him drive away and me sink to the floor. You didn't have to see me stay there, unable to cry because I knew people were watching me. You didn't have

to help me up. You didn't have to help me into a car. And you didn't have to see me curl into a ball on my way home.'

'Ava…' he whispered.

She heard the horror in his tone. But all desire for simplicity had gone out of the window now. She'd been captured by her own tale. Ensnared by the emotions. The memories.

'I think the worst thing for them was that I was determined not to show anyone he'd hurt me. Halfway to my house I uncurled from the ball and demanded we go back to the church. And then I marched back in and told everyone we had food and alcohol and the party would go on.'

She laughed at her audacity now, and the sound was harsh.

'I made sure I spoke with every single person who attended that reception. I explained to them that Milo and I had made a mistake and decided to go our separate ways. That I was fine and he was fine, and I assured them they could enjoy themselves. Even though I hadn't spoken to Milo I already knew we wouldn't get back together. He'd humiliated me. And he didn't have the decency to tell me why. He didn't deserve me.'

'He didn't,' Noah said fiercely. 'He didn't deserve you.'

'Except,' she said softly, almost as if he hadn't spoken at all, 'I couldn't believe that. Not entirely. I could only think that there must be something wrong with *me*. That *I* didn't deserve *him*.'

'He told you that when he eventually spoke with you, didn't he?'

'Not in so many words.' She took a breath. 'He came to my house the next day. I'd sent my family away because I needed time. I wanted to stop pretending. I didn't want to be "on", and with them I felt like I had to be.'

She paused.

'He said I was too much work.' She blinked, and felt wetness fall down her cheeks. 'As if I were a project that needed tackling. As if I were a dilapidated house that needed to be rebuilt.' She looked at Noah now. Noted the fierce look in his eyes. Heard it echo in her tone. 'We were together for five

years, and on our wedding day he discovered that he didn't want to work on this *project*. This *house*.'

'Please tell me he's somewhere in the world missing a digit.'

She gave him a look, though his words steadied her. 'If I'd removed something from his body, it wouldn't have been a finger or toe.'

He grimaced, and then laughed. 'Fair point.' He walked to her now, apparently not noticing he was soaking his trousers in the process. 'You're not too much work.'

'I might be.' She swallowed, and stilled when he brushed a thumb across her cheek, spreading the wetness of her tears over her skin.

'Not too much. Just…work. We're all work.'

'Not all of us are left at the altar because of it.'

'Because some of us are too scared to take that chance.'

He frowned, and she realised he was talking about himself. Perhaps he'd just discovered it about himself, and was reassuring her about something he didn't really believe was true.

'Taking chances is overrated,' she said under her breath.

He laughed, breaking the tension. 'I doubt most people in the world would agree with you.'

'Most people in the world haven't been left at the altar,' she said again. 'I have the moral high ground here, Noah. You don't want to mess with—'

She stopped as a huge wave of water washed over her. Partly because she was surprised—they were in a dam; there were no waves—and partly because all her efforts to keep her dress dry were now in vain.

'Did you—' She wiped the water from her face. 'Did you just *splash* me? When my hair and face are *perfectly* made up? When my dress—which is *very* expensive—is still—'

She was silenced by another wave of water. This time she didn't bother coming up. Instead, she sank under the water, knowing that inevitable panic would cause Noah to come closer.

Just as she'd thought, she felt his leg against her belly, and before he could do anything she'd come up in front of him and was pulling him down with her.

A part of her knew that he was letting her drag him down. He was much too strong for just the weight of her arms to pull him under. But, as if he'd accepted his punishment, he stayed under the water for as long as she held him down.

When they came up, he flicked his hair back and wiped his face.

'Fair.'

She stared, and then laughed. 'Of *course* that's all you're saying about this.'

He lifted a shoulder. 'It *is* fair. I started it.'

'Why?'

'It seemed like the perfect way to distract you.'

Softening, she rolled her eyes. 'Yeah, well, it's not only going to distract me, but also the entire party when we go back up there in soaked clothing.'

He winced. 'I didn't think about that.'

'No, I didn't think you did.' She sighed and pushed herself deeper into the water. 'But we're here now, and we're probably going to get into trouble anyway, so we might as well enjoy it.'

He hadn't thought his actions through, but now, watching Ava relax in the water, he couldn't make himself regret it.

'What is it with you and water?' he asked suddenly, surprising himself. 'You've always been at your happiest when you're swimming.'

'I don't know,' she said, straightening where she'd been floating on her back. 'I guess it was all the family holidays we spent in the water. Beaches, swimming pools, dams...' She sighed happily. 'Good memories.'

'I agree.'

Her eyes met his and immediately the energy around them snapped. He could have sworn he saw the water boiling. Because, as he'd intended, his words had made her think about

the last time they'd been in the water together. About the memories they'd created then.

'No,' she breathed when he closed the distance between them.

Dutifully, he stopped. 'I'm sorry.'

'Don't be. I just… You mess with my head. And kissing you…' She shook her head.

And even though the curls on her head were misshapen with water—even though the make-up on her face was smudged—she was still the most beautiful woman he'd ever been drawn to.

'You don't think that's true for me, too? Because I guarantee what happened last week has kept me awake *every single night* since then. Fortunately, I'm only going back to the station after the wedding.'

'And you can take photos without having slept?'

'I can,' he confirmed, 'but I don't have to. I work freelance. According to my own terms. According to my own time. I've given myself some time off.'

She sucked her lip between her teeth and his body tightened.

'This isn't a good idea,' she said, but she swam closer and lifted her dress under the water, wrapping her legs around his waist.

'I know.' He put his hands under her butt and brought her tight against his body, so her mouth hovered just above his.

'Jaden could find us.'

'I don't care.'

'What about the warning?'

'I'm going to hell anyway, Ava. Might as well go down swinging.'

And with those words he kissed her.

No matter how many times he'd kissed her, it always felt new. Different. And yet somehow there was a familiarity that made every movement of their lips seductive.

The other times, he'd taken his time kissing her. Kissing was a leisure activity, after all. Created to be savoured,

enjoyed. And kissing Ava had strengthened that belief for him. Her tongue moved in intuitive ways, and sent shimmers of pleasure through him. Her lips were soft, inviting, and pressed against his as if they belonged there.

Kissing her leisurely gave him the opportunity to feel the softness of her body under his hands. To feel its contrast with the hardness of his own. To enjoy the curves of her, the lines of her. To have desire travel lazily through him. To have awareness torture him.

Which was why it made no sense that he was kissing her now as if there would never be any more kisses.

He could sense her surprise as he deepened their kiss. But there was no resistance, and she tightened her arms around his neck, angling her mouth and inviting him to take more.

So he did.

He took and took, and wasn't surprised when she demanded more from him, too. Because that was who Ava was. Power. Fire. Strength. She matched him with every stroke; returned every caress with equal passion.

His fingers—his body—wanted more, and he suspected hers did, too. Just as he suspected that they would have both taken more—given more—if they hadn't been interrupted.

CHAPTER SIXTEEN

SHE NEEDED TO STOP. To stop kissing Noah. To stop kissing him in water. To stop enjoying the feel of his body under her fingers. But most of all she needed to stop kissing Noah in water, feeling his body under her fingers and *getting caught*.

As soon as she heard the giggling she pushed away from him. And then, for good measure, swam a short distance out. She rolled her eyes at herself, knowing that no one who stumbled upon them was going to believe that they were just there to talk. Even if that *had* been what they'd been doing initially.

But if she'd thought being caught kissing her brother's best friend was awkward, she wasn't prepared for the awkwardness of being caught by her brother's best friend's *father*... and the woman he was clearly sneaking off to make out with.

If the water around them had heated when they'd started kissing, it had iced over now. Noah's face had gone completely blank, though there was a twitch at his eye that betrayed his feelings.

'Noah,' Kirk said, his hand firm on the small of his guest's back.

Ava didn't recognise the woman, so she assumed it was one of Leela's friends. If she didn't hate being in this situation— seeing what it did to Noah—she would have been amused.

'I didn't realise anyone was here.'

Noah didn't reply. He just walked out of the water, and turned to Ava, his hand outstretched. She immediately

started towards him—trying not to think about how her dress clung her body, or the fact that it was even more incriminating that she wasn't wearing a bra—and took his hand as soon as she could.

'We'll leave you two alone,' Noah said as they walked over and picked up their things.

'Noah—'

'It's fine,' Noah interrupted his father, giving him a smile that looked more like a grimace. 'I'll see you at lunch tomorrow.'

Her hand still caught in Noah's, she gave Kirk an apologetic look before following Noah to the car park. The journey was short, but the heaviness in the air around them made it feel endless, as if they were still moving through water.

She gave a sigh of relief once they got to the car park and saw that most of the cars were still there. Since she had her keys with her, she could leave without showing anyone what a mess she was. Or facing the inevitable questions when they saw who she'd got into a mess with.

'Are you okay?' she asked quietly, when Noah didn't take any steps towards his car.

'Fine.'

She winced. 'You don't have to pretend to be fine.'

'No?' When he turned to her, his eyes were cold. 'So you want to know what's going on inside my head after seeing my father sneaking off to—' He broke off on a curse.

'Yes. If it's going to make you feel better then, yes, tell me.'

'It won't make me feel better,' he said flatly. 'It's just going to annoy me even more.'

He walked towards his car then, but she hurried forward, blocking his path.

'Tell me.'

He didn't reply. Only moved to walk around her.

She shifted again. 'Tell me, Noah.'

'Nothing good will come out of it if I do, Ava,' he said in a warning tone. 'Just let me go.'

'I've confided in you—' she swallowed when the words caused her stomach to churn '—because I trust you. You can trust me, too.'

'And how is trusting you going to change the fact that seeing my father back there just reminded me that I can't run from my family's past?' he asked tightly. 'That no matter how much I want to, *I can't run*?'

The despair in his voice was the reason Ava didn't stop him when he walked past her this time. A few minutes later, he drove away. It happened so quickly that she was still staring at the dust his car had left behind long after it was gone.

And then, when she heard voices, she hurried to her own car and left, too.

It was late that night before she allowed herself to think about it. It was a coping mechanism she'd developed that was conducive to productivity but a nightmare for sleep. She could do everything she needed to do and ignore her thoughts, her emotions, but the minute she got into bed she'd think about it all.

It meant that she'd got a lot done after the end of her engagement. It also meant that she'd had too little sleep to be able to function in those first few months. She'd been on leave at first—had gone on her honeymoon alone, forced herself to enjoy it, or at least pretend to—and had returned more tired than when she'd gone an entire year without a single break.

She'd tried to keep doing her job, but the words had swum in front of her face, and the copy she'd turned in had been so riddled with errors her manager had suggested she take the rest of her leave days to try and pull herself together.

It had hurt her pride, that request. It had also caused her to realise the pride she'd thought she'd lost after being jilted was still there, alive and kicking. It had spurred her to the animal shelter the next day, and prompted her to ask for their least sought-after cat.

When they'd shown her Zorro—and told her how he'd been abused as a kitten—she'd fallen in love immediately.

He was the ugliest cat she'd ever seen, but when he'd rested his steady gaze on her she'd seen something there she didn't think anyone else had. Feeling a pull to that—feeling it resonate within herself—she'd adopted him.

And from the moment she'd brought Zorro home she'd felt better. She'd been able to go back to work the next week, and had worked her butt off to make sure her team knew she wouldn't be making the same mistakes.

It hadn't mattered that she'd still cried at night sometimes. It hadn't mattered that there had still been days when she'd felt as if she were a collection of puzzle pieces unable to fit together again. The only thing that had mattered was that the world saw her as whole. And if the world thought she was, maybe she'd believe it, too.

It had worked for the most part. Until this stupid wedding had come along—until it had brought Noah back and she had been forced to face just how incomplete she was. She didn't need the added complication of falling for Noah. Of being reminded of her feelings for him. Or that once upon a time she'd dreamt about a wedding for the two of them.

He'd hurt her when he'd left all those years ago. And, like most things in her life, she'd avoided thinking about it until she no longer could. Because she knew that if she acknowledged that Noah had hurt her she would have to acknowledge other things, too. That she'd put herself out there to *be* hurt. Because she'd had feelings for him.

And, as annoyed as she'd been at Noah for entertaining her brother's protectiveness back then, she knew that Jaden's feelings had affected the way she'd felt about the situation, too. She hadn't been able to imagine unsettling their relationship for something that would go nowhere. And, based on the way both she and Noah had responded to one another seven years ago, she hadn't seen it going anywhere.

But she could now. And the events of that night—his support, their arguments, the revelations, the kissing—told her she was right. Except that she wasn't sure she *wanted* it to

go anywhere. Because if she did she'd have to face her very real fear: that she didn't deserve him.

Noah had known the lunch with his father was going to be awkward and long before he'd seen his father giggling with a woman half his age. But not that long before, he thought. In fact, the exact moment had been when his father had caught his eye as he'd been trying to get Ava's attention during the rehearsal dinner. Kirk had just raised a brow at him, but it had been enough.

So Noah wasn't too surprised at the silence that reigned during most of their lunch.

'Are you looking forward to the wedding?' his father asked, after their waiter had brought their starters and their conversation still hadn't consisted of much other than 'hello'.

'For Jaden's sake, yes.'

'But not for your own?'

He forked a crumbed mushroom with more force than necessary. 'Do people *ever* look forward to other people's weddings for their own sake?'

His father didn't reply, and Noah realised that was why silence was better. Everything was a minefield. An innocuous question about the wedding could lead down a very dark path. Noah had almost asked his father if *he* was looking forward to the wedding for his own sake. It *was* a decent place to pick up women, after all.

He popped another mushroom into his mouth and forced himself to chew. He didn't like the tone of the voice in his head. It sounded just like the part of him that still blamed his father, though he knew it wasn't fair.

'Ava tells me the two of you have struck up a friendship since I've been gone,' he said.

Oh, yes, because that *question won't explode in your face.*

'Yes.' Kirk's face softened. 'She's sweet. Didn't deserve the mess of last year.'

His father picked up his beer and took a long drag from it before shaking his head.

'I'll never forget the look on her face when that man walked out—'

'You were there?'

'Yes.' Kirk frowned. 'I thought you knew that?'

'I didn't realise your friendship had secured you an invitation to the wedding.'

'I was more her parents' guest than hers,' Kirk told him. 'We're friends, just like you and Jaden are. Though I think Ava was happy I was there.'

He chose not to reply to that, his mood too dark for him to trust what he might have said. Instead, he took a deep breath. And then he asked, 'Why didn't you tell me Ava was getting married?'

'Would you have wanted to know?'

'What kind of a question is *that*?'

'The kind a father asks when he knows that his son ignored his own invitation to said wedding.'

'That wasn't because I didn't want to know.' Noah clenched his jaw. 'I didn't get it.'

'Why not?'

'I—' He took a sip of water. 'I blocked her email address.'

'Why?'

'Because—' He shook his head. 'It's complicated.'

'Well, you'd better *un*complicate it, son. Ava's been through enough without you messing with her head.'

Noah stared at his father. 'You know *I'm* your son, right? You're not supposed to choose a random woman—' He broke off with a hiss. 'I'm sorry. I didn't mean that.'

'You probably did. And we'll get to that.' Kirk ate some of his salad before continuing. 'But in terms of Ava… You and I both know she's not "a random woman".'

Chastised—and more than a little jolted by his father's perceptiveness—he nodded.

'And I don't agree that my warning you against messing with her is choosing her over you. Especially since something tells me you're probably messed up about this, too.' He paused. 'So, if your plans don't involve you staying here long

enough to clean up any mess you've made, you shouldn't be out swimming with her at midnight.'

He couldn't argue with that. Besides, Kirk had just given Noah the perfect segue into telling him why he'd arranged this lunch in the first place.

'I'll be here,' he said slowly. 'I'm moving back home.'

His father blinked. 'Back home?'

'Yeah.' He rubbed a hand over the back of his neck. 'I'm taking a break from photography for a while. At least, unofficially.'

'Are you moving back or are you taking a break?' His father's voice was stern. 'Those are two different things.'

They were, but he was trying to find a diplomatic way of telling his father about his plans. Now he thought being honest might be easier.

'I'm moving back, Dad. Permanently. And I'm taking a break from photography while I figure out what I want to do while I'm here.'

His father nodded slowly. 'Why?' he asked after a moment.

'I've missed you.'

Kirk reached out and squeezed Noah's hand. 'I've missed you, too. And you know I'd love to have you home again. But you left for a reason. What's changed?'

'Me.' He'd answered without thinking and now he realised it was the truth. 'And—I hope—us.'

Kirk stared at him for a moment, and then nodded. 'Let's start with us.' He paused. 'How about you tell me why seeing me with that woman last night upset you?'

CHAPTER SEVENTEEN

'TORTURE,' AVA SAID, unashamed of how miserable she sounded. 'It's bad enough that I have to do all this wedding stuff at Christmas, but now there are unexpected little meetings like this? To do what? Fold boxes for Christmas cookies? You're torturing me, Jaden.'

Jaden grimaced. 'If I had a choice, none of us would be folding any boxes.' He paused. 'I *am* sorry that this is at Christmas, though.'

She sighed. 'No, you're just sorry that it's *this* Christmas.'

She'd arrived at Jaden's house early, so that she could scold him privately for all the things Leela had been demanding in the last week. After all, she could hardly complain to the bride. But she knew that part of her motivation was also because she was still annoyed at him for his overprotectiveness of her with Noah.

Which she couldn't talk to him about directly. Because that was *not* a conversation she needed to have.

She walked to the fridge, looked longingly at the wine, but dismissed the thought instantly. She didn't need any more reason to loosen her tongue. Instead, she took out a soft drink can.

'Would it have been better at any other Christmas?'

Ava took a sip of her drink and turned to her brother. It was the first time they'd got anywhere close to discussing what had happened the year before. Or how his wedding might be affecting her.

'I think so. Time always makes things easier.'

Jaden nodded. 'You probably hate me for all this.'

'I don't hate you. I'm annoyed, yes. But not at you. At myself for…for the entire mess.'

She didn't pull away from him when he walked over and put an arm around her waist, resting her head on his shoulder instead.

'I didn't ever think it would go bad. Now, after everything, I'm annoyed that it was Christmas and that a holiday I used to love has been tainted in this way. And I… I blame myself for all of it.'

Jaden's face tightened, and he pulled her into a hug. She let herself be comforted by him—knowing it would be the only time she'd allow it—before she pulled away and took a step back.

'Now, let's just get through the box-folding and whatever other delights Leela has in store for us before the wedding, shall we?'

He smiled at her, but she thought she saw something on his face that looked almost reckless.

A moment later it was gone, and then the doorbell rang and Ava pushed it out of her head. It wouldn't benefit her, so what was the point in thinking about it? Besides, she had enough to think about now that she'd said something to Jaden about how she felt. And then there was Noah, whom she hadn't seen or spoken to since the rehearsal dinner the week before.

She greeted Leela and Tiff, who had arrived at the same time, but didn't move to hug her future sister-in-law as she should have because she had no desire to hug Tiff.

Not that she had anything against the woman. She just—

No, she did have something against the woman.

Tiff had had Noah's heart once. And she'd stomped on it. Ava was pretty sure that was part of what he'd alluded to last week. But she was a civil person—most days—and she could be an adult.

An adult who won't hug a woman because of her past with the man you—

If Ava had ever experienced stopping her thoughts in their tracks, it was in that moment, when that very annoying voice in her head was taking liberties with the truth. *Liberties.* Because the actual truth was too terrifying to consider.

It tested her commitment to civility, so that when Noah and Ken arrived she only nodded at them, and simmered in her anger as she watched Tiff hug Noah.

'Well, everyone, thank you for coming on such short notice,' Leela said once everyone was settled with a drink. 'I know we've been putting you through the wringer with this wedding, but we really appreciate your help and support. So tonight—'

'So tonight, as a thank-you,' Jaden interrupted, ignoring the surprise on Leela's face, 'we're going to be taking you all to the Christmas carnival at the high school down the road.'

Ava couldn't help the chuckle that left her lips at this announcement. Jaden shot her a look—*I'm doing this for you. Please don't get me into any more trouble*—and she turned it into a cough before gleefully clasping her hands together.

'This is the absolute *best* news you could have given us, Jaden!' she said.

Again with the acting, Ava thought. But this time it was for a much nobler cause than when she'd been lying for her cat. Or teasing Noah.

She was saving her brother's future marriage.

'I can't believe you and Leela thought of thanking us in such a considerate way. By taking us to the carnival you and I used to go to every year at Christmas!'

Now she stood to hug both Leela and Jaden. When she got to her brother, she whispered, 'Thank you,' and then stood back and did a quick jump. 'This is *wonderful*!'

Leela gave her an uneasy smile. 'You're welcome.'

'Tricking us into believing we needed to fold boxes,' Noah added, smirking when Ava looked at him and realised that

Jaden had given *him* a look, too. 'You're sneaky, future Mr and Mrs Jaden Keller. But we love you anyway.'

'Yes, well,' Leela said, her smile fading somewhat. 'We should probably get to it, then.'

'On a scale of one to ten, what are the chances Leela is going to castrate Jaden tonight?'

'One,' Ava said immediately. 'She wants a big family. She wouldn't risk it. However, I can't say the same for his limbs.'

Noah chuckled, more from relief that she'd answered than from what she'd said. He hadn't heard from her all week, though he knew that was because they'd been busy. She was still working, and he'd been helping Jaden with the wedding, and editing some pictures he'd taken before he'd come back home.

But he wasn't sure that that was it. He hadn't spoken to her since he'd acted like an ass—and revealed why in his little outburst—the night of the rehearsal dinner. He'd told himself to call her, but that had required a courage he hadn't conjured up yet. He'd also spent a lot of his energy trying to process the conversation he'd had with his father that day at lunch.

All of which were, of course, excuses.

'I think you deserve some points for your acting back there.'

'You know, I'm not even going to argue that that's against the rules. I accept.'

'Firstly, of course you do. Secondly, it's not against the rules. I'm fairly certain you orchestrated this in defence of yourself, somehow.'

She smirked. 'Not orchestrated. Just told my brother that this hasn't been the best time for me. His guilt did the rest.'

'Fifty points,' he said, pride surging inside him. Not only because she'd been honest with her brother, but because Jaden had actually done something about it. Their talk must have helped.

'You know this puts me ahead now, right?' she said.

'One-thirty for you, one-twenty for me?' When she lifted

her brows, he shrugged. 'I've been keeping track, same as you.'

They were walking behind the rest of the group. Jaden and Leela were far in the front—arguing, no doubt. When they all reached the line to enter the carnival, things went eerily silent. And then Tiff turned around and began asking Noah about his travels.

He could feel Ava stiffen next to him, and his annoyance at his ex trying to make conversation with him—*flirting* with him—was kidnapped by another emotion: satisfaction. Ava was *jealous*.

He immediately took a step back so that Ava was between him and Tiff, and deliberately included her in the conversation. Though it would have been worth it based solely on the fact that Ava relaxed as soon as he did so, it also managed to annoy Tiff. As soon as they got inside the carnival, she and Ken went their own way.

'Should I ask?' Jaden said, looking pointedly at Tiff's back.

'You could,' Noah replied, 'but I don't think it's going to get you any bonus points with your fiancée.'

Jaden glanced back to Leela with a grimace. She was at the bar, and when she turned they saw she'd ordered a large beer. Which she then downed.

'Yeah, she's not happy about this.'

'Why would she be?' Ava asked. 'You *knew* this wasn't going to go well for you. With her, I mean. You have no idea what it means to me.'

She stood on her tiptoes and kissed Jaden's cheek, and the affection and gratitude in her action did something to Noah's insides.

He and his father had never been overly affectionate with one another. They'd showed their love through spending time together. Doing things together. Which explained why, when Noah had told Kirk he was moving back home, his father's reaction hadn't been what he'd hoped for.

But he knew he couldn't have expected no consequences

for leaving. He'd found that out the hard way with Ava. And now he'd found it out with his father. But they were dealing with it. Just as they were dealing with the aftermath of their first real conversation about how his mother's actions had affected them. And how his father's subsequent relationships had affected Noah.

Lunch had been a real hoot.

'I know I should have warned her,' Jaden was saying, 'but it was a spontaneous decision.'

'Clearly,' Noah commented. 'Though not a bad one.'

'Tell that to my future wife.'

'What you *can* tell your future wife,' Ava said, 'is that you're going to fold all those boxes by yourself in apology. And then you can drop them at my house tomorrow and I'll fold them for you.'

Jaden brightened, but then frowned. 'You have work until Friday, Ava. You can't fold a hundred and thirty boxes by yourself.'

'The office is quiet this time of year,' Ava replied easily, though Noah could tell that wasn't true. 'Besides, I can sleep after the wedding. And unless you want to fold those boxes yourself, so that you can a) make sure there *is* a wedding, and b) get your wife to sleep in the same bed with you afterwards— or before—you'll take me up on the offer.'

'I won't argue with that.' He kissed Ava on the forehead. 'Now—damage control.'

'Don't let her get too drunk!' Ava called after him, and Jaden glared at her when Leela looked over.

'You're enjoying this, aren't you?' Noah asked.

'The fact that I'm no longer going to have to pretend to be happy while folding boxes or the fact that we're here?'

'I was talking about how you're treating Jade, but, yeah, I guess the other two reasons work.'

She angled her head. 'I'm not going to lie and say I'm not enjoying how this is turning out for Jaden. But I feel like he deserves some of it—and that it's about time.' She shrugged. 'I'm only human.'

Noah smirked. 'Aren't we all?'

They began walking together, and he couldn't help but think what a perfect date it would have been under other circumstances. The carnival rides lit up the entire rugby field of the high school, and the Christmas theme meant that there were assorted Christmas characters running around. There were a couple of elves, a couple of reindeer, and all the stalls had workers wearing red Christmas hats.

It was ideal for someone who loved Christmas. For someone like Ava. But he needed to remember it *wasn't* a date. And that the only reason Jaden wasn't walking with them was because he had his fight with Leela to worry about.

So he'd use this opportunity of being alone with Ava constructively, and take his father's advice: he'd face the consequences of what had happened.

'Listen, about the night of the rehearsal dinner—'

'No,' she interrupted him.

'What?'

'My brother has put his relationship on the line to give me tonight.'

'I think that might be an exaggeration.'

'I don't,' she said solemnly, but her eyes twinkled. 'I'm not going to waste his sacrifice by talking about *that*. In fact, I'm sorely tempted to go find Tiff, just so that we can play the game again and I can beat you.'

'Now, we *both* know that's an exaggeration,' he said with a smirk.

'Yeah, you're probably right.' She tilted her head. 'Doesn't mean we can't still earn points, though.'

'How are you thinking of cheating now?'

'Not cheating,' she said haughtily. 'A bonus round, if you will.'

'I will.'

'You don't even know the terms.'

'Doesn't matter. I'm still going to win.'

'Ha! Well, now I'm tempted to tell you that you have to

enter the carnival pageant.' Her eyes widened. 'Actually, that's been my plan all along.'

'Over my dead body.'

She sighed. 'I suppose you're right. There's no way you could enter and win it, thus winning the competition between us, too.'

He narrowed his eyes. 'The point of this competition is that we distract each other from the wedding.'

'And we can still do that.' She lifted her shoulders. 'Let's compromise, then, and say you'll win five hundred points if you enter the competition for at least one round.'

'What if I get through to the next round?'

'You'll get another hundred points. And so on. And so forth.'

After considering, he said, 'Fine. But you have to enter, too.'

She laughed. 'Oh, bring it *on*, Giles.'

CHAPTER EIGHTEEN

AVA WOULD READILY admit that entering a pageant because of a dare wasn't the smartest thing she'd ever done. But it wasn't the stupidest thing she'd done either. Not when her wedding, staying over at Noah's place and making out with Noah—numerous times—were all contenders for that title.

And certainly not when she added falling for Noah into the race.

Hell, entering the stupid pageant didn't even make the top ten.

As she went through the process of entering the competition it became clear which of those things *was* winning that title. Why else would she be challenging Noah to a competition? To enter the *pageant*? Why else would she be so determined to distract herself from that feeling in her stomach that told her how fast she was falling?

So she would enter the pageant. Even though she hated the thought of going up there and having people ogle her. Even though her simple white dress couldn't compare to the beautifully patterned and coloured dresses of the women around her.

When she learnt that the women's pageant took place before the men's pageant, she told herself there was no point in complaining about it. *She'd* done this. And, regardless of how unsteady all of this—the pageant, her feelings—made her, she'd put on a show for Noah *and* the entire carnival.

She might as well.

'Contestant number seventeen—Ava Keller!'

Ava blew out a breath and then walked the length of the catwalk—shoulders back, legs slanting over each other, channelling the seven-year-old Ava who'd practised for this moment all the time. She heard cheering as she posed—from more than one person—and looked into the crowd to find the entire wedding party waving at her.

When her eyes landed on Noah's he gave her a wink and she narrowed her eyes, determined to find some way to get him back.

The only way she could think of to do it was to win the stupid pageant.

'I'm not sure how you convinced her to do this, but I am happy to pay you for it.'

Noah smirked, but it was more an act than anything else. He'd had no intention of having Jaden witness his humiliation, let alone Tiff and the others. But Jaden had found him, and had asked about Ava, and he hadn't been able to lie.

But now, seeing the look on Ava's face, he wished he had.

'Has she ever done anything like this before?' Leela asked.

She seemed to be better now—presumably because Jaden had told her he'd take care of the boxes.

Jaden shook his head. 'She didn't even want to take part in her school concerts.' His smile widened. 'I'm going to record this for posterity.'

He took out his phone, took a few pictures of Ava posing, and then chuckled to himself. 'Gold!'

They watched as she walked down the runway—pretty professionally, Noah thought, though he wasn't sure he was qualified to make that evaluation—and then Jaden asked, 'How *did* you manage to convince her to do this?'

'A bet.'

'A bet?' Leela repeated. 'She's doing this because of a *bet*?'

'Yeah. I mean, you know how she is.'

He hoped they did. Because he wasn't quite sure what he was talking about.

'It must have been some bet, man,' Jaden said with a quirked brow, his eyes sharp.

'Yeah. She and I have actually both entered tonight. Whoever gets furthest in the competition has to...' He paused, and then said the first thing that came into his mind 'Has to do a solo dance at your wedding.'

There was a long pause before Leela said, 'You mean *after* the formalities, when the dance floor is actually being used?'

'Of course,' he said immediately. 'It won't affect your wedding at all.'

'Well...' Jaden said after a moment. 'You'd better hope she wins. I've seen you dance.'

He pulled a face at Jaden, but his insides loosened in relief.

'I'm actually supposed to go out there and *speak* now?' Ava asked the man who'd brought her the bad news. 'I thought the extent of this was walking around and letting people judge me?'

'That's not how pageants work, ma'am.' He frowned. 'Didn't they tell you you'd have to speak when you entered?'

I wasn't paying attention.

'I don't think so, no.'

'Well, we have a pageant every night at the carnival to choose a carnival king and queen for that day. It isn't anything too demanding. You just have a couple of pictures taken with the crown,' he said, sounding almost bored. 'But the actual competition is judged on how much you entertain the crowd. You just go out there and introduce yourself. If they like you, you make it into the next round. That's a group dance—we teach you when you're out there, and it's more about having fun than anything else—and then in the final round you answer some questions. Got it?'

'Got it,' she said, but she felt dazed. All she could think about was that her fate in the stupid pageant was based on people *liking* her. 'I'm also pulling out.'

'What?'

'I'm sorry. I can't entertain people.' She gave the microphone back to him and stepped away. 'Trust me, you don't want me out there.'

She didn't give him a chance to reply, and instead took a route back to her car where she knew no one would see her.

She sat there for a moment, breathing hard and fast, and then she drove the short distance back to Jaden's house. She used her spare key to get in, scribbled a note for him, and then transferred the unmade boxes to the car.

And then she went home, messaged Noah that she was okay—and Jaden, too, for good measure—and switched off her phone. And cuddled with her cat.

'She's pulled out.'

Everyone in their small group looked at Noah, but Jaden responded first. 'What do you mean, she's pulled out?'

'I mean she just sent me a message saying that I've won the bet and she's gone home because she isn't feeling well.'

Jaden took out his phone, blew out a breath. 'She sent me a message, too. But mine just says that she isn't feeling well so she's left. I'll call her.'

Noah let him do that, but he knew Ava wouldn't answer the phone. She wasn't the type to just run away. And she hadn't backed out because she wasn't feeling well. Something was wrong.

'Her phone's off. Maybe I should go see if she's okay?'

'She's fine,' Tiff said. 'I'm sure it's just stage fright. You don't have to spoil our evening because of her.'

'She's my sister,' Jaden said in a warning tone.

'Tiff's right, though.' Noah forced himself to say the words. 'I'm sure she's fine.'

'See?' Tiff said brightly, as if Noah's agreement somehow absolved her of any pettiness that had been in her answer. 'I told you.'

'I think I'll be off, too, though,' Noah said, trying hard not to clench his teeth. 'Early start tomorrow.'

'We literally just got here,' Tiff protested. 'Besides, we haven't had a chance to speak yet. We could—'

'No, thank you,' he interrupted. 'I'm happy to be in this wedding with you because of Jaden and Leela, but that is the only reason we're seeing each other now. If I had my way I would never have had to see you again after what happened. I'll see you all later.'

He'd almost reached the exit before Jaden caught up with him.

'That was…*intense*.'

'Yeah, sorry.' Noah exhaled. 'I just don't understand why she keeps trying to talk with me.'

'Because she's a human being who regrets what she did when she was just a kid.'

'She's told you that?'

'Yeah.' He grimaced. 'We've been friends for a while now. I didn't want to tell you—'

'Because you didn't want to upset me.' Jaden nodded. He blew out another breath. 'Look, I get that. And I'll apologise for embarrassing her, but I don't regret saying what I said.'

'You don't want to talk to her? You don't want closure?'

'I don't *need* closure. Not from her. Maybe after what she did—' He broke off, shook his head. 'I wasn't in love with her. Or I was, but it wasn't… I don't know. Complete.'

Jaden didn't reply for a moment. Then, 'Is it complete now?'

He didn't have to say that he was talking about Ava.

'I—' Noah cleared his throat. Stood taller. 'I think so.'

'You'd better know what you're doing.'

I have no idea. 'I do.'

'Be sure,' Jaden warned, his lips stiff, as though saying the words cost him something. 'She's been through enough.' He gritted his teeth. 'And I've made it worse.'

'She's already forgiven you,' Noah replied after a beat. 'She wouldn't be doing any of this if she hadn't.'

'Which makes me feel worse.' Jaden rubbed a hand over his face. 'Please, Noah, don't make me have to punch you. I

have a lot of repressed anger that she didn't let me take out on her ex.'

'Understood.'

'And don't make me regret that you're back.'

His mouth curved. 'Can't guarantee that.'

Jaden's lips curved, too, though just a little. 'I guess it wouldn't be fair to ask. Not when I regretted your existence long before you even left.'

Noah laughed.

When the doorbell rang, Ava ignored it and snuggled closer to Zorro. Her cat was in one of his rare affectionate moods and was allowing her to put her arms around him. Not tightly enough to squeeze him, but enough to make the throbbing in her chest ease. She wasn't going to answer the door and mess that up.

But soon the ringing of the doorbell turned into a persistent knocking. And when the knocking became a pounding, Ava sighed and took a slow walk to the front door.

'What?' she said the moment she opened it.

Her heart swelled when she saw Noah, but then she remembered she could never be with him and it deflated almost as quickly.

'I could ask you the same thing,' he said, pushing past her into the house. 'Except I'd add "the hell" to the "what" to get my meaning across more clearly.'

She closed the door. 'Why don't you just say "what the hell?" then? It would sound a lot better than what you just said.'

'Fine. What the hell, Ava?'

'Actually, maybe it *was* better the other way,' she said, and lowered herself onto her couch. 'I could have just pretended I didn't know what you meant and sent you on your way.'

'Ava,' he said, his voice soft now. 'What's wrong?'

'Nothing. Fine,' she said when he gave her a look. 'Nothing that I have the energy to tell you about.'

'What happened at the carnival?'

'I told you, I don't have the energy to talk about—'

'Please.'

His tone had gone from soft to insistent, but it was the concern in that insistency that had her eyes filling.

She took a deep breath, and then stood up when it didn't make her feel any better. 'Tea?'

'No, thank you.' He paused. 'And you don't want tea either, Ava. You just want the distraction.'

'I *need* the distraction,' she said, and went to the kitchen before he had the chance to reply.

He didn't say anything as she made the tea, and the silence felt awkward. But he was there, she thought. And she took a moment to figure out how that made her feel.

It had been a long time since she'd had a rough night and someone had been there for her. She usually dealt with those nights alone, and once she was feeling stronger she'd visit Kirk. Or her brother, or her parents.

But having Noah there filled something inside her. And she'd forgotten what that felt like. Not to have to pretend. To want—despite how much she denied it—to talk. And not just to anyone—to *Noah*. It had always been Noah.

Damn it.

She hung her head as the kettle sounded, and could barely bring it up again so she could finish making her tea. She stirred the liquid for much longer than it required, and when she left the kitchen saw that Noah now sat on the seat she'd vacated, watching her.

Unwilling to think about whether he'd seen her have that moment in the kitchen, she set the tea down, sat and curled her feet under her body, and then waited for him to speak.

'I know what you're doing,' he said.

'Yeah? What?'

Please tell me because I have no idea.

'You're waiting for me to ask you what's wrong again.'

Her lips curved. 'You've always known me better than I've ever given you credit for.'

'Maybe not always,' he corrected her with a small smile.

'I think I've lost some of my ability since I left.' He paused. 'Help me to regain it.'

She looked down at her hands, watched as her fingers traced the lines of her palms as if she weren't the one controlling their movement.

'I don't know what went wrong. Or when.' Her fingers stilled, and then began to move again. 'I think I was too young when I met him. He was, too. We had ideas about who we wanted to marry and who we wanted to be, but when push came to shove neither of us were those people. Not for ourselves. Not for each other.'

'Ava,' he said slowly, on an exhalation of breath. 'Your life for the past seven years wasn't only tied to him. You've graduated since I last saw you. You have a successful career. Your family loves and supports you.'

'Those things aren't who I am. They're what I've achieved. And my family—' She exhaled sharply. 'They don't see the version of me who failed at my relationship. I mean, now they do, because I'm forcing them to. Because my quirky personality has turned surlier than usual and they have to tiptoe around me.'

'No one is tiptoeing around you.'

'*Everyone* is tiptoeing around me.' She threaded her fingers together. 'Jaden didn't speak to me about proposing to Leela until after he did it. And then, when they announced their engagement, they both glanced at me, checking to see how I would react. The pressure of that...' She shook her head. 'Trust me, I've been here this past year. I *know* how my family's behaviour towards me has changed.'

'And what about *your* behaviour?' he asked after a moment. 'I'm not talking about the surliness—we knew about that before, and we loved you for it. I'm talking about the fact that you've turned into this...this *unsure* person. That you don't trust yourself. That isn't you. You used to be the most self-assured person I knew.'

'Oh, no, that was just pretending. I was much too in love with you to show you I wasn't completely confident in myself.'

* * *

'You were…you were *in love* with me?'

Her mouth curved into a smile he'd never seen before. Shy, insecure, seductive. How could that even be a combination? he wondered. Or was that description just an indication that he was totally enthralled?

'Don't pretend you didn't know.'

'I *didn't* know. Trust me, if I'd known—'

'You would have what?' she interrupted. 'Kissed me? Freaked out? Moved away? Stayed away for the past seven years?'

'That's not fair.'

'But it's not untrue.'

'I didn't leave because of what happened between us.'

'Not entirely, no. But it was factored into your decision.'

She leaned forward, picked up her cup of tea. Gripped it between her hands. Why did it feel as if she was gripping his heart there, too?

'Though, of course, you won't give yourself the chance to think about the real reasons you left.'

'I *have* thought about them.'

'Have you, though?' She tilted her head. 'After everything that's happened over the last weeks?'

He narrowed his eyes, wondering what he'd done to put her in this mood. And then he remembered that she'd been in the mood before he'd got there, and because he'd been determined to check whether she was okay he'd put *himself* in this position now.

But that didn't mean he deserved this line of questioning. He didn't need to delve into his motivations for leaving— or his motivations for the other decisions he'd made in his life—any more than he already had.

Because for the past two weeks he'd done nothing *but* that. Because of her.

She'd reminded him that his father was human. Imperfect and human. Noah hadn't seen that before he'd left. Then, he'd wanted to leave because he hadn't wanted to see his

father heartbroken any more. He hadn't wanted to witness the pattern of it. Especially after his relationship with Tiff had shocked him into realising he might repeat that pattern, too.

But now Ava's words made him consider something else. Something that fitted now that he saw how his mother's cheating had affected him. He'd gone from being heartbroken over a cheating girlfriend to kissing Ava and feeling something for her within weeks.

He'd seen the pattern take root. He'd seen himself becoming his father. Being cheated on and then quickly moving from one relationship to the next. It had screwed with him. He could see that now. And it had forced him into ignoring the fact that what had happened with Ava hadn't been the same as his father's relationships.

But he'd been scared. The cheating and his feelings for Ava and everything to do with his mother and father had somehow meshed and he'd been *terrified*. Terrified of what Ava had made him want.

A relationship. A future. Things he hadn't thought he could commit to. Things he'd been scared to face. And so he'd run.

'How did you know?' he asked her quietly.

'Because we're something,' she said simply. 'And you told me about how your father's choices made you feel.' She paused. 'And about your mother.'

Noah swallowed and wished he'd accepted the tea so that he'd have something to distract himself with. As he'd known she would, she let the silence extend. She was waiting for him to speak.

'The thing with Tiff… It shocked me.'

'Why?'

'Because I fell in love. Quickly. Stupidly. I ignored logic and I fell in love.'

'It happens to all of us.'

'But it shouldn't have happened to *me*. Not after what I'd seen with my father—' He cut himself off. Sighed. 'My father's relationships have bothered me my entire life. Because of their

instability, yes, but also because I hated seeing my father hurt. That's one side of it.'

He lifted a hand, and then dropped it before he could do anything with it.

'The other side of it is I knew my mother had hurt him. And by doing that she hurt me with what she did, too—even though I only realised the truth of it after she died.'

He leaned forward, ran a hand through his hair.

'What happened with Tiff was like a perfect storm of… of *everything*.'

'The relationship moved fast, like your father's relationships. And then the cheating—'

'And you,' he interrupted, before he lost his nerve. 'Our kiss happened so quickly after Tiff—'

'And you thought you were turning into your father?'

He gave a curt nod. 'So I left.'

A long pause followed his words. 'You ran from it?' she asked softly.

He nodded again. 'And I called my *father* weak.'

'You're not weak. Neither of you are. You've both just had to deal with something tough.' She paused. 'But you can't run from it, Noah. It won't matter how far you go, or how hard you try to distract yourself. The fear, the pain… It stays with you.'

'Speaking from experience?'

'Yeah.' She lifted a shoulder. 'After I fell apart I tried to put myself back together again. But no matter how hard I tried, it didn't change the fact that some of the pieces had broken—had shattered—during the process. I'm still me—' she gave him a sad smile '—but there are some parts missing.'

'He stole them.'

She shook her head, and then she set the tea down and brought her knees up to her chest. Her position did something to him, and he was standing before he knew it, pushing her tea aside and sitting on the table opposite her.

'What is it? What are you not telling me?'

She shook her head again, and desperation—fear—made his tone insistent.

'Ava, I can't help you if I don't know.'

'You *do* know, Noah. I've told you—' She drew in a ragged breath. 'He didn't steal anything from me. He just saw what I couldn't—what I didn't before. That I'm...too much to be loved.'

the short chain at some add to mer of these fire

by the question

Do this whole sell from it given

by ammune on. Noah ... we held one of the day this

rupper with. "If you can, and speculations of he has

away last Friday—that later color." "...in and it was a

much at the hands ...

CHAPTER NINETEEN

'YOU CAN'T BELIEVE THAT.'

His disbelieving tone soothed Ava's heart, but a louder, stronger voice soon sounded over it.

If you were lovable—if there wasn't anything wrong with you—why did Milo leave? And why didn't Noah stay?

'I'm not upset about it,' she said, lowering her legs and straightening her shoulders. She'd had enough of the self-pity. 'I'm glad I know. Now I don't have to set myself up for failure. I can adjust my expectations.'

She stood now, and tried to move away. When he did the same it brought their bodies close together. She didn't want to feel the spark being close to him always brought. She didn't want to be reminded of the expectations she'd once had for the two of them. The expectations she'd admitted to him and he'd brushed off.

'That's the worst thing I've ever heard.'

'It's the truth.' She forced herself to look him in the eyes. Accepted the quivering of her stomach as she did so.

'It's not the truth. You're not "too much". And, while we're at it, there's nothing wrong with you either. You're kind and sweet. I mean, it's under a couple of layers of other stuff,' he said when she opened her mouth. 'The surliness and the fire. But you wouldn't have agreed to be in Jaden's wedding if there wasn't something sweet and considerate inside you. You wouldn't have offered to fold these boxes—' he gestured

to the cardboard she'd almost forgotten on the floor '—if you weren't a good sister.'

She didn't reply, lost in the longing for it to be as simple as he was making it out to be. But she wasn't the person he was describing. Or she *was*, but the balance was off. She was more surly than sweet. More blunt than kind.

She hated that those things came into her mind in the form of Milo's words. In the form of the expression on his face when he'd told her he didn't want to spend the rest of his life trying to avoid being snapped at. Or walking through it on eggshells because he was afraid of what she'd say.

'You don't believe me?' he asked.

'Because your perception is skewed. You...you care about me.'

'I do.' His voice was heavy with an emotion she didn't understand. 'Which is why you *should* believe me.'

'It's why I *don't* believe you. You're just like my parents. And, if I'm honest with myself, like Jaden, too. He gives me a hard time, but I know he loves me exactly as I am. And because of it he, my parents, and now you don't see me as someone who isn't perfect.'

He stared at her, and then laughed softly. 'You're not *perfect*, Ava.'

She frowned. 'Yeah, I know. I just said that.' But she hadn't expected him to agree.

'You *are* surly. And you're annoying. You needle me like no other woman I've met before. And your mouth is so sharp...' He lifted a hand, brushed his thumb over her lips as his other arm slid round her waist. 'And I wouldn't have wanted you so much if you were any different.'

And then he kissed her, and Ava's protests—her confusion— were engulfed by the emotions of that kiss.

His lips moved gently against hers, his tongue slipping between them. His hand moved from her waist up to her face, and it took her a moment to realise that he held her face in both his hands now. And that the embrace was as tender, as moving, as his kiss. She nearly wept.

Instead, she put her arms around his neck and told herself to fall into his light. She wished she'd put up her Christmas tree—wished she'd had the courage to celebrate the holiday she loved—so that the mental picture she'd always have of this moment would include Christmas. So that it would replace the broken picture she had of it now. Of Milo running from her. Of his face—ugly and twisted, and not the face of the man she knew—and his anger.

Determined to wipe it away, she pressed closer to Noah. And then she let her hands run over his body. The broad curves of his shoulders, the strength of his back. The slope between the bulge of his pecs, the valley between his abs. His body was the most extraordinary thing she'd ever touched, its lines and its curves a gift from heaven itself.

But the gift couldn't be for her. Even if he wanted to give it to her.

He felt the change in her and pulled back, hoping he hadn't crossed the line. But when he saw her face he realised that the line had been erased. No, that she was *about* to erase it. His heart jumped to his throat.

'You don't want this, Noah. Not really.'

Her breathless tone made the words all the more hurtful.

'You don't know what I want.'

'You don't either,' she said sadly. 'You think you want me because you want my body. But I can't—'

She broke off, shook her head. And then she cleared her throat and looked him dead in the eye.

Fire.

He was so in love with her.

'I can't give you my body without giving you more. And you don't want more.'

'Ava—'

'No, please, don't make this worse.' Despite the fire, her voice caught. But she didn't look away. 'Unless you're going to tell me that you're suddenly someone who wants to settle down. Who wants to stay in one place, buy a house—not

as an investment, as a *home*—and raise kids, don't bother lying to me.'

'I didn't… I thought you didn't want that.'

'I was going to get married.'

He almost smiled at the roll of her eyes.

'Of *course* I want that.' She paused, and again her voice hitched slightly. 'Just because I think there's something wrong with me doesn't mean I believe I don't deserve that.'

'You do deserve it,' he said softly, urgently.

But he didn't say what he thought next.

Do I?

He'd spent all his life judging his father's choices. Blaming his father for his decisions. Ignoring the way Kirk had been affected by a cheating wife. Ignoring the way *he'd* been affected by it.

He'd used teenage heartbreak as an excuse to run away from it all. And now he was back. Older, and thoroughly chastised for being so unforgiving of his father's imperfections.

He'd make up for it now that he was back home. He and his father had already started at their lunch the other day. But he was less certain that he could move past the fear of relationships that seemed lodged inside him. And, though he wanted to with all his might, he was afraid to let go of the control. He was afraid to fall. To let himself be hurt.

If anyone could help him overcome the fear it would be Ava. He felt it in a deep part of himself that was only complete when he was with her. But she didn't deserve a man who was still figuring it out. And he didn't deserve the sweetness and the fire of her as he tried.

It wasn't that he didn't want more. It was that he couldn't give *her* more.

'I know I deserve it,' Ava said again after a moment. 'Which is why I'm going to ask you to leave.'

She shook her head when he opened his mouth and he stopped, unsure of what he would have said anyway.

So he left, and tried to figure out how he'd gone from avoiding relationships to wanting one so badly it hurt.

It was progress, she thought. Figuring out that she deserved to have the things she'd always wanted even though she wasn't perfect.

I wouldn't have wanted you so much if you were any different.

No, no, no. She was *not* going to spiral down that hole again. She'd spent days thinking about it. Nights. And it had had more of an effect on her than being jilted at the altar.

But now wasn't exactly the time to think about that. There must be some rule forbidding members of a wedding party from thinking about the possibility of the groom or bride being jilted. Especially on the day of the wedding.

Though there was no rule that said someone who *had* been jilted shouldn't be afraid of walking down an aisle again, even if they weren't getting married.

'Can you give me a moment alone?' Leela asked with a nervous smile, pressing a hand to her stomach.

Photographs had been taken, the groom and groomsmen were in place, and they were now only waiting for some of the guests to arrive before Leela and Jaden would make their vows.

'Yes, of course,' she said.

She and Tiff headed to the door, but Ava stopped as Leela called her back. She heard the door click behind her as she turned.

'This is probably not the best timing, but I wanted to tell you how sorry I am.'

Ava frowned. 'For what?'

'All of it. Forcing you to be a part of this.' She lifted a shoulder, offered a smile. 'You look gorgeous, though.'

Ava looked down at the navy blue lace dress and smiled back. 'Thank you. So do you. Though you don't need to hear that from me again.'

Leela's Cinderella-type wedding dress took up a signifi-

cant amount of space in the room they'd got ready in, and Leela looked breathtaking in it.

'Thank you.'

'You're welcome.'

There was a pause.

'You didn't force me into this. I agreed. It was my choice.'

'I shouldn't have made you choose, though. I guess I got so swept up in wanting a Christmas wedding that I didn't give myself a chance to consider how much I could be hurting you. It wasn't until Jaden—' She broke off. 'I didn't tell him I was going to ask you to be a bridesmaid. I thought I'd surprise him because he loves you so much. He told me that I shouldn't have done it, and by then it was too late to take it back.'

'Thank you,' Ava said quietly. And felt the resentment she'd held for her brother—and for Leela—over the whole mess fade. 'I know I would have regretted letting Milo rob me of this moment if I hadn't agreed to it.' *Like he robbed me of so much else.* 'I'm glad you asked me. It's been hard, but it's been worth it.'

They smiled at each other, and then Leela let out a shaky breath. 'I'm so glad we're on the same page. I didn't want to enter my new family with the possibility of conflict lingering.'

Ava laughed. 'Oh, you're going to be a breath of fresh air for us. We don't talk about our issues,' she elaborated. 'In fact, I'm pretty sure if the roles were reversed Jaden would have carried this apology—and the admission—to the grave.'

'Oh, that'll change.' Leela winked at Ava. 'I have time.'

Ava left Leela alone then, joining Tiff outside.

'So,' Tiff said after a moment. 'You and Noah, huh?'

'No.' Ava frowned. Shook her head. 'No.'

'Yeah, you sound like you're telling the truth.' Tiff smirked when Ava looked over at her. 'Noah's father was… er…*entertaining* a friend of mine the night of the rehearsal dinner. At the dam, wasn't it?'

Hating that her skin was heating, Ava cleared her throat. 'Just a swim.'

'Sure.' There was a beat of silence. Then, 'I think part of the reason I did what I did was because I knew Noah didn't want me.'

'Oh, no. We don't have to talk about this.'

'I know.' Tiff smiled, and for the first time Ava thought it was genuine. 'But I guess I'm tired of being the bad guy. And of being jealous of you.'

'Bad guy—jealous? Of *me*?'

Tiff rolled her eyes. 'See, this is exactly what I'm talking about. The fact that you don't know how feisty and charming you are is *so* annoying. And then there's your face...' Tiff shook her head, but winked at her. 'Sickening.'

'I... I don't understand.'

'Noah never looked at me the way he looked at you, Ava. The way he *looks* at you.' Tiff's face tightened. 'I guess... I guess I was looking for someone to look at me that way. So I did something stupid—and I've done more, I promise you—and eventually I realised why. *Eventually*,' she said, tilting her head, 'meaning last week at the carnival.'

'I honestly don't know what to say.'

'So don't say anything.' Tiff shrugged. 'Or, no—do. Tell Noah I'm sorry. He'll believe it if it comes from you.'

And then they were being told the ceremony could start, and there was no more time to think about the bombshell Tiff had just dropped.

It was one of the worst things she'd ever done, walking down an aisle again. It didn't matter that it wasn't the aisle she'd walked down on her wedding day. It was just the *familiarity* of it. And the sympathy she felt coming from her side of the family.

It nearly caused her to stumble. But then she saw Kirk, and he nodded at her with a slight smile. And though her legs were still shaky she felt steadier.

And then her eyes met Noah's.

There was something on his face that made her want to

cry. But not because he was looking at her in pity. No, it was because he was looking at her as if he *saw* her. *Her*. The woman who'd grown up and taken chances. Who'd been bold enough to ask her brother's best friend to kiss her. Who'd eavesdropped on conversations. Who was fierce and honest and blunt.

He didn't look at her and see a failure. He didn't look at her and see what he needed to change.

I wouldn't have wanted you so much if you were any different.

And when her legs went wobbly this time, it had nothing to do with the fact that she'd walked down the aisle before. It was because she wanted to do it again. And this time she wanted to be walking towards Noah.

CHAPTER TWENTY

'I'M GOING TO regret this,' Noah said. 'I'm going to wake up every night for the rest of my life and regret this.'

'But hopefully this will mean you'll wake up every night next to Ava and you'll be able to entertain yourself!' Leela grinned when she saw Jaden's face. But mercifully—for all involved—she stopped talking.

'When did you become like this?' Jaden asked with a shake of his head. But he curved an arm around his wife's waist and nuzzled her neck.

'About four hours ago,' Leela said with a giggle. 'It came with the title of Mrs Keller.'

'Ooh, what else—'

'Please,' Noah begged. 'Don't make this worse than it already is.'

'Don't take your emotions over this stupid grand gesture out on us.'

'You need to talk me out of this.' He turned to Jaden. 'Tell me you don't want me to be with your sister. Tell me that I shouldn't do this and ruin your wedding.'

'I *don't* want you to be with my sister,' Jaden told him. 'But you can't ruin the wedding. Most of it's done, and I got what I wanted.'

He smiled at Leela, then turned back to Noah.

'Again, just so that it's clear: I don't want you to be with my sister. But...but you make her happy,' he said reluctantly. 'I've seen her smile more in the last two weeks than I have

in the last year. Maybe even before that.' He paused. 'And since you've been back, I've also learnt more about how she's feeling than I have in the last year. So, you know…' Jaden shrugged.

It was as much approval as Noah was going to get, and it warmed his heart—before he remembered what he was planning on doing.

'That doesn't change the fact that Ava's going to hate it. I'm going to embarrass her. Just like at her own wedding.'

'You're right. There probably *is* a chance she's going to hate it. And that she'll be annoyed that she's being embarrassed in front of her family again.'

'Wow. Thanks.'

'There's also a chance that she might *not* be embarrassed,' Jaden continued. 'There's a chance that she might love it and accept that you're in love with her.'

He rolled his eyes and Noah laughed.

'Besides,' Leela said, 'maybe you need to balance the bad embarrassment with the good kind.'

'There's a *good* kind?'

'Well,' Jaden said as they got a signal from the band, 'you're about to find out.'

With unsteady legs Noah made his way towards the band. He was still pretty sure he was going to regret what he was about to do, but he wanted to show Ava that he was serious about what he was going to tell her.

He winced when the singer handed him the microphone and he remembered he wasn't going to *tell* her anything.

'Excuse me, everyone,' Noah said.

The entire crowd looked at him, but he soon found the face of the only person he really cared about.

'I have something to say, and I have the bride and groom's permission, so I'm not stealing anyone's thunder.'

He saw Ava glance at Jaden and Leela—Jaden nodded at his sister and Leela blew her a kiss—before she turned back to him with a frown.

What are you doing? she mouthed, but he only shook his head, and continued speaking into the microphone.

'You see, today's been a bit of a rough day for some of us here. Particularly for some of the people in the wedding party.' Ava's eyes widened, and she shook her head at him. 'And I'm not ashamed to admit that I'm one of them.'

He took a step off the platform where the band was playing and walked into the crowd. And then he took a deep breath, because he didn't think there would ever be anything more terrifying than confessing his feelings in front of over a hundred people.

'You see, for the longest time I was afraid of falling for anyone. I had commitment issues, and I had a lot of excuses as to why.'

He took his eyes off Ava for a moment to look for Tiff, and nodded at her. Then he found his father and gave him a small smile.

'The truth is, I was afraid of being hurt. And having feelings for someone—real, deep feelings—terrified me even more. So I ran.'

Now he looked back at Ava.

'But I'm tired of running. You make me want to stand still, Avalanche. You always have.'

With another breath he turned back to the band and nodded.

'And now I'm going to win *all* the points to prove it to you.'

The band began to play.

He was a terrible singer. He was a less terrible dancer. And all in all it made Noah's performance well worth the thousand points needed to win the game.

She bit her lip to keep from laughing as he belted out a note that had the whole room cringing, and then didn't bother when he did a little jiggle to accompany it. In that moment it didn't matter that she was fairly sure Noah had lost control.

It only mattered that she was laughing, and that for the first time in a year she didn't care that people were looking at her.

He walked towards her, taking her in his arms and giving her a twirl before bringing her up against him. The song ended, and his face crinkled into a smile, but she saw the nerves.

'A thousand points,' she told him breathlessly. 'You win fair and square.'

'Yeah?' His smile widened. 'That's great.'

'Oh, yes. *Especially* since the videographer got it for the wedding video.' She nodded over to the woman, who winked at them with a smile.

He groaned. 'I *knew* I was going to regret this.'

'You shouldn't,' she said, her heart hammering. 'It was—' She cut herself off, decision made. 'Why don't I show you?'

She pulled his head in for a kiss, and heard applause and cheers from her family. Having no desire to give them a show—other than the one they'd already had anyway—Ava pulled back almost immediately and angled her head in acknowledgment to the crowd.

Noah grinned at her, and then handed the microphone back to the singer of the band before taking her hand. 'Can we go somewhere to talk?'

'We probably should.'

And just like that she was brought out of the little bubble of joy she'd been in since he'd started speaking into that microphone.

It was still light outside, the sky soft with orange and yellow as the sun made its way to the horizon. It made the vineyard look soft, too—the vines, the abundance of grapes, the green hills and slopes in the background. Romantic. Beautiful. The perfect setting for a promise of for ever.

'Did you really like it?'

They were on the balcony overlooking the vineyard now, far enough away from the reception that they had privacy.

'I loved it.' She rested her forearms on the railing, let out a breath. 'Though I'm still trying to figure out why you'd do it.'

'You know why.' There was a pause. 'Hell, every single person in that venue knows why.'

'Yeah.'

She dipped her head and told herself that now wasn't the time to cry. But even the thought of crying made her want to cry. She hadn't trusted anyone enough to cry in front of them since she was a little girl. She didn't know how many times she'd cried in front of Noah since he'd been back.

Quick and fast. Tell him and then get out of here and cry in peace.

'Today's been interesting.'

'What makes you say that?'

She laughed quietly. 'No need for sarcasm.' She paused as he mirrored her position on the balcony. 'What I mean is that it was harder than I thought it would be. But then there were moments when it was easier, too.'

You're not making any sense.

She cleared her throat. 'It was hard going through a wedding again. Up until Jaden and Leela were pronounced husband and wife I held my breath. Because last year up until that moment things were going pretty well for me, too.'

'He did it just before you said your vows?'

'Yes.'

He swore.

Her lips curved. 'It gets easier thinking about it. Or maybe not thinking about it, but talking about it.' She angled her body towards him. 'Or maybe it's just easier with you.'

She reached out, took his hand.

'Which is why some of today was easy, too. You didn't look at me like I was broken. You saw *me*, and I can't… I can't tell you how much that means to me.' She cleared her throat when emotion clogged there. 'So when I felt overwhelmed—when I struggled to breathe and my throat closed, when the tightness in my chest made me feel like I was going to snap—I looked for you. And even when you weren't looking at me you made me feel better.'

His hand tightened on hers. 'What does that mean?'

'It means—' She let the air of her lungs slowly as she pre-pared to say the words. 'I think it means I love you. And not in the silly teenage way I used to, but—'

Her next words were stopped by his kiss, and selfishly she let herself have it. If only for a moment.

'I love you,' he said.

'I know.' She wrapped her arms around his waist, rested her head on his chest and squeezed her eyes shut. And then she pulled back and took a step away from him, lifting a hand when he moved to come closer. 'I know you *think* that.'

'I think—' He frowned. 'No, I *know* that. I embarrassed myself in front of an entire room full of people. I'm taking this risk even though—' he broke off. 'I haven't done any of this because I *think* I love you.'

'Okay,' she said slowly, 'maybe I didn't phrase that prop-erly. I meant that…that what you feel for me is probably—'

'Love,' he interrupted flatly. 'I *love* you.'

'You *can't* love me, Noah. You can only love a whole per-son and I'm not… I'm not whole.'

'And yet here I am, offering you my love.'

'And your commitment?' she asked. 'Are you ready to commit to me, too?'

His expression tightened. 'Yes.'

She bit her lip. 'I don't want you to feel you have to say that.'

'No, that's not it.' The hand he had on the railing tight-ened. 'I'm…*scared*, Ava. I'm scared of being hurt. I didn't realise I could be until Tiff, after all the stuff with my par-ents—' He let out an unsteady breath. 'If you picked up hesitation it's because of that—not because I don't want to be committed to you. It's the same thing that happened the other night when you asked me about it.' He paused. 'I *want* to be in a relationship. I want to settle down, build a home, have a family. With *you*. Because you make me want it. Even though it still terrifies me, you make me want to risk it.'

A heady sensation passed through her, settling in her chest, and it took her a moment to realise it was hope.

'Why didn't you just tell me that the other night?'

'Because I thought you deserved more than me.'

His hands dropped to his sides and then he put them in his trouser pockets and stared out at the vineyard.

'I only realised my mom's cheating had affected me this deeply recently. I didn't—' He broke off, clenched his jaw. 'I want to give you everything you deserve, Ava. And I thought that because I'm still figuring things out I wouldn't be able to.'

'I think,' she said slowly, after a beat, 'that you've forgotten you told me I'm not perfect. And if I'm not perfect— and we both know I'm not—why would you think you had to be perfect for me?'

She could almost see him trying to formulate an answer, but he didn't respond and she bit back a smile.

'And since we're talking about it,' she continued, 'you said you had commitment issues earlier. I don't agree. I mean, you've had a relationship with the most difficult person I know—and I still question your taste for being friends with my brother—for most of your life. And you tried with your father, too. You didn't agree with him and yet you made sure to stay in touch. To see him every Christmas. You and I have had a pretty long relationship, too.' She let it linger. 'All of our relationships are forms of commitment. Not only the romantic ones.'

The features of his face relaxed slowly and the side of his mouth curved. 'I don't know how much of that is true. But I'd like to find out. With you. If you'll have me.'

'I want to. I want *you*.' She exhaled slowly. 'But I can barely look at myself in the mirror right now. All I see is... is a woman who was left at the altar.'

'So see yourself through my eyes.' He took a step closer, held her hands in his. 'See yourself through the eyes of a man who loves you.'

'I have.'

'He didn't love you, Ava. Not like I do.'

'I want—' She broke off and found herself struggling

against tears again. 'I want to believe you,' she said slowly, 'but it just feels like… *I* feel like… I can't,' she ended help-lessly, when she couldn't formulate her thoughts, her emo-tions, coherently.

She wanted to say she didn't deserve him—but then he'd believe *he* didn't deserve *her*, and she knew that wasn't true.

So why was it so easy to believe it of herself?

'So all of this was for nothing, then?' he asked in a care-ful tone, letting go of her hands. 'Why try to convince me that I can be what you deserve—what you want—if you don't want me?'

'Of *course* I want you. I just—' Again she cut herself off. She couldn't explain it.

Silence stretched so far, so thinly between them that Ava wondered what would happen if it snapped. And then she watched as it did. When Noah ran a hand over his hair and walked back to the reception.

'I can't believe you agreed to this, Dad.' Noah's hand tight-ened on the steering wheel. 'You *know* how things ended between Ava and me and you still agreed to have Christmas with the Kellers. *And* you dragged me into your invitation.'

'You need to face it, Noah,' his father replied, just as he had before. 'You knew there was a chance this would hap-pen, and you took that risk when you declared your love for your best friend's sister at his wedding.'

'Can you stop reminding me about that?'

'I've never been prouder,' his father said sombrely.

'So that's a no, then?'

Now Kirk grinned. 'Never.'

Noah grunted, and figured the only way he wouldn't rile himself up even more was if he kept quiet. He wasn't a glut-ton for punishment. He took no pleasure out of pain. And yet he'd agreed to attend the stupid Christmas party the Kellers were hosting, knowing it would be painful for him.

He'd returned to the reception at the wedding ready to put on the performance of his life. But when his feet had taken

him directly to Jaden and Leela, and then to his father, and his mouth had told them that he was leaving, he'd realised he'd had his fill of performance for the day.

And so had Ava, it seemed, since Jaden had later told him—very sympathetically—she hadn't returned to the wedding either.

It had made things easier for them both, he'd realised when he'd thought about it. Because it would have seemed as if the two of them had escaped the wedding to be romantic. Which would have been his preferred ending to the day.

Instead he'd gone home feeling like a fool, and now he was being forced to see her again.

The Keller house was decorated as if the Wise Men themselves were coming to Christmas lunch. There was tinsel, stockings, Christmas elves, a giant, beautifully decorated Christmas tree, and a nativity scene. And outside on the porch—where he was informed they'd be eating—was a long table fully decked with red and green, along with the requisite Christmas crackers.

The lamb he and his father had brought had been taken out of his hands, a beer placed in them instead, and still he hadn't seen Ava. And of course he couldn't be the one to ask where she was.

'Surely it can't only be the four of us today?' Kirk asked, almost as if he'd heard Noah's thoughts.

'You're right,' Ruth Keller told him. 'Jaden and Leela are coming. They're picking up Ava on their way.'

'Why isn't she coming in her own car?' he heard himself ask, kicking himself as he did.

'Oh, I don't think she wanted to drive alone today,' Ruth told him kindly. 'This is difficult for her after last year. We've had to force her out of the house.'

'Oh.'

'You're surprised?' Ruth said after a moment. 'I'm sure that's because Ava's given you the impression that she's fine.'

'No, ma'am,' he said truthfully. 'She's never quite been able to do that with me.' He cleared his throat. 'I'm surprised

because she's given me the impression that you and Uncle Sam aren't aware she's struggling.'

Ava's parents exchanged a look, and then Ruth said, 'Of course she has. That girl would eat her own limbs to make sure we're not in pain.' She sighed. 'I wish she would just be honest with us.'

'I think she thinks—' Noah hesitated, wondering if he was betraying Ava's confidence by telling them this. But then he saw the expression on Ruth's face and continued. 'She thinks it's *her* fault that the wedding was called off. And she doesn't want to tell you the truth about how it's been affecting her because she's afraid you'll think poorly of her.'

Ruth's face blanched; Sam's tightened. For a moment an awkward silence thrummed in the room. Then the doorbell rang—of course Ava would arrive *now*—which broke the tension.

'Thank you for telling us, Noah,' Ruth said quietly, nodding at Sam to get the door. 'And, for what it's worth, we think you and Ava would make a lovely couple.'

She got up then as well, and followed her husband inside.

'That's a hell of a thing you just did,' Kirk commented.

'Yeah. I just hope I didn't make things worse.'

'I don't think so.' There was a beat before Kirk continued, 'You know her better than anyone else does.'

Noah looked at his father with a frown, but there was no time to discuss it further. Jaden and Leela walked in first—looking appropriately loved up—followed by Ava.

Concern immediately flared inside of him at the sight of her pale face. At her strained expression. When she saw him her eyes lit, before going dim again. And when she gave him a slight nod and kissed his father on the cheek, Noah thought he heard his heart shatter in his chest.

One day Christmas would feel like it used to.

At least that was what she told herself.

There wouldn't be tension as everyone avoided talking about the elephant in the room. Last year it had been her

wedding; this year it was her and Noah. There wouldn't be furtive glances at her. Those expressions of concern, of curiosity. And, in Noah's case, the complete avoidance of her.

She deserved it. But for a moment when she'd walked into the room she'd forgotten that she'd spoilt it all. She'd only remembered that they were in love and she'd felt that heady hope again. And then the memories had flooded back and she'd realised she'd only been fooling herself.

But some day Christmas would go back to being wonderful. She'd be happy again, and she'd feel festive. Her family's laughter wouldn't grate on her emotions; their happiness wouldn't make her ill with longing. It would just be a holiday she could spend with the people she loved and enjoy the festivity of it.

For now, she had alcohol.

'Maybe you should go easy on the champagne,' Jaden said as he joined her on the porch steps.

'I'm offended. This is only my third glass.'

'But you barely ate.' Jaden took the champagne from her and downed it, then handed her the empty glass. 'You're welcome.'

She grunted, and set the glass on the step next to her. He was right. And the whole alcohol thing had been more of a distraction than anything else.

'Why are you sitting out here alone with champagne anyway? Noah left an hour ago.'

'It's not about him.'

But it was. Partly.

'Ava,' Jaden said, in his *I'm your big brother* voice, 'I say this with the utmost love, but you have to stop feeling sorry for yourself.'

'Excuse me?'

He winced, but said, 'You heard me.' He waited a beat before he continued. 'It's been a year. Long enough for you to snap out of your self-pity.'

'I'm *not* feeling sorry for myself. And even if I were, who

the hell are you to tell me I can't? You, with your perfect wedding and your brand-new wife?'

'I'm your brother.' He put an arm around her shoulders. 'And I love you. Which is why I can be honest with you.' He squeezed her shoulder, then pulled his hand back. 'Look, no one is saying that what happened last year didn't suck. It did. But you're using it as an excuse not to move on.'

'Because of Noah?'

'Yes.' He was unperturbed by her surly tone. 'And because after last year, you think there's something wrong with you.'

'Who told you that?' she asked sharply.

'Heard it through the grapevine.'

'Noah.'

'Actually, from Mom and Dad—the moment you were out of earshot.' He tilted his head. 'But they heard it from Noah.'

'I should never have told him.'

'I'm glad you did. We all are. Or we wouldn't have the chance to tell you that you're absolutely wrong if you think it's true.' He paused. '*And* that you're feeling sorry for yourself.'

She sucked in her lip as it wobbled. 'It *is* true.'

'Ava—'

'No, Jaden, it *is*. Milo told me—'

'Milo was selfish. He always knew you were too good for him and yet somehow he managed to make you believe it was the other way around.'

She blinked. And then took a very deliberate breath when the air simply vanished from her lungs.

'I don't know… I don't know what to say.'

'Don't say anything. Just believe it.'

There was a long pause while she tried to figure out how she *could* believe it. No, first she was trying to figure out whether her brother had always felt that way about her ex-fiancé. Had her parents felt the same? And, if so, why had none of them told her?

'You wouldn't have believed us if we'd told you.' Jaden's eyes crinkled when her head turned sharply, and he gave

her a wry grin. 'I've known you for all of your twenty-five years, Ava. I know how your mind works.'

'Okay, as disturbing as that is, it isn't the most disturbing thing you've said to me today.' She paused. Exhaled. 'I wish you'd told me. It could have saved me a lot of heartache.'

'And then I'd have had to tell you "I told you so", and while I would have enjoyed it, I don't think you would have.' His lips curved, then his smile faded. 'It's something I'll regret all my life. I know what it's like to fall in love when you're young.' He paused. 'I think it was worse for you, because you were so determined to prove that that kiss I'd walked in on—' he shuddered '—between you and Noah didn't mean anything.'

'What is *happening*?' Ava asked, her eyes wide. 'Are you revealing every single thought you've ever had?'

'No. I'm just lifting the carpet we sweep all our opinions under.' He let out a breath. 'If anything I've said today isn't true, then by all means forget it. But I always thought you'd come to these realisations yourself. The fact that you haven't points to the whole feeling sorry for yourself thing.'

She sighed with a shake of her head. Paused to consider it. 'Maybe you're right and I *do* feel sorry for myself. But, freaking hell, my fiancé walked out on me at the altar. *Can't* I feel sorry for myself?'

'Of course you can. And you have,' he added. 'But if you let it interfere with this thing with Noah—' he rolled his eyes '—then maybe there *is* something wrong with you.'

Now she rolled *her* eyes. 'Ah, my ever-sensitive brother.'

'And my dorky—but perfect—little sister.' He kissed her on the cheek and then stood up. 'Now, take some time to think about your sins and then come inside and let Mom and Dad tell you exactly what I just did but in a nicer way.'

He took one step away, and then paused. 'And if you ever, *ever* make me advocate for a relationship between you and Noah again, please know that I will strangle you in the process.'

She laughed softly as he walked away, and then took a

deep breath and watched as the sun began to lower behind the mountains she could see from her parents' house. Her eyes stayed there as her mind whirled. As she realised that Jaden had been right about her relationship with Milo.

She'd known they weren't right for one another, though she hadn't quite thought that she was better than him. But there had been signs that had pointed to how mismatched they were long before she'd realised it. Signs she hadn't given herself permission to see even after he'd left.

She was too strong-minded for someone like him. And maybe that was why she hadn't listened when her gut had told her they didn't fit.

She hadn't listened to it for five years. *Five years.* Even when there had been an extra flutter of panic in her chest as they'd approached the wedding she'd ignored it. She could see now that the fluttering had been warning her. And it had stayed with her after, saying the *I told you so* Jaden hadn't wanted to.

How, then, had she managed to turn it into a critique of who she was?

Because it had been easier, she realised. Easier to believe that Milo was right, that she needed to be fixed. That way she'd been able to nurture the hurt inside her. She'd been able to hold it close and use it as an excuse not to move on. Because if she didn't move on she wouldn't get hurt again.

It took some time for the realisation to settle inside her. And for her to figure out what it meant that she and Noah had the same fears about being in a relationship.

They each thought they didn't deserve the other. They were both scared of getting hurt. But he'd taken a chance and proclaimed his love for her nevertheless. He'd been brave and she hadn't.

But she wanted to be brave. Because now she understood that she couldn't wait for her fears to disappear. She'd be putting her life on pause again if she did wait. She'd figure it all out, just as Noah would. And she was determined that they'd figure it out together.

But first she had to go inside the house and face her parents. And then she had to convince her brother to get involved with her and Noah one more time...

CHAPTER TWENTY-ONE

WHAT *WAS* IT with the Keller family and trying to get him to celebrate with them? It was enough to make him consider leaving again.

But when his father's face popped into his mind—and he thought of the ease their relationship had slid into since they'd had that talk—he knew that it was an exaggeration. He was just miserable because he was in love. And the woman he loved didn't want to be with him.

His only consolation was that Ava wasn't going to be attending Jaden's New Year's Eve party. After the Christmas tension he didn't think they'd survive another occasion together. His stomach still felt jittery because of it, and it had almost nothing to do with how unhappy Ava had been.

Almost.

Was she unhappy because she wanted to be with me?

He pushed the thought to the back of his mind. Thinking about that would do him no good now. Nor would remembering that light in her eyes when she'd first seen him.

No good. No good at all.

He pulled into the driveway at Jaden's house, and was surprised to see only three cars there. He recognised one as belonging to Jaden's parents, but the other two he wasn't sure about. Until he realised he'd seen them there before and groaned.

The rest of the wedding party. *Great.* Now Tiff would be able to see his unhappiness.

Not that it mattered, he told himself, getting out the car. He'd come to accept that his relationship with Tiff had been a teaching moment in his life. And he'd resented her more for his own reasons than for anything *she'd* ever done to him.

He needed to move on.

He thought he had.

He grunted at the unwelcome thought, and then rang the doorbell. He was surprised to see Tiff open it.

'Hi,' she said.

'Hi.' He waited as she stepped back, and then he moved past her. 'It's good to see you again.'

'It is?'

Her surprise made him feel guilty. Until it was replaced with confusion.

'Ah, she told you,' she said.

'I'm sorry?'

'Ava. She told you I was sorry.' She smiled at him. 'I told her you'd listen to her. But I'm still glad I have the opportunity to tell you in person. I'm sorry…about everything.'

It took him a moment to process all the information, but then he nodded. 'I'm sorry, too. For how I've handled things…since.'

'Great.'

'Great.'

There was a pause. Then, 'Well, you can just go through. Everyone is on the deck.'

After that surprising exchange, the rest of the night was uneventful. The conversation was easy for the most part, except for the unexpected mentions of Ava's name and the uncomfortable glances at him, which he ignored.

Half an hour before midnight his father strolled in.

'Dad?' He stood. 'What are you doing here?'

'I couldn't let the first New Year's Eve my son spends at home in seven years pass without us being together.' He slapped Noah on the back.

'So, what? You pitch up half an hour before midnight?' he teased, but he was pleased.

'Yeah, well… I had some things to take care of.'

He winked at Noah, and then the lights went out and a familiar song began to play.

Noah's jaw dropped when he saw Ava walk onto the deck.

She felt a new appreciation for the embarrassment Noah had put himself through at Jaden's wedding. Here, she was only performing in front of her family—and Tiff and Ken, though they didn't really count. But then, none of them did when she made eye contact with Noah.

Her cue came and she lifted the microphone Jaden had plugged into his sound system and began to sing the song Noah had sung to her at the wedding. It was a silly Christmas song, about Father Christmas and his elves, and when she'd been practising she'd realised that Noah had chosen the song because of the jokes they'd made with one another when she'd been staying at his place.

The singing had been easier to perfect than the dancing. She'd watched the video of Noah's performance that Kirk had recorded on his phone and graciously sent her over and over again, but some of the moves were Noah originals and hard to imitate. Not to mention the fact that she was wearing his firefighter uniform.

No one could accuse her of not going all out for love. She only hoped it would work.

She beguiled him—and heaven only knew why. Though he knew she was a good dancer, she couldn't move very well in his uniform, and his helmet kept falling over her face during the song.

But still she was beguiling. So much so that he only realised they were alone when the music stopped and she stood in front of him.

'Pretty decent show,' he commented. 'Not as good as mine, though. I'd give you nine hundred points.'

'I'm pretty sure that still makes me the—' She cut herself off as the helmet slipped over her face again.

Grinning, he took it off her head. 'You were going to say winner, and even my helmet knew you'd be lying.'

'Fair enough.' She paused. 'It wouldn't be the first time, I guess.'

'That my helmet knew you were going to lie?'

'That I lied,' she said, with a smile that turned his heart over.

'What do you mean?'

'I mean— What do you *think* I mean?' she asked. 'What do you *think* me getting your father to get me your fire-fighter's uniform and send me the video of you performing that ridiculous song so that I could perform it and also getting my brother to invite you to this party means?'

She was out of breath when her speech was over, and while she caught it his mind played catch-up.

'You're saying you planned this?'

She rolled her eyes. 'Duh.'

'Why?'

'Why do you *think*?'

He opened his mouth, then shook his head. 'That's not fair.'

'Really?' Her brow furrowed. 'Okay, fine. I love you, Noah, and I want to be with you.'

His stunned silence slithered into her chest and gripped her heart.

'What...what changed?'

She was prepared for this. She exhaled. 'I realised I was scared, too. Of not being what you deserve. Of being hurt. I couldn't bring myself to move on because of it.'

He didn't reply immediately. 'You know what I think?' His voice was quiet. 'We should stop getting in our own heads about this and just admit we deserve each other.'

She smiled, the pressure in her chest easing. 'I agree.'

He smiled back. 'I won't hurt you, Avalanche.'

'I know.' She lifted a hand to his cheek, and then dropped it. 'It's still terrifying. All of this is.' She slid her fingers into

her hair, puffing out her curls where they'd been flattened by his helmet. 'Milo and I weren't right for one another. But... but I can't deny he made some good points.'

'Ava—'

'It's not just going to go away,' she said softly. 'These insecurities are here. The fears are, too. I have to work through them. But I won't let them keep me from being with you, if that's still what you want. Especially since my dear brother has reminded me of how getting into a relationship with the first man who was interested in me after you left might have been a sign of how much I was running away from my feelings for you.'

'I...' He dragged the sound out. 'I did *not* see that coming.'

She laughed. 'Neither did I. *Jaden* had to point it out.' She did a mock shudder. 'He wasn't happy about it.'

'I can imagine.' He let out a breath.

'It was easier for me to stop living,' she said after a moment. 'It meant I didn't have to get hurt again or do anything about the brokenness inside me.' She took a step forward, her heart hammering. 'But if you're willing to be patient as I put myself together again—properly this time—'

He cut her off with a kiss.

It was relief more than anything else, but he sank into the passion, the fire, the *home* of kissing her. And then he pulled back, told himself he needed to be sure.

'I don't want you to do this because when we're together things are awkward. We can go back to...to being friends.'

'I thought you said we weren't ever really friends?'

He acknowledged the hit with a nod. 'You know what I mean.'

'I do.' Her smile faded. 'I do miss you. And I don't want things to be awkward. But, more importantly, I love you and I want to be with you. It's that simple.' She drew in a breath. 'If that's still what you want.'

'It is.' He paused. 'If you're willing to be patient with me as I work through my own stuff.'

'For as long as it takes.' She smiled. 'Thank you for not drawing that out.'

'I wanted to.'

Her smiled widened, heating his insides. 'Can't blame you for it. I wanted to, too.'

'Except you didn't want to do it to someone you love.'

'I guess.' She lifted a hand, brushed his lips with her thumb. 'I wouldn't know.'

'Because you've never really been in love before?'

'Not like this, no.'

He slid his arms around her body, drew her closer. 'Me neither.'

They stood like that for a moment, and then she said, 'My brother must be hating having to watch this.'

'They're watching?'

'Every single one of them.' Her eyes shifted to behind him, and then moved back to his face. 'Should we give them something to look at?'

'You mean besides the fireworks?'

As he said it, the first set of fireworks went off.

He smiled. 'Happy New Year, baby.'

'Happy New Year,' she replied, and pressed her lips to hers.

EPILOGUE

Two years later, Christmas Day

'LOOK, YOU OWE me this. I saved your life. It's the least you can do.'

Zorro stared at Noah, only one message clear in his eyes. *I hate you for doing this to me.*

Which was a fair point, Noah thought, amusing himself by playing with the bow around Zorro's neck. But then his phone beeped and his heart jumped into his throat.

Showtime.

He picked Zorro up, and thanked the cat for not resisting. Then he tentatively put the cat on the kitchen counter, which had now been cleared of the Christmas spread that had been there only a few hours ago.

He and Ava had hosted their families at his house this year. His father had come with his girlfriend—a woman he'd been dating for over a year now and was 'taking it slowly' with, as he'd told Noah—as well as Ava's parents, Leela and Jaden and their new bundle of joy.

Throughout the day Noah had watched Ava. Watched as she'd laughed, as she'd joked. He'd watched as she'd teased her brother, as she'd played with her niece. And all he'd been able to think about was how far she'd come. About how a short two years ago she'd been in so much pain that she hadn't even managed to smile at her family.

That Ava was gone.

And because he could see the version of himself from two years ago had disappeared, too—how he no longer feared being hurt, or shied away from his mother's memory—he knew it was time for the next step in their relationship.

He heard her car pull into the driveway and silently thanked his father for giving him the heads-up that she'd left his house. They'd made up some reason for her to take a quick trip to Kirk's after everyone had left. He didn't remember what that reason was now, though that was probably nerves. But because of that made-up reason, he was now ready.

'Honestly, I love your father, but he needs to figure out what's important in life. Particularly at Christmas.'

Noah smiled when she walked in, but his eyes were on Zorro, who'd leapt off the counter and was now searching the kitchen floor for food morsels.

'He asked me all the way back to his house to give me a box of chocolates. *Chocolates.*'

So *that* was what it had been, Noah thought.

'He could have just brought them with him.' She frowned at him. 'What are you doing?'

'I have drinks, popcorn and dessert for a night in.' He walked to her and gently pushed her towards the living room, away from the cat. 'I thought you might want a quiet evening after the busyness of today.'

'Sounds amazing.'

But she didn't sit when she got to the couch—just turned and put her hands on her hips.

'You're acting weird.'

'No.'

He walked back to the kitchen and blocked the cat from darting into the living room. There was a beat when Noah thought Zorro would try again, but then the cat sat down and started licking his leg.

'Something to drink?'

'Noah, you *are* acting weird. Either you tell me why, or I start the Christmas karaoke up again.'

'Oh, please, *no*.'

Deciding that all he needed for it to be perfect was her, him and the damn cat, he sighed.

'Fine. But I *had* hoped it would go better than this. You and I would be watching our movie. You'd sigh, tell me how I've helped you to love Christmas again, and in would trot Zorro…'

She narrowed her eyes. 'Some of that might happen. But I don't understand—'

She stopped when Noah picked up the cat, her eyes widening as she took in the bow around his neck.

'Oh, he's *festive*.' She walked over to him and took the cat from his hands, just as he'd anticipated she would. 'How did you manage to get him to sit still?'

'I asked very nicely. Told him that if he did I'd legally adopt him.'

'Adopt—'

She broke off as Noah lowered to his knee and her eyes filled. True to who she was, she tried to blink the tears away, but she drew the cat in closer. When Zorro protested, she moved to put him down.

And then she saw the ring.

'Noah.'

It was both a gasp and an exhalation of air, and he didn't think he'd ever hear as beautiful a sound again. He took Zorro from her, untied the ring from his neck and gave him a little scratch on the head before letting him go.

True to who *he* was, he ran and hid under the closest table, unimpressed with the past few minutes.

'Ava, you know how much—'

'Noah,' she said again, and her voice was impatient this time. 'I love you, and I'm sure whatever you've planned to say is going to be beautiful, but you can say it to me later, okay? There's only one thing I want to hear right now.'

When he grinned, she shook her head, took the ring from his hand and slid it onto her finger.

'Never mind. I don't even have to hear it. *Yes.* Yes, I will.'

He straightened with a chuckle, but it was cut off when she kissed him. When they pulled apart, she grinned.

'So, how do you feel about wedding planning? Because I vote we get a wedding planner…'

* * * * *

FROM VENICE
WITH LOVE

ALISON ROBERTS

To Fi, with lots of love.
Here's to friendship. And memories xxx

CHAPTER ONE

THE SOUND OF more than one person shouting got
steadily louder as Nico Moretti turned into the nar-
row Venetian alleyway that would get him to his des-
tination a little faster.

He tried to ignore the sound. He was in a hurry and
it wasn't as if the sound of shouting was anything un-
usual for a large Italian city but he could feel his frown
deepening. It was a disturbing echo of what was al-
ready occupying too much of his head.

The noise was loud enough to have people stopping
in the street now. Turning their heads and asking each
other what they thought it might be about. The slow-
ing pace and knots of people forming made it harder
to move forward and Nico heard a growl of frustration
escape his own throat.

He could tell them what it was about if he had either
the time or the inclination. It was about people who
wanted different things. People who were passionate
about what they believed in. People who weren't pre-
pared to even try and understand each other and left
broken lives in their wakes. But he didn't have the in-
clination. Not when he felt so out of place in this city
of his birth and with the sound of his childhood lan-

guage surrounding him and reinforcing that exclusion.
And he certainly didn't have the time. Not when the
real reason for his return to Venice was due to start in
less than thirty minutes.

At least he had the advantage of his height. And
plenty of practice in cutting through obstructions to
get to the heart of an emergency. All he needed to do
was take on the mantle of an expert consultant en route
to an urgent call in an emergency department or at an
accident scene.

'*Scusi.*' The word was a command, not a request,
and, as always, it had the desired effect. A path ap-
peared through the gathering crowd. Those closest to
him actually stopped talking to stare at him but that
only made the sound of whatever was happening ahead
clearer.

Whatever it was about, it wasn't simply a misunder-
standing or disagreement. There was a language bar-
rier as well. He could hear English being spoken by a
forceful, female voice.

'Stand back. Don't move him yet. Call an ambu-
lance. *Ambulanza.*'

More shouting. In Italian. Had someone called an
ambulance? Where was it? Why wasn't it here yet?
They were right beside the Grand Canal, for heaven's
sake. Practically a highway in Venice. Where were the
police? Where was a doctor when you needed one?'

'*Sì.*' The English woman had understood something
in the furore. '*Dottoressa.* I'm a doctor. Let me get
close. I have to find out if he's breathing.'

'He's not,' someone close to Nico muttered. 'He's
dead. He has to be, falling off the roof like that. He
must have broken his sorry neck. Who does that En-

glish woman think she is? An angel who can work some kind of miracle?'

'It's almost Christmas,' a black-clad Italian grandmother said sagely. 'A good time for a miracle to happen.'

'*Scusi.*' Nico schooled himself not to show any personal frustration as he recognised the inevitability of what he had to do. He raised his voice and spoke in Italian. 'I'm a doctor. Let me through. What's going on?'

Charlotte Highton heard the commanding male voice that overrode the almost hysterical barrage of Italian around her. She could also hear the faint sound of a siren. Please, God, she breathed. Let that be an ambulance.

Getting caught up in an accident scene had been the last thing she'd needed after getting lost in the back alleys of Venice, trying to take a shortcut to her destination near St Mark's Square, but what could she have done? She'd seen the man fall from the scaffolding. More than that. She'd been caught by the way he had been doubled over and clutching at his chest seconds before he'd fallen. There was no chance of him surviving any injuries the fall might have caused if he'd already been in cardiac arrest before it had happened.

But they wouldn't let her near and precious seconds were being lost. One of the man's workmates was probably the first-aid officer for the building company and he'd decided that the fall had caused a spinal injury. He was holding the victim's head still and shouting at anybody who so much as bumped the unconscious body.

Now he was shouting in response to a query from the newcomer, who Charlotte couldn't see because

other people were also trying to tell him the story and some were gesticulating madly—pointing to the roof of the house and circling their arms in the air to represent the fall. For a crazy moment Charlotte almost smiled.

Here she was in this beautiful, ancient city with the water of a canal lapping almost at her feet. Surrounded by the sounds of a language she loved but had never had the time to learn. Caught by the passionate involvement of people who were, for the most part, probably complete strangers to the unfortunate man who had fallen. This would never happen in England. It was *so* Italian.

Then a single, curt word from the newcomer and everybody fell silent. And shifted enough to make an opening. The man who stepped in to fill the gap was as Italian as everything else. Tall and dark. Strong featured and exuding a masculinity that was supremely confident. Such a stereotype that, for another crazy moment, Charlotte was sure she'd met him before.

Or maybe she just recognised that kind of confidence. It didn't come from any awareness of his effect on women. This kind of quiet power came from being in a situation where he knew exactly what needed to be done.

'You're a doctor?'

'Yes.'

'And you speak English?'

'Yes. I'm a specialist in emergency neurology.' He was bending over the unconscious man now. 'Did you see the fall? Has he been moved at all?'

'Yes, I saw the fall.' Charlotte was right behind the man and she was reaching for the victim's neck. The newcomer caught her wrist in a grip that was as power-

ful as everything else about this man. His confidence. His voice. The eyes that were locked on hers right now.

'What do you think you're doing?'

'I *saw* him fall.' Charlotte spoke the way she would to anyone who was preventing her doing her job. Or some unfortunate junior doctor who was getting the basics dangerously wrong. 'I saw him *before* he fell. He clearly had severe chest pain. He didn't trip. He *collapsed*. I need to see whether he's got a pulse.'

For a stunned heartbeat the dark eyes continued to hold hers. Charlotte could see how swift his comprehension was. She actually felt the moment when he stepped back from confronting her action and they became a team. He let go of her wrist.

Rapid instructions in Italian followed. The Italian specialist took over holding the man's head and guided a log roll that had the patient on his back with his airway opened in an admirably short space of time. The nearby siren was getting louder but it wasn't yet close enough. Charlotte was crouched with her cheek against the patient's mouth, one hand on his neck with her fingers searching for a pulse and the other resting gently on his diaphragm seeking the movement that would indicate breathing.

'Nothing,' she snapped. She wasn't exactly dressed for performing CPR. She had to hoist up her slim-fitting skirt so that she could kneel on the rough cobblestones of the alleyway. Her equally neat-fitting blouse beneath the skirt's matching blazer hadn't been designed for vigorous movement either. Charlotte felt a seam ripping within the first seconds of pushing her body weight down hard enough to depress the chest of the large man.

Her unexpected medical colleague was still communicating in Italian to those around him. Explaining what was going on perhaps. And then he was showing the person who'd been guarding his patient so effectively from Charlotte how to support the man's cervical spine but do a jaw thrust at the same time.

As she stayed in position, with her body weight directly over her straight arms, Charlotte could look sideways. She saw the way he demonstrated the required position, with his large hands splayed, the palms pushing against the angle of the man's jaw and his thumbs resting on his cheeks. She knew the pressure required to keep that kind of hold and yet he made it look like he was being gentle with the critically ill patient.

And then he let the first-aider take over the hold and shifted so that he was kneeling right beside Charlotte. The shafts of pain from the movement of her knees on the cobblestones seemed to fade as his body lined up so close beside hers their arms were touching.

That eye contact was extraordinary. Reassuring and encouraging at the same time. The almost invisible movement of his head told Charlotte that he was in sync with what she was doing. That he was ready for her to pause so that he could deliver a breath. With an equally subtle nod, Charlotte began counting aloud. She had no idea how many compressions she'd done already but it was standard international protocol to deliver two breaths for every thirty compressions and a lead-in was given so that minimum pumping time was lost.

'Twenty-eight, twenty-nine...thirty.' Charlotte raised her hands and sat back on her heels as her CPR partner bent down, pinching the man's nose and covering his mouth with his own. She watched the man's chest rise

and fall. Twice. And then she was back in position and the compressions continued smoothly.

Wow. Not only could this guy get air into someone without disturbing the protected position of a C spine, he was prepared to do mouth-to-mouth resuscitation on a stranger. A risk very few medical people would be prepared to take these days. And compressions were deemed the more important component of CPR now. If an ambulance was on its way and the compressions were effective, you had a window of ten minutes or so before the lack of extra oxygen would cause irreversible brain damage.

Charlotte was impressed. She was also sweating despite the deep chill of Venice in December, and her knees felt as if someone had attacked them with a baseball bat. She'd never been more grateful to hear the sound of a siren so close. Looking up, as she paused to let another two breaths be delivered, she was astonished to see that it was a jet boat, arriving on the canal, complete with flashing beacons and a uniformed paramedic, with a defibrillator in his hand, waiting to jump ashore.

She knew better than to stop what she was doing and wait for these emergency medics to take over the scene. Automatically, she rocked forward, her hands back in position on the centre of the man's chest with one flat and the other locked around the wrist to give her extra strength as she pushed down and began the count that would remain silent until the warning of breaths needed.

One...two...three...

Nico could hear the shouts of the paramedics arriving and securing the ambulance. Thank goodness! The dis-

comfort of kneeling on cold, hard cobbles to perform CPR was truly unbearable.

Not that the English woman was showing any signs of discomfort. Nico had been watching her, waiting for the signal to deliver another couple of breaths but also because she was so…so *in control*. So very British.

She had that English peaches and cream type of complexion and the kind of reserve that always felt so foreign to Nico, but he had spent so many years away from Italy it was very familiar. So familiar, in fact, that he could imagine he'd met this woman before. He'd certainly met the type.

Virtually the exact opposite of the type of women he preferred.

It was perhaps unfortunate that he'd inherited his father's taste in women. He liked them small and dark, curvy and vivacious. With an appetite for life and fun that could negate any tendency to take life too seriously out of working hours. But as long as he didn't make his father's mistake of marrying a woman like this, he wouldn't end up abandoned and broken-hearted when someone on another continent offered something more exciting. Like when his father's beloved Irish wife had simply taken their only child and made off for greener pastures.

Nico shook off the thought. Normally, snippets of family history would never distract him from a situation like this but his mind had been full of it until the moment he'd intervened in this rescue scene. Even now, he was aware of the small object in his pocket that the solicitor had insisted he take with him. It should be small enough to dismiss out of hand but unfortunately it carried a significance that could never be dismissed.

He had to push it firmly to one side right now, however. After a second glance to reassure himself that the paramedics were coming in the right direction, Nico took another look at the woman who hadn't missed a beat in performing the chest compressions.

Strands of her blonde hair had worked themselves loose thanks to her current physical exertion but the rest of it was still tightly bound into an intricate kind of knot that removed the feminine allure of long tresses. She had grey eyes that could have looked attractively smoky but she was so focused on the clinical aspects of this situation that they were devoid of an identifiable emotion.

Even now, as the paramedics set up the defibrillator and prepared to take over the management of this patient, he couldn't detect any sign of relief or distress, perhaps, that she'd been caught up in this traumatic event. She was watching what the paramedics were doing with hawk-like intensity. She might not speak Italian but Nico had the distinct impression that she wouldn't hesitate to correct these medics if she felt things were not being done to an expected standard.

He filled them in as they attached the patches to the man's chest. He provided the cervical spine support as preparations were made to secure the airway and the first shock was delivered, but then a second crew arrived, along with the police, and Nico found himself stepping back and merely watching, along with the crowd of people the police couldn't manage to disperse.

The English doctor was in the same position. Nico saw her tucking the hem of her blouse back into the tight waistband of her skirt. He noticed the holes in her tights and the red, grazed skin of her knees. He could

feel the ache in his own joints and it gave him an oddly
powerful feeling of connection with this stranger. He
tried to catch her eye and smile but she was looking at
her watch and frowning, as though she was running
late for something.

And then she looked over her shoulder and her
frown deepened. Whatever she was looking for was
obscured by the crowd of people who were watching
in fascination as the resuscitation scene reached fever
pitch.

The man's airway was secured and a paramedic was
delivering oxygen via a bag mask unit. An IV line was
in place and drugs had been administered. And then
the shout was given to stand clear and another shock
was delivered.

There was a collective gasp from the onlookers as
the man's body jerked in response to the shock and then
silence fell as everybody held their breath. Only those
closest could see the blip on the screen of the life pack
and then another and another as the rhythm picked up.
One of the paramedics felt the neck of the patient and
grinned at his colleague.

'We have a pulse.'

A cheer went up from the crowd and the atmosphere
only became more excited as the emergency services
prepared to transport the man to hospital as quickly
as possible. People were moving away in response to
the shouted instructions of the police officer and Nico
saw the English woman disappearing behind others.

He couldn't let her vanish. Somebody had to thank
her for her contribution to saving the man's life.

'*Scusi.*' Again, Nico pushed his way through the
human obstruction. He was going against the flow to-

wards the canal and where they were trying to manoeu-
vre the stretcher that now carried the still-unconscious
man into the ambulance, but that was also the direction
in which the woman was going. She was still looking
for something, her head bent as she peered around peo-
ple, and suddenly Nico spotted what she was after. A
black laptop case, propped against the wooden piling
the ambulance launch had been tied up to.

He could get to it first. She'd have to stop and talk
to him then and he could thank her. Get her address,
maybe, and then follow up on the patient and let her
know the outcome. With a determined effort Nico
stepped in front of a man and reached for the case.
He had it in his hand when someone bumped into
him from behind with such force that his hand simply
opened. The case fell, bounced on the cobbles and fell
again, in a graceful arc, to land in the canal. For a sec-
ond or two it floated on the surface. And then it sank.

Charlotte watched the laptop case disappear under the
murky water of the canal, its disappearance hastened
by the wash of the ambulance as it took off with its
beacons flashing and siren sounding.

If she took her shoes and jacket off...

Good grief...was she actually considering diving in
to try and retrieve it before it sank too far?

The downward glance towards her shoes had
hammered home the reality of what was happening.
Straightening and dusting off her skirt after she'd got to
her feet hadn't cured the creases and streaks of grime.
Her tights were shredded and one knee was grazed
enough for a trickle of blood to be obvious.

Her armour had been dented.

But worse than that—far, far worse than that—her shield had been ripped away from her and destroyed.

'Oh…my…God…' Charlotte had about a heartbeat before she knew the fear would try and kick in.

The man was turning towards her, clearly appalled at what had just happened.

She couldn't let him see her fear. Couldn't let anybody see it because if they did it would become real. It would take over and she would be sucked back into that place where she was utterly powerless. Where she became nobody.

It wasn't going to happen. Charlotte fought back, gathering fury as if it could repair the amour. Replace the shield.

'You *idiot*,' she snapped. 'Have you *any* idea what you've just done?'

The dark eyes widened, startled by her ferocity.

'I'm so sorry,' he said. But the apology in his eyes was being replaced by something more like astonishment. Anger, even, at being attacked for something that had clearly been an accident.

Charlotte knew that. She'd seen the person behind being pushed and stumbling, only prevented from falling by the safety barrier this man's back had provided. It didn't help, though, knowing that the action had not been deliberate. How could it, when the effect was the same?

'That laptop has my presentation on it,' Charlotte snapped. 'The presentation I'm supposed to be delivering to an international symposium in…' She jerked her gaze to her wrist. 'In exactly *ten* minutes.'

His face was changing again, along with the expression in his eyes. He was putting pieces of a puz-

zle together with the same kind of swiftness that had been obvious when they had become a team, working in sync to try and save the life of the unfortunate man who'd fallen from the scaffolding in the wake of his cardiac arrest.

They weren't a team now. They were on different sides of a battle and Charlotte felt as if she was fighting for her life. He couldn't possibly understand how important this was to her but he obviously knew more than she would have expected.

'Not by any chance the symposium on critical interventions in the emergency department? Being held at the Bonvecchiata hotel?'

'Yes. I'm Dr Charlotte Highton. Due to open the symposium in…' Charlotte had to swallow hard '…*eight* minutes.'

'*You're* Charlotte Highton?'

'Yes.' Charlotte glared at the stranger, who was looking at her as if he'd seen a ghost. As if he couldn't believe she was who she'd said she was.

He gave his head a sharp shake. And then he held out his hand. 'Dr Nicholas Moretti,' he told her. 'Nico. We've met before. Twice, in fact. At St Margaret's Hospital in London. And that night at The Cosmopolitan Club. It was a few years ago now…' His voice trailed off. He was frowning and still staring as if he could barely recognise her. As if he couldn't make sense of what he was seeing.

Well…no surprises there. He was talking about a lifetime ago. She'd been a different person then.

A person she couldn't afford to be reminded of because it would only make this situation even worse. How incredibly unfortunate was this? To not only lose

the protection she depended on but to meet someone who had known her back then? Before…

Before her life had turned so sharply it had virtually doubled back on itself to take the path she was now on.

For just a moment Charlotte could remember what it had been like at that crossroad.

She could feel the fear.

She didn't remember meeting him. Oh…she'd felt the beat of familiarity when she'd seen him. She probably *would* remember him if she allowed her mind to go back to that time. To when she'd been the rising star of a prestigious London hospital and her academic brilliance had been enough to erase the shadows of a painfully shy youth. To when she'd had the world at her feet and she had been courted by albeit distant royalty and wined and dined at places like The Cosmopolitan Club.

A time that it hadn't even occurred to her that she might be reminded of today.

Not only reminded of but stripped of any protection she would normally have to ward it off. How long had it been since she'd felt this vulnerable?

To Charlotte's *absolute* horror, she could actually feel the prickle of tears at the back of her eyes. Tears that could unleash weakness that might undo her completely. She blinked. Hard. She dragged her gaze away from yet another expression she could read in this man's eyes. He had such an open face. He was probably a very nice person but she didn't need anyone to be *concerned* about her.

She could look after herself. And succeed. She'd learned that long ago.

A police officer had come to stand beside them. This man who had an Italian name that matched his

looks but who, curiously, spoke perfect English with an Irish accent, translated his query.

'He wants to know if you need assistance of any kind.'

A snort of something akin to laughter escaped Charlotte. She alone was the only person who could provide the kind of assistance she needed right now. Unless by some miracle a police diving team could be available within seconds and an even more impressive miracle would reveal a laptop that could survive total submersion.

But a rapid conversation in Italian led to the police officer nodding and indicating, with a wave of his arm, that Charlotte should follow him.

Nick was also following. 'He's going to take us to the symposium venue,' he said briskly. 'In the police launch. It will only take a few minutes.'

Charlotte looked down at her ruined clothes. She couldn't appear anywhere looking like this.

'We will explain what's happened.' His hand was on her arm, guiding her through the crowd that was only now dispersing properly. 'Please let me help if I can. I feel responsible for this unfortunate turn of events and I will do anything I can to put things right. Perhaps they can rearrange the order of the presentations. And do you have a back-up of your material?'

Having a man step in and try and solve this problem was the last thing Charlotte needed.

'Of course I do. It's on a flash drive.'

'Which is where?'

Charlotte focused as the police officer offered her a hand to step into the speed boat. She ignored the hand, climbed aboard unaided and then turned back.

She had to speak through gritted teeth. 'It's in the side pocket of the laptop case that you *threw* into the canal.'

It was a totally unjustified accusation in the wake of an obvious accident. It was also an undeserved slap in the face given that he was trying so hard to help.

But Charlotte didn't care. She couldn't afford to.

'Please don't concern yourself any further.' She turned away and nodded to the pilot of the boat, who revved the engine. Waved at him imperiously enough to indicate that speed was of the essence and it was time to leave. 'This is my problem and I will deal with it.'

Nico watched the police launch speed away down the canal.

He could walk to the venue in only a few minutes longer than the boat trip would take. He hadn't actually told her that he was booked to attend the symposium himself so he couldn't really take offence that he hadn't been invited to share the ride.

Besides…he needed a few minutes to try and get his head around this extraordinary development.

She might not remember him but he remembered Charlotte Highton very well indeed. He'd been looking forward to seeing what that dynamic young doctor was like further down the track of her brilliant career.

Not that she'd been his type when he'd met her all those years ago but he'd been able to appreciate her attributes. The soft femininity that had been such a delightful contrast to the skill and intelligence she'd radiated as a young clinician. The sparkle of a woman who'd had the world and most of its men at her feet.

Now she was a female clinician who exuded power and control. There wasn't even the slightest hint of softness.

Or emotion, other than anger.

Except…just for a moment there, when he'd told her that he'd met her before, Nico could swear he had seen real fear in her eyes. A vulnerability that had been so out of place with the external appearance of this woman that he'd thought he'd been imagining things.

What he certainly wasn't imagining was the stark contrast between the woman he remembered admiring in the past and the one he'd just encountered.

What the hell had happened to Charlotte Highton?

And what was she trying to hide?

CHAPTER TWO

'CHARLOTTE...THERE YOU ARE! Thank goodness...I've
been seriously worried about what might have hap-
pened to you.' The tall, grey-haired man was hurrying
towards her. As he got closer, however, his step fal-
tered and his eyes widened. 'Oh, my goodness. What
has happened to you?'

The hotel Bonvecchiata had a water landing for gon-
dolas and motorboats so Charlotte had entered the foyer
moments after leaping out of the police launch. She
knew she looked a fright but there'd been no chance
to duck into a restroom and at least tidy her hair and
sponge some of the mud from her clothing. Richard
Campbell, the co-ordinator of this select symposium
and the man who'd invited her to open it, must have
been pacing the foyer as he'd waited anxiously for her
to arrive.

'Long story, Richard. I'm very sorry, but I got
caught up in an emergency. A man went into cardiac
arrest and fell off some scaffolding right in front of me.
I had to keep up the CPR until the ambulance got there.'

Charlotte was speaking quickly but her mind was
working even faster. There were about fifty people
who'd been invited to attend this symposium. Where

were they? Sitting in the conference room already, drumming their fingers on the tabletops and muttering about the substandard organisation of this gathering?

Richard was an old friend. Charlotte felt terrible about letting him down like this by being late and he didn't even know the worst of it yet. How was she going to tell him that she'd lost her presentation material?

He'd noticed her gaze sweep the foyer.

'They're serving coffee and cake in the restaurant for everybody. As soon as I knew you were running late I put back the start time for half an hour. There's a couple of attendees that aren't here yet as well.'

'Oh...' Charlotte nodded. She had been given a small breathing space. Now she had to decide if there was any way in the world she could rescue the situation. 'Richard...about my opening address...'

The older man smiled. 'Catchy title. "Miracles or Mutilation?" It's caught everybody's attention already, I have to say. But, Charlotte...' Richard was frowning now, looking down at her shredded tights and grazed knees. 'Are you going to be able to deliver it?'

Richard Campbell's reputation was on the line here. There were people from all over the world who'd chosen to come to this satellite symposium—a breakaway group from the much larger conference that had finished in Rome yesterday—plus others who had chosen to come to this forum without attending the main conference. They were all leaders in the field of emergency medicine. Exceptionally busy people who would not be happy to have their precious time wasted.

Charlotte's presentation had been researched meticulously. The medical illustrations department of her university hospital had spent hours preparing the

graphics that represented the facts and figures, the trends and the controversies about cost-effectiveness. It didn't matter how phenomenal her memory was, there was no way she could do justice to her presentation.

If she could get hold of someone at St Margaret's they could find the presentation on her desk computer and email it to her, but that would take too much time. They only had a matter of hours to fit in the other presentations and discussions before the symposium dinner this evening. And someone needed to open the day's programme.

How would it look it she backed out? Even with the best excuse in the world it would still dent her reputation as a young leader in this field, and Charlotte *needed* that reputation. It was who she was. The professional Charlotte Highton was strong enough to hide the *real* Charlotte. The inadequate, shameful one who wasn't a real woman at all.

She was caught between a rock and a hard place here. If she explained that there was no way she could do this, she would tarnish her reputation with the taint of failure and that chink in her armour might never be mended. It might grow, in fact, and eventually split open and the whole world would know what she was hiding.

They might look at her the way Nico Moretti had. As if they knew she was a fraud.

Charlotte could feel her heart thumping rapidly and there was a sinking sensation in her stomach that threatened to spiral into nausea.

'I've got a small problem,' she confessed to Richard. 'I've lost my presentation. My laptop ended up in the canal.'

'Oh...Lord...' Richard shaded his eyes with his hand. 'Can you manage without it?'

Charlotte opened her mouth to tell him how unlikely that was, but before she could force the words out she was distracted by the sound of her name being called from somewhere near the reception desk.

'*Charlotte Jane Highton...*'

The voice was as familiar to her as her own but Charlotte didn't want to believe that there was yet another problem she had to deal with. She kept her gaze on Richard, who gave her a rueful smile.

'Sorry. I hadn't got around to telling you. Your grandmother's here.'

Charlotte shook her head sharply. 'No. She's not supposed to arrive until tonight. After the symposium. We're travelling back to London together tomorrow.'

But the voice was much closer now. It couldn't be ignored.

'Charlotte Jane... What on *earth* have you done to yourself, child? You look like you've been run over by a gondola.'

Charlotte closed her eyes. She might be thirty-one years old but her grandmother could make her feel like a child again in a heartbeat. Flame-haired and larger than life, Lady Geraldine Highton was never one to stand on ceremony.

'Gran...what are you doing here?'

'I'm supposed to be here. I booked a room for us tonight.'

'Yes, but you were flying in this evening.'

'I changed my flight and arrived first thing this morning. I decided I wanted to hear you speak and this

lovely man has told me I can sit in with all the transla-
tors and hear you on some headphones.'

Richard was nodding now and his smile was in-
tended to reassure Charlotte that this problem, at least,
had been dealt with. Clearly, he had been charmed by
Lady Geraldine. Or intimidated. Either way, she had
made arrangements that she now deemed satisfactory.

'But, Gran, you hate hearing anything about medi-
cal procedures. You've never wanted to hear me talk
about my work.'

'Today's different.'

Something *was* different. With the kind of skill
Charlotte found invaluable in her dealings with peo-
ple in traumatic situations, she could sense that there
was something important her grandmother was keep-
ing to herself.

'I might not like hearing it,' Lady Geraldine contin-
ued, 'and I might not understand it, but it won't stop me
wanting the chance to be proud of my granddaughter.
Who knows? It might be the only chance I ever get.'

Yes. There was a shadow there in her grandmother's
eyes. Eyes that usually sparkled with the determination
to squeeze the best that life had to offer out of every
opportunity. What was going on?

Charlotte knew she was staring. She also knew that
her grandmother could read her like a book.

'We'll talk later,' Lady Geraldine said crisply. 'What
we have to do now is get you tidied up. Thankfully, I
have spare hosiery in my bag. And a hairbrush. Come
on, Charlotte. Where's the nearest bathroom? There's
no time to waste. You don't want to keep all these im-
portant people waiting, do you?'

'But…'

There was a plea on Richard's face now. 'You don't have to give the presentation you prepared,' he said quietly. 'I have every confidence that you can think of something to say that would be an appropriate way to open this symposium. Could you do that, Charlotte? Please?'

The space between that rock and hard place suddenly got so small that it squeezed the breath out of Charlotte's lungs. She couldn't think. Maybe because she had no choice.

'I'll do my best.'

So it was that Charlotte found herself looking almost presentable again fifteen minutes later, standing in front of a room full of people who sat at a huge, U-shaped table. Some wore headphones to receive the translation service. Most had laptops or tablets on the table in front of them, along with pads of paper, pens, pitchers of iced water and even bowls of mints.

Charlotte had nothing other than a microphone clipped to the lapel of her jacket. From the way her heart was pounding and how exposed she felt, she could have been standing here stark naked.

She tried to smile at the group but failed. She did, however, manage to introduce herself and apologise for the delay in starting.

'I'm sure you've all heard by now of the reason why I was delayed and you, more than most, will understand that emergencies happen.'

Oh, help. Charlotte could hear the sound of her own voice, magnified by the loudspeaker system. Where was the calm, professional tone she always used in public?

What would her grandmother think of this? The niggling worry that there was something wrong that her grandmother wasn't telling her couldn't be allowed to surface until this was all over but it was impossible not to have a flash of shame that the pride her only living relative had taken in her achievements was going to be dented.

'Ah…' Charlotte stared at the group, totally at a loss for what she could say next. Please, God, let the ground open and swallow me up, she thought.

The ground didn't open but the door of the conference room did, to admit a latecomer. Everybody's head turned at the interruption but Charlotte's gaze had got there first and now it was stuck.

The worst moment of her life had just taken a dive to a new low.

How on earth could Nicholas Moretti have the nerve to show up here, knowing he'd ruined her preparation for this talk? He'd already revealed his disbelief that she was who she said she was. Did he now want to see if she was going to make a fool of herself and confirm that disbelief?

He was about to get what he came for, then, wasn't he?

Nico gave a very European hand gesture, apologising for his interruption as he took the empty space at the table. His body language conveyed complete confidence that he had the right to be here, though. That he was, in fact, eager to take part in the proceedings. And then his gaze locked with Charlotte's and that weird spinning sensation in her gut seemed to catch fire.

Anger?

Quite possibly.

Charlotte Highton wasn't about to let the actions of a man even threaten to destroy her.

Not again.

She took a deep breath, jerking her gaze away from Nico and vowing not to let it return to that section of the table until she was finished. In a way, he'd done her a favour. His entrance had covered her stumble and now she was fired up. Whether it was from anger or desperation was immaterial.

'Some of you might be asking whether I should have let myself become involved in that emergency situation, especially when the result has deprived you of the audiovisual accompaniment you were supposed to have this morning.'

A ripple of sympathy went through the gathering.

'It's a fair question,' Charlotte continued. 'How far should any of us go in getting involved? How far should we go as emergency medicine specialists? Out in the field or in our own departments?'

Her words were clear and her tone as professional as ever now. Everybody was listening. Looking at her. She could feel one gaze in particular so strongly that she knew exactly who it was coming from. Good. Let him watch and listen. Let him see who Charlotte Highton was now.

'We can do so many things that can be done in an operating theatre in our emergency departments or out in the field. Burr-holes, tracheotomies, amputations, thoracotamies, Caesareans.' Charlotte paused for effect. 'Extreme measures in desperate circumstances. How many are justified? Does the weight of evidence

suggest we're performing miracles? Or guilty of per-
forming mutilations?'

Another pause. This was the moment that would
make or break this talk.

'I had a presentation that was full of statistics about
these kinds of extreme procedures and graphics to
show you the controversial relationship between pa-
tient outcomes and cost-effectiveness. Obviously it's
not possible to do those facts and figures justice from
memory, so instead…' The solution to this problem
came to her in a flash of inspiration. 'I'm going to
present a case history.'

Nico sat back in his chair.

He could feel the surprise of the people around him.
What was this? They were all intelligent people who
were hungry for new knowledge. They wanted to be
presented with the results of cutting-edge research that
they could use to improve what they did for a career.
But they were going to be told a *story*?

'The man I'll call Bernie was forty-three years old,'
Charlotte was saying. 'He went to the corner shop very
late one night, because his pregnant wife had a craving
for chocolate ripple ice cream. The timing was unfor-
tunate. The shop was held up and Bernie got stabbed.
A small knife with a short blade was buried to its hilt
in his chest, deflected by the sixth rib, maybe five or
six inches to the left from the midline.'

Nico could sense the interest picking up around him.
The injury had been dangerously close to the man's
heart.

'The ambulance crew knew not to remove an im-
paled object. Bernie's still conscious when they arrive

but his blood pressure's dropping. Fortunately, this corner shop is only about two minutes' drive from St Margaret's hospital. They put a doughnut dressing around the knife to stabilise it, give Bernie some oxygen and load and go. They establish IV access en route.'

The way Charlotte had changed to the present tense drew them all into the urgency of this case. Clever. Or were they all drawn in, as he was, by the sound of her voice? Soft, but as clear as a bell. As under control as her hair was again, all scraped back into that complicated knot thing.

Nico had preferred it the way he'd seen it after that resuscitation scene, with enough loose wisps to suggest that the whole knot could be released if you buried your fingers in it, wiggled them and then dragged them gently through the length of the hair. How long was it when it was loose? he wondered. And then he sharply dismissed the errant speculation and concentrated again on what she was saying.

'By the time Bernie comes through our doors, he's lost consciousness. His BP's unrecordable. His cardiac rhythm goes from SVT to VF to asystole within thirty seconds of my team getting him hooked up to the monitors.'

Nico was really listening now. So this was a case that Charlotte herself had managed? He could imagine her there, in the emergency department of St Margaret's. Wearing scrubs, probably, with a white coat over them. No…she'd been expecting a major trauma. She'd have a plastic apron on. And gloves. And a head covering that probably had a plastic face shield to protect her from blood spatter. She would have been in

charge. In control. Her voice might have been louder than it was right now but just as clear.

'We know our protocols inside out but how do we start CPR? This man's got a knife in his chest that's probably punctured his left ventricle. He's bleeding out. We can pull the knife out and push fluids but there's a hole in his heart so that would be futile.'

Nico was holding his breath without realising it. Everybody here knew that the only option was to do one of the most invasive procedures that could ever be done out of an operating theatre. Cracking open this man's chest and getting to the heart of the problem, so to speak.

'He's dead already unless we do something major and do it fast.' Charlotte's tone told them she agreed with the conclusion they'd all reached. 'A thoracotomy is the only option but I know as well as everybody else in the team what the odds are for a successful result. Virtually nil. But, hey…we have to try, don't we? This man is about to become a father. Right now, his pregnant wife is probably wondering why it's taking him so long to get back with her ice cream.'

Charlotte seemed to straighten her back. 'I'm the one who has to make the call and, as far as I'm concerned, it's a no-brainer. We take out the knife and I do a clam-shell thoracotomy. There's a gaping hole in the left ventricle and I suture it shut while we deal with more blood in a thorax than I've ever seen before.'

Nico closed his eyes for a heartbeat. He could picture it. A nightmare scene. The tissue of the myocardium would have been slippery. The visual field would have been impossible to keep clear with all that blood so you'd have to work almost blind.

'We start pushing fluids and begin CPR. I'm riding that stretcher to Theatre with my hand inside Bernie's chest, doing internal compressions and praying that my rough suturing is going to hold.'

Oh, Nico could imagine that scene too. Charlotte would have had to have been astride the man's legs, with one hand on the side rail to steady herself. Amongst the bank of monitoring and ventilation equipment that would have been in place. Speeding along with her team running to get them to Theatre as fast as possible.

It felt like he was standing in one of the wide corridors of St Margaret's right now, watching the dramatic spectacle rush past him. Opening his eyes again, he knew that he was looking at Charlotte with growing admiration. This was some woman.

'The cardiac surgical team is waiting for us. They do a much better job than me in repairing the damage. They replace the blood volume and get Bernie's heart started again. By this time his wife is at the hospital. Bernie's taken to the intensive care unit. He's still alive but what none of us know is whether we've done the right thing in saving him. Will he wake up? And, if he does, how much brain damage has been caused by the lack of oxygen? His wife is distraught and, just to add to the tension, she goes into labour three weeks before her due date.'

A soft groan came from her audience. This might be nothing like what they'd expected as an opening talk but they were all invested in the story now. They had to know the outcome.

'I've told you this story because it does, unlike so many, many others, have a happy ending. Bernie did

have a degree of neurological compromise. His cognition and speech were affected and he had a unilateral weakness on his right side.'

It was the first time Nico had seen Charlotte smile. He felt his own lips curve in an unconscious response.

'But his weak arm didn't stop him being able to cradle his newborn daughter a couple of days later. His difficulty in finding words didn't dim the way he could communicate his joy to his wife.'

Dammit. Was that a *lump* Nico could feel in his throat? He swallowed it away. His own career was full of success stories like this, wasn't it?

'The bottom line,' Charlotte continued quietly, 'is that our job is about the people who come under our care. Bernie was a miracle. But if he hadn't made it, that resus scene in my ED could have been denounced as unnecessary mutilation. We couldn't know how it would go before we started but is it just a coin toss?'

Charlotte was looking around the room. Nico was waiting for her gaze to cross his. He was oddly disappointed when it didn't.

'No.' She answered her own question. 'That's what our chosen specialty is all about. Working towards being the best we can be in our field of expertise. Knowing when there's a choice that pulling out the big guns is going to make the difference between life and death.'

Nico saw Charlotte take a deep breath. She was wrapping up now and the unusual introduction had clearly been a huge success. Everybody was leaning forward, totally engrossed and eager to participate in the programme that was about to start.

He felt the same way so how on earth could he be

distracted by the way that deep breath pushed Char-
lotte's breasts against the material of the plain blouse
she wore under that tailored jacket? The way a hint of
cleavage struggled to appear over the top button. Good
grief. She was so buttoned up with that hairstyle and
the fitted clothes she wore, it was almost as if she was
trying not to look remotely feminine.

Maybe she was batting for the other team. Nico
tucked the thought away with satisfaction. That would
explain a lot. Maybe she had been trying to deny her
true preference when he'd seen her out with that man
in The Cosmopolitan Club all those years ago. And
even if she was now comfortable with who she was, in
her position Charlotte probably wouldn't want to come
out of the closet and travel in the company of her girl-
friend. Or wife, perhaps. It was none of his business
and it didn't bother him.

So why did that curious feeling of disappointment
in not making eye contact with her a second ago sud-
denly deepen several notches?

'The papers you are going to be privileged to hear
today are from invited speakers who are leading their
particular fields. I'm looking forward to hearing the
discussions that will follow the presentations. Again, I
must apologise for my unorthodox keynote speech but,
on behalf of Dr Richard Campbell, our chairman for
today, and the others involved in organising this sat-
ellite session, let me welcome you to our symposium
on critical interventions.'

Nico joined the round of applause. His neighbour
leaned sideways to say something about how moving
the story had been and how good it was to be reminded
of the human aspects of their science. But Nico merely

murmured agreement. He couldn't take his eyes off Charlotte. As if she felt his intense gaze, she looked up from her position at the front of the room.

So there, her gaze seemed to say. *I did it—even if you did do your best to stop me.*

After the awkward start to the day things were running smoothly. Richard was delighted. He smiled at Charlotte as they were preparing to follow the others out of the conference room for the lunch break.

'Do you know, I think your introduction has allowed for some very interesting questions to be raised that people might not have considered appropriate otherwise. You've given this whole forum an informality that has brought people closer together. It was a stroke of brilliance.'

'Thanks.' Charlotte rubbed the back of her neck, trying to ease the tension that still hadn't gone away completely. 'It could have taken things in the opposite direction. I was lucky.'

'I think everyone was impressed.'

Had Nicholas Moretti been impressed? And why did it matter so much that he had been?

'I'm sure they'll want to tell you that themselves, over lunch.'

Charlotte wasn't at all sure she wanted that to happen. She might be used to talking to colleagues while balancing a plate of food and eating but the idea of doing that in Nico's company seemed disturbingly… intimate?

Whatever. She had the perfect excuse.

'I'm going to skip lunch, if you don't mind, Richard. I'll grab a sandwich or something but I really need to

check on my grandmother and make sure she's being taken care of. And that she has something to do for the afternoon. Goodness knows what kind of mischief she could get up to otherwise.'

Richard was grinning now. 'She's quite something, your grandmother. How old is she?'

'Eighty-two. Going on about sixteen, I think. I often feel as if I'm in the company of a wayward teenager.' Charlotte's smile was fond. 'And then, at other times, she comes out with the kind of wisdom and advice that only someone who's experienced life to the full could have. She's amazing.'

Richard patted her arm. 'Go and catch up. I'll give your excuses to anyone who asks.'

'Thanks.' Charlotte hurried out to the reception area, away from the dining room, and asked whether her grandmother had left a message for her.

'No. But she's had lunch delivered to your room. Would you like your key now?'

The room was massive and decorated in Venetian style with sumptuous drapes, bed coverings and deep armchairs all in tones of silver and soft bronze. There was a Persian rug on the floor beneath the chandelier hanging from an astonishingly high ceiling. A small table with spindly legs supported a silver tray that had plates of delicate-looking sandwiches and cakes, a pot of tea and cups.

The first thing that struck Charlotte was that the tray hadn't been touched.

Almost at the same time she noted how tidy the room was. Where were the clothes strewn about that always happened when Geraldine was choosing her

next outfit? The open guidebooks as she chose her next adventure?

And why on earth was her grandmother lying on a bed in the middle of the day? Lady Geraldine Highton might be eighty-two but she didn't *do* naps. 'Life's too short,' she always said. 'And it's getting shorter for me by the day. Why waste it by sleeping? I can sleep when I'm dead.'

'Gran...' Charlotte moved towards the bed. 'What's wrong?'

'Oh...' Geraldine clearly hadn't been expecting a visitor. She sat up swiftly, looking...embarrassed. No, make that *guilty*. 'Charlie...I didn't think I'd see you until this evening.' The odd expression vanished, to be replaced by a beaming smile. 'That was a wonderful talk you gave, darling. I can't tell you how proud I was. And I understood every word. Well, almost every word. The next speaker was terribly dull in comparison. I went for a walk and watched the gondolas for a while. I might go for a ride in one after lunch. It's been years...'

Charlotte sank down onto the edge of the second bed, facing her grandmother. Something here was off-key. Terribly off-key.

'Gran...' She reached out and took hold of a soft hand decorated with several diamond rings. 'What's going on?'

'Whatever do you mean? Nothing's going on, Charlotte. Come and have lunch with me.' Lady Geraldine got to her feet but then her face changed. She couldn't hide a grimace of pain and her hand went to her stomach.

'You're not well,' Charlotte gasped. 'That's why you haven't touched your lunch. Why didn't you *tell* me?'

'I'm fine. There's nothing wrong with me.'

'Lie down,' Charlotte ordered. 'I want to have a look at you.'

For a long, long moment Geraldine looked unde- cided. But then she quietly lay down and answered the barrage of questions. Yes, she had abdominal pain. No, it wasn't the first time. Yes, she'd been to see a doctor about it. She'd had a scan. She was booked to have a biopsy between Christmas and New Year.

A *biopsy?*

With absolute dread giving her a chill that almost made her shiver visibly, Charlotte quietly asked if she could feel her grandmother's tummy and when she did, the hard edges of the mass she could feel confirmed her worst fear.

'Did…did your doctor tell you what he thought it was after the scan?'

'Oh, yes…' Lady Geraldine took hold of Charlotte's hand with both of hers. 'He's sure it's some form of bowel cancer.' Her voice wobbled. 'I didn't want you to find out, darling. Not yet.'

Charlotte's voice was thick with tears. 'Why not? You should have told me. I should have been there with you when you had your appointments.'

'We've been planning this trip for so long. Going on the Orient Express has been on my bucket list for far too long.' Unbelievably, Geraldine was smiling mis- chievously. 'And what better time to fulfil a bucket list item than when you've been told the end probably isn't that far off?'

'Gran… We can't spend thirty hours on a train. We have to fly back to London tonight. I'll talk to people.

We'll find a way to bring that procedure forward so
we can start treatment earlier.'

'No way, Jose.' The way Lady Geraldine's eyes nar-
rowed was a warning that she was not about to be con-
tradicted. 'I've taken some painkillers. I'll be as right
as rain after a little rest. You're not going to spoil this
for me, Charlotte. Are you?'

It wasn't really a question. And the look coming
from those faded blue eyes wasn't disapproving. It was
full of absolute love. The kind of love Charlotte had
received from this remarkable woman ever since she'd
been orphaned as a small, terrified child.

This was why her grandmother had wanted to hear
her speak today. Why she'd wanted to tell her how
proud she was of her. Well, that cut both ways, didn't it?

'Let's enjoy this time together,' Lady Geraldine
added softly. 'Before we know anything for sure. Let's
pretend you didn't find me like this. The way I wanted
it to be. Go back to your conference, darling. I need a
little rest and then I'm going to choose my outfit for
the dinner tonight.'

Those words stayed with Charlotte during the after-
noon's symposium proceedings and it was the hard-
est thing she'd ever done, to keep up her professional
image. The papers being presented were fascinating
and the discussions lively, and Charlotte had learned
long ago to firmly shut the door between her profes-
sional and personal lives, but today it was impossible.

Today had started badly. She thought she'd made the
best of a bad situation and survived but now it felt as
if the world had tilted far too sharply on its axis. What
did her brilliant career matter if she was about to lose

the person she loved most? The only person she truly loved, come to that.

The conference attendees were invited to a cocktail session before a break to get ready for the dinner but Charlotte quietly slipped away from the group. She had to pull herself together. Had to find the strength to deal with what was undoubtedly coming. Did she really want to deprive her grandmother of the long-awaited pleasure of the train trip tomorrow and whisk her back to London and into hospital? Did she have that right?

The balcony leading off the now deserted dining room offered a private space with the bonus of an idyllic canal view where more than one ornate gondola could be seen floating past.

One of the gondolas held a pair of young lovers who were locked in a passionate embrace, oblivious to their surroundings for the moment. Maybe they were practising. Wasn't there a bridge here in Venice and if you kissed while going beneath it, it meant that your love would last for ever?

If her grandmother was here on this balcony with her, she'd be poking Charlotte with a bony finger right about now. Clicking her tongue.

That should be you in that gondola, Charlotte Jane, she'd be saying. *Kissing some gorgeous young man whose baby you can't wait to have. You don't know what you're missing, child, and it's the most important thing in life.*

But Charlotte knew all too well what she'd be missing far too soon and hearing her grandmother's voice so clearly in her mind was the final straw.

Tears rolled down her cheeks. Hot, burning tears that felt like acid. No surprise there. They were pretty

concentrated given that she hadn't shed a tear for six years now. They were such a sign of weakness. Feminine weakness.

She knew there was no point in trying to stop them.

Thank God nobody could see her.

The room Nico had been given at the hotel Bonvecchiata was luxurious. He eyed the huge bed, pulled at his tie to loosen it, and looked forward to putting his feet up for a while before heading off to the symposium dinner.

What a day!

Shedding his jacket, Nico walked to the tall windows of his room and looked through the ornate iron grille to find he had the bonus of a canal view. A gondola floated past with a young couple locked in each other's arms.

Nico smiled. Nice. His gaze drifted lazily and then it caught.

His smile faded.

There was a balcony on the floor beneath his. Charlotte Highton was standing there, her shoulders bowed as if she carried the weight of the entire world on them.

And she was *crying*?

Dio, but this woman was so full of contradictions. For a moment Nico stared in fascination. He would never have believed that she was capable of showing such a depth of emotion. But why was she so upset?

Did it have anything to do with being unable to present what she'd intended to present this morning?

Because of the trouble he'd unwittingly caused for her?

For another, long moment Nico kept staring, un-

sure of how to unravel the conflicting emotions being stirred in his own gut. Why did he feel such a strong urge to try and help this prickly, complicated woman? It was more than having contributed to a bad start to her day. More, even, than being curious about how someone's personality could have changed so much in just a few short years.

Being aware that there was some indefinable extra motivation should be enough of a warning to stop him getting involved any further, but did he want to listen to that warning?

He turned away. Stared at the huge, inviting bed for a moment. And then, with a soft growl, he turned on his heel and headed for the door.

CHAPTER THREE

OH...NO.

As if she could cope with her day getting even worse!

Of all the people to discover her at her lowest point in so many years, it had to be Nico Moretti.

Charlotte did her utmost to stem the tide of her tears. She turned her back on Nico and leant on the balustrade of the balcony, gripping the roughened concrete so hard she could feel tendrils of pain in her fingers that flickered into her arms. She fixed her gaze on the canal beneath and blinked again and again, trying to clear the wetness that didn't want to stop. Why couldn't it go back where it had come from, instead of continuing to roll down her face in these humiliating tears?

He didn't say anything. He just came to stand beside her. He, too, seemed to be gazing at the view and he spread his hands on the balustrade as if the only reason he was there was to admire their surroundings.

Charlotte's panic ebbed a little as he just stood there, a silent presence.

She'd never had company during the most unhappy periods in her life. Her first instinct, even as a young child so bereft at the loss of her parents, had been to

hide. To cry alone. And feel alone. To accept that life
was a terribly lonely business and you just had to deal
with that.

There *was* comfort to be found in simply being close
to another person. To feel the presence of another liv-
ing, breathing human.

The fact that Nico wasn't saying anything made it
easy to accept his presence. She didn't have to try and
find excuses or explain anything, and to have someone
there who was clearly prepared to accept the state she
was in made it feel as if it was okay not to be coping.
As if she had support.

Strong support. Bit by bit, Charlotte found her
thoughts creeping out from the dark knot in her head.
She was aware of how big Nico was. Well over six feet
in height and broad with it. His hands against the an-
cient concrete looked huge and powerful but his fingers
were long and artistic looking. Clever hands, no doubt
capable of performing the careful, intricate movements
that were needed when you were dealing with some-
thing as precious as brain tissue.

Charlotte blinked again and, amazingly, her vision
wasn't blurred any more. Without raising her head from
its bowed position, she could study his neatly trimmed
nails and olive-brown skin and the smattering of dark
hair on the backs of his hands that disappeared under
the turned-back cuffs of his white shirt.

Her head turned, as if her gaze was being pulled
up by an external force. Up his arms, across his chest,
where a loosened tie hung like a necklace and the top
buttons of his shirt were undone. It was impossible not
to flick her gaze up to his face now, but it was safe.
He was still staring down at the canal so Charlotte let

her gaze linger for a moment on the strong profile. Unfairly luxurious eyelashes that brushed his cheeks when he blinked. A nose that made no apology for the space it took and deep creases on each side that ran down to meet a mouth that looked as if it smiled often and easily.

A jaw that looked like it hadn't seen a razor in a fair few hours. And a firmness to it that suggested tension. Was he gritting his teeth? Was he standing there not knowing what to say? Wishing he was somewhere else?

'I'm sorry.' The words came out as a whisper. 'I've had… It's been…' she had to take a tiny gulp of air '…a weird kind of day.'

'I understand.' Nico moved finally, but only his head. He angled it a little towards Charlotte. And then he smiled at her.

And…dear Lord…*what* a smile. Slow and so full of warmth. The most genuine smile she had ever seen. And it was for *her*. She had to catch her breath again.

'And I have a horrible feeling I might have contributed to your day not being the one you hoped for,' Nico continued. 'I really must apologise again.'

His voice was as warm as that smile. The Irish lilt was unmistakeable but, if he had been in Ireland, they would hear something else. An Italian inflection that made it unique. An astonishing accent colouring a depth that was as masculine as his size and aura of power.

How many women had fallen in love with that voice already?

Not that she was about to join the ranks. Charlotte cleared her throat.

'No…really. Losing my laptop was nothing com-

pared to...' Oh, help. Had she really been about to break one of her most ironclad rules and share personal information with a professional colleague?

'Compared to what, *cara*?'

It was the endearment that did her in. An endearment in a foreign language that somehow made it inoffensive and genuinely caring.

'My...grandmother is here. She's not well and... and it's possible she might not have...' Charlotte's intake of breath was a small sob. 'Might not have much time left.'

'Ohhh...' The sound was a drawn-out note of understanding. Empathy.

This man was a stranger even if they *had* met before. She would probably never see him again after today. So it didn't really count as sharing personal information, did it? Nobody would be giving her meaningful glances at work or gossiping about her in the cafeteria at St Margaret's. As if it would help with the anonymity, Charlotte fixed her gaze on the canal again. She could be simply talking aloud to herself.

'She's the most important person in the world to me,' she said softly. 'My parents both got killed in a horrible accident when I was eight years old. I was in the accident too and came out as a terrified shell of a child who wouldn't even speak to anyone for months. Gran never cared how tough it got, she was always so patient and so loving. So proud of any achievements I managed.'

'She would have had a lot to be proud of.'

Charlotte's breath came out in a huff of incredulity as she twisted sharply to glare at Nico. He was so used to giving women compliments, wasn't he? Meaning-

less compliments that demeaned what she was trying
to tell him about her wonderful grandmother.

'What makes you think you know anything about
me?' The words came out tight and accusing. And then
Charlotte shook her head and swallowed fresh tears.
'You know *nothing*.'

There was a flash in his eyes but, while he might
be startled by the verbal attack, he didn't look away.

'I know that a few years ago I met a woman who
would have made anybody who loved her immensely
proud,' he said calmly. 'But you're correct…I know
nothing about you on a personal level.'

His gaze still held hers and there was something
else in his eyes now. Respect? Curiosity?

'So tell me,' he invited. And then he smiled again.
'I'm listening.'

She was about to walk away.

Nico could sense the internal struggle but, dam-
mit, he *wanted* to hear more. He knew perfectly well
he was taking advantage of finding Charlotte in a state
that made her vulnerable but he wasn't about to use
the situation to his own advantage. Quite the opposite!
His only motivation for coming out to this balcony and
interrupting an obviously private moment had been to
offer assistance.

He owed her that, surely?

Even though she had dismissed any contribution
he'd made to her having such a bad day, he knew he
hadn't helped it get off to a good start. And it was
frustrating not to be able to think of a way to make up
for that. Nico Moretti was an expert in making other
people's lives better, even in the most dire of circum-

stances. He firmly believed that you could find at least a little patch of joy anywhere if you didn't take life too seriously.

Maybe that was why he knew he had the reputation of being a playboy. But play was the key, wasn't it? Like when he took the time to actually play with one of his smaller patients or do something silly enough to make them smile. And…good grief…he'd never encountered a woman who couldn't accept a compliment, even if it had been an automatic and possibly less than genuine response.

Nico had a strong sense that anything Charlotte told him would be completely honest, no matter how badly it reflected on herself. In his experience, this was an unusual trait, particularly for a woman on first acquaintance.

What really surprised him, however, was how much he wanted to hear more about her. His curiosity about Charlotte Highton was increasing rapidly. He remembered the brilliant young doctor. He'd seen the icy-cool clinician in action. He'd seen a speaker not only cope with facing an international audience having been deprived of her resources but engage them to the point where she'd had them in the palm of her hand.

And now he'd seen a glimpse of a loving granddaughter. Beneath all the layers he could detect there was an orphan who'd been a desperately unhappy child. A woman who currently looked alone. And lonely.

Just who was the real Charlotte?

He tried to send a silent message with his smile. And his eyes.

Talk to me. Please. You never know, I might be able to help. I'm good at helping.

It wasn't working, though. It was as though he was trying to hold a wild creature in his hands and it was struggling to be free. An injured wild creature that wanted to crawl away and lick its wounds somewhere it felt safe.

He needed something more to keep her here. He needed to tap into something that would give them a bond, however tenuous.

'I've met many people at many conferences over the years,' he told her. 'They are often accompanied by their husbands or wives. Or their lovers. Sometimes by their children. You are the very first I've met who is accompanied by a grandparent. That's…intriguing. Special.'

He watched Charlotte take a ragged breath. He heard her sniff and had to hide a smile because it sounded so…unprofessional. Childlike, even. It wasn't as if he'd never witnessed a grown woman crying, of course. They usually did, when he told them things were over, but this was different. The tears had nothing to do with him and they touched a spot in his heart usually reserved for those younger patients or their families. Something poignant.

'Gran *is* special,' Charlotte said, her words a whisper. Then she cleared her throat. 'But she doesn't usually accompany me. In fact, I'm not allowed to talk about anything remotely gruesome or medical when I'm around her. She says that you can always find something uplifting to talk about if you try hard enough.'

'A woman after my own heart,' Nico smiled. 'A finder of joy who can make people around her feel better.'

He let out a quiet breath as he sensed Charlotte re-

laxing. He knew she was almost smiling herself because he was watching so carefully and he could see the softening of her lips. The imperceptible curling at their corners.

'She always has something to look forward to. A new adventure planned. That's why she's here. As soon as she knew I was going to be speaking in Venice she looked up the timetable for the Orient Express going from Venice back to London and when the dates were perfect she said it was meant to be and I couldn't say no because it was well up the bucket list.'

'The bucket list?'

'You know…' Charlotte really smiled this time, as she looked up and caught his gaze. 'The list of things you really, really want to do before you kick the bucket?'

'Kick the…? Oh…' Just occasionally, the fact that English was a second language tripped him up. '*Sì…*' The Italian word slipped out unconsciously as he contemplated the euphemism for dying. 'I understand.'

Her eyes were grey. A dark, stormy sort of grey at the moment. He always expected blonde women to have blue eyes so the colour struck him as different. As unusual as this woman was herself, perhaps?

'But it's a crazy idea. How can we take a slow train trip across Europe when she's so sick? We should fly back to London tonight. I could have her in a hospital by tomorrow, getting the kind of investigations she needs to plan treatment.'

'Is that what she wants? Your grandmother?' It was a relief to be given a problem to solve at last and Nico was more than ready to focus on it, but he needed more information. 'What is her name?'

'Geraldine. Her friends call her Jendi.'

'And what are the symptoms of her illness?'

'I don't really know. She's kept this from me. I wouldn't have known about it at all yet except I found her resting and could see she had abdominal pain. And...I could feel a mass...'

'She has medication for the pain?'

'Yes. She seems fine now. She totally refused to consider cancelling the train trip and getting a flight to London. She told me to go away so she could have a bath in peace and get ready for the dinner tonight. She wants to dress up.'

'If there are no obvious signs that it would be detrimental to her condition, then maybe that's exactly what she *should* do.'

Charlotte's jaw dropped. 'And the train trip? You think that's a good idea, too?'

'Another day or two will not make any difference to the course of her illness,' Nico said. 'And look at it from her point of view. What would be better? To be lying in a hospital bed waiting for possibly a painful procedure or being able to forget about what lies ahead for a brief time and enjoying a wonderful experience in the company of someone you love?'

'But...' Charlotte caught her bottom lip between her teeth and tugged on it. It was another childish gesture that caught Nico in that soft spot in his heart. But then she let go with her teeth and soothed her lip with her tongue and suddenly it was quite another, very unexpected spot that Nico could feel waking up. 'How could *I* forget enough to help her enjoy it?'

'Because you have that kind of strength.' This time the compliment was completely sincere. Nico already

knew enough about Charlotte to be convinced of it. 'You can choose the part of you that you want other people to see and the rest you can keep hidden.'

Something very odd flickered across Charlotte's face. The kind of expression that suggested...guilt? As though she'd been caught out trying to hide something huge and important?

No. The expression was gone as fast as it had appeared. And now Charlotte was turning away. Nico wasn't ready to let her go. Not just yet.

'I think you should make the most of any time you can have together. Be proud that you can help her achieve this bucket-list thing. Maybe you can find out what the other things on her list are too and tick another one off soon.'

A rueful laugh escaped Charlotte. 'Oh, I know what's on the top of that list and it's not something that's ever going to be ticked off.'

'Oh?' Nico tilted his head encouragingly. 'They say that nothing is impossible.'

'*This* is.' Charlotte was looking up at the sky now. Assessing the clouds to see if the forecasted snow might arrive or was she seeking divine inspiration? She flicked Nico the briefest glance. 'Gran's greatest wish is to see me get married. Settled down and ready to present her with her first great-grandchild.'

'Ohhh...' Nico nodded slowly. 'That could be tricky.'

'Impossible.' The word was final.

'Hmm.' He had solved the problem of the train trip. Surely there was a way of at least getting around this one? 'Would there be any harm in letting her *think* it might be possible?'

'Gran's not stupid. She knows perfectly well that I'm not in a relationship. I haven't been for years. I'm hardly likely to get away with pretending I've met "Mr Right" within the next few months, am I?' She took a step away from him, raising her hand to smooth her already perfect hairstyle. 'And I really can't believe I'm having such an astonishingly ridiculous conversation.'

Nico had been distracted for a split second, wondering again what Charlotte's hair would look like if it wasn't so tightly coiled and clipped into place. He wanted to pull out some of those pins. To force her to loosen up a little.

'Because it's not so ridiculous,' he said. 'What if you attended this dinner tonight with...with your new boyfriend? How happy would that make your grandmother?'

This time it was real laughter that escaped. A delicious, totally unexpected chuckle of real mirth. 'Is there a "hire a boyfriend" agency in Venice that you know about?'

'There's no need to hire anybody.' Nico's grin stretched his mouth. 'It's the least I could do to make up for this morning's unfortunate happenstance.'

It was perfect. Here it was on a plate. The opportunity to not only make up for contributing to any distress caused by this morning's incident but to do it in a manner that would be *fun*.

Except that Charlotte was looking at him as if he was totally crazy.

This was surreal.

Just having a personal conversation with a profes-

sional acquaintance would have been weird enough but this incredibly good-looking stranger seemed to be offering to pretend to be her *boyfriend* for an evening.

Imagine that!

Unfortunately, Charlotte *could* imagine it. She could imagine herself introducing him to her grandmother as a...as a *friend*...and Nico turning on his most charming smile and Gran putting two and two together and letting wishful thinking make the impossible a reality.

Oh...God...how happy would she be?

The distraction of a train trip to take her mind off what was coming was nothing compared to the joy she would have if she thought Charlotte had finally found 'the one'.

It was crazy. Wasn't it?

'That's crazy,' she said aloud, hoping the spoken words would confirm it.

'It's only for an evening.' Nico shrugged as if it was no big deal. 'We could tell her we've met before, which is perfectly true. We could say that there's something about Venice being such a romantic city and we've realised we can't fight the attraction any longer. It was meant to be.'

Oh...my... If the look he was giving her right now was any indication of the performance he could put on for her grandmother, she would be totally convinced.

For a skipped heartbeat kind of moment, Charlotte almost believed it herself. She could feel it right down to her bones. How could anyone be so good at looking as if they had just fallen madly in love with someone? It was doing very strange things to something deep inside her. A process that had to be stopped immediately.

He's acting, she reminded herself. And he's only this good at it because he's clearly had a lot of practice.

'You may be an expert in pretending,' she snapped, 'but it's not something I could carry off. I wouldn't even want to try.'

He was still giving her *that* look.

'I watched you this morning,' he said softly. 'I think you can carry off anything that's important enough to you.'

There was a glint of mischief in those dark eyes. Good heavens, he was actually *enjoying* this, wasn't he? He *wanted* to do it?

'You might be surprised at how easy it is,' he continued. 'You might enjoy it.'

Charlotte snorted. 'I don't think so.'

'And wouldn't you even want to try? For your grandmother's sake?'

'No. It would be completely dishonest.'

'Completely?' Nico injected a hurt tone into the word. 'Could you not summon even a tiny bit of attraction to me to work with?'

He tilted his head, moving it closer to her own, his gaze dropping from her eyes to her lips.

And, heaven help her, but Charlotte could actually feel a curl of desire unfolding deep in her belly. It escaped from that place that was locked away. A place she could never enter because, if she did, she would have to remember... Have to face up to what was so wrong with her...

'No.' The word came out like the slamming of a door. It was time to get away from there.

Away from this man who was making her think about ridiculous things.

Feel things she had no desire to feel.

'At least think about it.' His words followed her as she almost ran to get off the balcony. 'I'll see you at dinner.'

CHAPTER FOUR

'*OH, MY...*'

'What's wrong, Gran? Are you all right?' The lighting wasn't so great in this dinner venue. A restaurant within easy walking distance of the conference venue, this ancient stone vault of a room had been transformed into a winter wonderland in honour of the season.

White church candles with multiple wicks, in a nest of holly leaves and poinsettia flowers, made a centrepiece for each of the small tables set for four. Sheets of fairy lights in icicle form hung from the high ceiling and, on one roughened stone wall, a slide show of Christmassy scenes was softly fading in and out as the scenes changed.

It was a beautiful setting for a dinner but the flickering light levels made it impossible to see things as clearly as Charlotte would have liked. She was convinced her grandmother had suddenly gone pale.

'Stop fussing, Charlotte, for goodness' sake.' Lady Geraldine gave her a surprisingly sharp poke with her finger. 'If you weren't half-blind, you would have noticed what I just noticed.' Her smile was almost gleeful as she lowered her voice. 'Eye candy...'

'*Gran*. Wherever did you learn an expression like that?'

'I blame television,' Lady Geraldine sighed. But she was still smiling. Still watching a point well beyond Charlotte's shoulder. The entranceway, most likely, because Charlotte had deliberately chosen a table as far away from the door as possible. A nice, dark corner. With a bit of luck, Nico Moretti would be late and either he wouldn't be able to spot her or the two unoccupied settings at their table would have been taken by another conference attendee and his or her partner.

But no. With a sinking heart Charlotte realised that to have grabbed her grandmother's keen interest, this 'eye candy' would have to be spectacularly good looking. And judging by the way her elderly relative was practically fanning herself with her hand now, he was coming in their direction. Slowly, she turned her head.

*Oh, my…*was an understatement. Dr Moretti was wearing a beautifully fitting dinner suit, which always made men look good, but so were most of the other male guests here. Maybe the soft lighting had something to do with the way he stood out. Or more likely, it was the man's sheer presence as he wound his way through the tables, pausing to smile at people he knew or share a few words in greeting.

He seemed to have a spotlight on him, in any case, and Charlotte knew her gaze was as transfixed as her grandmother's. As focused as every other woman in this room.

If Nico was scanning the room, looking for her as he kept moving, he certainly gave no indication of it. Anyone watching would assume he knew exactly what table he was expected at. Charlotte could feel

her grandmother's interest sharpen into astonishment as he finally made a beeline for their corner, his face lighting up in a smile of sheer joy.

'Carlotta. *Cara*…' With his gaze locked on hers, Nico reached out and cupped one side of her face with his hand. It was an exquisitely tender touch. Overwhelmingly so. Charlotte had no hope of collecting her thoughts, let alone expressing them. His gaze suggested that if she didn't want him to play this game she only had to say the word, but how could she when she couldn't even draw a breath?

And she saw the moment the question in his gaze turned to delight.

Game on.

With a smoothness that suggested Nico was far too good at acting, he turned his charm onto the unsuspecting Lady Geraldine. He gently picked up the hand with its diamond rings flashing in the candlelight. He pressed his lips to it.

'And you have to be Carlotta's *nonna*. I've heard so much about you. This is…*such* a pleasure.'

And then Nico took hold of one of the two spare chairs and moved it so that it was as close to Charlotte's as possible. He sat down and adjusted the silverware and then nodded at a nearby waiter, who instantly came to fill his champagne glass.

Lady Geraldine was watching this little show with rapt attention and she seemed as lost for words as Charlotte. Until Nico raised his glass, tilted his head in a silent toast to the women, took a long sip and then… smiled.

'Um…Charlotte?'

'Yes, Gran?'

'Is there something you haven't told me?'

This was her chance to pull the plug on this crazy plan that Nico seemed perfectly happy to put into action. To pretend—in public—that they were a couple in love.

Trouble was, even for the short time it had been happening, it was casting a spell that was unbelievably powerful.

They said that falling in love was magical. Maybe even pretending to be tapped into some of that incomprehensible power.

Whatever. Charlotte could feel the waves of envy coming from the other women in this space. She could see the gleam of joyous disbelief in her grandmother's eyes. Worst of all, she could almost feel what it *would* be like having someone like Nico head over heels in love with her.

And, God help her, she wanted more.

Just for an hour or two.

Just enough to give her a bubble of whatever this magic was so that she could remember it when times were bleak.

And there *were* going to be bleak times ahead.

Could there possibly be a greater gift she could give her beloved grandmother than to let her die with the peace of believing that the child she had raised was happy at last? That she would be loved and cared for in her absence?

It was a very strange feeling, this…giving in. Living in the moment without trying to weigh up any consequences or complications. It was incredibly liberating. *Fun*—like Nico had suggested it could be? Something was certainly lifting the corners of Charlotte's mouth.

'Gran…this is…Nico.' Her words sounded hesitant. Breathless. The way they would if someone was about to reveal something secret. Something personal and precious.

'Nico Moretti,' he expanded. He laid his hand over Charlotte's on the crisp, white linen tablecloth as he smiled at Lady Geraldine. 'I am Charlotte's…' He hesitated, clearly at a loss for the right word to describe his relationship to her, and she held her breath. Could he really pull this off?

Nico turned his head and she could swear his sigh was one of pure happiness. 'I am whatever Carlotta will give me the honour of being,' he murmured.

'Charlotte?' The gentle word belied the 'please explain' undertone.

'It's been s-sudden,' Charlotte stammered. 'I was going to tell you today, Gran, but…'

'But then you started worrying about me.' Lady Geraldine clicked her tongue. 'For heaven's sake, child. This is *far* more important. I want to know everything.'

Oh, help… Charlotte tried to buy some thinking time by picking up her champagne glass. The Italian prosecco being served was astonishingly light. Delicious. She took another long sip.

'We actually met years ago,' Nico said into the expectant silence. 'At St Margaret's in London. It was my bad luck that Carlotta was unavailable at that time.'

Uh-oh… It took Lady Geraldine less than a split second to work out exactly what time Nico was referring to and that earned Charlotte a glance she would rather have avoided.

Gran knew there had been far more to the break-up of that relationship—the only one she'd ever known

Charlotte to have—than she'd ever been privy to. It was the only aspect of Charlotte's life she'd ever been shut out of and it was a cloud that had hung over them ever since. Something that was never mentioned but always there.

Charlotte drank the last of her wine and barely noticed the waiter refilling her glass as she listened to Nico continuing to talk.

Why hadn't she thought that this pretence could open that particular can of worms?

And it was too late to stop it now. She was already in too deep.

About to drown?

He knew he'd said the wrong thing.

Nobody could have missed that electric glance that Lady Geraldine had speared her granddaughter with when he'd said that she had been otherwise attached when he'd first met her.

What the hell was that about?

Never mind. He knew he could redeem himself. He'd been quite confident of pulling this off from the moment he'd walked into this exclusive restaurant and spotted the table he needed to aim for.

The table where the two most beautiful women in the room were sitting.

Maybe Charlotte often wore an elegant silver dress to such a formal occasion but Nico had a strong sense that it was not usual practice for her to leave her hair loose like that—a tumble of soft waves that gleamed an ash blonde in the candlelight. Had she be thinking of him when she'd brushed it out and chosen not to wind it back into its prison of pins?

And the grandmother! Nico had expected an English dowager of some kind. Tall and forbiddingly aloof. He had smiled the moment he'd set eyes on the old lady sitting beside Charlotte. Even from a distance he had caught the flash of her bejewelled hands and even a small tiara nestled in fiery red hair. He could sense her interest in the people around her and an ability to see beneath the surface of social niceties. This was going to be a much more entertaining evening than he could have hoped for.

'I can't tell you how often I've thought about her since then,' he told Lady Geraldine with palpable honesty. 'And then fate brings us together in the most romantic city in the world.' He shrugged, his smile suggesting he hadn't made much of an effort to stand firm against the winds of fate.

Was he overdoing things? Judging by the mistiness in Lady Geraldine's eyes, she was swallowing this very happily, but from the corner of his eye he could see that Charlotte was simply sitting there, staring at him, her lips slightly parted and her expression dazed.

He still had his hand covering hers, so he picked it up. Such a soft hand. Such elegant, long fingers and neat nails that were not disguised by any unnatural colours. He touched his lips to her hand and then leaned forward as though drawn irresistibly to kiss her lips next. They looked soft, too, and when Charlotte unconsciously dampened them with the tip of her tongue, Nico realised that he actually *did* want to kiss her.

Dio... That wasn't meant to happen. He closed his eyes for a heartbeat to take control of the unexpected shaft of desire but then he let his breath out in a soft sigh. Did it matter? Charlotte wouldn't need to know

it was anything other than good acting and it would certainly make his performance more believable. He opened his eyes and focused on the owner of the hand he still had imprisoned in his.

'It was meant to be,' he said softly. 'I'm lucky enough to have been given a second chance and even luckier that this beautiful woman seems to feel the same way.' He added a few words in Italian, knowing how limited Charlotte's grasp on the language was, and hoping that it would add to the impression of sincerity.

It had more of an effect than he had anticipated. Lady Geraldine sniffed delicately and picked up her linen serviette to dab at the corner of her eye.

'*Bella*,' she said, her Italian accent flawless. '*Carlotta è una ragazza fortunate.*'

Beneath his fingers, Charlotte's hand stiffened with tension. 'What?'

'She said you are a lucky girl,' Nico murmured. 'That the story of how we met is beautiful.'

'At last...' Lady Geraldine smiled mistily at her granddaughter. 'Oh, darling. I can't begin to tell you how happy this makes me. This...this is the best night of my *life*.'

Charlotte's lips trembled but she managed to smile. In the instant before she turned to look at her grandmother Nico caught the flash of emotion in her eyes that told him how huge this gift of happiness was.

And she couldn't have given her grandmother this if it hadn't been for him. It made him proud.

It made him want to give *more*.

The interruption of the first course of their dinner arriving was a welcome distraction that gave Charlotte

time to try and collect herself. Not that she had the slightest appetite and she couldn't help her gaze straying sideways to look at Nico at noticeably frequent intervals as she wondered how he could be so incredibly good at this pretence, but that was just the sort of behaviour a woman who'd just fallen head over heels in love would display, wasn't it?

No wonder Gran believed it all. Charlotte had been sucked in herself. She'd totally forgotten the fear of the conversation touching on that no-go period in her life. And the way she'd felt when he'd picked up her hand and kissed it… No. What had been utterly shocking had been the way she'd felt when he'd leaned closer and looked as though he was about to kiss her on the lips.

The hum of conversation around them and the elegant strains of the Christmas carols being played by a quartet in the restaurant foyer had faded into nothing more than background static. The flickering light of the candles seemed to mirror the tiny flames licking her skin. Heating her blood and pooling somewhere deep in her belly.

A moment's madness, fuelled by what she could swear was an equal level of attraction in Nico's eyes. But they were dark eyes and the light was low. She couldn't possibly have seen his pupils expand and she must have imagined the electric charge that came through her fingers where his skin was still in contact.

The shock of hearing her grandmother respond to Nico in Italian had been enough to break the extraordinary spell being cast, which was just as well. Nico was enjoying himself quite enough. How appalling would it be if he knew he was having a genuine effect on her?

Lady Geraldine wasn't eating much either, and that

was enough to send Charlotte's thoughts in a darker direction. Her grandmother might be in her eighties but she had always been a woman of amazing energy who lived life to the full. Nobody would deny her the maximum extent of whatever modern medicine could do to prolong that colourful life, but you had to balance additional time earned by what the quality of that life would be. Major surgery and chemotherapy would be a miserable time and it was possible that the end would not justify the means.

Something like despair gathered in a cloud over Charlotte as she toyed with her entrée. Thank goodness Nico and her grandmother were so engaged in conversation. Nobody would thank her for destroying the joyous atmosphere that had been created at this particular table.

'So your mother is still living in Ireland?'

'Yes. With husband number four.'

'Good gracious! What was wrong with the first three?'

'My mother has trouble resisting offers that seem to give her a better opportunity to experience the best that life can give. She is a free spirit, Lady Geraldine, who is not bothered by what others think. A bit like yourself, I'm guessing?'

Gran actually laughed with delight. If she'd had a fan in her hand, Charlotte thought, she might have smacked Nico's hand with it. Instead, the old lady gave him an almost shy smile.

'You can call me Jendi, dear,' she told him. 'As my friends do.'

'I'm honoured…Jendi.'

'And your father? Is he still living, too?'

'No.' Charlotte saw the way Nico laid down his fork as though he had caught the lack of appetite around him. 'He died some years ago now.'

'Oh…' The sound was one of sympathy. 'Too young. Was it an accident?'

'A broken heart.' Nico's voice was expressionless. He was stating a fact.

Charlotte couldn't help her eyebrows rising at such a non-medical notion from a man with his training. She didn't say anything but maybe her breath had escaped with a disparaging sound because Nico flicked a glance in her direction. His words, however, were directed at Lady Geraldine. His new *friend*.

'They called it a heart attack, of course,' he said. 'But his heart broke when my mother left him and on every visit I made back here, I could see his slow decline.'

'That's terrible,' Lady Geraldine declared. She was frowning now. 'But at least it hasn't put you off marriage, Nico.'

'M-marriage?'

The word was so shocked that Charlotte knew the game might be up. Had it not occurred to him that it was a natural direction for someone's thoughts to go in when faced by two people who were 'meant to be together' and had made the connection at last?

'Early days, Gran,' she said in a stage whisper across the table. 'Don't frighten the poor man.'

'Frightened? Me?' To give him credit, Nico recovered fast. He actually winked at Lady Geraldine. 'We men like to pick our own time, that's all. The element of surprise, you understand?'

'Oh, of course.' Lady Geraldine beamed at him. 'I promise I'll be surprised.'

She wouldn't be the only one. Nico was only supposed to be posing as her new boyfriend, that's all. Something that would make Gran happy because it offered hope for her not having a lonely future. This was getting out of hand. He was sharing family secrets as though he was already a prospective grandson-in-law.

How on earth was she going to explain what had happened here tonight if, by some miracle, her grandmother's treatment was effective and she lived for years after this?

The interruption of formal speeches in praise of the symposium and its organisers filled in the time between courses and prevented any further bonding between her gran and Nico, but it didn't lessen the increasing tension Charlotte was experiencing. It only got worse as people began to mingle between the tables and Richard Campbell came to say hello.

'Did you enjoy listening to Charlotte this morning, Lady Geraldine?'

'Oh, I did. So much. Thank you for arranging things, Dr Campbell. I am the happiest woman in the world tonight.'

'So I see.' It was impossible not to respond to the glow her grandmother was exuding. No one would believe that she could be facing confirmation of a terminal disease within days. And the misty look she was giving the young couple at her table was just as easy to read. Richard's jaw sagged visibly as he followed her gaze.

'Charlotte? You and...?'

* * *

'Nico Moretti,' Nico said, extending his hand.

A new challenge, then. Could he pull off this pretence with the people who worked with Charlotte?

'Delighted to meet you, Richard. Although I think we met some years ago. At St Margaret's?'

'That was where he first met Charlotte,' Lady Geraldine put in.

'Mmm.' Richard was giving Charlotte a strange look and Nico's heart sank. He remembered that impression he'd had when he'd been listening to her speak this morning. That her playing down her femininity might reveal a sexual preference that didn't include men. Maybe her closest colleagues were aware of something that was kept strictly private. Something she didn't want her grandmother to know, either.

Was that what had been hidden beneath that absolute conviction that she would never be fulfilling her grandmother's dearest wish of settling down and having babies? Suspicion on Jendi's part might also explain that charged glance directed at her granddaughter, which he'd inadvertently provoked.

Charlotte certainly seemed bothered by something. As soon as possible after Richard moved on to another table, she excused herself, muttering about needing a bathroom. He saw her ask a waiter for directions and then head out a door that led to a long balcony. Presumably the bathrooms opened off the balcony to one side of the restaurant.

Which meant that Nico could also excuse himself and head in that direction. He could catch Charlotte before she came back into the dining room and just check that he wasn't causing even more trouble for

her, although exactly how to broach the subject of her sexuality in a sensitive manner was entirely beyond him at the moment.

The balcony ran right along the canal side of the restaurant. It was quiet out here with the added darkness that came from the still water of the canal. Nico didn't need to use the facilities so he paced back and forth, waiting what seemed an interminably long time for Charlotte to reappear. What was she doing in there? Twisting her hair back into some impossibly tight 'hairdo'? He hoped not.

A gondola drifted past below with just a single light making the ornate brass ornament on the prow of the boat gleam. A couple sat, wrapped in blankets against the cold and silent as they gazed in wonder at the magic of touring this city at night with only the ripple of the boat to disturb the serenity.

The tap of high heels on stone disturbed the moment for Nico. He turned and Charlotte's step faltered.

'What are you doing out here?'

'Waiting for you.'

The only light now that the gondola had passed came from the fairy lights of the restaurant and a small Christmas tree that was being used to reveal where the door to the bathrooms was. Silver light that made Charlotte's dress shine and cast a spotlight on the way the fabric clung to her body and revealed noticeable curves. It also caught matching strands in her hair. It would look golden in the sunshine, Nico thought. Chameleon hair. He could imagine her eyes could create that illusion too. Maybe they would take on a blue hue under a summer sky. Or when she was happy?

Right now they were a stormy, slate grey.

'Why?'

She sounded nervous and added to that impression by pushing her fingers through her hair. The gesture ruffled the loose waves. It was a supremely feminine movement. Confusing, given what Nico was there intending to find out. The reminder made him shake off his focus on how unexpectedly attractive Charlotte was looking. He cleared his throat.

'I...um... It seems to be going well. Your *nonna* is happy.'

'Mmm.' He could see Charlotte swallow. A ripple that ran the length of her elegant neck. 'Too happy, maybe.'

'Is there such a thing? Especially at a time like this?'

Charlotte sighed. 'She *is* happy. I don't think I've ever seen her look so...so contented.'

'There you go, then. It's been a good thing to do. A reprieve from thinking about less happy things. One that you may be able to use for some time.'

Charlotte looked away, watching the tail end of the gondola as it turned a corner. 'But I didn't think things through. I thought other people would just think you were sharing our table for dinner.' Her voice rose and the words sped up a little, revealing how unsettled she was. 'I didn't expect to start a rumour that will follow me back to St Margaret's. I have no idea what I'm going to do about that.'

'You don't have to do anything.' Nico paused, trying to select his words carefully. 'Unless it's going to cause personal distress?'

She frowned at him. 'What kind of personal distress?'

'Well...you might have someone in your life that

wouldn't be happy to know about this...this illusion you're creating.'

'I don't...' She was trying to process his meaning. Then she made an impatient sound. 'I told you I wasn't in a relationship.'

'Not with *Mr* Right,' he murmured.

There was a moment's dead silence and then Charlotte's eyes widened. 'Oh, my God...you think I'm a—' An incredulous huff broke her words. 'Are you *serious*?' And then she turned away but not before Nico had seen a fierce sparkle in her eyes.

Oh...*Dio*... He'd really put his foot in it now, hadn't he? Was she about to start crying again?

No matter. He had come prepared. He reached for the neatly pressed handkerchief he'd pushed into his jacket pocket just before he'd left his room. He pulled it out and, as he did so, something glinted in the light and bounced on the stones with an audible *ping*.

Charlotte turned her head. 'What was that?'

'Nothing important.' Nico knew what it was. It had been weighing his pocket down earlier today. But then he'd forgotten all about it after he'd arrived at the symposium. After he'd been swept along by listening to the story Charlotte had told them. Weirdly, it hadn't occurred to him to think about it again all day. Or remember to take it out of his pocket.

His grandmother's ring. The one his father had given his mother. The one she'd left behind when she'd broken the marriage and Nico's true family. Maybe it was better if it got left behind at the bottom of a Venetian canal. Drowned and lost. Like his belief in true love and marriage and happy families for ever had been lost so many years ago.

But no. This ring was the only thing his father had left him as his inheritance. The only link he could touch that went back to his early childhood. It was important. Nico ignored Charlotte and his gaze raked the rough stones as he searched for what he'd dropped. It must have come out of his pocket at speed, propelled by being caught in the folds of the handkerchief. Had it already bounced irretrievably into the waters of the canal?

Like Charlotte's laptop?

No. There it was, precariously balanced right beside a stone balustrade on the very edge of the balcony. He would have to be careful not to nudge it over the edge, he realised as he stooped. Trying to slow his movement, Nico dropped to one knee and reached for the ring.

'What on *earth* are you doing?' Nico could see the ripple of the long, silver dress as Charlotte stepped closer. He sighed and held the object up to show her.

'It's my grandmother's ring,' he said heavily. 'It's a long story…'

He wasn't going to get a chance to tell her any of it, however. A startling shriek cut through the night air.

'Charlotte! Nico! Oh, my goodness…' Lady Geraldine had come out through the restaurant doors and was standing there, her hands clasped in front of her as though in prayer. 'Is this…? Are you…? Oh…how *romantic*. A proposal. In Venice, of all places…'

It took a long moment for the full horror to sink in but, yes…here he was, on one knee. Kneeling in front of a beautiful woman with a backdrop of a Venetian canal, holding up what was obviously an engagement ring in his hand.

He bought a fraction of time by getting to his feet

somewhat awkwardly. He caught the panicked look in Charlotte's eyes. They were going to have to confess now, weren't they? Ruin the happiest night of this sick old lady's life.

No. He could fix this.

With the ghost of a wink to let Charlotte know he had things in hand, Nico grabbed her hand and shoved the ring onto her finger. It was a tight fit but he gave it an extra push to get it over her knuckle. Was it pain that made Charlotte gasp? Maybe it was the shock of how fast he'd moved or this unexpected twist in the show they were putting on. That didn't matter either. Maybe people would think she was simply shocked at how quickly he had managed to sweep her off her feet.

He kept hold of Charlotte's hand and gave it a squeeze. She dragged her gaze up from the ring and met his eyes and he tried very hard to give her a silent message.

Trust me. We can get through this without hurting anybody.

And then he turned and pasted a smile onto his face.

'Jendi… What wonderful timing. We wanted *you* to be the first to know.'

CHAPTER FIVE

'I KNEW ALREADY.' Lady Geraldine was coming towards them with surprising sprightliness given her age and state of health. 'Nobody can hide the glow of true love…' Tears were running down her wrinkled cheeks as she got close enough to embrace Charlotte. 'Oh, my dear…I'm *so* happy for you.'

She must feel like she was hugging a tree, Charlotte realised, but she couldn't make her body soften. Or even raise the arms now hanging by her sides like dead branches. One of them was even weighed down with an enormous rock. No… She had to be dreaming. He couldn't *really* have shoved that ring on her finger, could he?

Still dazed, Charlotte lifted her left arm. It looked like she was returning her grandmother's effusive hug but, in reality, she was getting her hand to a position where she could see it.

Yep. There it was. On her third finger. A quite respectably sized solitaire diamond in an antique gold setting. Definitely an engagement ring. What on earth did Nico Moretti think he was playing at, walking around with an engagement ring in his pocket?

Words floated into through the sludge in her head. His grandmother's ring. *A long story.*

No story could be long enough to rescue her from this escalating nightmare. What was that saying Gran used to deliver with a wagging finger? Something about the complicated web you weave when first you practise to deceive. Charlotte shook her head to clear the mist. This had to end. Now.

'This isn't what is seems, Gran. I'm not engaged. This is...ridiculous.'

'Oh, I know, darling.' The grip Lady Geraldine still had on her increased a notch. 'You weren't expecting this, were you?'

'Of course I wasn't.' A snort of something like laughter escaped her throat. 'Nico and I have only just met. We're not even...' Charlotte raised her gaze as she searched for the right word to explain the total lack of a genuine relationship between them. It brought her line of vision directly over her grandmother's shoulder. And it locked with Nico's gaze.

He had one eyebrow raised and a curiously disappointed stillness to the rest of his face . What dismissive word was she going to come up with here?

That they weren't even *friends*?

That they weren't connected in any way, shape or form?

Except they were, weren't they?

They'd become connected totally by chance when they'd formed a united medical team to help the man who'd had the cardiac arrest and fallen from the scaffolding. Having him present when she had been floundering in front of so many distinguished symposium attendees this morning had been what had given her

the strength to give any kind of presentation at all. The thought that he might have been impressed had made her feel like she hadn't failed.

Having him right there when she had been already starting to grieve for Gran had been what had given her the strength to try and make whatever time her beloved grandmother had left as happy as possible.

And the way she'd felt when he'd looked at her like that at the table. As if he was in love with her. As if he'd wanted to kiss her.

Oh, yes…she couldn't deny a physical *and* emotional connection to him even if she didn't want it to be there. Somehow Nico had broken through her safety barriers. Despite the short time they had known each other—less than a day, for heaven's sake—he was already enmeshed in her personal life in a way that no man had ever been.

'I know, darling.' Lady Geraldine's soothing words took her back. Way back to when it had seemed that nobody could ever understand. Or put things right. And yet the words had always been sincere. And Gran had always put things right, no matter how long it had taken. 'People will think it's too soon. *You* think it's too soon.'

'Of course I do. It's…it's…' *Ridiculous*. But Charlotte's gaze was still holding Nico's as she tried to read the silent message he was sending. It was a reassuring message, whatever it was. How was she supposed to interpret that? Or believe that this was somehow okay.

'It's love at first sight, that's what it is,' Lady Geraldine said happily. 'The best sort. Wearing Nico's ring doesn't mean you have to get married next week, dar-

ling. It's just a promise of commitment. You can take all the time you need to make sure that it's perfect.'

All the time they needed to keep Gran happy for as long as she lived?

Time.

That's what Charlotte needed.

'It will take time.' Nico's voice was strong. Amazingly calm, considering. 'And you're right, Jendi. I have…what's that expression? Jumped the gun.'

Something about the way he recited the phrase made Charlotte think his choice of words was deliberate. He was reminding her of the euphemism she'd used about kicking the bucket. Reminding her of what was important here. And maybe it was a warning, too.

If she destroyed this illusion she would be ruining not one but two of the items on Gran's bucket list. There was no way the train trip could provide the slightest pleasure if the number-one item on the list was revealed as a deception.

Geraldine let Charlotte go with a final pat. She turned and looked up at Nico, who smiled at her.

'We will have to be apart a lot in the coming weeks,' he said sadly. 'I have commitments in the United States and Europe. In Australia, even. But I had to do something to make my intentions as clear as possible. To achieve what I know will make us *both* happy.' Make us *all* happy, his glance reminded Charlotte.

'Of course you did.' Lady Geraldine beamed.

Charlotte's mind was clearing rapidly. Nico was presenting an easy way out here. He could be her fiancé but he would be absent. She could keep her grandmother happily believing that a wedding was on the cards without any further awkwardness of them hav-

ing to keep up the pretence for real. Or, if she couldn't bear to be less than honest, she could say that things had fizzled out in a few weeks and use the excuse that it would never have worked. They would never have enough time together to keep the relationship alive.

'Mmm.' The sound came out in a strangled fashion. 'I'm still not sure—'

'Of course you're not.' Lady Geraldine slipped her arm through Charlotte's and began to lead her back to the restaurant. 'You like to be in control, child, and you've been swept off your feet.' She slipped her other arm through Nico's. 'Come on. We'll all go and have another glass of that lovely champagne and give Charlotte time to get used to this delightfully unexpected state of being an *engaged* woman.'

Dio mio…

What, exactly, had happened there?

It wasn't the unexpected twist of events that had led to Charlotte now wearing his grandmother's ring that was disturbing Nico most as he followed the women back to the restaurant.

No. It went far deeper than a pretence that was now a little more complicated than intended. Something had happened when Charlotte had been caught in that loving embrace and had looked at him over her grandmother's shoulder. When she'd been searching for a way of trying to explain that this was all a lie. That there was nothing of any significance between them.

She hadn't been able to, had she? Because she'd felt the same thing he had when their gazes had touched and locked. Somehow, over the course of this crazy day, they *had* connected. And on a level that was to-

tally alien to Nico. Inexplicable and deeply disturbing but, at that moment, he would have overturned heaven and earth to protect Charlotte. To extricate her in a dignified fashion from this mess he had created.

He had no idea what had triggered such a strong urge. Guilt from knowing he'd pushed her into this? Or maybe he'd caught another glimpse of that lost and frightened child in her eyes. He'd certainly seen desperation that had been coming from not wanting to hurt somebody she loved so much. Maybe that explained why he was feeling as though the ground was shifting beneath his feet and that the rules he lived by were no longer relevant.

Knowing that Charlotte was capable of that kind of love when, to outward appearances, she was incapable of that much emotion. Knowing that she was such a different woman from the one he'd met years ago. Curiosity was a powerful motivating force and Nico wanted to put as many pieces of this puzzle together as he could before he moved on.

Maybe when he had the full picture he would be able to understand why he was feeling as if he was caught in some invisible web. And then he would be able to avoid it happening again. He liked his life exactly the way it was, thanks very much. He did not like this feeling of long-held beliefs wobbling and his footing being less than secure in his world.

Back at the table, Lady Geraldine waved a bejewelled hand and waiters willingly rushed to refill glasses and serve exquisite-looking desserts. Charlotte was sitting very still, staring at the chocolate creation on the small plate in front of her as though unsure whether it was, in fact, edible.

Or maybe she was unsure whether anything was real. Perhaps she was hoping to wake up and find that this whole evening had simply been a bad dream. Her grandmother was also watching her and then she turned to Nico and smiled. It was an expression of understanding. And reassurance. Charlotte just needed a little more time, the glance suggested. And then she would be able to embrace the joy of this new event in her life.

She certainly needed something. A gentle reminder of why they'd started this charade in the first place?

Nico smiled back at Lady Geraldine. 'Tell me about tomorrow,' he invited. 'I hear you have an adventure planned. On the Orient Express?'

Lady Geraldine beamed at him. 'It's been a long-held dream of mine. One of them, anyway.' She slid another glance at Charlotte and there was a moment's pause as she sighed happily. Then she collected herself and focused on Nico. 'Have you ever travelled on the Orient Express yourself?'

'No. I've heard of it, of course. It has a wonderful history, doesn't it?'

'Right back to 1883.' Lady Geraldine nodded. 'It's the world's most famous train and it's been totally restored to its original glory. You step back in time and travel in the kind of elegant luxury that only the very privileged could afford a hundred years ago. It's an experience everybody should have at least once in their lifetime, don't you think?'

'Absolutely.' Nico was happy to agree. This was what this evening was about after all. To make Charlotte's grandmother happy. To encourage her to make the most of whatever time she had left in her own life-

time. To tick off those 'bucket-list' items. 'I hear that the food is amazing and isn't there someone that plays a grand piano in the bar?'

'Oh, yes.' Lady Geraldine's smile was misty now. 'Everybody dresses in their best and is on their best behaviour. We'll all be thoroughly spoiled as we glide through Italy, Austria, Switzerland and France and back to London just in time for Christmas.'

She eyed Nico over a spoon containing a tiny portion of chocolate mousse. 'I expect you'll be visiting your mother for Christmas Day, Nico?'

'Ah…no.' Nico shook his head. 'I believe her new husband has whisked her off to New Zealand to have Christmas in the sun.'

'But you have other family?'

Uh-oh… Any moment now he was going to be invited to have Christmas dinner with Charlotte and her grandmother. He needed to head this one off at the pass.

'Sadly, I have work commitments in London I can't break. That's partly why I'm taking a day or two at my leisure in Venice now.' This was true enough, wasn't it? He was always happy to work over family-oriented holidays to give his colleagues time off. He didn't have a family to spend time with. And he didn't want one. Nico shifted in his seat, which brought his knee into contact with Charlotte's. He heard her sudden intake of breath and she finally seemed to become aware of her surroundings again.

Good. He needed some help here to avoid being pressured into joining the Highton clan for Christmas dinner. Who knew how many other distant but for-

midable relatives Charlotte might have waiting in the
wings?

Lady Geraldine had a very benign smile on her face
right now as she apparently enjoyed her taste of the des-
sert but Nico had the distinct feeling that the impres-
sion of a sweet old lady was probably deceptive. There
was an ironclad will beneath that perfectly groomed
exterior and that improbable red hair. What Lady Ger-
aldine wanted, she would no doubt get. Except, maybe,
the chance to live to an even riper old age.

He reached for his glass of wine. He increased the
pressure on Charlotte's knee a little to encourage her to
say something but she was watching her grandmother,
who was shaking her head as she put down her spoon.

'Absolutely delicious,' she said sadly. 'But I can't
eat it.'

Nico could feel the tension in Charlotte's focus.
'You've hardly eaten anything, Gran.'

'I'm too excited,' Lady Geraldine said.

'About the Orient Express?' This was a good direc-
tion to steer the conversation back to. A safe one. 'I'm
not surprised. It's probably a good idea to save your
appetite for all that wonderful food.'

'Mmm…' Lady Geraldine nodded thoughtfully. 'I
am excited about the train trip but not nearly as excited
as I am about this engagement.' She reached over and
took hold of Charlotte's hand, bending the fingers so
that the diamond ring took centre stage. 'I don't think
I've ever been so happy.' She was locked in eye contact
with her granddaughter. 'You will be, too, Charlotte
Jane. I just know you will.'

Charlotte's indrawn breath was ragged. 'But…'

'I know, darling.' Nico could see the way Charlotte's

fingers were being squeezed. Lady Geraldine's voice was soft. 'And it doesn't matter if I don't live to see the wedding. This is enough. To know that you've met such a wonderful man and the attraction is strong enough to be totally irresistible. It's a promise of a happy future for you…and I intend to enjoy every single moment of it.'

She straightened in her chair and turned her gaze to Nico. 'I have two cabin suites booked on the Orient Express,' she said unexpectedly. 'I wanted both Charlotte and myself to enjoy this trip as much as possible, without being cramped.'

'Good thinking.' Nico nodded. Thank goodness the topic of conversation was getting back onto safe territory. 'I'm sure you'll enjoy every moment.'

'Oh, I will. Especially now.'

There was something in the gaze from those faded blue eyes that made Nico feel like a small child again. A small child confronted by someone in ultimate authority.

'Because of the engagement?' Nico's smile was a little forced. He should be pleased because this represented exactly what he'd set out to achieve but he had a sinking feeling that he wasn't going to get off quite this easily.

'Exactly,' Lady Geraldine purred.

Maybe he was. Nico's smile widened.

'I can't think of a better way to celebrate,' Lady Geraldine continued, 'Can you?'

'No. What could possibly be a better way to celebrate than the very best of food and wine while you travel in ultimate luxury?'

'I'm so pleased you agree. I'll let the train manager know that you'll be joining us.'

'What?' Both Nico and Charlotte uttered the horrified exclamation simultaneously.

'It's perfect,' Lady Geraldine said calmly. 'You don't have commitments until Christmas Day, Nico, and we'll be back in London by Christmas Eve. As you said yourself, what better way could there be to celebrate? It sounds as though you and Charlotte are going to have a lot of time apart in the near future and I'm sure we all agree that we should all make the most of every moment we can have together. Who knows how many of them there will be?'

Her voice wobbled just a little as she finished speaking. Charlotte's jaw had been dropping but now it snapped shut.

'You can't do this, Gran,' she said slowly. 'You can't use something like your illness to make people do what you want them to do. It's…it's emotional blackmail.'

'Nonsense.' Any hint of frailty vanished from Lady Geraldine's demeanour. 'It's common sense, that's what it is. You're both important, busy people. You'd never make the time for something like this unless someone pushed you into it. And this is a once-in-a-lifetime opportunity. Do you have any idea how hard it was for me to get a booking on this train? And *two* cabins. If it had only been one, I would have given up my place so that you and Nico could have done the trip together.'

'But this is *your* dream, Gran.' Charlotte was shaking her head now, looking bewildered. 'Why would Nico and I want to do it?'

'Because it's the most romantic journey on earth,' Lady Geraldine said. 'You've found each other in the

most romantic city and by astonishing good fortune
you now have the chance to build on that by travelling
together to the destination you were both heading for
anyway. I'm not going to take you away from Nico the
day after you've just become engaged, Charlotte. This
is my engagement gift to you both—some more time
together. If he won't come with us on the train, then
you can stay here and I'll go by myself.'

'No…you can't do that. I won't let you. You're not
well enough.'

It was a stand-off. Nico didn't need the combined
effect of both women looking at him to know he was
expected to say something to defuse the tension but, for
the life of him, he couldn't think of anything to say. For
heaven's sake, all he needed was an excuse that would
keep him at least somewhere in Europe for the next
twenty four hours but his mind was blank. Stunned at
the way this…diversion had taken on a life of its own.
Moving at a pace that appeared as unstoppable as the
train he was now expected to board tomorrow.

Tables were being cleared around them and any
moment now the waiters would come and interrupt
this awkward silence, but clearly it wouldn't be soon
enough for Charlotte. She made an exasperated sound
as she pushed back her chair and got to her feet.

'I need some air,' she announced. 'I'll leave *you* to
talk to Gran, Nico.'

Her tone suggested that he was unlikely to get any-
where but that it was his problem. He'd got himself
into this mess and now he could get himself out of it.
Her body language as she headed towards the balcony
suggested that she was washing her hands of the whole
situation because it was clearly uncontrollable. The

slump of her shoulders said that she didn't believe he could do it without causing harm.

And maybe she was right. Maybe now he was going have to confess his part in this deception. Was there a way he could do that and convince Lady Geraldine at the same time that it had been done with the very best of intentions and that Charlotte had only gone along with his stupid idea because she loved her grandmother so much?

Nico took a deep breath and opened his mouth but Lady Geraldine got there first to fill the silence.

'Oh, dear…' she murmured. 'And there I was, hoping that she'd finally got over it all…'

Nico couldn't help himself. 'Over what, Jendi?'

Lady Geraldine looked uncomfortable. 'That's the problem, Nico. I've never been able to find out.' She raised her eyebrows. 'I was hoping you might be able to tell *me*.'

'*Scusi?*' The Italian word popped out, as they often did in moments of great stress or surprise.

'There's only been one other occasion when I've thought that Charlotte might have found the right man for her. The person she was going to spend the rest of her life with. To raise her own family with. And it was *years* ago. Back when she was just a baby doctor and everybody could see how brilliant she was. *Is*,' Lady Geraldine corrected herself but she was frowning. 'I don't know what went wrong,' she continued softly, almost as if she was talking aloud to herself, 'but Charlotte…changed.'

Yes. He was getting to the heart of the mystery now.

'That was the time I first met her,' he confided to Jendi. 'When she was the star of the emergency depart-

ment and nobody could sing her praises highly enough. And she was so happy. There was a sparkle about her that lit up a room. A smile that advertised such confidence...' His voice trailed off as he realised the extent of how radically Charlotte had changed.

The confidence was still there but it was only professional. Cold. That's what had hit him this morning—that lack of sparkle for want of a better word. It was only when he had pushed himself beyond any acceptably professional boundaries that he'd seen a hint of a woman capable of *real* emotion. That buttoned-up outward appearance was like a suit of armour around the old Charlotte.

Whatever had happened had killed her personal confidence. Her hopes for a future outside her work ambitions. Had she been brutally dismissed by a man she'd been deeply in love with?

How could the man have been such an idiot to pass up a woman like Charlotte?

And why did the thought of her being passionately in love with another man stir up a nasty sensation in his gut that he couldn't identify? Was it jealousy? No. That was absurd. He had never felt jealous in his life.

'I saw her out with that man,' he told Jendi. 'At a very exclusive London club. I think we were even introduced. Was he a *prince*?'

Lady Geraldine made a dismissive sound. 'That's what he called himself. He was a long way down the tree of some obscure European royal family. He was certainly a very charming young man. And very sure of himself.'

'So what happened?'

'Charlotte will never talk about it. I didn't see her

for a few weeks. She said she had flu and didn't want to pass it on. And then she always had an excuse of being too busy at work to come to see me and when she finally did I was…shocked.'

'Why?' Nico leaned forward, unconsciously holding his breath.

'She looked…ill. So thin. And…' Lady Geraldine shook her head very slowly and when she raised her gaze to Nico's he could see tears in her eyes. 'You hit the nail right on the head, my dear. Her sparkle had gone. It was like it had been when she first arrived in my care as an orphaned child. When she was so lost and unhappy that she wouldn't even speak. For *months*.'

'She wouldn't speak to you?'

'Oh, no. She wasn't a tiny child any more. She would talk but only if we didn't talk about *him*. Siegfried. All she would say was that the relationship was over and it wasn't important. The only thing that mattered was her work.'

Lady Geraldine looked away. 'I thought if I gave her enough space that she would eventually talk to me about it, but it's been nearly six years and after the first attempt or two I had to give up. It's the one thing that's never discussed but is always there. The elephant in the room, you know?'

'The elephant?' How many odd English phrases were going to test him today?

'The huge thing. You can't ignore it because you always have to walk around it to get anywhere. But you're not allowed to mention it because, if you do, the door gets slammed shut and you can't get anywhere at all.'

'Hmm…' Nico was digesting the information. He was silent for a long time and when he spoke, his voice

was uncharacteristically grim. 'He hurt her,' he said softly. 'He hurt Charlotte badly, this *Siegfried*.'

'Yes.' Lady Geraldine dabbed at the corner of her eyes with her napkin.

'Physically?'

The gasp was shocked. 'Oh, *no*… If he'd done that, she would have gone to the police, surely?'

'But you said she looked unwell.'

'She'd had flu. There was a very bad flu going around that year. One of those bird varieties, I think.'

Nico wasn't listening. How could anyone have wanted to hurt Charlotte? She had been so beautiful. A girl testing the wings of womanhood. In love and totally trusting. What kind of bastard had he been and what had he *done* to her? Nico didn't believe the 'flu' excuse for a moment. And something was telling him that the pain of the broken relationship had not been simply emotional.

'I need to talk to Charlotte,' he said, his chair scraping on the stone-flagged floor as he pushed it back.

Lady Geraldine caught his arm as he turned to leave. Her age and state of health disappeared from Nico's awareness as he read her expression. It was the look of a mother as well as a grandmother. Ageless. She needed to protect her child and she wasn't sure if she should have spoken about her concerns. There was a plea in her eyes that Nico could read only too well.

'I'm not going to hurt her.' The words came out like a vow and Nico meant every one of them. 'I never would. That I can promise you.'

Charlotte was freezing.

An evening dress was entirely inadequate for a win-

ter's night in Venice but she couldn't go back inside. She could see that the evening was winding up now and people were leaving.

Good. If she waited a little longer, there would be no audience for when she had to go back in and face her grandmother after Nico had explained why he couldn't accompany them on the Orient Express.

She could see them through the tall, arched window. Their body language was intense as they leaned towards each other, oblivious to anyone else in the room. The fairy lights made the room seem like another world and Charlotte could see the Christmas images still scrolling against the far wall. Snowmen and sleighs. Christmas trees and prettily wrapped parcels. Happy people. Families. Parents with excited children.

Parents who had once been lovers. Engaged couples.

Charlotte was twisting the ring on her finger without realising it. She gave it a tug. Good grief…it was a tight fit. She was going to need soap to get it off. Maybe she should go into the bathroom and find some.

But then she saw Nico get to his feet abruptly and she saw the way her grandmother caught his arm. For a moment that seemed suspended in time she saw the way they looked at each other and the light was enough for her to see the expression on Nico's face. Such a *kind* expression. Loving. Intense. The kind of look someone might have if they were making a promise they intended to keep.

Or maybe he'd been apologising. Was he coming out to tell her it was safe to go back in now?

Charlotte's heart picked up as Nico came out onto the balcony. He moved with such grace, this man. A calm assurance that he could command his environ-

ment and protect anyone within it. Powerful but not intimidating because there was a softness about him. That slow, easy smile. The glint in those dark eyes that advertised the ability to find joy in life. To play.

That's what they'd been doing tonight and Charlotte couldn't deny that, for a while, it had been…fun. No. Fun wasn't the word. What had drawn her in had been the illusion. The need to taste something that was so seductive it was irresistible. The illusion of being in love.

With Nico.

She had to turn her head and stop staring at him as if the charade was still continuing.

'Did you talk to Gran?'

'I did.' Nico was close to her now.

'Did you tell her the truth? Does she understand why you can't come on the train with us?' Charlotte couldn't repress a shiver. Was it the cold or the disappointment of failure?

'Not exactly.' Nico was shrugging off his jacket. He stepped closer and draped it over Charlotte's shoulders.

Her first instinct was to shrug the garment off with a dismissive shake. She wasn't a child who needed someone to take care of her. She could look after herself, thanks very much.

But the gesture had been unexpectedly thoughtful. *Caring.*

And the warmth was astonishingly comforting. Charlotte could feel her fingers creeping to the edges of the jacket to pull it closer around her. The warmth was the warmth of Nico's body. The slide of the silk lining against the bare skin of her arms and shoulders made it feel as though *he* was touching her.

It was disturbingly intimate now. Charlotte could

even catch a whiff of a scent that was pure male. Pure Nico? She had to close her eyes for a heartbeat as she tried to stop herself inhaling deeply.

'Your grandmother loves you very much,' Nico said quietly. 'She does not want you to be hurt…again.'

Again? Her eyes snapped open. Oh, my God…what had they been talking about in there? But Gran didn't know the truth so she couldn't have told Nico. She was safe.

So why didn't she *feel* safe?

'W-what did *you* say?'

Nico looked more serious than she'd seen him look all day. Even when he'd been arriving at a potentially fatal incident. The subdued look didn't sit well on a face that was made for laughter. Her heart skipped another beat.

'I told her that I would never hurt you.'

'So she still thinks that we're…we're *engaged*?'

Nico's mouth twitched. 'I'm afraid so. I couldn't bring myself to cause her pain.'

It shouldn't be such a relief. Not when Charlotte couldn't see any way out of this.

'And the train?'

Nico shrugged. 'I have a free day. I have to get back to London. Why not?'

'Because…it's impossible. How could we keep this up for thirty hours?' Charlotte had another try at tugging the ring off her finger, looking away from him as she did so.

She could see past Nico to where the final guests for the evening were leaving. Only her grandmother remained and the maître d' was looking concerned, helping the elderly woman to her feet. Lady Geraldine

was pointing towards the balcony. And now she was walking towards the door.

'Nothing is impossible,' Nico was saying.

'She's coming. She'll guess. She's not stupid.'

'She won't guess if you stop trying to remove that ring.' Nico caught her hands. 'If we…'

His hands moved, pulling hers up to his neck before he let them go. His hands kept moving, though, burying themselves in her hair. Cupping the back of her head and tilting it as he leaned in to cover her mouth with his own.

He was *kissing* her.

Just for show. To cover an awkward moment when Gran might have picked up on the tension between them.

Except…it didn't feel like a pretend kiss.

Or maybe it did, for that first, startled moment as their lips made contact, but then Nico's lips moved with a kind of question that Charlotte couldn't help responding to on some deep, instinctive level that totally overruled any conscious thought. Her lips parted beneath his and when she felt the touch of his tongue against hers all ability to control her thoughts vanished.

A fleeting hope that her grandmother would see them and stay well away to give them a private moment evaporated, along with any awareness of what was around them. Charlotte was completely lost in this kiss. Transported to a place she'd never been. A place where passion and tenderness combined to create an all-consuming fuel that could burn away anything and everything and leave only peace and fulfilment in its wake.

A kiss that promised everything. So much more than this touch of lips and tongues.

More...

And that was when Charlotte stopped being lost.
She couldn't do more. If she tried, Nico would find
out and he would know what was so wrong with her.

That she could go so far and no further. Because
she was not a real woman. Real women liked going
further. They weren't...*frigid.*

That did it. Just the tiniest echo of that hateful word
was enough. Charlotte wrenched herself back from
Nico's touch. His jacket slid from her shoulders and
puddled on the stone terrace. She could turn to see what
had happened, scoop up the jacket and try to collect
herself before acknowledging her grandmother stand-
ing in the restaurant doorway.

'Oh...Gran... I'm so sorry. I...lost track of time.'

'So I see.' Lady Geraldine's smile warmed the win-
ter's night.

Nico was rubbing his lips slowly with his fore-
finger, staring at Charlotte, but now he also turned
towards the door.

'You must be tired, Jendi. Let me see you both back
to your hotel.'

'That would be lovely, Nico. Thank you. We have
an early start tomorrow. I think we have to be at the
Santa Lucia station by nine a.m. to catch the train.'

It was Charlotte's turn to stare at Nico but he didn't
meet her gaze. Instead, he put an arm around her waist
as they began moving.

'No problem,' he told her grandmother. 'I'm an early
riser.'

CHAPTER SIX

'WHERE IS HE?'

'I don't know, Gran.' Charlotte allowed a small seed of hope to blossom that Nico might fail to show up in time. Or maybe that odd squeeze in her chest was disappointment?

Yep. There was definitely an internal struggle going on here. The safest thing was to never see Nico Moretti again and that's what she should want. And, yes, she could try and convince herself that she only wanted him around, continuing this pretence of a relationship, because it was such a joy to see her grandmother so happy, but there was no way of hiding the real truth. Part of her—a big, rebellious part of her—simply wanted to be close to him again.

'Maybe something came up.' Like a bout of common sense? 'He doesn't have our phone numbers so he might not have been able to let us know.'

The train was already here at the station, the sleek, dark blue carriages with the gold trim, the coat of arms featuring two rampant lions and the lettering announcing that this was, indeed, the Venice Simplon Orient Express. As if anyone could mistake it! Among the ordinary modern European trains in the station, this

one stood out like a beacon. So did the attendants. The gold-trimmed blue uniforms looked positively military and the pillbox hats the stewards were wearing made them look ready for a fancy-dress party.

The check-in desk stood out on the grey concrete of the platform in equally startling contrast. A red carpet, of all things, with brass posts holding tasselled ropes to create an oasis of luxury amidst the mundane. Even the people milling around looked different. Like that young woman in a long coat that belonged to another era, its fur collar turned up around her neck. The people were generally better dressed, certainly, but that wasn't the only difference. There was an air of excitement that encased this part of the station and separated it from the rest. From the real world.

'I knew we should have offered to let him share our water taxi.'

'It would have been a bit of a squeeze with all your luggage, Gran.'

It had, in fact, taken an impressive tip to get the water taxi driver to leave his boat tied up and carry Gran's bags up the daunting flight of stairs leading into the train station from the road beside the canal. 'You did know you're only supposed to have one cabin bag and one piece of luggage to be checked in, didn't you?'

Her grandmother sniffed. 'If you're going to do the Orient Express, it must be done in style. Everybody knows that. Goodness knows how you get away with nothing more than an oversized handbag.'

Cabin luggage hadn't been all Charlotte had been carrying on her way to Venice, of course. She'd had her laptop bag to contend with as well. An accessory that was now lying on the bottom of a Venetian canal.

She could remember the expression on Nico's face as he'd realised what had happened. So apologetic, even though it hadn't exactly been his fault. The willingness to do whatever he could to put things right.

He was a kind man. And a generous one. The tailored suit jacket Charlotte was wearing again today suddenly felt tight. Scratchy, almost, as her senses replayed the sensation of the silk lining of Nico's jacket against her bare skin. A sensation that morphed almost seamlessly into remembering that kiss.

How kind was he? Kind enough not to reveal astonishment...*disgust*...when he found out what Charlotte was lacking?

And then there was that very tiny seed of what was definitely hope because that kiss had made her feel things that no other kiss ever had—even Siegfried's. And if just a kiss felt that different, maybe other things would feel different too and maybe...just *maybe*...she'd be able to—

Oh, *help*... Wasn't it enough that her memory of that little scene had kept her awake virtually all night? She couldn't allow it to keep distracting her like this. Charlotte balanced her cabin bag on top of Gran's biggest suitcase and grabbed the handle of the other with her free hand. With a determined shove she began moving the luggage towards a check-in desk that looked suspiciously like an antique mahogany piece. Lady Geraldine pulled the handle of her smaller bag as she followed.

'You're going to have to wear the same dress for dinner tonight that you had on last night, aren't you?'

'What was wrong with my dress?' It had been the first time Charlotte had worn the slinky, silver num-

ber but she'd been delighted with how it had looked when she'd put it on. How good it had made her feel.

'It's a lovely dress, dear. You just need more than one of them.'

It was a lovely dress. And if Charlotte was honest, she'd felt way more than simply 'good' in it. The way Nico had run his eyes over it more than once, as though the experience was a pleasure all in itself. Yes…that dress had made her feel *beautiful*. An odd experience for a woman who did virtually nothing to enhance her appearance in order to attract the attention of the opposite sex.

'Nobody's going to know I'm wearing it two nights in a row.' Charlotte smiled at the woman behind the desk and handed over the tickets.

'Apart from your fiancé.'

The woman behind the desk was smiling. 'You must be Lady Geraldine. We got your message. We're delighted to be able to welcome Dr Moretti on board to accompany you and your granddaughter.'

'Um…there could be a small problem…' Charlotte began. But the woman wasn't listening. She wasn't even looking at her and the expression on her face suggested that she was looking at something far more interesting.

A tall and extremely attractive man, perhaps?

'Cara…' The endearment was a caress. 'I'm so sorry I'm late.' Nico pulled Charlotte into his arms and then bent to brush her lips in a perfectly acceptable kiss for a public place. Except it lingered for just a heartbeat too long. And his eyes lingered on hers even longer. Charlotte dragged in a breath. The part of her that wanted to be close to Nico was winning. Doing a happy dance

inside her chest that made her heart thump and send extra blood up to warm her cheeks. The wash of relief was unmistakeable and hot on its heels was something she hadn't felt in years.

Excitement. The kind a small child would have creeping downstairs too early on Christmas morning and seeing the magic of the gifts under the tree. Gifts for *her*.

Did she dare to pick one up and rattle it? Tear off a tiny piece of wrapping paper to see if she could guess what was inside?

But what if it wasn't what she wanted? Maybe the anticipation was better than reality.

'I went to the hospital,' Nico explained. 'I knew you'd want to know how our man from yesterday was getting on.'

To her shame, no doubt due to the emotional rollercoaster the day had presented, Charlotte had barely given the man another thought. So much for her heartfelt presentation yesterday about the medicine they practised being about the people. But Nico was right. She could feel her face light up in her eagerness to know the outcome. This was the kind of excitement she was used to. *This* was what she needed to focus on.

'He's doing well.' Nico's smile was one of pure delight. 'He had an angioplasty and half a dozen stents put in. His broken leg's been sorted and he's sitting up in the coronary care unit and you'd never know he'd been dead for a while. No evidence of any brain damage even.'

'Really? That's...astonishing. Our CPR must have been up to standard, then.'

'A little more than that, I think.' Nico put his arm

around Charlotte's shoulders as he turned towards Lady Geraldine. 'We are an amazing team. And here we are, about to have an adventure. I am the happiest man on earth.'

Lady Geraldine was beaming at them. The check-in clerk was smiling mistily but then she collected herself. 'Here are your boarding passes. We'll take care of the suitcases and you can take your cabin baggage with you. I wish you the happiest of journeys.'

Lady Geraldine merely nodded. 'It will be,' she said softly. She winked at Charlotte. 'All that remains to be seen is which of us is the happiest *woman* on earth today.'

Lady Geraldine needed some assistance to climb up the steps and negotiate the narrow corridor of the train carriage. The first impression was the glow of polished wood and brass. And lights. Lamps casting a soft glow. Fairy lights in honour of the season, looped at ceiling height on the internal wall and twinkling merrily. The doors had small wreaths festooned with artificial cherries and tiny golden bells.

Even more overwhelming than the warm glow of the wood and lights was a sense of confinement. The cabins were tiny with no more than a richly uphol-stered double seat and a tiny table beneath the window. A washstand was cleverly incorporated into a corner.

For most passengers this would have been their total space but with a suite, a door beside the washstand cab-inet was open, leading to the adjoining cabin where the seats had already been turned into comfortable-look-ing bunk beds with crisp white linen and soft-looking towels folded on the ends.

For one person, it would have been the ultimate

in spaciousness aboard the train. For a couple, it still would have been more than enough. To share this amount of space with Nico Moretti was something entirely different. There didn't seem to be enough oxygen in the small spaces.

Their personal steward served champagne as the train pulled out of Santa Lucia station while Charlotte was checking that Lady Geraldine was settling comfortably into her suite. Nico joined them as the steward pointed out features of the cabins, including the bell that would summon him for assistance at any time of the day or night.

'The maître d' will visit your cabin soon to take your lunch and dinner reservations. Our restaurant cars have tables for two or four people.'

'We are a party of three,' Charlotte informed him. And how lucky was that? No chance of an intimate table for two with soft lighting and too much champagne. If she could put up good enough barriers around that part of her that was so drawn to this man she would be safe from making a complete fool of herself.

Was that a significant look that her grandmother was sharing with Nico?

'This is your gift,' Charlotte added, for good measure. 'And we intend to share every possible moment of it with you. Don't we, Nico?'

Nico seemed to be relishing the champagne and he merely lifted his glass in a toast of agreement.

There wasn't room for three people to sit in one cabin. Charlotte sat beside her grandmother as they opened and perused the map of the journey. Nico stood near the door, apparently enjoying the scenery through

the corridor windows and chatting to other passengers as they went past.

They chose the first sitting for lunch and it was Nico who insisted on helping Lady Geraldine negotiate the route and cope with the sometimes jerky motion of the train. It took a long time to get through several carriages and through the bar car before they got to one of the restaurant cars, especially when everything had to be explored and admired.

'The bathroom is amazing,' Lady Geraldine declared after their first stop to wait for her, which was right beside her suite at the end of their carriage. 'The toilet seat is made of mahogany and everything else is brass. Even the cover for the paper. And it's all so clean and shiny.'

The resident pianist was not yet playing the baby grand piano in the bar but they had to stop there as well.

'Play something, Charlotte,' Lady Geraldine commanded.

'I can't do that.' Charlotte was horrified. 'I haven't played a piano for years and I'm quite sure it's not allowed, anyway.'

But the handsome young man polishing glasses behind the wooden bar grinned. 'Go ahead,' he invited. 'It's too early to bother anyone.'

'Please, Charlotte.' Lady Geraldine was heading for a nearby seat. 'For me? It's so long since I heard you play.'

And she might never hear her again?

'Yes… Please, Charlotte.' Nico's smile was mischievous. 'I'm curious about your splinter skills.'

Oh, for heaven's sake. Charlotte realised she wasn't

going to win and the best way of avoiding stress in getting through this voyage was clearly going to be taking the path of least resistance. She slid herself onto the piano stool and raised the lid on the gleaming keys. She had taken lessons for years as a child and playing for pleasure had been a feature of every visit to her grandmother's house. Until…until her life had changed overnight.

Her hands shook for a moment as she held them over the keys. Maybe the least stressful response would have been to refuse to do this but now it was too late and if she didn't, she might be expected to provide an explanation.

Flicking a glance upwards Charlotte knew that Nico had seen the tell-tale tremor of her hands. She willed them to be still. Willed herself to continue, much as she'd forced herself to start that presentation in Nico's presence yesterday. The only piece she could think of to play by heart was Beethoven's 'Moonlight Sonata'.

The first notes were tentative but the piano was beautiful and within a few bars Charlotte was drawn in to the haunting sound of the music. Her stiff fingers relaxed as she remembered the release that this had once brought her. The pleasure of doing something for herself that had nothing to do with work. Mindless and satisfying and restorative. Just…pleasure…

'Bravo…' Nico's eyes were full of admiration as the last notes died away.

'I knew those piano lessons were worth every penny.' Lady Geraldine held her hand out for Nico to help her to her feet. 'Now, let's go and have some lunch.'

The lunch was three courses of beautifully prepared

and presented food but Lady Geraldine only picked at hers and didn't touch the tarte tatin served for dessert.

'I'm a little tired,' she confessed. 'I think I'll go back to my cabin and rest for a while.'

'I'll come and keep you company,' Charlotte offered immediately.

'No. I might need some help to get back without being knocked off my feet but I need some quiet time. I might have a nap.'

Charlotte felt her level of concern ramp up. Gran hadn't eaten much and now she looked pale. Was she in pain?

It was Nico's arm that Lady Geraldine chose to lean on to keep her balance and they had to stop at frequent intervals to allow other people to pass on their way to the restaurants.

One of those people was another elderly woman whose head turned in surprise as she took another look.

'Lady Geraldine? Jendi?'

'Oh, my goodness. Winsome Black. What on earth are you doing here?'

'I could ask you the same thing. What an astonishing coincidence.'

Lady Geraldine's head shake was incredulous. 'It's a small world, isn't it?' She turned to Charlotte. 'Winsome's an old friend that I haven't seen for years. We worked together once on a huge fundraiser for that children's charity.'

'One Last Wish.' Winsome nodded at Charlotte. 'Such a worthy cause. They made wishes come true for terminally ill children.'

'This is my granddaughter, Charlotte,' Lady Geraldine said.

'And this is my grandson, Connor.' The good-looking young man, who was clearly aware of how much space they were all taking up in the narrow corridor, smiled at Charlotte and offered her his hand.

She shook it with an equally conspiratorial smile. They had something in common, didn't they? Here they both were in the company of grandmothers with… personality.

'Charlotte and her fiancé are keeping me company,' Lady Geraldine was confiding in Winsome. Her smile was poignant. 'This trip is my last wish…'

'Oh, surely not.' Winsome smiled. 'I seem to remember you telling me that age is only an attitude.'

Lady Geraldine opened her mouth but then noticed the human traffic jam they were creating in the corridor. 'We'd better get a move on,' she said. 'But we must get together, Winsome, and have a proper chat.'

'That would be lovely.'

'How about afternoon tea? We could meet in the bar at, say, four o'clock?'

'See you then.' With a smile, Winsome continued on her way.

Charlotte wondered if the arrangement might be too much given that her grandmother had already said she needed a rest, but the sparkle in the elderly woman's eyes chased away the worry that her condition was deteriorating and that this trip would prove too much for her.

'Oh, look…the queue at the gift shop has gone. Let's see what they have.'

Charlotte was quite happy to linger and look at the souvenirs available. The more time they spent doing

things like this, the less time she would have to spend
with Nico, alone in their cabin while Gran had a rest.

You could buy hand-blown crystal glasses and
crockery with the Orient Express insignia. There were
salt and pepper shakers, travel accessories in blue vel-
vet, photo frames and even jewellery.

Lady Geraldine chose a specially bound copy of
Agatha Christie's *Murder on the Orient Express*. And
then she ordered Charlotte and Nico to choose a gift
for themselves.

'A selection of wine glasses would be a lovely en-
gagement present,' she suggested.

'You are celebrating an engagement?' The tall man
with a heavy accent who ran the gift boutique sighed
happily. 'I tell everybody that this is the train of love…'

'This trip is the gift, Gran. Remember? We don't
need anything else.'

But the tall man was putting things on the counter in
front of Nico. 'For your beautiful lady?' he murmured.
'A special memory, perhaps?'

Blue velvet cases were being opened to display pearl
necklaces on silver chains that had clasps engraved
with the train's insignia. Silver and gold bangles were
similarly engraved. A chain bracelet had tiny silver
charms like a train carriage, a conductor's whistle and
a pillbox hat but Nico was picking up another bracelet.
He held it up to show Charlotte.

'Do you like this, *cara*?'

Tiny silver hearts linked together. A delicate piece
of jewellery.

Romantic.

Charlotte opened her mouth to tell him that she
didn't wear jewellery but out of the corner of her eye

she saw the way her grandmother was pressing a hand to her throat. Holding her breath as she witnessed evidence of the love her granddaughter had finally found?

'It's…lovely.' Let him buy it, she told herself. She could reimburse him later.

Nico not only purchased the bracelet, he insisted on putting it on Charlotte's wrist. His fingers brushed her skin as he fed the rod of the clasp through the silver circle engraved with the name of the train.

He smiled at her then. Just the way he had when he'd sat at their table last night. As though she was the only woman in the world for him. As if he was so deeply in love that nothing else mattered.

She knew he was going to kiss her. The tall man wanted it to happen. Her grandmother wanted it to happen.

And, God help her, *she* wanted it to happen.

It was just a kiss and her lips were ready for it this time, already soft and slightly parted. If she sat down at a piano any time soon again, she would probably find that her fingers were instantly ready for the release of music too. The pleasure to be found. The connections between her fingers and her brain and her heart had unexpectedly been woken up after a very long sleep.

Like her lips had been?

Not that it was a passionate kiss, of course. Just a gentle pressure. But the promise was there. And no matter how fiercely Charlotte told herself that she didn't want this and couldn't go there, her body was defying her. The shaft of desire was so much more intense after last night. How on earth was she going to cope with the rest of this journey? Where were some new barriers when she needed them?

At least Nico left her alone to do some more exploring after Lady Geraldine was settled back into her cabin behind a closed door. It gave Charlotte time to try and rebuild her defences. To plan how she could get through the next hours. Maybe one of them could sleep in here, on the seat? At the very least she could choose the top bunk so that she wouldn't have Nico climbing past inches away from her face. What did he wear in bed? Oh, God…imagine him climbing up wearing nothing but a pair of silk boxers or skin-hugging cotton knit underwear. And even with the highly unlikely possibility that he had a pair of flannelette pyjamas in his bag, she'd still be aware of him sleeping beneath her, wouldn't she? She would hear his breathing. Feel the warmth of his presence. *All* night.

Heavens, it was warm in here. Charlotte adjusted the central heating radiator beneath the window and even opened the top window a little for some fresh air. She was just beginning to feel calmer when Nico returned to the cabin.

He was carrying a bottle of champagne in a silver ice bucket. Two crystal glasses dangled from his other hand. He leaned against the door with a smile of invitation curling the corners of his mouth.

What woman would be able to resist?

Charlotte, that's who, with her grandmother safely shut away and all the good work of calming herself down undone in an instant.

It wasn't hard to glare at Nico as though he was committing an unpardonable sin. 'What on earth are you thinking?' she snapped. 'I hope you're not planning to get me drunk so you can take advantage of me again.'

* * *

Again?

Nico shoved the cabin door shut with his foot. The champagne had seemed like a good idea. They were supposed to be celebrating their engagement, weren't they? They didn't have to drink the damned stuff. And what was wrong with trying to make this journey as pleasant as possible, anyway?

What *was* Charlotte's problem?

'Take *advantage* of you?' He kept his voice quiet but allowed it to cool noticeably. 'Is that how you see this?'

Her voice was small. 'No.'

At least she had the grace to look embarrassed but it wasn't good enough.

'On balance, I suspect most people would consider you to be taking advantage of *me* right about now.'

'You agreed.' Charlotte had two bright spots of colour on her cheeks and her tone was accusing. 'This was all *your* idea—'

'I have gone out of my way to help you,' Nico interrupted, dumping the ice bucket and glasses on the table by the window, oblivious to the glorious scenery of the Italian Dolomites rushing past in the distance. 'And it is *not* because I have any intention of "taking advantage" of you. You are the complete opposite of the type of woman I find attractive.'

A curious expression changed Charlotte's features. She looked…hurt? Disappointed? Surely not. The expression was gone as quickly as it had appeared but it took the wind out of Nico's sails. His anger evaporating, he sank down onto the seat beside her. 'Do you want to know the real reason?' he asked.

'Mmm?' The sound was somewhat strangled but

Charlotte was looking at her hands, which were clasped tightly together in her lap.

'You fascinate me,' Nico said simply. An honest statement, dragged from a deep place, possibly against his better judgement.

There was a long moment of silence but Nico let it ride as he tried to shut down the implications. Why did this interest feel so very different from the attraction a woman usually had for him? Was it a threat?

Very slowly, Charlotte finally raised her head. Her eyes were a dark, stormy grey and they were wide and puzzled. Fearful, almost.

'Why?' The word was a whisper.

Why indeed?

'You're a beautiful woman, Carlotta.' The Italian version of her name came to his lips unbidden. 'You are also very intelligent and successful. I have a great admiration for your professional abilities.' He could feel a corner of his mouth quirk. 'You are also surprisingly talented at playing the piano.'

A snort of mirth escaped Charlotte as she shook her head, encouraging a lock of hair to escape the tight ponytail she was wearing today.

Nico couldn't resist catching that lock and smoothing it back behind her ear. 'I believe that people come into your life for a reason,' he added quietly. 'I find myself in an extraordinary place, if only for a limited time, and I have to wonder if fate has brought us together because we have something we can learn from each other.'

She was looking at him now as if he'd grown two heads. 'Like what?'

'I don't know.' Nico shrugged. 'Maybe it's your as-

tonishing grandmother I was destined to meet. To learn how one can make the most of life until the very end. Or how to face the prospect of that end with such dignity and courage.'

'Oh…' Charlotte caught her top lip between her teeth but it wasn't enough to stop tears rushing to her eyes.

Dio…he hadn't intended to make her cry. Nico extracted one of her still-clasped hands and held it between his own.

'Or maybe I need to learn about family,' he said. 'The love you have for your *nonna* touches me very much. Right here.' He brought her hand up to press it against his heart. 'I don't have a bond like that. Perhaps I pushed my mother away because of the childhood sadness of losing my father. Maybe that's why I never want to marry or have a family of my own because I can't imagine inflicting that kind of pain on children.

'But half of me is Italian and it doesn't feel right. I've ignored that sense for many years but seeing you with your *nonna* opened my eyes.' His smile was wry. 'I don't know if it will change how I live my life but it feels right to be helping you.'

'But you wouldn't inflict that pain on your own children.' He could feel the pressure as Charlotte started holding *his* hand instead of just letting hers be held. 'Because you'd know what it was like. And even if the marriage didn't work, you'd still keep your bond with your children. You'd fight for it. And win.'

She believed that. She believed in *him*. It gave Nico an odd frisson of…what, pride? Invincibility? Oh, yes…he could conquer the world if a woman like Charlotte truly believed in him. Except…

'It's not going to happen…' The admission was being torn from somewhere that had been so well locked away maybe he hadn't even been aware of it himself. 'The kind of love that leads to marriage… and children…can only happen if you can fall in love. I think…I think that I'm not capable of doing that.'

There it was. His deepest, darkest secret. Something that he'd never said to anyone. From the shocked expression on Charlotte's face she must realise the significance of his confession. But she didn't believe it.

'Why not?'

Nico had to swallow hard. Why was he putting himself through this? Because it seemed like a pathway to get Charlotte to open up about herself? If he stopped now, he'd never reach his goal.

'I love my mother,' he said quietly. 'I can't blame her for wanting to find happiness in her life and the men she falls in love with don't seem to be able to provide that for very long. But I loved my father too and, even as a child, I could see that he was destroyed by losing the woman he loved so much. Falling in love can create so much pain. You either end up being destroyed yourself, like my father, or destroying others, like my mother has—more than once.'

'That doesn't have to happen. Not if you choose the right person who can give you what you need.'

'What if you don't know what it is that you need? How can you possibly make the right choice of a person to be with for the rest of your life?' Nico shook his head. 'No. It's safer to never fall in love. Perhaps I'm lucky that I have that inability.'

Charlotte was still staring at him, a crease of concern between her brows.

'But you don't want to end up like Gran,' she said, with a wobble in her voice. 'Old and sick but with no-body to care about you. No child. No grandchild.' Her voice trailed away as if Nico wasn't supposed to hear her next words. 'That's what terrifies *me*...'

'So why are you alone?' Nico turned so that he could look directly at Charlotte. 'A beautiful, talented woman who should be thinking of having children of her own so that she can have grandchildren one day.'

There was no response other than a withdrawal Nico could both see and feel. As if the white witch from Narnia had waved her wand and turned his companion to stone.

Nico had bared a part of his soul here. A part that had never been shared before and never would be again. Charlotte wasn't going to be allowed not to take her turn.

'Tell me about Siegfried,' he said.

'No.' The refusal was absolute. Charlotte pulled her hand away and turned to stare out of the window.

Nico leaned back against the seat, letting his head rest on the lace-covered cushion. 'I'm a patient man,' he said lightly. 'We have the rest of today. And *all* night.'

He couldn't miss the way Charlotte's chest heaved as she gasped silently. Struggling for control? Interesting. He was getting somewhere, at least.

Nico watched her profile closely. 'We are in this extraordinary place and time and we never have to see each other again after tomorrow. I believe I have something to learn from you, Carlotta. And I think that maybe you have something to learn from me.'

He touched her arm and she flinched. Nico sighed. He should give up. Accept that Charlotte wasn't pre-

pared or ready to learn anything. Except he didn't believe that. She just had to unbutton herself a little more. And if she did that, maybe he would get the answers to the mystery of why she'd changed so much. And then his fascination with her would fade and his life could get back to normal.

'In order to learn something,' he offered carefully, 'maybe you have to be prepared to admit that there's something you don't know. To be open. And honest. Being honest makes you vulnerable, I know that. But I've been honest with you.'

Charlotte nodded. 'You have.'

'More than honest. I've told you something that I've never told anyone else. That I never *will* tell anyone else. Something that I see as…shameful. What kind of man am I if I cannot fall in love or be the kind of husband and father a woman would want?'

She was still struggling. Did she even realise that she was shaking her head very slowly? That her hands were gripping each other tightly enough to have cut off any useful supply of blood?

'You have the power to hurt me, Charlotte, if you chose to share that information with anyone. I'm trusting you not to do that.'

The slow headshake turned into an equally measured nod. A promise.

Nico lowered his voice to something just above a whisper as he touched her again. And this time she didn't flinch. 'You can trust me.' He cleared his throat and spoke more strongly. 'So…will you do me the honour of being honest with me?'

Dio, that had disturbing echoes of some kind of marriage proposal. Except it wasn't, of course, so he

didn't need to feel as if he was getting completely out of his depth.

Even when Charlotte raised her eyes to his and he could see that she wanted to tell him.

Wanted to trust him.

She was just having to gather so much courage that it broke his heart to watch.

'I loved him.' She finally choked the words out. 'I thought he loved me. But he wanted… I couldn't…' There was agony coating the words now. 'We weren't… *compatible*.'

There was another message in her eyes now. One that said Charlotte was unbearably alone in the world but that there was nothing she could do about it.

Nico sighed again, more heavily this time, as though utterly defeated. He held out his arms and gathered Charlotte to his chest.

And held her while she cried.

CHAPTER SEVEN

'THERE'S NOTHING LIKE a *proper* afternoon tea, is there?'
Lady Geraldine sighed happily as she stirred sugar
into her second cup and listened appreciatively to the
sound of silverware tapping against real bone china.
'Did you know you can buy these lovely cups and sau-
cers from the gift shop?'

'I'll have to have a look. I'm planning to go there
after this.'

Lady Geraldine couldn't help noticing the glow of
Winsome's smile. Her old friend certainly looked very
happy these days. She could return the smile easily.
She had a lot to be happy about herself at the moment.

Like meeting an old friend unexpectedly. Being on
her once-in-a-lifetime dream journey. Actually sitting
in this famous bar carriage with the pianist now in res-
idence playing some soft, classical music interspersed
with Christmas carols. Remembering Charlotte playing
on the beautiful instrument earlier when it had been
the first time she'd heard her in so many years. Could
it be that it was Nico who was bringing back the part
of her granddaughter she'd been missing for so long?

She picked up the elegant white cup with the blue
ribbon pattern around its rim and the VSOE logo under

a small crown. 'Maybe a set of these would make a lovely engagement gift for my Charlotte and her Nico.'

'You said they'd only met yesterday? In Venice? When they both saved that man's life?'

'Yes...' Lady Geraldine pushed aside that tiny niggle of doubt. 'But they'd met before. Years ago, at Charlotte's hospital. Fate has just thrown them back together and...' She sighed again. 'It's obviously meant to be. Like your Connor and...what was her name again?'

The conversation paused for a moment as the steward removed the plates that had contained tiny sandwiches and replaced it with a platter of warm scones, adding small silver pots of jam and clotted cream.

'Mmm...' Lady Geraldine eyed the cream. 'Proper Cornish clotted cream, by the look of that.'

'Kelsie,' Winsome said as she followed her friend's example and picked up one of the scones. 'Kelsie Summers. But I don't think she and Connor are about to fall into each other's arms like your Charlotte and Nico. She jilted him, in fact, fifteen years ago and I have the feeling he hasn't forgiven her.'

'Really?' Lady Geraldine had spread the jam and clotted cream onto her scone and was just about to take her first bite but the conversation had just become more enticing than the calorie-laden treat. 'They must have been very young. Oh, *do* tell...'

They both dropped their voices to a more discreet level and Lady Geraldine listened to the story with avid interest. Young love could be such a fragile thing, couldn't it? She had to hope that there wouldn't be any unforeseen twists in the road ahead for Charlotte and Nico.

She finally turned her attention back to her scone but her expression was thoughtful.

'We might be able to help things along,' she suggested.

'What do you mean?'

'The dinner seating is very strict, I hear.'

'It certainly is. I've tried to change tables at the last minute on some of my previous journeys and it almost never happens.'

'It's not the last minute yet,' Lady Geraldine said firmly. 'And if we both had a little chat to the maître d', I'm sure we could persuade him to juggle things a little.'

'In what way?'

'By making an extra table available. We've still got a lot of catching up to do, haven't we? We haven't even started talking about that terrible business with Deirdre Wilkins defrauding the charity so that she could run off to the Maldives with that "personal" trainer of hers.'

Lady Geraldine knew her smile would reveal how much she enjoyed an occasional bit of juicy gossip. 'If we asked to be seated together, that would mean leaving both your Connor and this Kelsie and my Charlotte and the lovely Nico alone at their tables.'

'Yes… If we could make sure they gave them a table for two or didn't put another couple to join them at one of the bigger tables.'

'It would be so romantic, wouldn't it? Everybody dressed up and the lighting all soft and lots of delicious champagne to add to the atmosphere?'

Winsome was smiling. 'Why don't we ask our nice steward to go and see if the maître d' might be able to spare us a minute or two?'

* * *

Charlotte drifted towards consciousness with reluctance.

She had never felt so comfortable. So relaxed. So *safe*. She was floating, supported by a strength she knew she could trust. Cradled against it and it was warm and…moving?

Yes. A steady, gentle movement like breathing. And there was an equally steady but gentle thumping against her ear.

A sound she normally only heard through a stethoscope.

Awareness of where she was kicked in. Or should that be who she was with?

Asleep on, in fact?

'Ohhh…' Charlotte pushed herself upright with a groan. 'I fell *asleep*?'

'You did.' There was amusement in Nico's tone. And a tenderness that touched something that felt raw inside Charlotte.

The last thing she remembered was bursting into tears and Nico holding her. She'd expected him to want more information about what had gone so wrong with her relationship with Siegfried. For her to define what she'd meant by being incompatible. But he hadn't asked anything. He'd offered her comfort instead, as though he understood. As though everything could somehow be put right.

And it had been too much for Charlotte. Her defences had collapsed completely and she'd sobbed out the tears that had been bottled up for years and years. And then she must have been overcome by sheer exhaustion and fallen asleep.

And he'd just continued to hold her?

'How long?' Charlotte put a hand to her hair, which felt like a rat's nest. She closed her eyes in disbelief and found that her eyelashes felt all clumpy when she blinked. She probably had mascara all over her face. She opened them again. The short winter's day was ending already and it was dark outside but their cabin was glowing in the soft light from a lamp on the table. 'How long have I been asleep?'

Nico was tilting his head to one side and then the other, stretching his neck. 'I wasn't watching the clock.' He smiled. 'I may have dozed off myself, in fact.'

Charlotte could feel a smile stirring. A joke about them sleeping together forming.

'Only until the steward woke me to tell me about Jendi.'

The smile and joke evaporated. 'What? Oh, my God…and you didn't wake me? What was wrong? Why—?'

Nico put a finger against her lips and the gentle pressure stopped her anxious flow of words.

'He merely came to ask if I could accompany her to the bar for the afternoon tea she had arranged to have with Mrs Black. As soon as he saw that I was… ah…otherwise occupied, he said it was no problem, he would accompany her himself and ensure that she didn't lose her balance.'

Charlotte couldn't believe she could have slept through the whole exchange. 'I'm sorry,' she muttered. 'I must have been more tired than I realised. I…um… didn't sleep much last night.'

'Of course not. You're worried about your *nonna*.'

'Mmm. That, too…'

She saw the flash of understanding in his eyes as he considered what else might have been keeping her awake. Like that kiss…

Distraction was needed. Charlotte looked around. The bottle of champagne was still sitting in the bucket. There were a few small cubes of ice floating on the water inside. Nico must have followed her glance.

'It may still be cold enough,' he said. 'Shall we have a toast?'

'To what?'

'To making this evening as enjoyable as possible? For everyone involved. It will be time to get ready for dinner before long, I expect.' Nico was dealing with the foil on the champagne bottle. 'We need to prepare ourselves to put on a good show.' The cork came out with a satisfying 'pop'. He smiled that slow, easy, ir-resistible grin as he filled the glasses and held one out to Charlotte. 'Dutch courage?'

'Will I need it?' And then Charlotte remembered what her hair and face must look like and she smiled ruefully. 'Don't answer that. I know I look a complete mess.' She took a sip of her drink. 'It's just as well I won't see you again after tomorrow. I would be morti-fied. I can't think of anyone who's ever seen me look this terrible.'

Apart from Siegfried, of course. Charlotte took a longer sip of the wine.

Nico touched his glass to hers. 'You are beautiful, Carlotta.'

He looked as though he believed the words. He was giving her *that* look again. Like the one he'd given her last night. And again, in the gift shop. But why?

There was no one around to see. He didn't have to pretend here.

And hadn't he told her that she was safe because she was so completely not *his* type?

She wanted to be his type. Heaven help her but she wanted Nico to kiss her again.

Dammit. Where were her safety barriers when she needed them? At the very least she needed to break their eye contact but it seemed impossible.

Charlotte searched for a barrier she could put up to protect herself but couldn't find a trace of one. All she could find was a memory of how it had felt to know that Nico had shared his shameful secret with her and how cathartic it had been to finally share her own with another living person. How it had felt to wake up in Nico's arms.

How was it possible to feel so vulnerable and yet so safe at exactly the same time?

She still couldn't break the eye contact either. And Nico wasn't looking away. Charlotte could feel the distance between them closing. The kiss that she wanted so badly was only a heartbeat away.

Until a knock sounded on the cabin door.

'Dr Moretti? Dr Highton?' The steward sounded as if the matter was urgent. 'I'm sorry to disturb you, but you are both needed.'

It was just as well the moment had been broken by the interruption.

Perhaps it had been a mistake to let Charlotte sleep in his arms for so long but what else could he have done?

The depth of pain he'd heard in those words '*not*

compatible'. They couldn't have had anything other than a sexual reference and for it to be so hard for Charlotte to have uttered them meant they were the key to the puzzle of what had changed her so much.

A horrible suspicion had formed in Nico's mind. Something unthinkable. So dark it couldn't be given a name. So horrific all he'd been able to do was hold onto this damaged woman as he'd tried to fit in the other pieces of the puzzle and control the rush of pure fury on her behalf.

He had to control it. Nico hadn't known if his assumption was correct. Maybe Charlotte would never tell him and even if she did, what on earth could *he* do about it?

Nothing, that's what. It was none of his business. Not his problem. But it would provide an explanation to the mystery and that was what he'd wanted, wasn't it?

So Nico had done nothing. Said nothing. As the minutes had ticked by he'd continued to do nothing and that was when he'd felt Charlotte's heartbroken sobbing subside. When the exhaustion in her body had taken over. When she'd slipped into a peaceful, bone-deep slumber.

He could have eased himself away at that point, found a pillow and blanket to make her comfortable on the seat. Or carried her to a bunk, maybe, and left her to sleep for an hour or two. What was it about this bizarre situation he'd been caught up in since early yesterday morning that made it impossible to walk away?

He could have ignored Charlotte when he'd first seen her crying on the terrace below his window. He certainly hadn't needed to come up with the dangerous notion of posing as her lover, let alone shoving a ring

on her finger. And he could have found an excuse not
to accompany the women on this train journey.

But he hadn't. Every step of the way he had hesi-
tated and then been drawn in deeper by something
he couldn't explain. And if the steward hadn't rapped
on the door at that particular moment, he would have
kissed Charlotte again.

More than kissed her, actually. He could have asked
gentle questions with his mouth and his hands that
would have confirmed what he suspected was the an-
swer to the puzzle that had intrigued him ever since
he'd recognised Charlotte on that cobbled Venetian
street.

He would have got answers to those questions, he
was sure of that. Just as sure as he was of the fact that
Charlotte had *wanted* him to kiss her. He had seen that
desire darken her eyes and soften her lips and he'd felt
that knowledge kindle his own flame because it was
part of what intrigued him so much. The contradic-
tions. The ice queen on the surface and the woman
capable of such deep emotion within. Was the single,
ultimately professional doctor desperately in need of
physical release, possibly without being consciously
aware of it?

Whatever. The desire had been wiped from her eyes
the moment that sharp rap had sounded on the door and
the tone of the steward's voice had told them that they
were not only needed but needed urgently.

Charlotte's assumption was, of course, that Jendi
had become ill. She moved swiftly to wrench open
the cabin door.

'It's my grandmother, isn't it? She needs us?'

The steward nodded. 'Only you, Dr Highton. She's asking for assistance to get dressed for dinner.'

'But you said you needed both of us.'

'Yes. I'm hoping that Dr Moretti could come with me to see another passenger in the carriage who requires a doctor. He thinks he might be having a heart attack.'

Nico could actually feel his professional persona taking over. Smothering anything personal, like his desire to kiss Charlotte. There was still a flicker of something personal there, though. He stepped closer, needing to touch her, and put his hand on her shoulder.

'You go and help your *nonna*,' he told her. 'I'll deal with this.'

'But…' Was it his imagination or did Charlotte lean into his hand a little, as if she was trying to return the touch? Her gaze caught his and he could read the message so easily. She was reminding him of what he'd told her grandmother only hours ago. That, together, they made an amazing team.

'I'll send for you,' Nico said softly. 'If I need you.' He stepped past Charlotte into the corridor, where the steward was waiting anxiously for Nico to follow him. The last personal thoughts evaporated. 'What equipment do you have on board?' he queried. 'Oxygen? A defibrillator?'

'Yes. We have oxygen. And an AED.'

'Good.' Nico picked up his pace as they made their way to the cabin at the far end of the carriage. 'Show me which cabin and then fetch them for me, please.'

The man in the end cabin was in his sixties. His colour wasn't good and he was clutching a small red and white canister of glyceryl trinitrate spray in his hands.

His wife was beside him, looking even paler than her husband and virtually wringing her hands.

'How long is it since the pain came on?' Nico asked.

The anxious woman checked her watch. 'Nearly fifteen minutes.'

'And how many doses of the spray have been taken?'

'Two? Maybe three... I've lost count.' The woman was struggling to hold back tears. 'It's not working and...and they said that if it didn't work it could be a heart attack and we'd have to get Douglas to the hospital as quickly as possible.'

Nico had his fingers on the older man's wrist. His pulse was a bit rapid but quite strong and regular.

'Tell me about the pain.'

'It's like a bus parked on my chest. Right here...' Douglas pressed a fist to his sternum. 'It's hard to breathe.'

'Just in your chest?'

'Yes.'

'Have you ever had a heart attack?'

'Yes. Ten years ago. That's when this whole business started. But it's been stable. Always comes on the same way...and if I sit down and use the spray it... does the trick.'

He was starting to sound breathless. Thankfully the steward had returned now. He was carrying an oxygen cylinder in one hand and the small red case of an AED in the other. Hopefully the automatic defibrillator wouldn't be needed but it was great to know that such a lifesaver was available if it came to that. Even with the best team in the world performing CPR, it could only buy time. The only way to restart a heart was through defibrillation.

The best team in the world. Unbidden, a memory of
Charlotte working with him on the man at the build-
ing site flashed into the back of Nico's mind. He shook
it off as he uncoiled tubing and fitted nasal prongs to
give Douglas some oxygen.

'This may help the pain,' he said. 'Are you on any
medications?'

'Yes. Too many.'

'Can you tell me what they are?'

Douglas shook his head, closing his eyes and screw-
ing up his face as though the pain was becoming un-
bearable. A sheen of perspiration was beginning to
show on his bald head. Nico's heart sank.

'I've got them.' The anxious older woman was rum-
maging in a small suitcase. She pulled out a plastic bag
containing numerous packages of medication. They
were all things that a cardiac patient could be expected
to be on.

'Have you had your aspirin today?'

'Yes.' It was his wife who answered. 'He's taken
everything.'

'Let's try another dose of the GTN.' Nico took the
canister from the man's hands. It was a bad sign if the
spray that normally worked on his angina was failing
to be effective but was it possible that it hadn't been
used correctly? Nico rolled the canister in his hands,
making sure the contents were mixed and then sprayed
a dose into the air to check that the metered dose mech-
anism was working. The spray came out but, oddly,
Nico couldn't smell anything.

He held the canister up and peered at the base. 'This
spray expired two years ago,' he exclaimed.

'Oh, my goodness!' Douglas's wife clapped a hand to her mouth. 'Really?'

'Really.' Nico reached for the portable pharmacy in the plastic bag. Yes. There was a small box in there that contained a replacement canister. And the expiry date was a year away. He ripped open the box, took the lid off the canister and squeezed off a test shot. 'Open your mouth,' he directed Douglas, 'and lift your tongue.'

He gave Douglas two sprays under his tongue and then kept his fingers on his patient's pulse and watched his breathing while they waited. Within a matter of minutes Douglas started breathing more easily and deeply. The lines on his face relaxed and when he opened his eyes he actually smiled.

'It's almost gone,' he said.

'Oh…thank God…' His wife was crying. 'I'm so sorry, Doug. This is my fault. I should have thrown that old spray away as soon as we had the new one.'

'Waste not, want not.' Douglas patted his wife's hand. 'If you weren't so good at being thrifty we'd never have been able to afford this trip, would we?' He turned to Nico. 'Thank you, Doctor. I'm not having a heart attack after all, am I?'

'It certainly looks like nothing more than an episode of angina. Let's keep the oxygen going for a little while and see how you go. Someone can always come and find me later, too, if you're worried.'

The only person looking worried now was Douglas's wife. 'I'm so sorry to have disturbed your trip,' she told Nico.

'It's not a problem.'

'Is it your first time on the Orient Express?'

'It is.'

'Isn't it wonderful? Are you enjoying it?'

'Of course.' But Nico had to consciously smile instead of allowing a puzzled frown to crease his forehead. Enjoyment wasn't a word that he would have chosen to describe his state of mind so far. He'd started out being intrigued and then he'd been impressed by Charlotte's piano playing. He'd had a spell of being angry when he'd been accused of planning to take advantage of her and then he'd had that cold chill of horror when he thought he'd guessed her secret.

But the overwhelming emotion that he would remember from this trip was going to be the way he'd felt sitting in that cabin and holding Charlotte while she slept. The feeling of protecting her. Of knowing that she trusted him enough to fall asleep in his arms like that. That he could trust *her* enough not to ever share the personal information he had given her.

A good feeling.

An incredibly powerful feeling.

Even more powerful than the desire that had kicked in when he'd realised that Charlotte had wanted him to kiss her as much as *he'd* wanted to kiss her?

Yes. Strangely, it was. He was used to desire and he knew there were countless women in the world who could make him feel like that.

But that other feeling was completely unfamiliar. And deeply disturbing. Powerful enough to feel like it had a life of its own and could take control. Was this what falling in love was all about?

Nico couldn't answer that because he'd never been in this space before. He wasn't capable of falling in love. He knew that. But maybe he was getting a glimpse of what it might be about.

And it was disturbing enough that he never wanted to experience it again so maybe it was time to take charge and make sure he wasn't ambushed by any other strange emotions. The distraction of being a doctor for a little while was definitely helping. The fact that the train seemed to be coming to a halt was less helpful.

Had something happened? Maybe there was engine trouble or something on the tracks and he'd end up being on this train for a lot longer than expected. Just how long could he keep up the level of control he might need when he was sharing a compartment with Charlotte?

The steward, who'd been hovering outside the cabin while Nico treated Douglas, stooped to peer through the window. 'We're coming into Innsbruck,' he announced. 'I need to attend to other duties.'

Nico nodded. 'Thanks very much for your help.'

'I can put the AED away now?'

'Yes. Thankfully, I don't think we need it.' Nico raised his eyebrows as the train jerked and came to a complete halt. 'Why are we stopping?'

'We have to change engines whenever we come to an international border. This is a thirty-minute stop and most people like to get off the train and stretch their legs a bit.' The steward hurried off, probably to open doors and then to stand, looking very smart in his blue uniform, to give people another photo opportunity.

Douglas certainly wasn't going to be jumping off the train to stretch his legs right now. Nico adjusted the setting on the oxygen cylinder and settled in to watch the progress of his new patient.

The contents of Lady Geraldine's larger suitcase were spread out over the seat and hanging from the edges of the bunks as she chose her outfit for dinner.

'The long black taffeta skirt,' she decided. 'With the black, silk camisole and the velvet bolero jacket.'

'Very Gothic,' Charlotte smiled. 'Shall I do your hair so that you've got a bit of fringe covering one eye?'

'Don't be naughty, Charlotte Jane. The black is merely a canvas to show off my diamond jewellery. I'm going to need my necklace and the brooch that goes on the jacket. And I've got my bracelet and best rings in my jewellery case. Oh…we mustn't forget that darling little tiara either. The one I wore last night, remember?'

'How could I forget?'

Lady Geraldine eyed her granddaughter suspiciously. 'I don't think you're taking this seriously, Charlotte. This is the dinner of my lifetime and I intend to look the part.'

'Sorry, Gran.' Charlotte kissed her fondly. 'I want you to enjoy tonight as much as possible. Are you sure you're feeling all right? Did you have a good rest?'

'I had a lovely rest. And then I had an even better time having afternoon tea with my old friend, Winsome. We still have lots to talk about.'

'Maybe you'll see her again after dinner.'

Oddly, Lady Geraldine looked evasive now. 'Help me into my skirt, child. And then you'd better start doing something to get ready yourself. Fancy suggesting I wear my hair over my eye. Have you looked in a mirror recently? What have you and Nico been up to in your cabin?'

'Gran…' But Charlotte couldn't help thinking about the look in Nico's eyes just before the steward had interrupted them. About how much she had wanted that kiss to happen. Even now, the curl of desire the memory could evoke was enough to make her close her

eyes for a heartbeat. To make her lips curl in pleasure at the memory.

If that kiss had happened, would it have stopped there? Would she have wanted it to? The bite of fear that kicked in was enough to make her shake her head as if she could banish the hateful sensation.

She needed to try and locate at least a shimmer of her old armour. To pretend to be in control. Normal. Maybe it would help to make a joke of it. 'Have you *seen* the size of those bunks?'

'You're young,' Lady Geraldine said with a smile. 'I'm sure you'll cope.' She reached out and stroked Charlotte's cheek. 'Oh, darling. You're so in love with him, aren't you?'

Charlotte had to turn away. To find something solid to focus on as she felt the ground shifting beneath her feet with a curious spinning sensation. She lifted the hanger holding her grandmother's astonishing skirt with the ruffled hem down from the top bunk and pretended to notice some lint that needed brushing away.

In love?

Ridiculous. Nobody fell in love that quickly. She felt safe with Nico, that was all. He knew more about her than anyone. More than her grandmother, in fact, in a rather significant area.

She liked him. A lot. Who wouldn't? He was clever and kind. So kind that he'd sat, getting cramp, for hours, holding a woman in his arms because he hadn't wanted to wake her?

She trusted him, too. Who couldn't trust someone who put the kind of trust in you that led to sharing the kind of secret she could so well understand him wanting to keep to himself? Not that it was true, of course.

Nico was more than capable of falling in love if he'd only let himself.

And that feeling when she'd woken up in those arms. As if she had been floating in the most blissful place on earth. She'd never felt so safe.

So *protected*.

Superimposed on that memory came that look of desire in Nico's eyes when their lips had been drifting closer together in the moments before that rap on the door.

That mix of safety and desire was a chemical combination that could only mean one thing.

That…yes. She *was* in love with Nico Moretti.

No. Maybe it meant two things.

She was not only in love. She was in trouble.

CHAPTER EIGHT

MAYBE IT WAS her new awareness of how she felt about Nico. Or perhaps it was the incongruity of him appearing in these surroundings looking impossibly gorgeous in his dinner suit. Whatever it was, it completely stole Charlotte's breath away when she opened the door of her grandmother's compartment to his polite knock.

Did her grandmother actually bat her eyelashes?

'It's been a long time since I was escorted to dinner by such a handsome young man,' she said with delight. 'Charlotte Jane? You can have him later but I really do need Nico's arm while we're walking. This train is remarkably jerky at times.'

'No worries, Gran.' Charlotte smiled. 'He's all yours.'

But then her gaze caught Nico's and the smile got stolen away like her breath had been. Oh...Lord...that look in his eyes.

'I love that dress,' was all he said. 'I'm so glad you've worn it again, *cara*.'

Lady Geraldine made a tutting sound. 'I'm trying to train Charlotte to expand her wardrobe, Nico. It won't help if you tell her you're happy she's worn the same thing two nights running.'

'But it's true, Jendi.' Nico's smile for her grand-

mother was so warm and genuine that Charlotte's heart squeezed painfully. How could she not love a man who was clearly already so fond of her beloved gran? 'And I am an honest man.'

The comment did something strange inside Charlotte. Echoes of his voice telling her that he'd been honest with her and asking her to give him the honour of being the same with him. It was a bond she knew she could never have with another person. Did he feel the same? No. How could he when she hadn't shared the most shameful part of her secret? When she'd been less than completely honest?

But his gaze flicked past Charlotte's again. 'Most of the time,' he added.

All the time, Charlotte suspected. This pretence they were engaged in was an aberration. Sure, Nico had approached it as an amusing diversion but any control had been lost very quickly, hadn't it? At about the time he'd pushed that ring onto her finger, probably.

No wonder he was feeling uncomfortable but Lady Geraldine didn't seem to pick up on the loaded comment. 'I'm ready to go,' she announced. 'I want as much time to enjoy seeing everybody else dressed up as I can before I start feeling too old and tired.'

Or before she felt too sick and sore? Charlotte followed Nico as he carefully escorted Lady Geraldine through the rocking carriages towards the dining cars. She needed a break, she said, when they reached the bar car. She wanted to sit for a few minutes and enjoy listening to the piano. And…how nice…her friend Winsome was sitting at one of the side-facing seats and seemed to be saving space for her. Perhaps Charlotte could order a nice cocktail for her?

Charlotte perused the cocktail menu while Nico made sure her grandmother was seated comfortably. Heavens, but there were a lot to choose from. She'd never even heard of a Moscow Mule or a Planters Punch. Both her grandmother's favourites were there, though, so all she really needed to choose between was a Singapore Sling or a Gin Fizz.

Nico came back to the bar as she ordered a Gin Fizz. When he was only a step or two away the train gave a sudden and rather dramatic lurch. A cry rippled through the carriage as people spilt their drinks but the pianist didn't miss a beat of the Viennese waltz he was playing. And Nico's arm was right there to steady Charlotte as she lost her balance.

It was the first time he'd touched her since that almost kiss when they'd been interrupted earlier and it seemed to ignite a peculiar magic. How else could Charlotte explain the fact that a steadying touch morphed into an embrace that moved in time to the music?

They were dancing?

Yes. On a minuscule patch of blue carpet, in the space between the bar and the piano, Nico was very competently leading her through a confined version of a Viennese waltz. Charlotte could have laughed out loud. Except that this was giving her the same kind of feeling that she'd had when she'd woken from that deep sleep in Nico's arms, and she wanted to recapture that bliss for just a few seconds.

So, instead of holding her head in the correct position for a waltz as she'd been trained to do in those lessons Gran had insisted on when she'd been a teenager, Charlotte let herself droop enough to put her head

on Nico's shoulder. And he tilted his head so that it rested against hers. It was no waltz now. Just a slow, close dance.

To anyone watching, and no doubt that included Lady Geraldine and her friend, they must look like a couple madly in love. Nobody, meaning Nico, needed to know that it was actually genuine on her part now.

And maybe that was a good thing. Maybe…just a very small maybe…this didn't have to end when they got off the train in London tomorrow.

No. That tiny, unbidden seed of hope died away as Charlotte remembered Nico saying he never wanted marriage or children. That she was safe because she was so completely not his type of woman.

Oh, well…at least if Gran lived long enough for her to have to confess that the relationship wasn't going to work long term, she wouldn't have to pretend to be heartbroken, would she?

Oh, God…she really was in trouble now.

Released from Nico's arms to a round of applause from the crowded carriage, Charlotte headed back to the bar. She was going to order one of those potent-sounding cocktails for herself because she needed something strong if she was going to cope with the rest of this journey. She needed some bottled courage. Or stamina.

Moving towards Lady Geraldine's seat to wait for the bartender to bring the drinks, Charlotte found that introductions were being made. Winsome's grandson Connor was with a young woman called Kelsie, who was now sitting beside Lady Geraldine. They were discussing seating arrangements.

'Winsome and I have arranged a table for ourselves,'

Lady Geraldine said. 'We don't want to bore you young things with our gossip.'

The implications were immediately obvious. Nico and Connor exchanged a glance as if they were measuring each other up and considering the prospect of a foursome for dinner. Kelsie was watching the older women as if she knew there was more coming. And there was.

'So, instead, we have three tables,' Lady Geraldine smiled. 'One for each couple.'

Charlotte almost groaned aloud. 'I don't think you're allowed to change arrangements like that, are you, Gran?'

Lady Geraldine merely tapped the side of her nose. 'Wait and see where the maître d' puts us all,' she murmured. And then she winked at Winsome. 'Being old doesn't entirely deprive us of our ability to charm men into doing what we want, does it, Winnie?'

'Not at all, dear. As you say, age is only an attitude.'

Charlotte caught Connor's gaze and his expression said it all. This was a done deal and there was absolutely no point trying to make changes now. She was now faced with the prospect of being alone with Nico for a dinner that might go on for hours. An intimate, romantic kind of dinner. Her heart sank. One strong cocktail was not going to be enough.

Nico had to admire the persuasive powers of older women. Tables had to be at a premium on the train, even if there was more than one sitting for dinner, but here they were at a table that could seat four people and it was only set for two.

It was beautifully set with crisp, white linen, spar-

kling silverware and immaculate crystal that caught
the soft light of the Tiffany lamp on the window side
of the table. The carriage might be crowded with other
diners but it felt like he and Charlotte were enclosed
in a bubble of their own. He was glad that she hadn't
had a different dress to wear because this silver sheath
was gorgeous and so very appropriate for the season. It
made her eyes look like a dark shade of silver instead
of grey. Or was that because they were catching such
a warm glow from the light?

Or perhaps it was the champagne he had ordered.
She certainly seemed to be enjoying the Moët, even if
she wasn't clearing her plate with each delicious course
that arrived. He had polished off the entrée and then
demolished the main course of traditional roast turkey
with chestnut stuffing.

Conversation had proved easier than he'd expected,
having been deprived of Jendi's company. They'd
started out with the practical matter of sleeping ar-
rangements for the night.

'I'll stay in the bar for a while,' Nico had told Char-
lotte. 'And then I'll come back to the cabin and sleep
on the seat. You can close the connecting door when
you go to bed.'

He'd asked if she knew what would happen tomor-
row.

'We get to Paris around dawn,' she'd told him.
'When we get to the end of the French line for the
Orient Express, we have to get off and there are spe-
cial buses that we stay on for the channel crossing. The
English branch of the train takes us into Victoria Sta-
tion. I think we get in at about five p.m.'

As the plates for the main course were taken away,

Charlotte allowed her champagne glass to be refilled. Did her smile look a little forced as she held it up to Nico in a toast?

'What will you do?' she asked brightly. 'When we've arrived back in London? For Christmas Eve, I mean.'

Nico shrugged. 'I expect I'll go to work and catch up on any inpatients. I'm covering a big area for the next few days. I like to give my colleagues as much time as possible to be with their families over Christmas. And you? What will you be doing?'

Charlotte turned her head to look out the window, although there was nothing to see in the darkness.

'I'll go out to Gran's. Her estate is a good hour out of London. I'll stay with her for Christmas Day, of course, and then it'll be time to face up to what needs facing up to.'

Jendi's cancer. Dio…but it was going to be a difficult time ahead for Charlotte. Nico wanted to reach across the table and catch her hands. To offer to be there for her as a friend in the weeks or months ahead.

But this faux relationship wasn't supposed to continue, was it? Charlotte wouldn't want it to. Having her in a committed relationship with a potential family in the future might be at the top of her grandmother's bucket list but Nico could still hear the vehemence in Charlotte's voice when she'd declared that it was never going to happen.

So he said nothing. Instead, he followed Charlotte's example and stared out of the window. There were sparkles of light swirling outside in a mesmerising kaleidoscope.

'Look at that,' he exclaimed. 'It's snowing. It'll be a white Christmas for some people.'

'I love a white Christmas,' Charlotte said softly. 'It makes you feel like you're living inside a Christmas card. I think the best Christmas I ever had was one where Gran and I got completely snowed in and the electricity went off. We ended up cooking the chipolatas that were supposed to go in with the turkey on sticks on the open fire. I was only about nine but I was so impressed that Gran knew how to do stuff like get the fire going and cook sausages.'

'Sounds special.'

'What's the best Christmas you remember, Nico? Was it white?'

'No. It never snowed in our part of Italy.' Funny that to remember his best Christmas he automatically wiped out any year after he'd been whisked off to Ireland. 'It would get cold, though. I think the best Christmas I can remember was outside. We had a terrace with a long wooden table that was under grapevines. In the summer it was leafy and cool and in the winter there was an open fireplace big enough to roast an ox. For some reason we had Christmas dinner outside that year. Possibly because so many family members had gathered. There were aunts and uncles and cousins I never knew I had.'

'How old were you?'

'About six.'

'Did you have turkey?'

Nico shook his head. 'That wasn't traditional. We have the feast of the seven fishes on Christmas Eve and then on Christmas Day we have lots of pasta and then roast meat like chicken or beef. And potatoes.' He frowned. The food hadn't been what had made that Christmas memorable.

'There was music,' he continued softly. 'My father was at the head of the table and he was *so* happy. Between courses he would drag my mother away from the kitchen and dance with her in front of the fire. There were so many people. So much laughter. So much love…'

'Family.' The word was a whisper and Charlotte's eyes were as bright as he'd ever seen them when Nico turned from the view of the snow. 'It's what Christmas is all about, isn't it?'

'It was once…' Nico had to clear his throat. The memory of that particular Christmas was disturbing because it evoked a yearning he'd thought he'd put behind him many, many years ago. Part of the heartbreak he would never want to inflict on a child. Or a woman. Or have inflicted on himself ever again.

Dessert of a classic plum duff with crème anglaise and brandy butter came and went with a noticeably more sombre mood at their table. It was a relief when a steward came to tell him that Lady Geraldine was ready to be escorted back to her cabin whenever it was convenient for him.

'Or I can arrange another escort?' The steward tilted his head to include Charlotte. 'If you and your fiancé wish to stay longer?'

'No.' It was Charlotte who spoke up quickly. 'We can finish now.' She didn't meet Nico's eyes. 'If that's all right with you, Nico?'

'*Sì.* Of course it is.

The last thing Charlotte expected when she returned to her suite after helping her grandmother get undressed

and settled into her bunk for the night was to find Nico still there.

She had thought he would be long gone. Having a nightcap in the bar and ready to wait until he thought she was safely asleep before coming back to get what rest he could on the seat in this compartment. Not that she expected to get much sleep herself but it would have been a relief to shut the connecting door and have a space entirely to herself for a good few hours. No chance of losing control and making a fool of herself that way.

Now she was distinctly unsettled. Not only was Nico here but he'd taken off his dinner jacket and rolled up the sleeves of his dress shirt. His bow-tie was undone as well, hanging down beside the undone top buttons of his shirt. His hair was rumpled, as if he'd thrust his fingers through it more than once, and it was long enough since he'd shaved to give his jaw a dark shadow. He looked ever so slightly disreputable lounging on the padded upholstery of the seat.

And ultimately desirable.

Maybe that was why Charlotte's words came out more sharply than she'd intended. 'I thought you were going to the bar.'

Nico raised an eyebrow. 'It occurred to me it might be a good idea to wait until Jendi was asleep. What if she wanted to go to the bathroom and saw me abandoning my beautiful fiancée?'

Oh, God…this was getting way beyond a joke. Charlotte had had enough.

'It's not funny, Nico.'

'No…it's not.' Nico got to his feet. 'Shall I tell you the real reason I haven't gone to the bar?'

He took a step closer and Charlotte was pinned by the heat in his gaze. She still had a hand on the door to help her keep her balance as the train rocked, and Nico was swaying on his feet but his gaze didn't waver in the slightest.

She couldn't respond to the question but it didn't seem to matter. Nico was going to tell her anyway.

'I didn't want to,' he growled.

Charlotte didn't have to ask why not. She could see the see the answer in his face. Could feel the flicker of heat spiral deep in her belly. The words forced themselves out anyway, though, as she tried to buy enough time to process what was happening. 'W-why not?'

'Because I wanted this instead.' Nico closed the gap between them. He steadied himself with one hand over Charlotte's against the door but he slid the fingers of his other hand behind her neck and then up into her hair as he cradled her head and dipped his own so that their lips could touch.

His mouth felt familiar now. Safe. Charlotte knew that the touch of his tongue against hers would provide a pleasure so intense it was almost pain but her lips parted eagerly and her tongue met his halfway to begin the dance. And this time the give and take of the kiss changed into more than an exploration and taste of pleasure. This time it had an urgency that demanded more.

And that was enough to make Charlotte pull away. To snatch a gasp of breath and then shake her head.

'I...I don't understand...'

'Yes, you do, *cara*,' Nico said very softly. 'I want you.'

She shook her head again, more insistently. 'But...*why*?'

Nico leaned against the door. He still had a hand cradling her head and she felt his fingers move in a caress. 'Why wouldn't I?'

'Because I'm...not your type. You said so.'

Nico smiled *that* smile. The slow, lazy one. Except that this time it seemed to be gentle. Reassuring? 'I say stupid things sometimes.'

Charlotte had to drop her gaze. Dammit. The train seemed to have picked up speed and the way it was rocking made her more acutely aware of the proximity of Nico's body. Of how it would take nothing for her to fall just a little closer and mould her own body against his.

'This can't go any further,' she said.

'Why not?' The words were a whisper. A question, not an accusation. If she said the word Nico would stop but he genuinely didn't understand, and why would he? He must have seen her own desire for him. He had to be well used to reading those kinds of signals from women.

'Because...' Charlotte couldn't look up. She couldn't stop herself continuing either. Good grief...far from giving her the stamina to maintain control in a difficult situation, the amount of champagne she'd knocked back this evening was having the opposite effect. Her control had slipped so far she'd lost the handle for the door behind which she kept her secret so well shut away. She hadn't been completely honest with Nico earlier, had she? *He* had been with *her*. Guilt bubbled up inside her and something snapped.

'I can't do it,' she whispered. 'I...can't have sex. I'm...' No. There was no way she could utter that horrible word. A shudder went right through her entire body.

Nico's hand slipped out from her hair and he let go of the door. This was it. He was going to excuse himself and go to the bar for a stiff drink, and who could blame him?

But, instead, he gathered Charlotte into his arms and held her close to him. His mouth was close to her ear and he spoke softly.

'You've been hurt, *cara*,' he said. 'I know that. You've been raped, haven't you?'

Charlotte's gasp was shocked. 'No…it…wasn't rape. How could it have been? He was my…my boyfriend. I had chosen to be with him. I'd chosen to go to his apartment. It might have been my first time but I knew what was going to happen.'

For a long moment Nico simply held her in silence. Then he spoke gently. 'But it didn't happen the way you wanted it to, did it?'

'N-no.' Unbelievably, the tears were gathering again. After not having cried for so many years, she was certainly making up for it now.

'And when you wanted him to stop, he wouldn't, would he?'

'H-he said it wasn't his fault if I was frigid. He wasn't going to have his evening ruined by a—a tease.' There. The word had come out all by itself. 'And—and he was right. I hated it and…and when I tried again, more than a year later, with someone else…I couldn't do it…so he—'

'Was a stupid, arrogant bastard,' Nico whispered vehemently. 'Who had no idea what he was talking about and didn't deserve to be in the company of any woman, let alone someone like you.'

Charlotte felt his lips press against the top of her head. And then she felt Nico's hand under her chin and a pressure that made her raise her face to meet his gaze.

'It's not true,' he told her. 'You are a beautiful, *passionate* woman and all you need to do is believe that.'

Maybe there'd always been a glimmer of hope deep inside that that was true. Maybe when she'd tried again, it had been too soon. Or with the wrong person. Charlotte had always thought that she might have conquered her demons if she could have talked to someone professional about it but the shame of anyone knowing had always stopped her.

And now Nico knew. And he was still here.

And he was gorgeous and kind and he'd said that he wanted her.

They wouldn't be seeing each other again after tomorrow so would it really matter if it didn't work. She might never have an opportunity like this again. To find out...

Charlotte licked suddenly dry lips. 'Did you really mean it?' The words were incredibly hard to utter.

'That I want you?' Nico's eyes were so dark they looked black. His hands on her back slid lower until they cupped her bottom. He pulled her even closer so that she had no need of any verbal confirmation of his state of arousal.

'Oh...' Charlotte couldn't look away from his eyes.

'Do you trust me, *cara*?'

She didn't have enough breath to say anything. Instead, Charlotte stretched on tiptoe so that she could reach Nico's lips with her own. She slid her arms

around his neck at the same time as she felt herself being lifted off her feet and carried into the adjoining cabin and a bunk that would simply have to be big enough.

Well...

He'd been right, hadn't he?

Not just about the reason why Charlotte Highton's personality had changed so much.

He'd been right about the fact that she was a beautiful and passionate woman.

It was well after midnight when Nico eased himself out of the bed that was far too small for two people to sleep together comfortably. He got dressed again and let himself quietly out of the cabin with the intention of going to the bar for that long-postponed nightcap.

Charlotte was deeply asleep again, which wasn't surprising. She'd been on an emotional roller-coaster for the last two days and she'd had rather a lot of champagne tonight.

Had he taken advantage of her lack of inhibitions?

Or would she thank him for proving what she should have been able to believe in all along? That there was nothing wrong with her. Nothing she needed to be afraid of or hide from.

That was a minefield in itself. Charlotte was a passionate woman. The way she'd responded to him had been a joy. No...it had been by far the most tender lovemaking he'd ever experienced. So overwhelming that he could only hope Charlotte hadn't noticed she hadn't been the only one with tears wetting her cheeks in the aftermath. The way he'd felt when she'd started to touch him back... To offer herself so completely...

Even now Nico had no idea what to do with the sensations that made it hard to breathe. It had made him feel like he was the most special person on earth. As though she was the only woman in the world he ever wanted to be with again because he would never experience anything like this with anyone else.

He knew how ridiculous that was. The world was full of beautiful women who were eager to share his bed. But Charlotte was naïve in such matters. She might believe he was the only man who could make her feel like that. She might mistakenly believe she had fallen in love with him when she was now capable of having a fulfilling relationship with any man she chose.

It didn't have to be him.

He didn't want it to be him.

So why was he feeling so…uneasy? So in need of a stiff drink?

Because there was a voice in his head that was trying to insist that being with Charlotte for just a little longer wouldn't hurt? That he could, at least, have one more night like last night? Just to check whether it had actually been so extraordinary?

He knew perfectly well how wrong that would be. *That* would, without any doubt, be taking advantage of Charlotte, and Nico had far too much respect for her to even consider it.

The strange sound Nico heard as he made his way through the seemingly deserted carriages in the early hours of the morning only added to his disturbance.

He'd heard that sound before. The cry of a baby who'd only just entered the world.

A newborn on the Orient Express? Impossible.

The echo of that cry of new life stayed with him, though, imagined or not. And Nico didn't like it.

He didn't want a new life.

He wanted his old one back.

CHAPTER NINE

CHARLOTTE KNEW SHE was alone even before she'd surfaced from sleep enough to open her eyes.

Had it been a dream?

Her memories certainly had a dreamlike fuzziness to them. Sensations rather than clear thoughts, and the gentle rocking of the train beneath her seemed to encourage her to close her eyes and explore them. She could feel each one as clearly as if it was happening all over again.

The surprise of finding Nico in the cabin when she'd finally got Gran settled, so closely followed by a breath-robbing fascination generated by seeing him with his shirt buttons undone and his tie hanging loose. As if she'd interrupted him in the process of getting completely undressed…

The explosion of that sensation that had sent shafts of desire into every cell of her body when she'd seen the reflection of her own desire in Nico's eyes. When she'd felt his fingers steadying her head for the kiss that had sent her straight over the edge.

Into that abyss of fear and self-loathing. The feeling of falling without a parachute, knowing that death was

inevitable, as she'd uttered the words that had been her confession of her inadequacies as a woman.

The soft cloud that had gathered and cushioned that fall…first with Nico's words of reassurance and then the physical invitation to see how right they'd been.

And…oh…Charlotte had never known it could be like that. Maybe she'd had fragments of glimpsing it from haunting, erotic dreams but this had been reality.

Or had it?

Shifting a little in her bunk, Charlotte could feel the sweet, inner tenderness that could only be the result of having been passionately loved. With a small sound that was almost a groan, she let herself sink into the last sensation she remembered. Of falling asleep in Nico's arms again but this time feeling as though it was the only place in the world she could ever want to be. Falling asleep with the utter bliss of knowing those arms would still be around her when she woke.

Except they weren't.

How had Nico managed to extricate himself from this tiny space without waking her? He must have been very determined not to, which meant that he'd wanted to be alone.

Why? Did he regret what had happened between them?

Well…why wouldn't he? For heaven's sake, he'd been sucked into her private life because of her meltdowns in front of him. She'd cried all over him. Twice! He'd seen her with her panda eyes and he'd heard all the sordid details of her mortifying past. He must think she was needy and pathetic virtually all the time.

Did he think that she might remain clingy? That she

ALISON ROBERTS 157

would try and keep him in her life longer than the pe-
riod they'd agreed on? Ask him for more than he was
prepared to give?

It was odd but the notion of being seen as pathetic
and clingy was worse than revealing herself as physi-
cally frigid. Nico had shown her that what she'd be-
lieved about herself had been so not true.

What she needed to do was show him that any fears
about how else she might behave were also untrue. She
was in love with him, certainly, but that was *her* prob-
lem. It didn't need to be Nico's and he didn't deserve
it to be. Not after giving her a gift so far beyond price
by restoring her self-esteem.

Creating the magic that had been her night on the
Orient Express.

She would have to thank him, of course, but she had
to do it in a way that let him know he was not under
any further obligation to her. And she needed to make
him believe it. To present herself in a way that showed
confidence and independence. The way she presented
herself at a conference might be a good start.

With a determined shove Charlotte got rid of the bed
covers and climbed out of the bunk. Finding herself
naked was a reality check that made her blush. She'd
never slept naked in her life and the comfort zone of
well-fitting clothes had to be her first priority. Washing
her face in the tiny corner basin a short time later, she
eyed herself in the mirror. The smudged make-up and
rat's-nest hair that advertised a night of totally wanton
behaviour were the next things she had to take control
of. Only then would she be able to face her day.

And Nico.

* * *

He was going to have to face Charlotte at some point. Having caught a few hours' sleep on the seat in the daytime area of the suite and making sure he was not there when Charlotte woke up, Nico had successfully whiled away a good portion of the morning with coffee and newspapers in the bar car.

Brunch was being served already in the dining cars and there was still no sign of Charlotte or Lady Geraldine. It wouldn't be that long before they reached Calais and would have to board the buses for travel to England via the channel tunnel. There would be no private cabins on the train leg to London, during which they would apparently be served afternoon tea, and they would be going in different directions as soon they reached Victoria.

Nico could well imagine how chaotic it was going to be in that huge station on Christmas Eve. It probably wasn't going to be much less private from the time they had to share a bus with dozens of other people. If he wanted a conversation alone with Charlotte, he would have to do something about it now. Clearly, she wasn't planning to come and find *him* this morning.

Their suite was empty and Lady Geraldine's door was closed but Nico tapped on it anyway. It was after ten a.m. Surely Jendi would be up and about by now?

Charlotte opened the door. For a long moment they simply stared at each other. Nico had to process the startling change from when he'd last seen Charlotte, asleep with her glorious hair spread across the crisp, white pillowcase, her lips devoid of any artificial colouring and swollen from so many kisses.

He was facing Dr Highton right now. Dressed in that

power suit he'd first seen her in when she'd been on her way to the symposium. She had her hair scraped back into that complicated knot arrangement that gave her the look of an air hostess and her make-up was perfect. No smudged mascara from tears being shed and her perfect lipstick made it look as though her lips had never been licked, let alone kissed.

And, apart from a flash of something that was gone too quickly to analyse, even her gaze looked professional. Impersonal enough to make Nico take a mental step backwards, at any rate.

'Is everything all right? It's…getting quite late.'

Charlotte wasn't meeting his gaze now. 'I can't believe I slept so late,' she said, loudly enough for her grandmother to overhear. 'No wonder you went off to find some breakfast. There's something about the motion of a train, isn't there? It makes you sleep so well.'

Nico raised an eyebrow. Surely Charlotte would realise that *he'd* had virtually no sleep.

'Is that Nico?' Lady Geraldine called. 'Bring him in, Charlotte Jane, for goodness' sake.'

There wasn't room for three people to sit. Charlotte remained standing as well.

'How are you this morning, Jendi?' Nico enquired politely. 'Did you sleep well, too?'

'Not bad.'

Nico could feel the tension emanating from Charlotte. She didn't believe that and she could be right. Lady Geraldine did look rather pale and she was gripping the windowsill with one hand, as though the movement of the train was making her uncomfortable.

'Apparently there was a baby boy born on the train last night, have you heard?'

'No...*really*?' Lady Geraldine turned and was unable to disguise her wince of pain. She ignored it, however, and her expression suggested that everybody else had better follow her example. 'How do you know?'

'The steward in the bar told me when he gave me the newspapers. He said that we'd be reading about the unexpected event on the Orient Express very soon. I actually heard it crying late in the night when I was walking through the carriage. Apparently the young girl had disguised her condition very well, by wearing a large, old-fashioned coat.'

'Oh...I think I saw that girl at the station in Venice,' Charlotte said.

'What on earth were you doing, walking around the train in the middle of the night?' Lady Geraldine asked.

'I needed to stretch my legs,' Nico said, after a moment's awkward silence. 'The bunks are...rather small, aren't they?'

'Depends on what you're doing.' Lady Geraldine managed a smile. 'I'm delighted that Charlotte felt the need to sleep in, I must say. It's probably been years since she hasn't been up at the crack of dawn.'

There was a very noticeable flush of colour on Charlotte's cheeks now and when she flicked a glance towards Nico the shutters were down. She was most definitely thinking about what had kept her awake last night. The relief at seeing what he now knew to be the real Charlotte peeping out was enough to make him try and hold that gaze. And convey the message in his smile that he agreed it was well worth remembering. Unforgettable might be closer to the mark.

'Oh, for heaven's sake...' Lady Geraldine flapped a hand at them. 'Go and make sheep's eyes at each other

in your own cabin and leave an old lady in peace.' The tone was authoritative but she was still smiling as she delivered the order.

Charlotte looked as though she was about to refuse but then shook her head and signalled Nico to go ahead of her. He stepped into their suite and she barrelled in straight after him, closing the door behind her.

'I don't want to leave her too long,' she said. 'I'm pretty sure she's not feeling nearly as well as she's trying to make out.' Biting her lip, Charlotte stared down at her hands. 'I *think* she wants me out of the way so she can take another dose of her painkillers.'

'Is there anything I can do to help?'

'I don't think so.' Charlotte shook her head. 'But… thank you…'

Nico had the distinct impression that the hesitation meant that Charlotte had something else she wanted to say. So he waited. Sure enough, her chin rose as she took a very deep breath.

'I don't mean just for offering to help with Gran…' The movement of Charlotte's facial muscles suggested acute embarrassment. 'Thank you for…you know…'

Nico raised an eyebrow. Was this it? So much for fearing that Charlotte might think she'd fallen in love with him! Was last night going to be a polite 'Thank you' and 'You're most welcome' kind of exchange?

He felt distinctly piqued even though he knew he should be relieved. But it deserved something more than that, surely?

He stepped closer. Close enough for them to be breathing the same air. He bent his head as if he was about to kiss her but stopped halfway there.

'I can assure you it was very much my pleasure.'

Her eyes widened and he heard her catch her breath but then she stepped back. Only a tiny step, admittedly, but it was enough to send a very clear message. Charlotte didn't want to be kissed again this morning. And there was enough tension in the air to make Nico wonder if she was trying to get back into her old comfort zone. That might explain the way she was dressed and the hairstyle that defied anyone to try and run their fingers through those long tresses.

'Don't....' The word escaped from him as a whisper. A soft groan almost.

'D-don't what?' she stuttered.

Nico had to close his eyes for a heartbeat. He hadn't intended saying this but maybe it needed to be said. 'Don't dismiss last night as a one-off.'

Oh... *Dio*...would she think he was asking to see her again?

Maybe he was...

With a mental shake Nico forced a smile to his lips. 'Don't ever stop believing that you're special. That what you have to offer would be more than enough for any man you chose to be with.' He straightened his spine and tried to keep his smile from faltering. 'There's a whole world of men out there, Charlotte. You'll find someone one day and you'll know he's the person you want to share your life with. Don't let your past hold you back.'

She was nodding. Blinking hard as though determined not to cry. And when she spoke, her voice was remarkably strong.

'Back at you, Nico Moretti.' Okay, her smile was a bit wobbly. 'Don't be afraid to fall in love in someone or let your past hold *you* back. You need to trust your-

self and find someone who can appreciate all you have
to offer because…it's a lot.'

Find someone?

Someone else, she meant.

It was Nico's turn to nod. To smile. This extraordi-
nary connection they had was because they'd shared
things they'd never shared with others. It was a new
experience—much as this train journey was new. To-
tally unrelated to normal life and it couldn't be ex-
pected to continue. They both knew that. At least, this
way, they could part with special memories of their
brief time together.

Charlotte was twisting the ring on her finger. 'I
should give this back,' she said.

'There's no rush.' Nico shrugged. 'Despite your wise
words, I'm not about to go hunting for a wife. And even
if I found someone, I don't really think she'd want to
wear such an old-fashioned ring.'

'It's a beautiful ring,' Charlotte said immediately.
'A family heirloom. A symbol of what's held you back
even. *I'd* wear it.'

'You *are* wearing it.' He had to smile. 'Not that I
gave you much choice about that.'

Charlotte's breath came out in a huff. 'I mean, you'd
have to make sure that whoever you really give it to
understands its significance. The promise. You'd have
to tell her everything you told me.'

As if he was ever going to find someone to share
soul-deep secrets with again. Once was enough. Like
this train journey.

They were both staring at the ring.

'I'll have to take it off as soon as I get back to work,'

Charlotte said. 'I wouldn't be able to wear a ring like this even if I *was* engaged.'

'There's no rush,' Nico said again. 'Just see how things go with your *nonna*. You know where I work.'

Charlotte nodded again. 'At the Hammersmith, yes?'

'Yes. And it doesn't matter if I'm not there for some reason. You could just leave it with my secretary.'

'But...' There was a lot not being said here. About how long she might want to keep up the pretence. How long it would take for her grandmother to die. Her lips trembled. 'But it's precious...'

'I trust you.'

It wasn't hard to sound sincere. He'd trusted Charlotte with far more than a family heirloom, hadn't he?

The only sound for a long moment was the clack of the train wheels. Rhythmic and steady. Like a heartbeat. And then Charlotte raised her eyes.

'I trust you, too,' she whispered.

That was a lot bigger than the trust he'd placed in her, even by confessing what he knew could be seen as an inadequacy. Being a commitment-phobic male was far more socially acceptable than the stigma of having been labelled a frigid woman. Or having been raped. He was holding a secret that could potentially wreck her carefully ordered world. It was huge.

A gift that no one else could have given him.

Like the one he'd given her by showing her that it wasn't true? Being the man who'd had the privilege of holding her as she'd come apart in someone's arms for the first time?

They were even. Equals.

And, as long as he didn't do something stupid and make a fool of himself, they could keep this respect

for each other. Part as friends. They would get back to reality and their own lives soon enough.

It was time to lighten the atmosphere.

'I'm hungry,' Nico announced. 'Would you care for breakfast in the dining car?'

'Gran's ordered cabin service. I need to stay with her and see if she actually eats anything. You go.'

So the separation was to begin already. The countdown was on.

Fine. Nico knew that was sensible. What they both wanted. There would be plenty to distract them for the rest of the day because it was unlikely that they would be alone again together. They would probably never be alone together again. This was it. The last intimate moment he would have with Charlotte Highton.

He had to kiss her. Just a soft farewell.

'I won't forget.' It was a promise. A deliberately ambiguous one. Charlotte could assume he was talking about her wise words regarding his future. She didn't have to know that he meant *her*.

Her quiet words followed him like an echo that seemed to be picked up by the train wheels as he made his way to the dining car.

'I won't either.'

The rest of the journey seemed interminable.

Lady Geraldine was keeping up a brave face but she ate virtually nothing of her brunch and didn't touch the champagne or afternoon tea on the English leg of the trip. The weather was cold enough to make her look pinched and it was clearly a struggle to join the excited conversations around them that were predicting

a genuine white Christmas as fat snowflakes began to fall more and more heavily.

'I'm just tired, love,' she told Charlotte. 'But I wouldn't have changed anything about the last couple of days. Not a thing.'

And Charlotte had been able to smile back and tell her grandmother that she felt exactly the same.

Victoria was heaving with people desperate to get to where they wanted to be for Christmas Day. It was Nico who helped collect their luggage and carve a pathway through the crowd to where Lady Geraldine's chauffeur had arranged to meet them.

They offered Nico a lift but he declined with palpable regret.

'I've made an appointment with a colleague at the Hammersmith,' he told them. 'You need to go in the opposite direction and it'll be bad enough already. I hope you don't get caught in a traffic jam or the snow. If I can't find a cab, I'll take the tube.'

He took Charlotte in his arms to say goodbye. For her grandmother's sake? Was that why he said that he was going to miss her and that seeing her again couldn't be too soon for him?

It wasn't why Charlotte returned his kiss and agreed that it couldn't be too soon for her either.

She meant every word.

The bleak feeling of watching the crowd swallow Nico only got stronger as they inched their way out of London.

Lady Geraldine took her hand and gave it a squeeze.

'I know it's hard, darling. It's such a shame that Nico's going to be so busy for a while.'

'Mmm…'

'You're lucky, though.'

'Oh?' Thank goodness her grandmother couldn't possibly have any idea of just *how* lucky her grand-daughter had been.

'Yes. Much luckier than back in my day. You've got your mobile phones and…and Scope.'

Charlotte smiled despite herself as she sighed. 'Skype, Gran.'

'Whatever.' Her hand got another squeeze. 'It's not quite the same as the real thing, though, is it?'

'No. It's not.' There was an odd pain in Charlotte's chest as she tried to draw in a new breath.

Her heart starting to break perhaps?

CHAPTER TEN

CHARLOTTE'S FAVOURITE CHRISTMAS ever had been the one she'd told Nico about when they'd been snowed in and Gran had cooked sausages on sticks over the open fire in the drawing room.

Maybe, some time in the future, somebody would ask her about her *least* favourite Christmas and she knew that, coincidentally, it would also be one of the rare, truly white ones.

This one.

She stared out of the V-shaped gap in the snow piled on the sill of her latticed window and there was the eerie, early morning light that only a thick blanket of snow could create. There was nothing to disturb the perfection of the Christmas-card scene in the gardens of Highton Hall. The footprints on the lawn below had probably been made by a fox but if her grandmother had seen them in years gone by, she would have told a small Charlotte that they were the tracks left by Santa's reindeer.

The thought should have brought a poignant smile to her face but instead Charlotte felt the lump in her throat get bigger.

She had never felt this…bleak.

This lonely.

This...*empty*.

As if she'd lost something huge that she would never have back again. Like her heart? Or maybe it was part of her soul. The part that she'd shared with Nico. Yes. That's what it felt like. He had brought light into the darkest part of her being and, by touching it, it had somehow become his, even if he didn't want it.

Was that what love was? Giving away the most important part of yourself?

No... Charlotte found her picture-perfect view becoming blurry. It was finding someone who recognised that part. Accepted it. Made it better than it had been before simply by being there.

And it wasn't one-sided, that had been the clincher. Nico had shared that part of himself with her. The lonely little boy who was still there deep inside. The one who'd been hurt and had seen people he loved get hurt, and was determined to never be the cause of such hurt himself.

Nico thought he didn't know what he needed. That he couldn't possibly make the right choice of a person to be with for the rest of his life. He thought he was incapable of falling in love.

And maybe he had the kind of strength to hold himself back from that kind of surrender but it was blindingly obvious what he needed.

A tiny robin, its bright red breast a decoration in itself, fluttered into view and landed on the windowsill, tilting its head and to give Charlotte a cheeky glance.

'He just needs what we all need,' she informed the robin. 'To be loved.'

The robin fluttered off like an echo of laughter.

As if it was that simple…

It was. Charlotte had found that person, hadn't she? She had given him that part of herself she could never give to anyone else.

But it was that impossibly difficult at the same time.

Because finding someone that you connected with at a soul-deep level wasn't enough. They had to feel the same way or it could never begin to work.

And Nico didn't feel the same way. How could he when they'd only known each other for a couple of days?

But he didn't even want to *see* her again. Good grief, he'd told her that she could leave the ring with his secretary, if he wasn't around.

It had meant nothing. A bit of harmless pretence to make an old lady happy before she died. Repayment for the imagined debt of losing her laptop. A bonus of a one-night stand as well?

Charlotte forced herself to move. She couldn't stand here dwelling on how miserable she felt. It was Christmas Day after all. And her toes were freezing. Dressing quickly, she chose clothes for warmth, donning black woollen leggings and an oversized crimson pullover on top of a black bodysuit. No doubt her grandmother would expect her to change for dinner but that was a few hours away yet and it would be warmer downstairs when the open fires were stoked up.

Maybe Christmas dinner wasn't so far away after all. The rich aroma of roasting meat caught Charlotte's nostrils as she went downstairs. Betty, the cook, must be busy in the kitchen, probably under Gran's strict supervision. Charlotte would probably be given a laden

plate of bacon and eggs and an admonishment about the perils of laziness and sleeping in.

The Christmas tree in the huge foyer of this grand old house had coloured lights twinkling merrily and there were gifts beneath, enticingly wrapped in pretty paper and tied with bows of satin ribbon.

It looked like one of the festive pictures that had played against the wall of that Venetian restaurant... good grief, only three days ago? On the evening when she'd given in to the temptation of pretending that Nico was her lover. When she'd accidentally become 'engaged' to him.

The ring was still on her finger. Touching it, Charlotte found she could twist it more easily now. Because she was away from the efficient central heating of the Orient Express and in a huge, chilly ancestral home?

Or was it because she felt so cold inside? So bleak...

Whatever. She couldn't take it off yet, could she? Not on Christmas Day, when it would be the first thing Gran would notice. She would have to find a solution to this situation but not today.

And she couldn't let Gran see how miserable she was either. Pasting what she hoped was a bright smile on her face, Charlotte walked past the Christmas tree and went down the long hallway to the kitchen.

Betty was basting an enormous turkey. Her husband, John, was polishing silver serviette rings over newspaper spread on one end of the kitchen table. Her daughter was peeling Brussels sprouts and scoring an X into the stalks.

'I was just about to put some breakfast on trays and bring it up,' Betty said after Christmas greetings had been exchanged. 'I was getting worried.'

'Has Gran not been down yet?'

'Not a peep from her. And she's always the first up on Christmas Day.'

'I'll take her up a cup of tea,' Charlotte said. She was worried herself now. 'I expect she's just tired out after her big adventure.'

'You look a bit peaky yourself, pet.' Betty and her family had been a part of Highton Hall for as long as Charlotte could remember. They were more like relatives than staff. Family. Charlotte's smile was genuine this time.

'I'm fine, Betty. I just need a cup of tea, too.'

Betty had been patting her hand. Her jaw dropped.

'Oh…my…. Is that what I *think* it is?'

Charlotte held up her hand and the diamond flashed as it caught the light. Her heart sank. The game had to go on a little longer no matter how much worse it was going to make her feel.

'I guess I had a bit of an adventure myself, Betty. You'll hear all about it as soon as Gran's up, I'm sure.'

'I'd better.' Betty busied herself with a teapot and a china cup and saucer. She added a couple of tiny gingerbread stars to the saucer. 'Go on…tell Lady G that we're waiting to hear all about it.'

Her grandmother's bedroom was still dark.

'You awake, Gran? I've got a cup of tea for you.' Charlotte balanced the cup in one hand as she drew back the heavy drapes to let the bright, mid-morning light into the room.

And then she turned, and didn't notice how much tea she was spilling on the Persian carpet as she raced to her grandmother's bedside and dropped the cup and

saucer on the bedside table. Gingerbread stars floated in a saucer full of tea.

'*Gran...*'

Lady Geraldine was lying with her knees pulled up and the bedcover gripped between clenched fists. Her face was white with a sheen of perspiration on her forehead. Her pulse was racing. And weak. Her abdomen was swollen and hard to the touch. And it only took the lightest touch to make her cry out in agony.

'Oh...*God...*' Charlotte picked up the phone beside the half-empty cup of tea. She dialled only three numbers.

'I need an ambulance,' she said crisply as soon as her call was answered. 'It's urgent.'

Emergencies like heart attacks and strokes were no respecters of what day it happened to be.

Extreme weather was more of a problem on days when people simply had to be somewhere else for an important occasion and the number of accidents rose.

And there were plenty of people like him who had no family to be with and no desire to celebrate Christmas and carried on with stupid behaviour like getting into fights and getting beaten up or stabbed.

Worst of all, there were the people who found the season too much of a reminder of what they didn't have so the rate of attempted suicides always went up, too.

It was not a good day to be in charge of an emergency department but the staff always did their absolute best to make it as cheerful as possible, and Nico had always managed to join in and encourage them.

Why was it *so* hard this year?

Why did he feel so...bleak?

So…*empty*?

It was *ridicolo*. Ridiculous.

He had his life back the way he wanted it to be. *Needed* it to be.

So why did he feel so off-kilter? So *perduto*, almost?

And why was it always Italian words that came into his head when something stirred him deeply? The past was behind him and best forgotten. Even dredging up happy memories, such as the favourite Christmas he'd shared with Charlotte, was not a good thing to do. No wonder he couldn't settle into doing what he most loved to do and lose himself in the demands of his work.

He would go and do another thorough neurological check on the elderly gentleman in cubicle three who had fallen when he'd gone outside to sweep snow off the steps in preparation for his family arriving. He'd hit his head hard enough to need a period of observation before they could consider letting him go home to his Christmas dinner. Maybe it hadn't just been the slippery steps and the fall responsible for him losing consciousness either. Perhaps a more thorough cardiovascular work-up would be justified.

Imagine what would have happened in Venice if Charlotte hadn't been there to see beyond what others had seen?

'Incoming, Dr Moretti,' a nurse told him as she hurried past. 'Eighty-something-year-old female with an abdominal mass and acute bowel obstruction. She's tachycardic, short of breath and vomiting. GCS of thirteen.'

Dio… An elderly woman with a bowel obstruction that could potentially be due to a tumour? Was every-

thing today going to remind him of either Charlotte or her *nonna*? They were probably sitting in front of an open fire right now. Drinking mulled wine or eggnog, perhaps and listening to Christmas carols. Maybe there was a piano and Charlotte would be playing carols. Or maybe they were opening their gifts to each other.

Or…maybe something terrible had happened. Nico could see the ambulance team coming through the doors of his department now. He couldn't see much of the figure on the stretcher because she was bundled up in warm blankets and her face was covered by an oxygen mask. The person holding the bag of IV fluids aloft wasn't part of the paramedic crew, however.

It was Charlotte.

No. Could this be the beginning of the end for Jendi? Surely not today, of all days…

'Resus One,' Nico ordered, before the triage nurse had a chance to consider priority. 'And get a surgical consult down here stat.'

He ushered the entourage into the resus area reserved for major cases. There was no time for any more than brief eye contact with Charlotte as Nico listened to the handover from the paramedics and prepared to launch an investigative and stabilisation protocol that could deal with this emergency. There was no way he was going to let Lady Geraldine Highton die in his department on Christmas Day.

As awful as it was, this was just the kind of challenge he'd needed. That disturbing, *empty* feeling had completely vanished and Nico had never felt more in control. Or more determined to do his absolute best for his patient. And her family.

* * *

The waiting was the worst.

At least all the tension and drama and fear since the moment she'd found Gran in such a dreadful state had been balanced by the swiftness of action and the company of others. The paramedics had been brilliant, using a four-wheel-drive vehicle to get to the estate and then transferring Gran to a faster ambulance to get her into the city. The roads had been appalling with all the snow and traffic jams from a big accident on the M1. They'd had to stick to routes that had been cleared in the city and get to an emergency department that was not only open on Christmas Day but prepared to accept a major case.

It had taken too much time and all the while Lady Geraldine's condition had been deteriorating. It was becoming hard for her to breathe and her level of consciousness was slipping. By the time they'd arrived at the totally unexpected destination of the Hammersmith—*Nico's* hospital—she was unconscious and the situation was looking bad enough for Charlotte to be unaware of anything except the relief of getting to a place where they might be able to help her grandmother.

And then there'd been the drama of trying to get Gran stable enough for the surgeon to consider that operating might be an option on an eighty-two-year-old woman. There'd been fluid resuscitation and ventilation assistance, blood tests and scans and ECGs. People rushing in and out with the kind of controlled chaos Charlotte was all too familiar with, but this was her *gran* being treated and she'd never felt less like a doctor.

Waiting like this in an area set aside for the families of patients undergoing surgery was a new experience too. It was nerve-racking and felt interminable. There were only one or two theatres being used for absolute emergencies today and just a skeleton staff on duty so it felt like she was completely alone and she'd been here for what felt like hours. Surely the surgery was over by now? Why hadn't someone come to tell her what was going on?

Had they forgotten she was even here?

No… Charlotte could hear footsteps echoing in the wide, empty hallway outside. Coming closer. Someone was coming to see her and what they had to say could possibly be devastating news.

She couldn't move. Could only stand there, with her fingers pressed against her mouth to stifle a cry. Afraid to breathe. Unable to blink even.

And then a tall figure filled the doorway. A powerful presence entered the small space of the waiting room and…

And Charlotte wasn't alone any more.

'Carlotta…*cara*…' Nico gathered Charlotte into his arms and held her close. '*Grazie a Dio ho trovato voi.*'

He'd had to come even though he had no real news for her yet. Standing there, in the observation deck of the operating theatre, it had come back with a vengeance.

That empty feeling.

Had it really been the challenge of fighting for Jendi's life that had made it go away? The focus on medicine that was the most important thing in his life? Or

had it had been because Charlotte was so close to him again?

He had to find out. His shift in the emergency department was finished and there would be no professional distraction for him now. If he found Charlotte and that empty feeling disappeared then he would know the truth.

And it had. *Dio mio*, but it had evaporated like mist in hot Italian sunshine as soon as he'd gathered her in his arms and held her close to his heart.

The truth was irrefutable. It wasn't work he needed like the oxygen in the air he breathed. It was this woman. *Charlotte*. Without her, he would have that horrible, empty feeling for the rest of his life.

'*Carlotta...*' The word was a breath that got lost in her hair.

'I don't understand,' she said.

Neither did Nico. But it was wonderful. So joyous.

'I can't speak Italian, Nico...' She was wriggling in his arms, pulling back so she could see his face. 'What's happening?' Her breath was a fearful gulp. 'Where's Gran?'

How could he be so selfish? Nico stroked her hair and focused enough to change languages.

'There's a break in surgery. They're doing a biopsy of the tumour. It will be a bigger operation if they decide to try and remove it all and it would be too much of a risk if it's...'

She knew what he was saying. If the tumour was aggressively malignant, they would only attempt a palliative procedure to deal with the bowel obstruction.

But Charlotte's eyes had widened. 'The surgeon

thinks there's a chance it's not malignant? That it's…
benign?'

Was it cruel to give her hope or a gift that he could
share with her for at least a little while? The point was
moot because she knew the answer. They wouldn't be
interrupting surgery for the length of time it took to
use a technician on Christmas Day if it wasn't a good
possibility.

'Are you going back? Can you find out?'

Nico shook his head. 'They'll come and tell us. I
want to wait here with you. I…I *have* to.'

'You *have* to?' Charlotte's tone was as odd as his
had been. A note of wonder? *'Why?'*

'Because…' There was no point in being less than
honest with her. There never had been and never would
be. 'Because being with you…it makes the empty feel-
ing go away.'

'Oh…' Charlotte's gaze was holding his and he
could actually see it melting. Getting misty. 'It does…
It *so* does, doesn't it?'

'*You* feel it too?' A surge of emotion was threaten-
ing to explode inside Nico's chest. Gratitude? Relief?
Hope? No. It was bigger than any of those. 'I've never
felt like this,' he confessed. 'I don't know what this
is…but it's…it's…'

'I think it's love,' Charlotte whispered. 'I'm in love
with you and that's why I have the empty feeling when
you're not here.'

'I'm in love with you…' Nico tested the words out
loud. Strange and new but…yes…they felt right. He
tried them in Italian to make sure. *'Cara mia, innamo-
rata di te.'*

And that made them real but still unbelievable. 'How?' he whispered. 'How did this happen? So fast?'

'I don't know...' But Charlotte was smiling. Almost laughing, but there were tears in her eyes at the same time. 'But it's Christmas...and it's the most wonderful gift I could ever have been given. I love you so much, Nico. I've never felt like this before. It feels like everything that's ever happened to me, even all the bad things, were worth it because it led me here. To *you*.'

He had to kiss her then. Slowly. Tenderly. The bursting feeling inside him intensified and turned to molten joy. It was a long time before he could lift his head to look into Charlotte's eyes again.

'When I was in Venice,' Nico told her with a smile, 'a moment or two before I saw you at the accident scene I was having to push my way through the crowd and I heard this old woman and you know what she said?'

'No.' Charlotte was smiling up at him. A tear escaped and Nico let go of one of her hands so that he could brush it away for her. 'What did she say?'

'That it was almost Christmas. A good time for a miracle to happen. I think that's what this is, Carlotta. A miracle.'

Charlotte sniffed and the sound was so unromantic that Nico could feel himself fall even deeper in love with her. Had he really thought he was incapable of doing this? He was good at it. With a bit of practice he would be the best.

When Charlotte scrubbed at her nose, he caught her hand. The one with the ring on it. He seemed to remember it had been quite a struggle to get it onto her finger but it came off quite easily.

Charlotte went very, very still.

'You know what this is.' Nico had to clear the sudden gruffness of his voice away. 'Of all the people in the world, you are the only one who can know the symbolism of this ring. The…' His voice cracked again. 'The promise it carries.'

Her gaze clung to his. Her head dipped and rose again in a slow, solemn nod.

'I didn't give you a choice about wearing it before,' Nico continued. 'I'm giving you that choice now. Will you wear this ring, *inamorata*? Will you accept my promise?'

'Oh…*yes*, Nico.' Her hand was shaking as she held it out for him to slip the ring back on her finger. 'But…'

He stilled her words with a gentle finger on her lips. 'It's like your *nonna* said,' he murmured. 'It doesn't mean we have to get married next week. It's a promise of commitment. We can take all the time we need to make sure it's perfect.'

The sound of footsteps outside the waiting room sent a sudden chill down Nico's spine. Someone was coming to give them news.

What if it was bad news?

The only way this could be truly perfect would be to have Jendi at their wedding, wouldn't it? To see her, at some point in the future, cradle her first greatgrandchild in her arms.

To know that the biggest thing on that bucket list of hers had been well and truly ticked off.

It was the surgeon, who'd come straight from Theatre to find them. He'd stripped off his gown and gloves but he was still in his scrubs and white gumboots. He still had a hat covering his head and neck.

But he was smiling. 'Your gran's a real trouper,' he

told Charlotte. 'Tough as old boots, in fact. She's come through this astonishingly well. You'll be able to go and see her in Recovery very soon.'

'Oh…thank God…' Charlotte was clinging to Nico's hand with a vice-like grip. 'And…and the tumour?'

'Benign. We got it all out. Can't see any reason why she won't keep ticking along for a good few years yet.' The surgeon's smile widened. 'Merry Christmas.'

Charlotte was sobbing in his arms now. Nico had tears on his own face.

Buon Natale, indeed.

The best ever, without a doubt.

EPILOGUE

CHRISTMAS WAS LONG GONE.

Lady Geraldine Highton didn't remember it at all. She remembered Venice, of course, and the magic of the Orient Express journey. How could she ever forget when it had made her most cherished dream come true? Her beloved Charlotte had found the love of her life.

And here they were, in the gardens of Highton Hall, in the springtime. Surrounded by daffodils and blue-bells with the gentle perfume of apple blossom and tiny puffs of cloud in an otherwise blue sky making this day perfect.

Their wedding day.

They'd waited until she was fully recovered, bless them, and these last few months had been a gift in themselves. She hadn't been allowed to rely solely on the wonderful care Betty had co-ordinated. They'd both moved into Highton Hall themselves, despite the hassle of commuting to London for their busy working lives.

And somehow Nico had got out of all those overseas commitments that had threatened to keep him and Charlotte apart for the foreseeable future. They hadn't had to rely on that new-fangled Scope thing at all. It

had been, in fact, as if they couldn't bear to be apart from each other for a heartbeat longer than they had to.

And when they were together, they couldn't keep their hands off each other. Not that anyone minded today, of course. It was only expected that they would link hands when Charlotte had wound her way through the chairs set out in the bluebell woods under the ancient oak trees to join her husband-to-be in front of the celebrant. That Nico had immediately bent his head to place a lingering kiss on her lips might have been a tad premature but…he was Italian. What could one say?

And it wasn't as if Charlotte was wearing a veil to cover her face. She may have chosen a traditional, stunning white dress that made her look beautiful enough to bring a tear to anybody's eye, but she'd left her hair loose and flowing.

It had been a joke when Geraldine had offered her beloved tiara as the 'something borrowed' but there it was, sparkling in her blonde hair as a shaft of sunlight found a way through the unfurling leaves of the oak trees. A glint of silver on her wrist was the only other adornment Charlotte had chosen. That tiny ring of hearts that had the emblem of the Orient Express engraved on its catch.

Geraldine eyed the rings on her own fingers as she smoothed the skirt of her lovely new pink silk dress. Maybe she should tone down her own accessories? No. That would be tantamount to curbing all sorts of things. Acting her age even, and that would never do, would it?

She had to shift a little on her chair in the front seat as the proceedings started. There were still moments of discomfort as she recovered from the major abdom-

inal surgery that had removed that thankfully benign growth but she would never complain.

This was more than a bonus of time that she hadn't expected to have.

What had occurred during this last Christmas season had been the most amazing gift ever.

Although…

She'd interrupted something last night. A moment between Charlotte and Nico that had looked like more than an intimate goodnight on the eve of their wedding. Nico had had the palm of his hand on Charlotte's belly. She'd had her hand resting on top of his and the look they'd been giving each other was one of those that could speak volumes.

She hadn't let on that she'd seen them.

And she certainly wouldn't advertise the fact that her bucket list now had a new item on the top.

She was already the luckiest woman in the world, even though she knew her granddaughter would dispute that title. It would be her secret that she would be keeping her fingers crossed for another amazing gift next Christmas.

A gift they could all share.

A *baby*…

* * * * *

CALLIE'S
CHRISTMAS WISH

MERLINE LOVELACE

Many, many thanks to Machaelie Halsey,
who let me pick her brain about counseling
techniques during lunch at Chili's, then read
several chapters while we were cooking Easter
dinner. Thanks, too, Christy Gronlund, who
filled me in on the joys and stresses of Children's
Advocacy. You both made this book so rich in
detail and rewarding for me to write.

Chapter One

It started with the fountain.

That damned Trevi Fountain.

Callie and her two best friends *had* to take a long-dreamed-of trip to Italy this past September. Then she and Dawn and Kate *had* to defy the tradition that said just tossing a coin in the fountain would bring them back to Rome someday. Oh, no. The centuries-old tradition wasn't good enough. They *had* to make separate, secret wishes.

Kate's came true while the three friends were still in Italy, when she and her husband reconciled mere weeks away from a divorce. Dawn didn't realize her wish had been granted until she was back in the States and acting as surrogate nanny for a lively six-year-old. A few short weeks later, the laughing, flirtatious redhead had made the surprising and completely unexpected leap from carefree bachelorette to deliriously happy mother to Tommy and wife to hunky Brian Ellis.

Callie had made a wish in Rome, as well. One she hadn't shared with anyone. Not even her BFFs. It was too silly, too frivolous. And so not in keeping with her usual level-headed self.

That ridiculous wish was coming back to haunt her now. Every part of her thrummed with nervous anticipation as she helped Dawn and Tommy loop fresh pine boughs into Christmas wreaths for the doors of the Ellises' home. Luckily, the determined efforts of Tommy's three-month-old wheaten terrier pup to get into the action kept both the boy and Dawn so amused that neither noticed Callie jump when the doorbell rang.

The sound of the bell sent the pup into an immediate frenzy. His butt end whipped around. His claws skittered on the pine plank flooring. High-pitched yelps split the air as he careened out of the kitchen and down a hallway fragrant with the scent of the cloves and cinnamon and oranges in the Christmas potpourri.

"That'll be Joe."

Pushing to her feet, Dawn dusted the pine needles from the moss-colored turtleneck that clung to her generous curves and made her eyes appear an even deeper shade of emerald.

"His message said his plane would touch down at three and he'd be here by four." She slanted Callie a sly look. "Tall, dark, handsome *and* punctual. What more could a girl ask for?"

Nothing, Callie agreed, her stomach fluttering. Not a single, solitary thing.

Except…maybe…

There it was! That absurd coin toss again. How juvenile to wish Joe would let just a tiny smidgen of romance sneak through his solid, masculine, don't-mess-with-me-or-mine exterior. Hadn't he put his highly lucrative

business interests on hold for her? Devoted considerable time and expense to tracking down the source of the ugly emails she'd begun receiving a few weeks before the trip to Italy? Shaking her head at her own foolishness, Callie followed Dawn, the wildly yipping terrier and Tommy down the hall.

"Joe promised he'd bring me a real, live boomerang from Australia," the boy reminded them as he charged for the door. "Hope he remembered it!"

He would. Callie didn't doubt it for a second. In the few short months she'd known Joe Russo, she'd come to realize that nothing ever escaped the steel trap of his mind.

They'd first met during a never-to-be-forgotten jaunt to Venice. At the time Joe headed a highly specialized personal security team guarding Carlo Luigi Francesco di Lorenzo, aka the Prince of Lombard and Marino, who also happened to be one of Italy's most decorated air force pilots. Carlo, Kate's husband, Travis, and Dawn's now-husband, Brian, had been involved in testing some hush-hush, super-secret modification to NATO special ops aircraft flying sorties from a base in northern Italy.

Callie and Joe had met again in Rome, when Travis surprised Kate with an elegant ceremony to renew their marriage vows. At that damned fountain! It must have been the stars in Kate's eyes as she reaffirmed her love. Or the mischievous sparkle in Dawn's when she announced she was flying home with the Ellises to assume duties as Tommy's stand-in nanny. Whatever the impetus, Callie gave in to her friends' urging that they all toss one last coin over their shoulders. Which was when she'd made that stupid, *stupid* wish.

Not ten minutes later, she'd found herself separated

from her friends and yielding to Joe Russo's quiet but relentless interrogation. As she'd soon discovered, the man hadn't transitioned from military cop to soldier of fortune to head of one of the world's most exclusive personal protection agencies without learning how to extract secrets from even the most reluctant interviewees.

He'd watched her, Joe had revealed. Saw how her shoulders braced every time she checked her email. Noted, too, how her eyes would flicker with distress before she withdrew even farther into her seemingly serene shell.

Callie tried to deny it. Tried to shrug aside his laser-sharp perceptions. She was too used to safeguarding the privacy of the children she'd represented as an ombudsman for the Massachusetts Office of the Child Advocate to spill their—or her—secrets. At that point Joe reminded her that she'd walked away from her job some weeks ago. He also pointed out that he could tap into any legal and/or law enforcement agencies necessary to resolve whatever was scaring the crap out of her.

Callie still couldn't believe she'd broken down and told him about the threatening emails before she'd shown them to Kate and Dawn. Neither could her two best friends, for that matter. They'd let her know what they thought about that in some pretty forceful terms. But they got over their snit in short order and promptly threw a protective shield around her.

First, Kate insisted Callie stay with her in DC after their return from Italy. Then, when Dawn married and moved out of the elegant gatehouse designed for Tommy's live-in nanny, *she'd* insisted Callie take up residence there while Joe investigated the emails. And when the emails escalated from ugly to really scary, Joe tried to hustle her into protective custody.

Callie had drawn the line at that. She was staying in DC, hundreds of miles from her Boston home. She had four fierce watchdogs in the persons of Kate and Dawn and their spouses guarding her day and night. She'd turned over every threatening communication to the authorities, and Joe had exercised the legal system to gain access to the juvenile court cases she'd worked.

Enough was enough.

But her heart had still pounded each time she checked her emails. It pounded even harder every time Joe called or flew in to update her on his investigation. The kiss he'd laid on her last time he was in DC might also have something to do with the fact that she was holding her breath while Tommy yanked open the front door.

"Hi, Joe. Didja bring the boomerang? Didja?"

"You bet."

One of Joe's rare smiles flickered across his face. His cheeks creased, almost hiding the scar slashing down the left side. All Callie knew was that it was the legacy of a mission he wouldn't talk about to anyone, not even to Brian, Travis or Carlo. The angry red slash had faded in the past few months but still drew occasional startled glances.

Callie barely noticed it anymore. The rest of the package was too compelling. The broad shoulders now encased in a leather bomber jacket that had seen its share of wear, the square chin, the ice-gray eyes, the dark brown hair with its barest hint of a curl.

"Don't forget what I told you," Joe instructed as he stepped through the door and handed over a package wrapped in brown paper. "It's not a toy."

"I remember! Boomerangs are more than ten thousand years old. The aber...um...abra..."

"Aborigines."

"Yeah. The aborigines used to hunt with 'em."

While the boy tore at the brown paper, Joe nodded hello to Dawn before shifting his gaze to Callie. In their short time together, she'd discovered that his silvery eyes could turn as opaque and impenetrable as a Massachusetts coastal fog when he wanted, which was most of the time. But they glinted now with a triumph so clear and sharp that she knew instantly his sudden trip Down Under had yielded results.

"The emails!" she exclaimed. "You nailed the sender."

"To the wall," he replied with such savage satisfaction that Dawn whooped and flung up a palm for a joyous high five.

"All riiiight, Russo!"

The exuberant exclamation startled Tommy and the pup. Blue eyes wide, the boy clutched his boomerang to his chest and demanded to know what was going on while his pet made indiscriminate lunges at any and all adults.

"Down!"

Joe's low command caught the terrier in midlunge. It dropped instantly onto its haunches, looking as uncertain as a cuddly, curly-haired puppy could.

"Let me take your jacket," Dawn said in the sudden, blessed silence. "Then we'll go into the kitchen and you can tell us every detail."

"Mooooom."

Tommy stretched the single syllable into a mile-long protest that stopped Dawn in her tracks. Despite the butterflies in her stomach, Callie had to smile at her friend's goofy expression. The bubbly, irrepressible Dawn still wasn't used to being a mother to anyone, much less a blue-eyed imp with the face of an angel and

enough energy to propel the Hubble Space Telescope into extended orbit.

"Joe's gotta show me how to make my boomerang come back," Tommy insisted. "Or..." He assumed an air of patently false innocence. "I guess I could take it outside and figure out how it works myself."

"Yeah," Dawn snorted. "Like I'm going to turn you loose with an ancient hunting weapon."

The Ellises' home was in an older part of Bethesda, just over the Maryland border from Washington, DC. The neighborhood consisted of gracious brick and stone houses set on large, tree-shaded lots. Their backyard was enclosed in mellow brick and graced by a fanciful gazebo now dusted with a light snow. It was also overlooked by a half dozen plate-glass windows, all of which were at risk despite Tommy's assurances that he would be *real* careful.

"We want to hear Joe's news," Dawn told the boy firmly. "Then we'll all put on our jackets and go out with you."

His lower lip jutted mutinously. "But..."

"Chill, dude."

Always a man of few words, Joe got his point across without raising his voice. Dawn flashed him a rueful smile as she created a diversion for boy and dog.

"Why don't you go into the den and get on the computer? You can pull up that website on the aerodynamics of boomerang flight your dad bookmarked for you. I bet Joe would like to see it after we talk."

Reluctant but outnumbered, Tommy caved. "'Kay. Just don't talk too long."

Still clutching his prize, he scampered off with the pup hard on his heels. Joe shrugged out of his jacket and

raised a brow as Dawn hooked the well-worn leather on the hall coatrack.

"Aerodynamics of flight, huh?"

"What can I say? Brian and his first wife were both engineers. It's in Tommy's genes."

It was a measure of Dawn's basic warmth and security in her two-month-old marriage that she didn't want Tommy to forget his birth mother. Caroline Ellis had died of a brain tumor less than a year after her son's birth. Tommy had no real memories of her except those captured in the exquisite digital book Dawn had made for him using all her skills as a graphic designer.

"C'mon. I'll brew you some coffee while you tell us all."

Dawn turned to lead the way down the hall, so she missed the casual hand Joe laid at the small of her friend's back. Callie, on the other hand, felt the light touch right through her baggy purple sweater and cotton camisole.

When Joe called to say his plane had touched down, she'd almost dashed to the gatehouse to change, slap on some lip gloss and drag a brush through her mink-brown hair. She'd been thinking about taking Dawn's advice and getting the shoulder-length mass shaped at one of DC's elegant salons. With her life pretty much on hold these past weeks, though, she'd settled for just pulling it back in a ponytail or clipping it up.

She made a futile effort to tuck back some of the wayward strands as she and Joe settled in high-backed stools at the kitchen counter and Dawn plugged a fresh, single-cup, dark arabica blend container into the coffeemaker. As hot water steamed through the cup, the coffee's rich aroma competed with the sappy tang of the fresh-cut pine boughs on the kitchen table.

"Okay," Dawn demanded when the super-fast appliance delivered a steaming mug. "Talk! We've all been speculating like crazy since you took off so suddenly for Sydney. Tell us who the creep is who's been sending those emails and why."

Joe swiveled to face Callie. "Do you remember acting as ombudsman for a girl named Rose Graham?"

Frowning, she flipped through a mental filing cabinet of the cases she'd worked in her six years with the Massachusetts Office of the Child Advocate. Some files were slender; others were fat and crammed with tragic details. Still others were truly horrific. As best Callie could recall, though, Rose Graham's case file was one of the thinner ones.

"I remember the name."

"She was five when her parents duked it out in divorce court."

From the corner of her eye Callie saw an all-too-familiar mask slip over Dawn's normally expressive face. Her friend had been a young teen when her parents' increasingly bitter arguments led to an even more acrimonious divorce, with their only daughter caught smack in the middle. Kate and Callie had acted as buffers as much as possible, but sharing Dawn's heartache had been a significant factor in Callie's decision to pursue a master's degree in family psychology and accept an appointment as a children's advocate.

"The mother worked as a paralegal," Joe prompted. "The father was a software developer at one of Boston's ultra-high-tech medical research companies."

The details seeped back. Callie could visualize Rose Graham—fair-haired, small for her age and very bright.

"I remember the case now." Her forehead crinkled. "As best I recall, it was pretty open-and-shut. The child

was well adjusted, doing fine in preschool and clearly adored by both parents. Judges are predisposed to leave a female child that young with the mother unless there's evidence of gross neglect or abuse. But…" Her frown deepened. "I'm pretty sure I recommended generous visitation rights for the father."

"You did, which was why we didn't give the Graham case as much scrutiny as some of the others. Only after I had my people go back and do a second scrub did we learn the father's company transferred him to their Australian office earlier this year."

"Uh-oh."

With a sinking sensation, Callie sensed what was coming. Otherwise amicable divorce and custody agreements could turn ugly when overseas travel was involved. The cost of the travel itself was often prohibitive, and the court couldn't discount the possibility a child taken outside its jurisdiction would not be returned. For that reason, Callie's report to the judge had contained the standard caveat requiring review if either of the parents should relocate outside the US.

"Rose's mother flat refused to let her daughter fly all the way to Australia," Joe confirmed.

"And the law firm she worked for tied her ex up in legal knots," Callie guessed. She'd seen that too many times, too.

"The father had to come back to the States so often for hearings and court appearances that he wiped out his savings and was forced to take out huge loans. As a result, he fell behind on child support."

Callie grimaced. "And that in turn led the state to institute proceedings to garnish his wages from his home company in Boston, only adding to his legal woes and burden of debt."

"He asked his company to transfer him back to Boston. He's been waiting for six months for a position to open up."

"In the meantime, his anger at the system festered."

"And then some." Joe shook his head in disgust. "I can't believe it took my people so long to break through the series of firewalls he erected. The man's damned good at what he does."

"But your people are better," Dawn commented.

"That's why I pay 'em the big bucks."

"So what happened when you confronted Graham?" she wanted to know.

"Pretty much what I'd expected. He acted astonished, then indignant. Then, when the Aussie cybercrimes detectives who accompanied me to his place of employment laid out the electronic evidence, he wouldn't say another word without an attorney present. After his lawyer showed up it still took some persuasion," Joe said with what both women suspected was considerable understatement, "but he finally admitted to fixating on the caveat in Callie's report as the root cause of his problems."

"Right," Dawn snorted. "Not the judge who signed the visitation order. Not his ex-wife or her team of lawyers. And of course not himself."

"Of course." Joe's silver-gray eyes frosted with icy satisfaction. "Bastard's in a world of hurt now. He'll be sitting in a cell for months while the US and Australia work out jurisdictional issues. Years, maybe, since the investigation and prosecution of terror-related cybercrimes takes far higher precedence in both countries than his threats."

Callie might have felt sorry for Rose's father if his vicious emails hadn't disrupted her life for the past three

months. She'd have to pick up the pieces and get on with it, she realized. But first...

"Thank you." Reaching across the counter, she laid a hand over Joe's. "I appreciate all you've done for me. More than I can ever say. I hated involving you in the mess, but..."

"Hated me butting in, you mean."

"Well, yes. At first." She had to smile. "After all, we barely knew each other."

"A situation I've been trying to remedy."

He had. He most definitely had. Just remembering the hard press of his mouth on hers the evening before his sudden trip to Australia brought a wash of heat from the neck of her sweater. The heat surged even higher when Joe turned his hand, enfolded hers and brushed his thumb over her wrist in slow, easy strokes.

Callie didn't dare glance at her friend. Dawn wasn't the least bit hesitant to dish out advice or offer opinions. She and Kate had both already suggested—several times!—that strong, silent, super-macho Joe Russo had a serious case of the hots for the quiet, seemingly demure member of their trio.

Thankfully Dawn refrained from commenting on either Joe's thumb movements or the heat now spreading across Callie's cheeks. Instead she invented a quick excuse to depart the scene.

"I'd better go make sure Tommy isn't trying to test those aerodynamic principles in the den. Give a shout when you're ready to, uh, take the action outside."

The door to the den swished shut behind her, and a sudden silence descended. Callie was the first to break it. Her hand still in Joe's, she tried to ignore the skitter of nerves his stroke was generating and smiled up at him.

"I meant what I just said, Joe. I'm really, really grateful. And so relieved it's finally over."

"Me, too. It's been keeping me awake at night."

"I've lost sleep, too," she admitted. "I can't ever repay you for the man-hours you and your people put into the investigation."

"If it gets the shadows out of your eyes, I'll consider the debt paid."

His gaze locked on hers. "Your eyes are the damnedest color," he said after a small pause. "Not purple, not lavender. Sort of halfway between the two. First thing I noticed about you."

Well, Callie thought with an inner grimace, it wouldn't have been her ebullient personality or luscious curves. Dawn had the corner on those. And any stray male glances the flamboyant redhead didn't instantly capture, Kate's lustrous, sun-streaked blond hair and mile-long legs would.

"Thanks," she said for lack of a better response.

"I tried to find the right way to describe the color when I gave my folks your vitals," he said with a rueful grimace. "Couldn't bring myself to go with hyacinth or heliotrope. Their jaws would've smacked their chests."

Callie's own jaw almost took a trip south. These were the most words she'd heard Joe string together in one sitting. They were also the most surprising.

"So what *did* you go with?"

"Pansy."

Her nose wrinkled. "Lovely."

"Yeah, they are."

His hand tightened and tugged her closer. His other hand came up to slide under her hair. His palm felt warm on her nape, the skin hard and ridged in spots. She'd once read that expert marksmen fired thousands

of rounds weekly to maintain their skills and developed shooter's calluses as a result.

Okay. She'd read that just a few weeks ago. When she was trying to weave a more complete picture of Joe Russo from the scant threads of his past that he'd shared with her. She was thinking of the still-gaping holes in that picture when he reclaimed her attention with a gruff admission.

"Those damned emails weren't the only thing keeping me awake."

He lowered his head but didn't swoop in and catch her by surprise, as he had the night before his abrupt departure for Australia. He gave her plenty of time to pull away, to ease out of his loose grip. So much time she was the one who leaned into the kiss.

That was all the encouragement he needed. With a low grunt, he pushed off his stool. She came off hers eagerly. The hand still wrapped around her nape moved up. He tipped her head back for a better angle and used his other arm to fit her against him. She strained even closer while his mouth worked hard, hungry magic on hers.

Within moments, Callie was aching for more. She wanted him out of his shirt. Out of his worsted-wool slacks and his Italian leather boots and...

"Caaal-lee."

She jerked her back and looked over her shoulder to find Tommy glaring at them with equal parts indignation and accusation. His pup wedged through the door with him and yipped, as if wanting to add his two cents to whatever was going on.

"Mom said you guys were still talking. But you're not. You're kissing 'n' stuff."

They hadn't actually gotten to the "stuff" part, but

Callie was thinking about it. Thinking hard. So was Joe, judging by the wicked tilt to his mouth.

"Yeah," he admitted, "we are."

Scowling, Tommy planted his fists on his hips. "When are you gonna be done?"

Joe slanted Callie a wry look. "How about we finish our...discussion...later? Somewhere private. Inaccessible to kids and dogs."

"Deal."

"All right, kid. Get your jacket and your boomerang and we'll go outside."

Chapter Two

When Joe stepped outside, he welcomed the clean, sharp bite of a DC winter. December was midsummer in Australia. During his flying visit, Sydney had been sweltering through usually high temperatures. As a result he enjoyed the brisk chill almost as much as he did Tommy the Terrible's determination to get his boomerang to fly.

Before making the first attempt, though, the boy fingered the fine-grained wood surface and gravely explained its aerodynamic principles to Joe. "See, this is a nonballistic missile."

"That so?"

"Uh-huh. It's different from ballistic missiles. They're, like, spears 'n' arrows 'n' bullets 'n' stuff. When you throw them or shoot them from a gun, they fly up in an arc till gravity pulls them down."

Which was about as cogent a distillation of ballistics as Joe had ever heard. He hid a grin as he thought of the

hours he'd spent on the range as a raw recruit learning to calculate distance, velocity and trajectory.

"But a boomerang's different," Tommy continued, his face a study in fierce concentration as he fingered the intricate designs inlaid in the wood. "It's got this curved shape 'n' wide surface 'n' the top is conver... convey..."

"Convex?"

"Yeah, convex. Anyway, Dad says if you throw it right, it'll defy gravity as long as it has enough speed 'n' the rotation will bring it right back to you."

"Sounds like you've got the theory down. Want to put in practice?"

"Yes!"

Thankfully, Joe's Aussie contact had directed him to an indigenous arts and crafts store with a very accommodating owner. The man had hooked a Closed sign in his shop window and taken his customer to the soccer field just a half block from his store. It took patient coaching and several attempts before Joe eventually got the damned boomerang to return.

The Ellises' backyard wasn't anywhere near as large as a soccer field, but Joe figured it was adequate for Tommy's strength and throwing ability. Hunkering down on his heels, he shared his recently acquired knowledge.

"Okay, hold it in a two-fingered pistol grip."

"Huh?"

"Sorry. Hold it here with your thumb and two fingers. Tuck the other fingers into your fist. Good. Now lift the boomerang vertical to your shoulder. A little higher. Okay. It doesn't take a lot of effort to throw this. Just bring your arm back and hurl it forward."

Tommy's first attempt sent the boomerang plowing

straight down into the snow-dusted grass. The second whizzed past the pup's nose. The third actually flew off to the right, whirled and started to return before it ran out of speed.

"Joe! It was coming back!"

"I saw."

Thrilled with his throw, Tommy almost tripped over his pet in his eagerness to retrieve the boomerang. Joe figured he'd pretty well exhausted his expertise and leaned against the garden wall to let the boy enjoy himself.

He was a good kid. Make that a great kid.

Looking back, Joe could admit he'd harbored more than a few doubts when he'd heard Brian Ellis had brought his young son to Italy. At the time, Ellis, USAF Major Travis Westbrook and the playboy prince Joe and his team were providing special security for were in the final test phase of a highly classified NATO special ops aircraft modification. The mod had been designed by Ellis Aeronautical Systems, however, and the company's CEO was a widower who included his son and the boy's nanny on extended trips abroad whenever he could. Unfortunately, the nanny tripped and broke her ankle in the final and most critical phase of the test.

Joe didn't believe in luck. Not many men and women in his profession did. You considered every possible contingency, devised backup plans, worked out alternate escape routes and relied on training and instinct to get you out of tight situations. He was living proof that the formula worked...most of the time. When he looked in the mirror, however, he saw a graphic reminder of Curaçao and the one time his instincts were dead wrong.

Yet even he had to admit that chance or luck or whatever the hell you wanted to call it had played out in Italy. Kate and Travis Westbrook had hooked up again.

Fiery-haired Dawn McGill had stepped in as Tommy's temporary nanny. And Joe had met Callie Langston.

It hadn't been love at first sight. Not even, Joe recalled, instant lust. Callie would be the first to admit that most male glances slid right past her to snag on long-legged, tawny-haired Kate or laughing, flirtatious, extremely stacked Dawn.

Joe had experienced the same initial testosterone spike when introduced to the other two women. Right up until Callie had turned her head and nailed him with those purple eyes. But it wasn't until he saw her trying to disguise her reaction to those emails that she snagged more than a casual interest.

At first it was the cop in him. The military-trained investigator turned covert operator turned personal security expert. Then it was her insistence she could handle the problem herself. Then...

"Didja see that one, Joe? Didja?"

"I did. Good job, kid."

Then, Joe remembered, it was Brian and Dawn setting sparks off each other. And Kate and Travis getting back together. And the playboy prince putting the moves on Callie.

Carlo's heavy-handed seduction attempts had pissed Joe off more than they should have. They also got him thinking about things he hadn't allowed himself think about since Curaçao. Like someone to come home to. Hell, a *home* to come home to. And maybe, just maybe, a son like Tommy.

Suddenly impatient, Joe pushed away from the garden wall. "A couple more throws, kid."

"Not yet. I'm just gettin' good."

"Yes, yet. I want to finish talking to Callie. Besides," he added, taking a cue from Dawn's devious tactics,

"your dad should be home soon. You don't want to wear out your arm before you show him your moves."

"'Kay. Four more."

"Two."

"Three."

"This one," Joe said in a tone that brooked no further argument, "and one more."

Inside the kitchen warmed by the dancing flames from a brick fireplace, Dawn and Callie cradled cups of steaming cappuccino and watched the action through frost-rimmed bay windows.

They'd just placed several calls. The first to Dawn's husband, Brian, to break the news that Joe had ID'd the originator of the emails. Another to the remaining member of their female triumvirate.

Kate had whooped with joy and relief and insisted they celebrate. Tonight. Before Joe disappeared again on one of his bodyguard gigs for some rock star or South American dictator. She and Travis would bring the champagne and sparkling cider. Dawn and Callie could take care of the eats.

They accomplished their assigned task by calling in a to-go order for tapas and paella at Paoli, a top-rated Mediterranean restaurant just a few blocks from the house. Which left them plenty of time to sip their cappuccinos and watch the outside activities.

"Joe's really good with Tommy," Dawn commented casually.

Too casually. Callie recognized that okay-whatever-I'm-just-saying tone. She buried her nose in the frothy brew and waited. Sure enough, Dawn plunked her own cup down and cut to the chase.

"C'mon, Cal. Give. To paraphrase my precocious little imp, what was with all that kissing 'n' stuff?"

Callie lowered her cup and met her friend's eager gaze. Her own, she knew, no doubt mirrored the welter of confusing emotions Joe Russo roused in her.

"I'm not sure. It's just… Well… Look, you've known Joe as long as I have."

"But not as well, obviously."

The drawled retort raised a smile, followed by a rueful grimace.

"The truth is, I don't know him as well as it might have appeared. Aside from the fact he can't—or won't—talk about his past, he's not exactly loquacious."

"No kidding. But back to that kiss. It wasn't the first, was it?"

"No."

"And?"

"And what?"

"Don't play innocent with me, sister. You might come across as all demure and innocent to outsiders, but Kate and I were peeking through the blinds when you sweet-talked Pimple Face Hendricks into dropping his drawers and showing off his prized possession."

"For pity's sake! We were, what? Eight or nine years old?"

"Old enough to know Pimple Face didn't have much to brag about. So spill it. Do you want Joe to deliver a repeat performance?"

There was only one answer to that. "Yes."

"Hallelujah! It's about time you took the plunge."

"Wait! I'm not exactly plunging into any—"

"The heck you're not. I can't count the number of studs Kate and I have fixed you up with in the past few years. After every date you've smiled your enigmatic

Mona Lisa smile and sent them on their way. Joe's the first male you've invited back for seconds."

"Dawn," Callie protested, half laughing and half embarrassed at how close that barb had hit to home. "It was only a kiss. Although…"

"Although what, Langston?"

She played with her half-empty cup. She couldn't understand her reluctance to share her silly wish with Dawn. God knows, they'd shared everything else in their lives. She hesitated another few seconds before yielding her secret.

"Okay, here's the deal. Remember when the three of us tossed coins in the Trevi Fountain that first time?"

"Of course I do. But you, Miss Priss and Boots, wouldn't make a wish. You insisted that just throwing in a coin satisfied tradition and we'd all return to Rome someday."

"Actually, I did make a wish."

"Which," Dawn guessed instantly, "involved Joe Russo."

"How could it? We didn't meet him until a week later, in Venice."

"Okay, okay. If you didn't wish for steamy, totally deviant sex with Mr. Macho out there, what was it? Please tell me it was something equally kinky."

"Since when are any of us into kink?"

When Dawn wagged her brows, Callie gave a rueful laugh. "All right. The wish was a little…fanciful."

"Are we talking satin sheets fanciful? Or whipped cream and melted chocolate? Or ice cubes and…"

"Dawn!"

"Ha! Do *not* go all prune-faced and prudish on me, missy. Just remember who advised Kate on the best brand of vibrator to buy when she and Travis separated."

"It was the same brand you recommend to me."

"Please stop annoying me with all these pesky details. Just tell me. What did you wish for?"

"Not what. Who. Louis Jourdan."

Dawn understood the reference instantly. She should, since she and Callie and Kate had drooled over the stunningly handsome '50s and '60s–era star during several all-night movie marathons as teens.

"God," Dawn breathed. "Do you remember him in *Gigi*? So suave and sophisticated and *hot*. The man made me want to jump straight from twelve to twenty."

"I think he was better in *Three Coins in the Fountain*," Callie mused.

She remembered the first time they'd watched the old classic. So many years ago. So many dreams ago.

"Did you ever notice how much Joe looks like him?"

That was met with a moment of startled silence.

"Now that you mention it," her friend said, recovering, "I can see the resemblance. Aside from that fact that Joe's eyes are gray, not brown, and he's probably four inches taller and considerably more muscled than our boy Louis, they're dead ringers."

"All right, I may be projecting a bit."

"Ya think? But, hey. Project away, girl. It's *so* romantic."

And *so* out of character. Despite the incident with Pimple Face Hendricks, Callie had always been the sensible, bookish one of the three. More into reading than boys in junior high. An honor student in high school. On scholarships all through college and her master's program.

Majoring in psychology had given her great insight into the vagaries of human behavior. Unfortunately, it had also reinforced her natural tendency to stand off to the side and observe. Six years at the child advocate's

office, where she was sworn to protect her young clients' rights and privacy, had only added to her natural reticence. The often heartbreaking cases she'd worked had taught her to wall off her own emotions. Except, of course, from Kate and Dawn.

And now Joe.

He'd pierced her shell in Italy when he'd convinced her to tell him about the emails. He'd taken another whack at it with that kiss before he'd zipped down to Australia. The one he'd laid on her just a few moments ago had pretty well completed the conquest. Watching him now, coaching Tommy in the fine art of boomer-anging, Callie could almost feel her outer barriers trembling like the fabled walls of Jericho.

"Well," Dawn commented in an obvious effort to validate Callie's wish at the fountain, "Joe certainly has what it takes to star in a few movies. They'd probably be more shoot-'em-up action flicks than romances, though." She hesitated a few moments. "It doesn't bother you, what he does?"

"It might, if I could pry more than the most superficial details about his clients out of him."

"Brian says Joe and his people were prepared to take a bullet for Carlo in Italy. Evidently the prince led a special ops raid that rescued some UN workers in Afghanistan. Or maybe it was Africa. Anyway, the group's leader put a bounty on Carlo's head. That's why he required beefed-up security when we first met him in Italy."

"Kate told me a little about that raid. Travis took part in it, too."

Dawn nodded. "I know I don't have to remind you that the constant fear and uncertainty, the never knowing where Travis was or how long he'd be gone or who was shooting at him, almost broke up Kate's marriage."

"No, you don't have to remind me."

Callie had been right there. She and Dawn both. Lending support and shoulders to cry on when Kate made the agonizing decision to end her marriage to the man she'd loved since high school. They'd been there, too, when Travis refused to let her go, insisting nothing else mattered if he didn't have her.

"Joe and I are nowhere near that stage," Callie said. "Or any stage, really."

"Tell that to your action hero." Dawn tilted her head in the direction of the window. "He looks like he has more than a kiss in mind."

Callie followed her nod and caught Joe's glance through the wide windows. He and Tommy and the pooch had finished and were heading in. When he jerked his chin in the direction of the gatehouse, she slid off the counter stool with more haste than grace.

"Kate said she'll leave work early," Callie reminded Dawn. "She and Travis should be here by six or six thirty."

"Brian's leaving early, too."

"Buzz me when they get here."

"You sure you want to be disturbed?"

Ignoring her friend's salacious grin, Callie met the three males at the back door. The pup danced around her while she dutifully praised Tommy's skills. Then Dawn lured her two boys into the main house with an offer of hot chocolate and whipped cream.

"Lots of whipped cream," she said with a wicked glance in Callie's direction.

Joe caught the less than subtle byplay. "Something going on I should know about?"

"Nothing important," she said as she led the way along the covered flagstone path to the gatehouse. Es-

caping the chill December air, she ushered him inside. "Here, let me take your coat."

She hung it beside hers on an empty hook. The well-worn bomber jacket carried his scent, she thought as she took a discreet sniff. Sharp and clean and leathery. It felt like him, too. Tough and resilient.

Oh, Lord! She had it worse than she thought if she was standing here smelling his jacket. Hoping to heck he hadn't witnessed the sniff test, she turned. Thankfully, he was looking around with interest.

"This is nice."

It was. Bright and cheerful, with floral chintzes and bay windows that invited the outside in. The gatehouse had provided Callie a cozy safe haven for almost two months now. She hated the idea of leaving but knew she had to pick up the threads of her life again.

The problem was, she had no desire to return to Boston or to her former career. Despite all the courses and training and advice to the contrary, she'd let too much of the heartache experienced by her young, helpless and too often abused clients get to her. Even before the emails, she'd decided to quit. Now all she had to do was figure out what to do with the rest of her life.

She had no idea how much Joe might play in that. If at all. The thought made her uncharacteristically nervous. To cover it, she responded to his comment with a lively patter.

"The Ellises had the whole gatehouse gutted and redone for Tommy's former nanny, Mrs. Wells. The one who broke her ankle in Venice. I don't think you met her."

"No, I didn't."

"Dawn's totally conflicted over that. She'd never wish anyone harm, but she wouldn't have met Brian and Tommy otherwise."

"And I wouldn't have met you."

Ohh-kay, Callie thought as he curled a knuckle under her chin. So much for small talk.

He tipped her face to his. "As I was saying before I got dragooned into boomerang duty, it wasn't just those damned emails keeping me awake these past weeks."

His voice got lower and huskier with each word. Combined with the brush of his thumb along her jaw, he managed to get every one of her nerves bucking.

"You're so beautiful."

The compliment touched a secret place deep inside her. She didn't lack confidence in herself or her abilities, but she'd spent a lifetime in Kate's and Dawn's more flamboyant shadows.

"When did you have your last eye exam?"

"I'm not talking the externals. I'm talking about what's inside. The quiet self-assurance. The serenity."

The happy glow faded a bit.

"I haven't felt all that self-assured or serene in the past few months."

"You hid it well, even from your best friends."

"There was so much happening in their lives. I didn't want to add to it."

"So you drew on your own inner strength, Callie. I admire that." His thumb made another pass. "You're the kind of woman I've been looking for. The kind I could come home to."

She didn't know why that doused the glow completely, but it did. She pulled back and searched his face. The scar didn't so much as enter into her thought process as she tried to interpret his expression.

It hit her a second later. Affection. That's what she was seeing. Admiration tinged with warm, genuine affection. Humiliatingly similar to what she saw on

Dawn's and Brian's faces when they played with their son's pup. The fact that Joe's was spiced with an unmistakable dollop of desire didn't soothe the swift, lancing hurt. Concealing her dismay, she eased out of his arms.

"Sorry, but I'm not sure I understand. What, exactly, do you mean by 'come home to'?"

"Well…" He paused, obviously searching for the right words and opted for a demonstration instead. "How about I just show you?"

He reached for her again and drew her closer. When his head lowered, Callie hesitated for just a moment before meeting him halfway. Her lips molded his. Her palms found his shoulders, circled his neck. It wasn't just affection, she told herself. She could taste his hunger, sense it in the arms that tightened around her waist.

When he widened his stance and positioned her between his thighs, she couldn't quite stifle a groan. She could feel him against her belly. A minor distraction at first. Then a hard, rampant bulge that shot heat from her midsection to every other part of her. She wanted this man. Ached for him. Would take him any way she could have him.

And when he scooped her into arms, she didn't hold back before responding to his gruff, "Which way to the bedroom?"

He undressed her with a skill that might have given Callie pause if she hadn't been so intent on matching him button for button, tug for tug. Her heart melted when he took time to sheathe himself. If she hadn't already been a little in love with him, his determination to protect her even in this most intimate act would've done the trick. That, and the fact that he drove her to sensual heights she'd never experienced before.

Every stroke, every kiss, every scrape of his late-afternoon bristles on her breasts and belly and thighs pushed her higher. She was panting when he parted her legs. Almost mindless with need when he entered her. Just enough sanity remained for her to take him along on the wild ride.

Her belly tight, she locked her calves around his. Her muscles contracted. *Every* muscle! She thrust her hips against his again, once more, and gave herself up to the roaring tide of sensation.

When they untangled, she came within a hair of succumbing to his offer of tomorrow and forever. Most likely would have, if he hadn't tucked her against him and stroked her hair. Slowly. Lazily. Again, with the same absent affection Dawn or Brian might stroke their son's puppy.

She didn't draw away. Didn't vocalize the return of her insidious doubts. Instead, she buried them deep as she and Joe took turns in the shower. He'd brought his carryall with him from the airport and changed into jeans and a misty-blue cashmere sweater that softened the steel gray of his eyes.

In deference to both the season and the occasion, Callie dressed up a bit in ballet flats, black tights with just a touch of silvery sparkle and a Christmassy green wool tunic. Twisting her hair up, she caught it with a jeweled butterfly clip she'd picked up on a foray to one of the DC area's many malls.

She was wearing her usual smile when she and Joe joined Dawn and Kate and their respective spouses to celebrate the end of her harassment.

Her calm smile stayed in place even when Kate and Dawn dragged her into the kitchen, using the excuse of

making coffee for a tête-à-tête. Kate barely waited for the door to swish shut before she pounced.

"Details! The fat, pregnant sow wants details!"

Neither Dawn nor Callie bothered to point out that her tiny pooch barely even qualified as a baby bump.

"Rumor has it you and Joe got all close and cuddly this afternoon," Kate said. "Then you disappeared for several hours."

"Rumor being our gossipy friend here?"

"Hey!" Dawn protested. "Since when is any area of our lives off-limits? Seems like I can recall you two demanding every intimate detail when I got engaged the first time."

"And the second time," Kate admitted.

"And the third," Callie conceded.

"There! See? Turnabout's fair play. So how was it?"

"Pretty amazing, actually."

"You can do better than that, girl. On a scale of one to ten?"

"Twelve and a half."

"Way to go, Joe!"

Kate raised both palms and got slaps from the other women. Callie's was just a fraction slower than Dawn's, but the other two women picked up on that millisecond instantly.

"What?" Kate asked. "Twelve and a half didn't ring your bells?"

"They rang. Several times."

"But?"

She'd shared too many ups and downs with these women to hide her silly, niggling doubt from them. Still, she felt foolish even putting it into words.

"Turns out I want Louis Jourdan, and he wants Lassie."

Chapter Three

Dawn understood the reference to their earlier conversation, but Kate was totally confused. "Lassie? What's she got to…? Oh!" Her eyes popped. "Calissa Marie Langston, you sly thing! Just how kinky did you and Joe get this afternoon?"

"Kate! I was speaking metaphorically."

"Okay, now I'm really lost. How about translating for the verbally challenged? Where does Lassie come into this equation?"

Callie searched for the right words to frame her confused thoughts of a few hours ago. "Joe said I'm the kind of woman he could come home to. Not conquer worlds with. Not stand side by side with to battle the forces of evil."

"Okay," Kate said dubiously. "I guess that's a start."

"Some start," Dawn snorted. "I like Joe. What I know of him, anyway. And I love how good he is with Tommy. But he's not half as smart as I thought if he

hasn't figured out Callie's the toughest one of the three of us."

"You and I know that," Kate agreed. "Travis, too. You gave him the most verbal abuse when he and I split, Dawn-O, but Callie sliced and diced him. The problem is, Joe hasn't seen that side of her."

"True." Dawn aimed a frown across the counter. "He stepped right into the role of big, strong hero to our helpless heroine. Okay, maybe not helpless," she amended when her friends opened their mouths on a simultaneous protest, "but you have to admit you haven't been yourself, Cal. Not since you quit your job." She cocked her head. "It wasn't just stress or the emails, was it?"

"No. I was… I don't know." She rubbed absently at a spot on the marble counter with a fingertip. "I guess the best way to describe it is feeling restless. As though life was passing me by. I needed a change."

"You don't think getting involved with Joe would provide enough of a change?"

"Yes. Of course it would." With a determined shrug, she shook off her odd mood. "Assuming, that is, he wants to get involved."

"Yeah, right," Kate drawled. "As if you *can* get more involved than twelve and a half."

"Maybe not," Callie agreed, laughing. "We'll see. In the meantime, we'd better put that coffee on and get back to the guys."

As much as Callie hated to admit it, Kate and Dawn were right. She *had* played the helpless heroine. Worse, she'd been more than willing to let Joe step right into the role of the big, strong protector while she hid out here in DC. It was time to take charge of her life again.

But first, she decided as her gaze rested on the man

she'd opened her arms and the quiet corners of her heart to, she needed to find out just where Joe thought things between them might go. That could well color her decision on where to live and what new career paths to explore.

She approached the issue in her characteristically straightforward way. Serene and unruffled on the outside and nervous as all hell inside, she invited Joe to the gatehouse after they'd finished their coffee. The door barely closed before he had her backed against it.

"I like your friends," he muttered, nuzzling her hair. "But they talk too much."

"It's…uh…called conversation."

Oh, for pity's sake! All the man had to do was blow in her ear and she stumbled over her own tongue.

"Not where I hail from," he countered as his lips grazed her cheek.

The gruff reply reminded Callie of her objective. "We need to talk about that, Joe."

He raised his head. "Where I hail from?"

"Among other things. Your security team dissected my life during the investigation. They checked out my Facebook friends. Where I buy my bagels. I don't know anything about you."

The withdrawal was so subtle, so slight. His expression didn't change. He still pressed hard against her. Yet Callie sensed a few degrees of separation instantly.

"What do you want to know?"

"More than I can absorb with my back up against a door and your mouth three inches from mine." She edged sideways. "Should I make another pot of coffee? Or would you like a brandy? Dawn left the bar pretty well stocked."

"I'm good."

"Okay. Well…"

She led the way into the combination living room, den and study. Like the rest of the gatehouse, it had been furnished with an eye for comfort and color. Periwinkle-blue hydrangeas and lilacs in full flower patterned the overstuffed sofa and easy chair. The sixty-inch TV was mounted at easy viewing level, and a small niche housed a built-in desk with hookups for all the latest electronic gadgets. As a tribute to both the season and the temporary nature of her occupancy, Callie had put up only a three-foot tree decorated with ornaments she and Tommy had made the previous Saturday morning.

Kicking off her ballet flats, Callie sank into the plush sofa cushions and tucked one foot under her. Joe took the opposite corner. She did her best to ignore the hard thighs and broad shoulders showcased to perfection by his jeans and that cloudy blue cashmere.

Joe met her gaze with a steady one of his own. "I can't tell you much, Callie. Most of the ops I participated in while I was in the military are still classified, and those I work for my clients are confidential."

"I'm more interested in the basics. Where's home?"

"Originally? A little town in Texas you never heard of."

"Try me."

"Bitter Creek."

"You're right. I've never heard of it. Did you leave there to go into the marines like Brian? Or was it the air force, like Travis?"

Again, his expression didn't change. Neither did his inflection. Yet Callie could sense the gap widening.

"Army. Rangers. Then," he added slowly, reluctantly, "Delta Force."

She had no idea who or what constituted Delta Force but decided she didn't really need to know at this point.

"How long were you in uniform?"

"Nine years."

Longer than she'd spent at the Office of the Child Advocate. Like her, Joe had changed direction in mid-career. More curious than ever, she probed deeper.

"Why did you leave the military?"

"It was time," he bit out.

Okay. That was obviously not something he wanted to talk about. Well, there was one subject he couldn't avoid. Raising a hand, she feathered a finger over his still fading scar.

"And this? Where did you get this?"

He froze her out. That's the only way she could describe it. The icy mask dropped over his face so swiftly, so completely, that she blinked.

"That's not open to discussion."

Joe smothered a curse when she reared back looking as though he'd slapped her. Which he pretty much had.

No way he could tell her about Nattat, though, or his desperate, futile attempt to keep her safe. Exerting every ounce of will he possessed, he blanked out the all-too-vivid images of the mountaintop resort in the Caribbean and focused on the woman regarding him with such a bruised look.

"Sorry."

He scraped a hand over his jaw and forced Curaçao to the black pit where it belonged. The clean feel of his chin reminded him that he'd shaved after showering. He must have bristled like a hedgehog when he'd hustled Callie into bed earlier, though. Wincing inwardly, he could only imagine the whisker burns he must have left on her tender skin.

Hell! That was the wrong direction to let his thoughts take him. Exerting an iron will, Joe slammed the door on the image of this woman soft and hot and panting under him.

"Look, Callie, you'll just have to accept there's a big chunk of my past I can't talk about. All that matters is what's between us here and now."

"Funny you should say that. I was actually wondering about that, too." Those purple eyes skewered into him. "What *is* between us, Joe?"

Christ! Where were his alternate escape routes when he needed them? Sweating a little, he reached out. Cupped her chin. Felt a weird lurch under his ribs.

"I can only repeat what I told you earlier. You're a calm port. A safe harbor."

"Right."

She lowered her glance. Her lashes fanned against her cheek, as thick and dark as her shoulder-length hair. Joe had fantasized about that silky mass for the past few weeks. He didn't have to fantasize now. The sight of the dark locks spilling across the pillow had been even more erotic than he'd imagined. It was a sight he intended—hoped!—to enjoy on a regular and frequent basis.

So when she raised her eyes, her calm announcement came down on him like a collapsing brick wall.

"I'm going back to Rome."

"What?"

"Carlo texted me last week." She eased her chin from his hold. "He's offered me a job."

The quiet response triggered a welter of savage reactions. Before agreeing to provide Carlo Luigi Francesco di Lorenzo the high-level personal security his government had requested, Joe and his people had thoroughly researched the prince. The man might be short,

balding and getting thick around the middle, but he'd descended from one of the oldest houses in Europe. He also commanded Italy's crack airborne special ops unit.

None of which mattered to Joe at the moment as much as the fact that di Lorenzo had racked up more hours in women's beds than he had hours in the cockpit of his C-130 Hercules.

"Did you know Carlo sits on the board of several charitable foundations?"

Her question brought a curt response.

"Yeah."

Grimacing, Joe raked a hand through his hair and fought to temper both his tone and his visceral reaction to the idea of Callie heading back to Italy on her own. Without Dawn or Kate. Or him.

"Di Lorenzo gave me a list of the organizations he's involved with when I agreed to provide enhanced security," he told her. "Most of his charitable activities are purely economic, but several…"

Joe caught himself. He'd built a reputation and a multimillion-dollar business based on absolute trust. He wouldn't breach a client's confidentiality any more than Callie would the privacy of the children she'd represented in court. Still, he couldn't hold back a terse warning.

"Several of the agencies he's involved with have ties to Africa and the Middle East."

"I know. The job he's offered is with one of those agencies. International Aid to Displaced Women."

Joe felt the tendons in his neck cord. Prince or not, if Carlo thought he could involve Callie in the type of activity he himself had needed protection from, the man had another think coming.

"IADW operates a sort of halfway house for female

refugees," she was explaining. "Women who've escaped or been driven out their own countries and have either lost their male protectors or been abandoned by them somewhere along the way."

"That right? And what does Carlo think you can do for them?"

The question carried more of a bite than he'd intended. So it was no surprise when Callie stiffened.

"Despite the impression I've obviously given you," she said coolly, "I'm neither helpless nor unskilled. At the least, I can help these women acquire a rudimentary English vocabulary, which many of them will need before being resettled in English-speaking countries. At best, perhaps I can ease some of the trauma they've gone through."

Cursing his lack of tact, Joe tried to recover. "Sorry. That came out wrong. What I meant was…"

What he meant was that he didn't like the idea of her working with or for Carlo di Lorenzo. Which was why he committed his second major blunder in as many minutes.

"Look, before you accept his offer, take some time to think about mine."

Her forehead puckered. "Did I miss something? What offer?"

"About coming home. To you."

Her jaw sagged. "Is this…is this a proposal?"

Her surprise knocked him back a step. Hell! He'd thought—been certain—she'd understood where this was going.

"Yes, it's a proposal," he said gruffly. "What'd you think it was?"

"I didn't… That is…" She gave her head a quick, disbelieving shake. "Joe, we barely know each other!"

"Not true."

She'd hit the mark when she'd reminded him that he'd had his people investigate every corner of her life. Joe suspected he'd uncovered a few things about her younger years she wouldn't want her parents to know. He chalked up those early escapades up to her more lively friends, though. Dawn, especially. The voluptuous redhead had started breaking male hearts while still a teenager. Luckily, she seemed to have met her match in Brian Ellis. As Joe had in this dark-haired, violet-eyed siren.

"I've seen your strength and grace under the pressure of threats, Callie. Plus," he added deliberately, "I'd say we got to know each other pretty well this afternoon."

"We certainly did," she agreed, recovering from her astonishment. "And it was wonderful. Off the charts, as Tommy's friend Addy would say."

He waited for the *but* he knew was coming.

"So I hope…I really hope…we can build on that mutual desire."

"With you taking off for Italy?"

"That's where we met," she reminded him, her gaze steady. "Where we can continue to meet. You may not be able to tell me much about your clients, but I gather Carlo's not the first European you've worked with. Nor, I suspect, will he be the last."

She had that right. Joe had put a number of potential clients on hold while he'd tracked the source of Callie's emails. He could pretty well choose the continent, the risk level and the degree of personal involvement in his next contract.

"We could see each other as often in Rome as we could in Boston," she said. "Maybe more often. If you want to make it happen."

Damned if Joe knew at this point.

He'd been so sure she would appreciate what he had to offer. Mutual respect. Sexual compatibility, which they'd more than proved earlier. Financial security. He knew she'd been living on her savings since she'd quit her job. Had thought she'd appreciate that while he wasn't the most expressive or demonstrative man in the world, he was rock solid. Unlike a certain Italian prince.

"I still don't understand. Why go all the way to Rome?"

She chewed on her lower lip. When she answered, Joe sensed she was revealing a part of herself she rarely shared with anyone other than her two friends.

"Your job takes you all over the world. But I grew up, went to school and have worked all my adult life within a ninety-mile radius of Boston. Aside from family vacations and a jaunt to Cancún with Kate and Dawn during one spring break, Italy was my first real adventure. I loved the color, the food, the people. And Rome…!"

A full-blown smile came out, so warm and radiant it slammed into his gut like a rifle butt.

"Oh, Joe! Dawn and Kate and I spent only a few days in Rome. I want more time to explore its rich history and culture. On my own…and with you whenever possible."

Okay. So maybe it wasn't such a bad idea after all. Wandering through the Forum with her. Sharing a bottle of chianti at the tiny trattoria he'd discovered a few blocks from the Spanish Steps. Making love in a hotel room with a view of the old city walls.

They could take the train up to the Lake District for a weekend at some opulent resort. Maybe zip over to Portofino, Italy's answer to the French Riviera. Now that the first shock had passed, Joe could see himself laying all Europe at her feet.

"I guess I can understand where you're coming from," he conceded. "I have one suggestion, though."

"What's that?"

"I think we should…"

He caught himself just in time. Dammit, he had to do this right. Had to appeal to this unexpectedly adventurous side of her personality. And that would necessitate a little more planning and execution on his part.

"I think we should sleep on it," he temporized. "See how we feel in the morning."

A gleam of laughter leaped into her eyes, but she answered with a solemn nod. "By all means, Mr. Russo, let's sleep on it. Your place or mine?"

His DC hotel room was modern and efficient but held none of the comforts of the gatehouse. Callie's smiling invitation to share it with him kicked his pulse into overdrive. It was hammering hard and fast when he tumbled her back onto the sofa cushions.

"Yours, Ms. Langston. Yours."

His internal alarm went off at its usual 5:00 a.m. He came instantly alert but had learned long ago to give no indication he was awake. That skill had saved his life several times, most recently in Curaçao.

Slamming the door on that memory, he kept his eyes closed and concentrated on recording sensory signals. He heard Callie beside him. Her breathy intake, her snuffling exhale. Not quite a snore but close enough to make him smile inwardly. He could feel her, too. Soft and pliant and warm against his side. Her scent filled his nostrils. The lemony tang of her shampoo. The faint, yeasty residue of their lovemaking. One whiff and he felt himself hardening. Only his self-discipline and

years of brutal training kept him from rolling her over and burying himself in her hot, tight depths.

He lay quiet, mulling over everything they'd talked about last night. Callie wanted to expand her world. He could understand that. He'd explored damned near every corner of it himself, both in the military and out. Before she went traipsing off to Rome, though, he intended to make sure she wore his brand.

He disciplined himself to wait an hour. It was close to six before he eased out of bed. No sign of the December sun poked through the bedroom shutters as he dragged on his clothes. He needed coffee in the worst way but decided not to wake Callie. Instead, he jotted a quick note and propped it on the kitchen counter.

He hit a Starbucks drive-through and infused the caffeine as he negotiated the still-light traffic in the southeast corner of DC. As early as it was, he knew Frank Harden would be at his desk.

He and Harden had served in Delta Force together before going their separate ways—Joe as a mercenary for some years before starting his own protective services agency, Frank as a civilian analyst with the Defense Intelligence Agency specializing in African affairs. Whip-smart and not shy about voicing his opinion, Harden had progressed steadily up the ranks at the DIA. His current senior executive service rank equated to that of a major general, but neither he nor Joe let that get in the way of the friendship they'd forged all those years ago.

Joe called Harden's private extension when he was almost to the sprawling complex now known as Joint Base Anacostia–Bolling. The base had been formed a few years back by cobbling together the Anacostia Naval Sup-

port Facility and Bolling Air Force Base. Since the two installations sat side by side and ate up a big chunk of this corner of DC, Joe guessed the consolidation made sense.

As he'd anticipated, his workaholic pal picked up on the first ring.

"Russo, you mangy dog," Harden drawled in that laconic, down-home Mississippi twang that disguised his needle-sharp instincts and encyclopedic knowledge of all things African. "Where the hell are you, boy?"

"About two blocks away."

"Hot damn! I'll call down to gate B and clear you in."

As promised, Harden got him cleared through the main gate leading to the massive complex that housed DIA headquarters and a slew of other intel activities, like the headquarters of the National Intelligence University and the Joint Functional Component Command for Intelligence, Surveillance and Reconnaissance.

Harden had an underling waiting to escort his guest into the inner sanctum. Joe surrendered the lightweight Ruger LCR-357 that nested in his ankle holster, accepted a signed receipt for it, clipped on a visitors' badge and passed through the metal detector.

Harden's office reflected his exalted pay grade, but Joe had little time to enjoy the view. Rail-thin and every bit as gaunt as the day the two of them had tunneled their way out of a Sudanese prison, the bureaucrat delivered a bone-jarring thump to Joe's shoulder.

"Haven't heard from you since the cows came home. What've you been doin'?"

"Had a job in the Caribbean earlier this year." Joe could feel his insides curl but kept his tone casual. "Most recently at a NATO base north of Venice."

"Yeah, I heard something about that." Frank gestured to one of the armchairs facing his desk. "Rumor

is your pal Ellis got a fat contract out of that gig. Some new avionics package for the entire NATO airlift fleet."

"Could be."

Joe knew damn well it was more than a rumor. He'd gotten to know Brian Ellis well during that NATO gig and at his request had recently completed a top-to-bottom scrub of his company's physical, industrial and cyber security. What had begun as a business association, however, had morphed into friendship.

"So what can I do you for?" Frank asked. "Or did you just come to gloat 'bout me being chained to a desk?"

"I need some info."

"Figured. Shoot."

"What can you tell me about a Rome-based charity called International Aid to Displaced Women?"

Joe left the Defense Intelligence Agency feeling marginally better about Callie's decision. Although Frank wasn't personally familiar with IADW, he had his people run a quick screen.

He also made a call to a contact at the State Department responsible for overseeing the US Refugee Admissions Program and the 6 billion dollars provided through the combined efforts of the Bureau of Population, Refugees and Migration and the US Agency for International Development. The contact's people in turn worked closely with a host of other agencies, including the Office of the UN High Commissioner for Refugees, the UN World Food Programme, the International Red Cross, the UN Children's Fund and the International Organization for Migration. Most of these organizations had special programs in place to protect the most vulnerable sectors of the population, including women and girls.

Harden's contact had verified that the Rome operation was legit. Equally important, there'd been no documented reports of terrorists or hard-core criminals infiltrating the population the agency cared for. That wasn't to say they couldn't. Given the growing number of women being recruited by groups like ISIS, the PLF and Sri Lanka's Tamil Tigers, programs that helped women enter or re-settle in other countries made tempting conduits.

Joe intended to go over the agency's refugee screening process with Carlo in some detail before Callie started work there. He made a quick call to his twenty-four-hour operations center and instructed the on-duty controller to check on an evening flight. The controller clicked a few keys and said there was a flight leaving Dulles at 5:40 p.m. Joe would have to hump to get everything done and be at the airport the required three hours early for international flights, but he figured he could make it.

"Okay, book it."

He then contacted the office of the director of the Na-ples film festival. Marcello Audi was worried that allow-ing a certain entry to be shown at this year's festival would put them on radical jihadists' hit list. He'd requested a thorough security assessment of all venues. Joe had planned to pass on the job, but Callie's little bombshell last night had triggered a swift reordering of his schedule. The Naples job would only take a few weeks, and it would put him less than an hour south of Rome. After that…

After that, he promised himself, he and Callie would settle on a permanent arrangement. One that gave them *both* a safe, comfortable haven. With that goal in mind, he steered his rental to the next stop on his hastily con-structed agenda.

Chapter Four

Callie sat curled up on the sitting room sofa, wearing loose, comfortable sweats and fuzzy slippers on her feet. She had fresh coffee in a Christmas mug and her iPhone within reach. She'd slept late—hardly a surprise given last night's strenuous exercise—and woken to find Joe gone. When she'd wandered into the kitchen, she found his note asking her to hold off calling Carlo until he got back.

She hoped he wasn't going to try to talk her out of Rome. He'd seemed to accept her decision last night, even admitted that he could see just as much of her in Italy as in Boston. She really wanted to contact Carlo and tell him she was accepting his job offer.

She itched to tell Kate and Dawn, too. And not just about Rome. There was this whole exciting, surprising, confusing matter of a proposal to share. They'd both already texted asking a) if she was awake b) if Joe was still there and c) whether she'd resolved the Lassie

issue. She wanted to go over to the main house, huddle with Dawn so they could FaceTime Kate together. The three of them had shared so many secrets, so many of life's ups and downs. But Joe's note had asked her to wait, so she'd held off, prey to a slightly disconcerting tug of divided loyalties.

She was still feeling the tug when she heard a car pull into the drive. A quick glance through the front windows confirmed Joe's return. Uncurling, she was halfway down the hall before the bell rang. When she opened the door, he walked in looking every bit as tall and strong as he had when he arrived from Sydney yesterday, but *so* much sexier. Which, of course, might have something to do with the fact that she'd explored every flat plane and hard ridge of the body that went with his steel-gray eyes and square chin.

God! Was she totally insane? What woman in her right mind wouldn't jump at Joe's offer? Why *not* settle into a comfortable nest with him? Why *not* be there, waiting patiently, when he rolled in from one of his unspecified, no-questions-allowed assignments?

When he greeted her with a quick kiss and one of his rare smiles, her uncharacteristic self-doubt spiked again. But before she could give in to the sudden urge to tell him she was reconsidering her options, he preempted her with a brusque announcement.

"I talked to a buddy at the Defense Intelligence Agency. The International Aid to Displaced Women operation's legit."

"Good to know. Although…" She lifted a brow. "Did you think Carlo would invite me to work for an organization that wasn't?"

"Doesn't hurt to check."

"No, I guess not. Aren't you staying?" she asked when he made no move to shed his bomber jacket.

"Can't. Have some things to get done before I fly out this afternoon."

"Fly where?"

She'd blurted it out without thinking and half expected another rebuff. This time, however, Joe provided details.

"First to Rome. I told Carlo I want to review IADW's refugee screening process before you arrive. Then to Naples. I'll be doing some work—"

"Wait! Back up." She couldn't believe what she'd just heard. "You told Carlo that I was coming to Rome? To work at IADW?"

He blinked, as surprised by her sharp tone as she'd been by his abrupt announcement a few moments ago. "You said last night that's what you wanted. Did you change your mind?"

"No." A surge of irritation smothered her earlier doubts. "I would, however, have appreciated the opportunity to tell my prospective employer *personally* that I'd accepted his generous job offer."

"Oh. Yeah. Sorry." He scraped a palm across his chin. "It's just…"

"Yes?"

"You've seen the news coverage. The attacks in France and Belgium and other parts of the world. Some of those terrorists got into place by posing as refugees and entering through legitimate refugee resettlement conduits. I just want to make sure IADW isn't one of them."

Her irritation melted. A little. Even more when he brushed a knuckle down her cheek. His touch was warm. Soothing. Possessive.

"Keeping you safe's becoming my number-one priority, Pansy Eyes."

She had to smile at the endearment. And she could hardly argue with his desire to protect her. Not after she'd burrowed in this admittedly luxurious hole while he tracked down the creep who'd sent the emails. Yet the little corner of her mind that rejected the prospect of being wrapped in cotton wool for the rest of her life reared its nasty head again.

"Thank you, Joe."

She meant that. She really did. Still, she took a small, instinctive step back when he extracted a small jeweler's box out of his coat pocket.

"I know this is pushing things, Callie, but I saw this before I flew to Australia and asked them to hold it. I wanted you to check it out, see if you liked it. Now, with this Rome deal, I figured I'd take a chance."

"Joe…"

"It's not as flashy or sparkly as some I looked at," he said, flipping up the lid, "but it's almost the same color as your eyes. And the setting is kind of nice."

More than nice, Callie saw on a little intake of breath. It was exquisite. White gold, she guessed, spun into a filigree bouquet to showcase a gleaming oval amethyst. The end prongs were long-stemmed roses, the side prongs delicate leaves with a tiny dove nested between them.

"Joe, I…"

She floundered, tugged in a dozen different directions by the whirlwind of emotions this man roused in her. He noted her confusion with a small smile and pounced.

"It doesn't have to mean anything more than you want it to, Callie. Here, try it on for size." He slid it

over her knuckle. "Good. It fits. I wanted you to have it before you took off for Rome."

She glanced up from the glowing amethyst and caught the glint of male satisfaction in his eyes.

"And," she guessed drily, "you wanted me to be wearing it when I meet with Carlo."

"Yeah, that, too."

The admission was totally unapologetic and so…so *Joe* that she had to smile.

"I like Carlo as a friend and now a prospective employer," she said. "That's all. Surely you know that."

"Of course I do. Doesn't hurt to reinforce the message, though." His gaze held hers, steady and unflinching. "You change your mind, or want to send a different signal after you get to Rome, just take it off. I'll understand."

Callie debated for some moments after Joe left. Her first instinct was to scurry next door, corner Dawn in her spacious home office and get Kate on FaceTime. A glance at the clock brought a swift revision to that plan. It was close to eleven o'clock, and her news was too momentous to share electronically. Two quick calls set up an emergency girls-only luncheon at an upscale eatery only a block from the thirteen-story high-rise on G Street where Kate worked.

Rushing into the bedroom, Callie exchanged her sweats and fuzzy slippers for boots, slacks and a roll-neck sweater. She angled a black angora beret sideways to keep her head warm and bundled up in a paisley scarf, gloves and the ankle-length khaki duster she'd snagged during a sale at Nordstrom.

She met a similarly muffled and extremely curious

Dawn on the flagstone walk connecting the main house to the guesthouse.

"What's the emergency?"

"I'll tell you and Kate together. You drive. You know your way around better than I do."

The light snow of the day before had pretty much turned to mush, but holiday decorations added bright touches of red, gold and green as Dawn negotiated DC's always busy streets. When she pulled up at the popular bistro and turned her Mustang over to the valet, the two women hurried inside.

It was still early, not yet eleven thirty, so Kate had been able to snag a booth by the round fireplace in the center of the restaurant. The noise level was still low enough for Nat King Cole's velvet-voiced rendition of "The Christmas Song" to provide the perfect complement to the crackle of flames.

Her tawny hair caught up in a smooth twist, Kate looked every inch the professional in a ruby blazer that hid her almost baby bump, white blouse and a flowing black skirt that draped over the top of her boots. She laid aside the menu she'd been examining and looked up expectantly as Callie and Dawn shed their outdoor gear before sliding into the booth.

"Okay, Miss Priss and Boots. What's so important that…oh, my God!" Jaw dropping, Kate grabbed the hand Callie was using to shake out her napkin. "This is *gorgeous*!"

Beside her Dawn gasped in surprise. "You stinker! Is that what I think it is?"

"Sort of."

"Sort of?" Kate angled Callie's hand from side to side. "What does that mean? Did you and Joe settle the Lassie question or not?"

"Not exactly. But we're working on it."

A server decked out in a sparkly red bow tie approached. Dawn waved him off with a quick smile.

"Give us a few minutes. We're talking some serious girl stuff here." She slewed around again. "Back to you and Joe and that hunk of quartz you're sporting. What's the bottom line?"

"The bottom line? Okay, brace yourself. I'm taking Carlo up on his offer of a job at International Aid to Displaced Women, and Joe wants me wearing his brand when I fly over to Rome on Thursday."

Her friends reacted with equal parts surprise and dismay.

"You're going to Rome?"

"This *Thursday*?" Dawn wailed. "You can't go this Thursday! Christmas is less than two weeks away. The three of us have gathered at one or the other's house every Christmas since, when? Fifth grade?"

"You've got Brian and Tommy to share it with now. And Kate and Travis. You'll have a house full."

"It won't be the same," she said stubbornly. "Wonderful, but not the same."

"The position I'll be filling has been vacant for several months," Callie explained. "The director—my new boss—is anxious to get someone in place."

"We're only talking another few weeks," Kate protested. "Surely your boss can wait until after the holidays."

"Evidently not." A small smile played at the corners of Callie's mouth. "From what I can gather based on my brief conversation with Carlo this morning, he's a bit intimidated by the woman."

Her friends shared another astonished look. Neither Kate nor Dawn could envision any mere female intim-

idating Carlo di Lorenzo. The cocky Italian Special Forces pilot with the string of royal titles after his name had racked up hundreds of combat hours. According to the paparazzi, he'd also charmed his way in and out of the same number of bedrooms.

"This director must be a real witch," Kate warned. "You sure you want to work for someone like that?"

"I'll be in Italy," Callie said softly. "Remember what happened to you there? And to you, Dawn?"

That silenced the other women for a few moments. Kate went all dewy eyed thinking of the surprise ceremony Travis had arranged at the Trevi Fountain to renew their wedding vows. Dawn could only grin at the memory of the sparks she and Brian had struck off each other when they'd met in Venice. She came out of her reverie in time to wave the waiter away again.

"What about Joe?" Kate asked. "He's content to let you zip off to Rome as long as you're wearing his ring?"

Callie gave a small huff. "Not hardly. By the time he got around to slipping it on my finger this morning, he'd already contacted a pal in the Defense Intelligence Agency and had them check out the organization I'll be working for. Then he told Carlo that he's flying in tonight to do a scrub of the center's screening procedures. And he set up a job for himself in Naples."

"Naples is only an hour south of Rome."

Kate should know. She'd researched train schedules and driving times and every possible tourist sight for their trip to Italy a few months back.

"So Joe informed me." Callie fingered the ring again. "He also informed me that all I have to do is take this off and he'll drop out of the picture, no harm, no foul."

"Oh, that's romantic," Dawn snorted. "Please tell me he didn't use those actual words."

"Pretty close."

"Well? Are you going to remove it?"

"No." Sighing, Callie shook her head. "Not now, anyway. I'm still trying to sort out how I feel about him."

"How *do* you feel? Right this exact second."

"Happy. Confused. Excited. And," she admitted with a reluctant laugh, "completely in lust."

Neither of her friends could argue with that. Or talk her out of relocating to Italy. Resigning themselves to the inevitable, they helped Callie tie up the loose ends she'd left dangling when she'd taken refuge in the Ellises' gatehouse.

"I'll zip up to Boston," Dawn volunteered. "I can sort through your closet and send you what you'll need in Rome. But what do you want me to do with rest of it? Your furniture, your houseplants, your ton and a half of books?"

"The books and furniture will have to go in storage. I'm pretty sure Mrs. Eckstein, my neighbor, will take the plants."

"How about your lease?" the fiscally minded Kate asked. "Does it allow you to sublet?"

"The lease is actually up for renewal at the end of next month. Since I'm not giving them the required sixty days' notice, I'll probably have to forfeit January's rent and my security deposit."

"Let me handle that. As for Rome, you shouldn't have any trouble using your credit card for purchases or withdrawing cash at an ATM. But you should open an account at a local branch and transfer some operating funds, just in case. I'll get the paperwork started, if you want."

"Thank you. Thank both of you!"

The gratitude came straight from Callie's heart. Yet

she had to suppress a stupid little twinge at how easy it was to cut all ties to the life she'd lived in Boston for six years.

Oh, for...! What was her problem? This was what she wanted. What she'd wished for at the Trevi Fountain! Adventure. Romance. A whole new chapter in her life.

"Won't you need a license to practice in Italy?" Dawn asked, still working the logistics in her mind.

"I would, if I was working in an Italian treatment facility or setting up my own practice. That's not the case here. The IADW center is physically located in Rome, but it's governed by an international body with different credentialing requirements. According to their standards, I'm actually *over*qualified for the work I'll be doing."

"And your parents?" Kate put in. "Have you told them you're zipping off to Europe?"

"Not yet. I wanted you guys to be the first to know. I'll call them after lunch."

They'd be surprised, Callie knew, but not particularly concerned. Since moving to a seniors-only retirement village in central Florida six years ago, her retired teacher mom and former postal worker dad had become totally immersed in new hobbies and activities. Including, she remembered with an inner smile, their latest passion for bird-watching. She hadn't told them about the vicious emails, and they'd voiced only mild curiosity about her extended stay in DC.

"So you're really going to do it," Dawn said, breaking into her thoughts.

"I am."

"In that case we need to celebrate with our favorite Italian drink." A smile and an uplifted finger brought the

patient server to the table. "We want three Bellinis—two regular and one virgin for the pregnant lady."

The young server looked confused. "I don't know if there is such a thing as a virgin Bellini."

"Tell the barkeep to improvise," Dawn instructed airily.

Despite her friends' wish that she would wait until after the holidays, Callie stuck to her decision to report to her new job the following Monday. She flew out of Dulles late Thursday afternoon and thoroughly enjoyed the unexpected and unaccustomed luxury of an upgrade to business class compliments of Joe. When she landed at Rome's Leonardo da Vinci Airport early Friday morning, she zinged off a text to let Kate and Dawn know she'd arrived.

She cleared customs with the intention of spending the day setting up the small flat that came with her new job and the weekend exploring the neighborhood around it. She hadn't included Joe Russo in her plans, however. Looking like Italy's answer to Patrick Dempsey in snug jeans, a black turtleneck and his tan bomber jacket, he met her in the arrivals terminal and welcomed her with a hard, hot kiss. She was still recovering from that when his take-charge personality emerged.

"Are you totally wiped?" he asked as he steered her to the baggage claim area.

"Not wiped at all. I slept most of the flight in lie-flat leather luxury." She hesitated, but innate honesty made her ask. "I saw that the upgrade was charged to JLR Security. It won't be billed as a business expense, will it? If so, I'll reimburse you."

He glanced down at her, amusement flickering in those stone-gray eyes. "Not to worry. I use a top-fifty

accounting firm. They keep my personal and professional accounts straight."

"Good to know. Except I'm used to paying my own way. I don't expect—or want—you to pick up the tab every time we're together."

"Well, we shouldn't have many expenses in Naples this weekend. I'm meeting with my prospective client, so my time will be charged to him."

"Naples? I can't go to Naples this weekend! I've got too much to do here in Rome."

"You might want to reconsider. Today's the feast of Santa Lucia. I'm told her day sort of officially kicks off the Christmas season. Marcello—my prospective client—has invited us to join him and his family for their traditional dinner tonight. It would give me a chance to get to know him in an informal setting, assess what kind of man he is."

"But…"

The rumble of the baggage conveyor belt cut off her protest. By the time Joe had snagged her two suitcases, she'd reassessed her priorities. From the sound of it, this meeting was important to Joe. Unpacking and settling into the apartment could wait.

Or not. To her surprise, he'd planned for that, too. After asking if she needed anything other than her roll-on for the weekend trip, he turned her bags over to the associate waiting beside a slick black SUV.

"This is Emilio Mancera, head of my operations here in Italy."

"Ciao, Emilio."

"Ciao, signorina. *Benvenuto a Roma.*"

Dark eyed, curly haired and the possessor of a proud Roman nose to go with the muscles that bulged under his fleece pullover, the thirtysomething Italian loaded the bags in the SUV.

"I will take these to your apartment, *sì*? And make sure the kitchen contains all you need."

"I, uh, *sì. Grazie.*"

He conducted a brief exchange with Joe in swift Italian before giving Callie another cheerful ciao and departing.

She glanced at Joe while he beeped the locks on a second SUV in the adjoining space. Why hadn't she picked up on the fact that he spoke the language when she'd first met him here in Italy? It was just one more gap in her knowledge about this man and his past. Gaps she intended to bridge. Starting now, she decided after they'd left the parking garage and hit the bright, brittle December sunlight.

"You sounded pretty fluent in that exchange with Emilio. Where did you learn Italian?"

"Here and there. My five-month gig with Carlo considerably expanded my vocabulary. Although," he added with a sardonic tilt to his head, "most of it can't be repeated in polite company."

"Do you speak any other languages?"

"Some Spanish. A little French. Enough Portuguese to ask directions to the closest bar."

"Portuguese? I'm impressed."

Shrugging, he aimed for the airport exit. "You take a job in Angola, it helps to be able to communicate with the local cops."

Callie tried to sketch a mental image of Africa. She knew Angola was near the continent's southern tip but couldn't place it on the east or west coast.

"What did you do there?"

He shot her a quick glance. Callie kicked herself, thinking she'd crossed the line again. She was suppress-

ing a twinge of resentment at being shut out of his past when he decided to let her in a bare inch or two.

"How much do you know about Angola?"

"Nothing, I'm embarrassed to admit."

"It sits on huge mineral and petroleum reserves, and its economy is among the fastest growing in the world. Problem is, a handful of wealthy elites control the economy."

"Which makes them prime targets," Callie guessed.

"Exactly."

Okay, he'd cracked the door. She pushed it just a little harder.

"Your client was one of these incredibly wealthy elites?"

His expression didn't change but Callie could sense him drawing into himself. Again.

"Dammit, Joe. You brought up the job in Angola. You can't just leave me hanging. Yes or no? Was your client one of these wealthy elites?"

"No."

Well, she'd set herself up for that one. She was about to let the grudging remark go when he surprised her with a terse follow-up.

"She was at the other end of the spectrum," he said, his jaw tight. "A young, passionate member of parliament who wanted to curb the elites' power. My team and I smuggled her out of the country the day before her appointment with a firing squad."

"Good grief! Where is she now?"

"Dead."

The single syllable hit like a glass of ice water to the face. When Callie recoiled against her seat back, Joe wrenched his gaze from the road.

"An assassin got to her in Curaçao." His tone was as cold as his eyes. "And I got to him."

Her breath stuck in her throat. She had to swallow twice before she got out a quavering, "Good."

As shaky as it was, her endorsement seemed to pull Joe from the dark cave of his memories. The taut angle of his jaw eased. So did the tension cording his neck above his jacket collar.

"Helluva a way to kick off what I'd planned as a fun weekend," he growled.

Still startled by the piece of his past she'd pried loose, Callie forced a smile. "I'm sure it'll be fun. How could a traditional Italian family dinner be anything but?"

Blessedly ignorant of the noisy, exuberant, exhausting evening ahead, she relaxed in her seat and vowed to keep the conversation away from dark subjects as they hit the autostrada and rolled south.

Chapter Five

Since Joe's client didn't expect them until late afternoon, they made the drive down from Rome in leisurely stages.

They stopped first at the Abbey of Monte Cassino. Perched atop a steep precipice overlooking the main road to Rome, the abbey had become a key objective in the Allies' push north during WWII. Their efforts to dislodge the Germans resulted in a murderous battle than caused more than 190,000 casualties and left the abbey and town at its base in smoking ruins. Rebuilt after the war, Monte Cassino now offered visitors a glimpse of its original medieval glory. The grim history of the battle and accompanying artifacts interested Joe, of course, but Callie delighted in the priceless manuscripts and religious treasures that had been taken to Rome for safekeeping and returned to the abbey after the war.

Closer to Naples, the warm Mediterranean currents

chased the chill from the air, and the temperature rose. Callie wiggled out of her wool duster and tossed it in the backseat. Joe did the same with his leather jacket. When they left the autostrada for lunch at a trattoria recommended by Joe's prospective client, they opted to sit outside on a vine-draped patio. The setting was idyllic but it was the cloud-wrapped mountain in the distance that held Callie's fascinated gaze.

"Is that Vesuvius?"

"Looks like it."

"Do we have time to visit the ruins of Pompeii?"

"Not if you want to do them justice. Maybe tomorrow. Or Sunday, before we head back to Rome."

Not quite believing that she was actually here, in the shadow of Mount Vesuvius, she took the friendly server's recommendation and ordered a local specialty of sausage served with broccoli rabe. Joe went the more traditional route of pasta in a red sauce, with meatballs served separately as the second course.

Feeling deliciously lazy afterward, she expected them to head into Naples. Instead Joe skirted the city's sprawling outskirts.

"Signor Audi lives in the city," he explained, "but his family's ancestral farm is another forty-five minutes south. Or more correctly, their ancestral ranch."

"They raise cattle?"

"Water buffalo. They've got about three hundred head on their ranch."

"What in the world do they do with… Oh! They make mozzarella?"

"The best in Italy, according to Signor Audi."

Despite her extensive reading, Callie couldn't imagine how the big, plodding, wide-horned water buffalo had migrated to Italy. From Asia, probably, herded

across the Mongolian steppes by nomadic tribes. Or maybe imported by the Arabs who'd invaded Sicily. But there was no denying mozzarella had pretty much become associated with all things Italian.

Still, she wasn't prepared for Campania's rich grasslands. Wide, rolling pastures bordered the road and stretched all the way to the sea that could be glimpsed through tall, thin cypresses and silver-barked eucalyptus trees. Dotting these pastures were herds of black buffalo grazing placidly or wallowing contentedly in man-made ponds with sloping ramps. The air wafting through the SUV's vents carried a mix of grass and salt sea air, along with an earthy hint of dung.

When the navigational system pinged a few minutes later, Joe turned left and drove through a pair of stone pillars. A cypress-lined road led them past more fenced pastures and ended in a broad yard bordered on one side by a long, narrow building with huge roller brushes at its entrance.

"Is that a car wash?" Callie asked in surprise.

Joe's glance flicked from the brushes to the gleaming stainless steel tank truck parked at the building's far end. "I'm guessing that's the barn where they milk the buffalo. They probably have to scrub 'em down first to make sure the milk stays clean."

Her mind boggled at the thought of one of those huge buffalo going through a series of washes and waxes like the family car. Trying to visualize the process, she looked around the rest of the yard with some interest. Older buildings and sheds constructed of local stone housed tractors and various other pieces of farm equipment.

A rambling, two-story residence sat a little farther down the road. Surrounded by ancient cypresses that

stood tall and spear straight, its varying levels suggested it had been added to numerous times over the years. Like the other buildings, it, too, was constructed of stone covered almost entirely with a pale yellow plaster. U-shaped terra cotta tiles delineated the varying roof lines, and bright green shutters framed its many windows. Flowers spilled from window boxes, stone urns, even the wooden bucket dangling over what must have once been a working well.

Adding to the color were the scattered children's toys…a red-and-blue plastic Big Wheel, a hot pink bike with training wheels and sparkly handlebar streamers, a forgotten doll with the pale hair and blue gown of Princess Elsa from *Frozen*.

Callie was thinking of all the times she'd watched that particular video with Tommy when two dogs raced from behind the house and offered a raucous greeting. One was a mottled gray and black of an indeterminate breed, the other a small collie. They were noisy but not vicious, as evidenced by the greeting they gave Joe after he exited the SUV and squatted to let them sniff his hand.

Callie climbed out as well and breathed in the pungent tang of a working farm overlaid with the perfume of so many flowers. She was letting the dogs scope her out when a woman strode out of the house. In boots, tight jeans and a loose-knit sweater, she moved with the careless, casual grace that seemed as natural as breathing to so many Italian women.

"Signor Russo, Signorina Langston, welcome. I am Arianna Audi de Luca." Her dark eyes were friendly, her handshake firm. "My father apologizes that he is not here to greet you. He and my husband are at the barn. One of our buffalo has gone into the milking chamber

and does not wish to come out. She can be very stubborn, that Domenica, but she'll usually come to Papà when he whistles to her."

"Domenica? Is that her breed?"

"No, no, it is her name."

Callie's glance swept past her to the hulking black animals in the pasture. "You name them all?"

"Not all. But this one is like a pet, yes? When she was but a tiny calf, she followed my brother and me everywhere." Head cocked, Arianna issued a smiling invitation. "If you're not too tired from your journey, perhaps you would like to meet her? And see something of the milking process?"

Callie wasn't about to pass up the chance to see the cow wash in operation. "I'd like that."

Joe seconded the idea, and their hostess gave them a quick history as she led them back toward the barn. With each step the scents of fresh-cut grass and dung edged out the flowers a little more.

"With Papà and my brother so busy in Naples, my husband and I manage the farm. It's been in our family since the sixteenth century. We have a framed copy of the original deed in the office."

Her expression turned serious.

"There are many cruelties in this business, but my family has spent much time and money over the years to make ours humane. As you'll see, we use the voluntary milking method. We also hold to the strict sanitary standards required for DOP certification. *Scusi.* DOP stands for *denominazione di origine protetta*. It means our mozzarella meets the highest government standards for quality and excellence."

Angling to the left, she pointed out a wide metal chute that led from the pasture to the giant roller

brushes. Several large bovines waited patiently in the chute while others milled near its mouth.

"The females come when they wish to be milked. Since it is all done by machine, they do not have to follow a set schedule. They enter here and…"

The sudden rumble of an engine starting and gears engaging interrupted her.

"Ah! Papà has convinced Domenica to leave the milking chamber. Now the others may enter. But first they take a little bath, yes?"

Streams of water arced across the barn entrance, the giant rollers whirred into action and the lead buffalo in the chute ambled up the low ramp. Tail swishing, it disappeared into the mist.

"Amazing," Callie murmured. "They're not afraid of it at all."

"I think they consider it a spa treatment," Arianna replied, laughing. "We give them jets of cool water in the heat of summer, warm water in winter."

Dodging the spray, she ushered them through a side door and into a spacious work area. "This is the office, where my husband takes care of all the necessary forms and endless paperwork. And here…"

She opened another door to show a small room with stainless steel counters and an impressive array of laboratory equipment.

"Here is where I spend much of my time."

Callie could see why. A quick glance at the framed degrees on the wall beside the door indicted Arianna Maria Patrizia Audi had earned a bachelor of science in organic chemistry from Stanford and a *laurea magistrale* in *biotecnologia agricola* from the University of Pisa.

"I'm working to increase the conjugated linoleic acid

content in our herd's milk," she informed them. "There's some evidence it possesses anticancer properties. It may also affect insulin response. Sadly, the science is not there yet. One can only keep researching."

After the high-powered cow wash and pristine lab, Callie wasn't surprised to see the single worker in the milking area wearing immaculate white coveralls, a hairnet and plastic booties over his shoes. He didn't appear to have much of a job, however. Just stood by as the newly scrubbed buffalo meandered into a narrow chamber. A second later, a robotic arm slid under her. The animal got another wash, this one from a gentle up-spray, then six flexible tubes snaked upward. Like cobras, they curled and wove and latched onto their prey.

"Good grief!" Astonished, Callie watched for some reaction from the buffalo, but she didn't so much as blink her long, curling lashes. "How did those cups magically attach to her udder?"

"They're equipped with optical cameras and lasers that detect the exact position of each teat. Once attached, the cup will rinse the teat again with warm water and gently massage it to stimulate the premilk. That gets flushed into a side line, then the rest will flow through the main milking line and empty directly into the truck you see outside for transport to our plant in town."

"No wonder Domenica didn't want to leave the chamber," Callie couldn't help commenting. "She must really enjoy all that flushing and massaging."

"She does," Arianna confirmed with a laugh. "What female would not?"

Both women glanced at Joe. He merely lifted his brows, but to Callie's surprise and secret amusement a faint tinge of red crept into his cheeks.

Would she ever understand this man? Only this morning he'd admitted taking out an assassin, and now here he was, embarrassed to hear two women discussing udders and teats. Smothering a grin, she listened as their guide continued.

"Once the milk stops flowing, the cups disengage and the udders are washed again, then sprayed with disinfectant."

They followed the chamber's current occupant toward the exit. The buffalo entered another chute that led to the pasture, and Arianna and her guests emerged into the yard.

"That was *so* interesting," Callie said. "I had no idea cattle milking had become so mechanized."

"Not all farms are as progressive as ours. And there… Ah! Here is Papà."

Callie's first, startled thought was that the gentleman who hurried toward them looked just like Rossano Brazzi, the hunky Italian actor who'd starred alongside Louis Jourdan in *Three Coins in the Fountain*. Tall, tanned, wavy haired and full lipped, he greeted Joe with a hearty handshake and Callie with a traditional kiss to both cheeks.

"I'm so pleased you could join us, Signorina Langston. I see Arianna has been showing you a little of what makes our mozzarella the best in Campania."

"She has, and I must say I'm very impressed."

"You will be even more so once you taste it. Please, let us escort you to the house and introduce you to the rest of the family."

Four hours, two dozen or so relatives, several glasses of wine, a ginormous platter of pasta and six different flavors of mozzarella later, Signor Audi asked his

daughter to entertain Callie while he took Joe into his study for a private discussion. Not that she needed entertaining. She was so stuffed she could barely move. She was also beginning to feel jet lag creeping up on her. Comfortably ensconced on the sofa, she was more than content to listen with half an ear to the buzz of conversation conducted mostly in Italian and watch Arianna's two young children setting candles into ornate ceramic holders to be lit in honor of Saint Lucia.

"It's a tradition for us," their mother explained, her feet up and her ankles crossed on a hassock. "One that dates back almost a thousand years. Lucia means light, yes? She was martyred on this day in December, which under the Julian calendar was then the winter solstice."

"The shortest day of the year," Callie commented.

"Exactly! So for us the lighting of candles signals the end of the dark winter as well as the beginning of the twelve days of Christmas. When we light the candles, we sing her song and give the children sweets and small gifts."

"'Santa Lucia.' I know that song."

She should. The famous Neapolitan hymn had been recorded by everyone from opera greats like Enrico Caruso and Luciano Pavarotti to modern-day classical crossover star Hayley Westenra. Even Elvis Presley had sung it in one of his most popular movies, *Viva Las Vegas*. Movie buffs that they were, Callie, Kate and Dawn had watched the classic starring Elvis and Ann-Margret a half dozen times.

"You have another interesting Christmas tradition."

Callie nodded to the A-frame crèche that occupied an entire corner of the room. It was the largest and most elaborate she'd ever seen. Five, maybe six feet tall, it contained several tiers of shelves filled with wrapped

gifts, fragrant pine boughs, small candles and far more figures than she was used to seeing in a Christmas nativity scene. Some of the exquisitely detailed and gorgeously painted figurines wore the simple robes of shepherds and goat herders. Others were garbed in what looked like costumes from a dozen different historical eras, including modern-day soccer garb.

"I've never seen soccer players in a manger scene before."

"That, too, is very Neapolitan," Arianna told her. "We add new figures to our crèche every year, and the new addition doesn't always have biblical significance. It could be a famous person from the past, a great opera star, even a president or politician." Grinning, she pointed to a figure in modern clothing. "Do you see that grim gentleman there, on the far right? That's our current prime minister. Papà added him this year. He feels the poor, misguided soul needs as much heavenly exposure as he can get."

"We have a few politicians in the States who could use more, too."

"You would probably see many familiar figures for sale on Via San Gregorio Armeno. That's where the artisans who make the cribs display their wares. You *must* stroll down that street while you're in Naples. You'll see nothing else like it in the world."

"I'll certainly check it out if I have time before we head back to Rome."

"Ah, yes. Papà tells me you are to work with Carlo di Lorenzo." Her voice took on a cautious note. "You've met him before?"

"Several times."

"*Bene.* Then you know to expect the most extravagant offers to jet away with him to Casablanca or Hong Kong."

"His last offer was Dubai," Callie confirmed.

"And Joe?" Arianna asked curiously. "He knows this about Carlo?"

"He does."

Callie didn't realize she was fingering her ring until it drew the other woman's gaze.

"That amethyst is gorgeous, and the setting so unusual."

"Thank you. I'm still not quite used to it."

"I begin to understand." Arianna's dark eyes danced. "If Joe Russo gave you that beautiful ring, not even Carlo di Lorenzo can mistake its message. Whether he will choose to heed it, however, is another matter altogether."

"Sounds like you know the prince pretty well."

"I, too, have been invited to fly away with him. But," she added on a merry laugh, "that was before I settled down with a husband, two bambini and three hundred water buffalo."

When Joe and Signor Audi returned, Callie confessed she was starting to feel the combined effects of her long flight, the delicious dinner and several glasses of wine. They made their farewells a few moments later and left with invitations to visit again, an exchange of phone numbers and a promise from Arianna to call Callie the next time she was in Rome. They must do lunch, the buffalo rancher declared, and shop at some of the city's elegant little boutiques.

"I hope she does call," Callie said as she settled in the soft leather seat. "It would be nice to hit the shops with a friend."

She wanted to stay awake for the short drive into Naples. She would really like to experience the city for

the first time bathed in moonlight. She was also eager to see the colorful Christmas lights Arianna said were strung from building to building in alleys so narrow that second- and third-story residents could almost shake hands with neighbors living across the street.

She remembered clicking her seat belt. Remembered her head lolling against the back rest. The next thing she knew Joe had opened the passenger side door and was unclicking her belt.

"Whrarwe?"

"At the hotel. C'mon, sweetheart, let's get you to bed."

The parking valet took the SUV, and Joe took her arm. While he checked them in, Callie registered sleepy impressions of a lobby with more marble than the pyramids of Giza, a wide circular staircase draped with exquisitely decorated garlands and a Christmas tree that soared three or four stories.

Once in their suite, her jet lag hit with a vengeance. Close to comatose, she left a trail of clothes from a sitting room graced by a massive sofa to a bedroom dominated by a four-poster bed draped with shimmering, champagne-colored silk. In bra and panties, she crawled under the covers. A sleep-starved corner of her mind registered the small thud of Joe placing their carryalls on the bench at the foot of the bed. The faint whisper as he undressed. The dip of the mattress when he slid in and pulled her against him. His chest was warm against her back, his thighs hard under her butt. With a sound halfway between a sigh and a whimper, she snuggled closer and sank into oblivion.

She woke to thin shafts of sunlight sneaking through the drapes and hazy realization she was still spooned

against Joe. She smiled in perfect contentment and went back to sleep.

It could have been moments or hours before she blinked awake again. Pushing up on one elbow, she discovered the other half of the bed was empty and the covers neatly smoothed. The only sound disturbing the stillness was the faint honk of a car horn outside the draped windows.

"Joe?"

No answer from either the bathroom or the spacious sitting room visible through open double doors. Tossing back the covers, Callie padded to the bath. Each step brought the delicious sensation of her feet sinking into inch-thick silk carpet. The room itself stopped her in her tracks.

The decadent bath was a symphony in marble— gleaming black-and-white squares on the floors, dove-gray patterned with what looked like real gold swirls on the walls, a matching slab of gold-toned stone on the countertops. The walk-in shower was as large as the kitchen in her Boston apartment, and the claw-foot tub sat in regal splendor on a raised dais.

Good grief! This hotel suite must cost a fortune. She felt an uneasy twinge thinking back to yesterday, when she'd insisted on paying her share of expenses. Then she remembered Joe saying his prospective client would pick up the tab. The mozzarella business must be booming.

Joe's business, too, if he catered to such super-wealthy clients. He and Callie had never discussed either the size or the financial base of his company. They'd had no reason to. Just one more aspect of the Joe Russo enigma she knew nothing about.

Thinking of the gaps in their knowledge of each

other, she padded to the shell-shaped sink with its gold faucets and arching swan's neck spigots. None of the fixtures showed a single water spot despite the obvious signs Joe had used them earlier—his razor, shaving cream and aftershave were lined up in precise order beside a leather shaving kit. He'd even folded back the top sheet of toilet paper, she noted with some amusement.

Her immediate needs attended to, she snuggled into one the hotel's plush robes and headed back into the bedroom to discover that Joe had picked up the clothes she'd discarded the night before. He'd also unpacked the rest of her things. They hung beside his at evenly spaced intervals in a wardrobe of ornately carved burled walnut.

"Well," she murmured to her reflection in the wardrobe's mirrored doors, "whatever else the man's done in his checkered past, he learned to pick up after himself."

Evidently you could take the man out of the military. Much harder to take the military out of the man, she mused as she surveyed the sitting room that he'd left in the same neat order. Newspaper folded. Glossy magazines aligned on the monster coffee table. Room service tray with its contents stacked, placed on a hall table near the door. Note folded and propped against the vase centered on a round table inlaid with a dozen different kinds of wood.

The message in the note, like the man himself, was short and succinct.

Checking out film festival venues with Sig. Audi.
Back by 3:00 p.m.

A glance at the mantel clock above a fireplace faced with green marble indicated it was almost 10:00 a.m.

She'd been out cold for thirteen hours. The basic need for sleep taken care of, she now had to deal with another. She'd left Audi Farms last night convinced she'd never eat again. Her stomach was now singing an entirely different tune.

She'd call room service, she decided, and grab a quick shower while waiting for breakfast to be delivered. After that she'd go explore. But first...

She searched the brocade curtains covering the entire wall, hunting for their pull cord then realized they operated electrically. She hit one switch, and the heavy brocade whirred back. A second switch opened the blackout curtain underneath. As soon as it parted, brilliant sunlight flooded in. Momentarily blinded, Callie took a step back and squinted through the glare.

"Oh. My. Lord!"

Stunned, she fumbled for the latch of the double doors that opened onto a wide balcony. A brisk breeze tugged at her hair. The balcony's marble tiles were cold against her bare feet. On the street below, traffic honked and diesel fumes tainted the air. What sounded like a jackhammer was going at it somewhere not too far away. Callie didn't see or hear or feel any of it. The view from the balcony utterly and completely enthralled her.

Naples in all its chaotic glory spilled down the hill below and spread its wide, sprawling arms to embrace the impossibly, incredibly blue Bay of Naples. Vesuvius towered above the far side of the bay. The clouds that had shrouded its peak yesterday had dissipated. Today the cone wore a wreath of glistening white snow.

Enchanted, Callie leaned her elbows on the stone baluster and reveled in her bird's-eye view of jumbled streets and narrow alleys strung with washing and ropes of colored Christmas paper. Far below was what she

guessed was the main piazza. A majestic cathedral dominated one side of the square. To its left was a 1890s-looking building with a fanciful glass dome. And facing the cathedral was a mile-long structure with a facade interspersed with dozens of statue-filled niches.

Whirling, Callie rushed back inside. The heck with breakfast. She'd grab a croissant or a roll and some coffee on the go. She had to get out and explore.

She scrambled into slacks and a lightweight sweater, bunched her hair into a scrunchie, slapped on some lip gloss and added a quick postscript to Joe's note. Then she was out the door.

Chapter Six

Callie was almost through the lobby before she remembered Arianna mentioning a street she shouldn't miss. A quick detour took her to the concierge's desk.

"But yes, madam," he said when she asked about a street where they sold crèches. "It is the Via San Gregorio Armeno. Let me show you where it is."

He pulled out a tourist map and circled what looked like a short alleyway but warned her it was difficult to find.

"It's best to take a taxi, madam. And may I suggest other sites nearby worthy of a visit?"

"Yes, please."

"Here, just a few blocks away, is the Museo Cappella Sansevero, with its magnificent statue of the Veiled Christ. And here is the Basilica of San Lorenzo Maggiore. It's located at the exact center of the ancient city of Neapolis. There is a new museum here that gives the history of this area, from the Greeks to the Angevins

and down to the present day. You can also visit the exca-
vation of the Roman market once located on this spot."

"Thank you, I will."

"But be careful, madam. These spots are very popu-
lar with tourists, and thus with pickpockets. I suggest
you drape the strap of your purse across your chest and
keep it in front of you, yes?"

Callie thanked him again and studied the map while
the bellman summoned a cab. Not that her studying did
much good. She gave up even trying to read street signs
as the cab rocked through a series of hairpin turns and
zoomed down the hill. With each turn the streets got
narrower, while the buildings got older, darker and a
little grimier.

The taxi driver let her off at the head of the street of
the crèche makers. As the concierge had warned, the
narrow lane was jammed with tourists. Callie kept a
careful hand on the purse she'd looped across her chest
and plunged into the throng.

Via San Gregorio Armeno was everything Arianna
had said it would be! In shop after shop, brightly lit
windows displayed crèches made of wood or cork or
gorgeously decoupaged cardboard. Some were small,
some huge and multitiered. A number of them featured
mechanical windmills or waterfalls or baaing sheep.
Artisans were hard at work in many of the shops, hand-
painting terra cotta shepherds and oxen and angels.

Other artisans crafted the figures from different eras
that fascinated Callie as much as they did the other tour-
ists. Arianna hadn't exaggerated. Statuettes of famous
political figures, rock stars and athletes crowded next
to the holy family, the magi and the shepherds. Callie
recognized a good number. William and Kate with their

own little angels. The US president. The Irish musician and world-renowned philanthropist Bono.

As one shopkeeper explained in excellent English, it was the ultimate goal of all Italian entertainers to find themselves on the Via San Gregorio Armeno.

"As soon as they become famous, they want the statue. Here is the great Pavarotti. And the young Anna Tatangelo, who sings like an angel. And this is Giuseppe Fabiano, the footballer who goes to jail for not paying taxes."

Callie dutifully admired the array of modern figures but decided to go traditional on a gift for Joe. The beautifully crafted four-inch statue of Joseph, Mary's husband and protector, depicted both strength and nobility of character. A fitting start to the crèche—and family—she and her very own Joseph might build together.

In another shop she found a Kristoff, the iceman from Disney's *Frozen*, for Tommy, and a flame-haired angel for Dawn. For Kate she chose a wicked caricature of a former US presidential candidate her friend had heartily despised. She left the street pleased with her purchases but not quite sure she fully appreciated the irreverent sense of humor that would juxtapose the sacred and profane so exuberantly.

The tantalizing scent of something hot and yeasty lured her to a bakery halfway down the next block. Since it was already past noon, the cases displayed both pastries and open-faced sandwiches. A slab of pizza bread tempted her, but she decided she'd rather share a real Neapolitan pizza with Joe and settled instead for coffee and a ricotta-filled pastry. Flaky and topped with powdered sugar, the roll melted in her mouth. She lingered over the coffee, people watching and enjoying the hustle of the busy street. She would've stayed

longer if not for the desire to be back at the hotel when Joe returned.

Once out on the street, she headed for her next stop. After several wrong turns and an appeal to a passerby for assistance, she found the entrance to Cappella Sansevero tucked off a side street. The printed brochure that came with the entrance fee explained that it had once been the private burial chapel of the prince of Sansevero, who'd hired some of Italy's most famous artists and sculptors to embellish his family tomb. The statues and frescoes and painted ceiling were magnificent, but the life-size statue of Christ draped in a thin shroud transfixed Callie. The veil was carved from the same marble block as the statue and was so seemingly transparent that the wounds on Christ's hands, feet and side showed plainly.

She stood by the velvet cord roping off the statue for long moments, only half hearing the Gregorian chant piped into the chapel through hidden speakers. When she finally turned to leave, she was sorry Joe hadn't been there to share the experience with her. So she was both surprised and delighted when a cab pulled up less than a half block later and a tall, broad-shouldered figure emerged.

"Joe! How did you find me?"

"The concierge said…"

The rumble of a truck drowned him out. He waited for it to pass before crossing the narrow street. He was in a suit today. Probably because he'd been meeting with the directors of the Naples film festival and touring the various venues. But he'd tugged off his tie, popped the top buttons on his dress shirt and hooked on a pair of mirrored sunglasses. Callie had to admit he looked as

hot in his big-important-executive uniform as he did in his jeans and bomber jacket.

When he'd crossed the narrow street, she greeted him with an eager question. "Have you seen the Sansevero Chapel? It's just down the block."

He hadn't, so Callie made a return visit. The Veiled Christ struck an even deeper chord on second viewing. Its vivid portrayal of Christ's suffering was deeply embedded in her memory when they reemerged into the sunlight filtering through the narrow alley.

"Did you have lunch?" Joe asked.

"Coffee and a roll about an hour ago. I was hoping we could share one of Naples's famous pizzas."

"So was I. Matter of fact, I asked Marcello Audi for the address of his favorite pizza joint. Let's grab a taxi."

His earsplitting whistle brought a cab whipping over to the curb. When he checked an electronic note on his phone and rattled off the address, Callie marveled again at his fluent Italian. She passed the short ride telling him about the mob on the street of the crèche makers and the incredible diversity of nativity figures offered for sale. Only after they'd been shown to a table on the second floor of a tiny restaurant overlooking the bay and placed their order did Callie remark again on the concierge's efficiency in putting Joe on her trail.

"He just told me where you were headed," he said with a shrug. "I tracked you via your phone."

"How?"

"It has a GPS chip."

"Yes, but I thought…"

Confused, she sat back as their aproned waiter delivered their caprese salads and a carafe of chianti. She poked at the thick wedge of mozzarella in the salad,

wondering if it came from the Audi farm, while the server poured the ruby-red vino into thick water glasses.

"You thought what?" Joe prompted when the waiter departed.

"I've used the Find My Phone app before to pinpoint its location when I thought I'd lost it. But I thought...no, I'm sure I had to enter my password to access the app."

"You do. I don't."

"Why not?"

"My tech folks developed a program that unscrambles the password."

He said it so calmly, so casually. As if hacking into someone's cell phone was just a routine part of his everyday routine.

"Doesn't the phone have to be turned on to be unscrambled?"

"No."

"So you can track anyone, just by the number?"

"Pretty much." A brief smile flitted across his face. "We offered the program to Homeland Security some weeks back. They want it but are still wrestling with the legalities."

Frowning, Callie poked at her salad again. Although she considered herself a liberal in most respects, the Boston Marathon bombing had tilted her to the right when it came to curtailing the civil liberties of suspected terrorists. She hardly fell into that category, however.

Still frowning, she met Joe's bland gaze. "I'm not sure I like the idea of being on an electronic leash."

"Comes with the ring, sweetheart."

The blunt, masculine possessiveness behind that statement left her sputtering indignantly.

"Dammit, Joe. The fact that I'm wearing your ring doesn't mean I want you to take control of my life."

A shuttered look dropped over his face, spurring her irritation.

"I appreciate your wanting to look out for me," she said firmly. "I do *not*, however, appreciate you preempting my decisions. Like letting Carlo know I'd decided to accept his offer before I had a chance to tell him myself. Or arranging this weekend in Naples, as delightful as it is, when I have so much to do in Rome. Or…"

"I protect what's mine." His eyes had gone cold. "Any way I have to."

A hot retort rose to Callie's lips. She bit it back as she remembered the little bit of his past that he'd shared with her on the drive down from Rome.

"The woman you smuggled out of Angola. The one killed by an assassin in Curaçao. Were you…were you in love with her?"

A muscle ticked in one side of his jaw. He sat unmoving, his expression so closed she thought he wouldn't answer. When he did, she had to strain to hear him.

"I'm not sure you'd call it love. Nattat was fiery and outspoken. And so damned uncompromising. We argued as often as we…"

He broke off, leaving Callie to fill in the blanks. Right. They'd argued as often as they'd indulged in wild, animal sex.

She dropped suddenly clenched fists to her lap. She'd never for one moment imagined she could be jealous of a dead woman.

"She wore her tribal headdress like a badge of honor," Joe continued after a moment. "She hated the Portuguese who'd plundered her country. Hated the native-born Angolans doing the same. As the youngest member

ever elected to parliament, she was an unrelenting thorn in their sides." His jaw worked. "It was only a matter of time until the bastards got to her."

The jealousy bit harder, sharper. Callie couldn't imagine a greater contrast between herself and a young, passionate Angolan member of parliament. She suspected Joe had never categorized this crusader for human rights as a calm port to come home to.

Ashamed of the thought and green-eyed monster nipping at her, Callie said quietly, "She sounds like an amazing woman, Joe."

"Yeah. Amazing. Also stubborn as hell and too prone to take risks."

"Which I'm not."

He hiked a brow.

"Okay, I may be a little stubborn at times," she conceded, "but I'm not inclined to take risks. So I don't need to be wrapped in cotton wool. Or kept on an electronic leash."

He didn't like it. She could tell by his closed expression.

"I mean it, Joe. We have to respect each other's boundaries."

He gave that a polite few moments' consideration before shaking his head. "I'm not made that way, Callie. I can't turn it on and off."

She stared across the table with a confusing sense of having reached an impasse. Intellectually, she flatly rejected the idea of being considered any man's possession. Training and experience, however, had taught her some primitive instincts were so deeply imprinted on homo sapiens' DNA that society's civilizing influences could never eradicated. The instinct to protect one's mate was certainly one of those instincts.

Unfortunately, she'd worked too many cases where that protective, possessive instinct spilled into jealousy and domestic violence. Could that happen with Joe? Given his admittedly violent past and dangerous present occupation, Callie couldn't deny the possibility. Yet every primitive instinct *she* possessed said she had nothing to fear from him.

Still, they needed to establish some of those boundaries she'd mentioned now, before they went too far down the path to misunderstanding or distrust. Their pizza arrived before she could marshal her arguments, however. Just as well, she decided. Better to finish this discussion back at the hotel, in the privacy of their opulent suite.

"Ecco! Pizza margherita."

The waiter positioned the pie on the stand in the center of the table with a dramatic flourish and proceeded to serve them a piece. The single slice slopped over the edge of Callie's plate and smelled of crusty dough, sweet tomatoes, mozzarella and fresh basil. Her first bite confirmed it tasted even better than it looked.

"Oh, God! This is unreal." She took another bite, swiping at strings of cheese and savoring the explosion of spices and sauce. "Do you know why they call it *pizza margherita*?" she asked Joe. "I read somewhere it's named after a queen."

"Right. The wife of King Umberto the first or second. Maybe third." He caught a wayward mozzarella strand, tucked it back on his half-devoured slice. "When Umberto and his wife visited Naples and tried pizza for the first time, she said the colors reminded her of the Italian flag."

Callie could see why. The bright red tomatoes. The white mozzarella. The green of the basil leaves.

"So they named it after her," she commented. "Would

those be the same royals who built that humongous palace in the main piazza?"

"Their descendants, I'd guess, a couple centuries removed." He downed another man-sized bite. "The palace is on the way back to the hotel. It's pretty impressive. We could tour it, if you'd like."

"I would. And tomorrow, we *have* to visit Pompeii before we head up to Rome."

"Deal."

They opted for a self-guided tour of the grand palace, aided by a free app they downloaded to their cell phones. The wide marble staircase was impressive enough. The opulence of the salons above boggled Callie's mind. The salons ran into each other, one after another. The blue room. The red. The gold. Each containing priceless works of art, lavishly decorated baroque furniture and some really strange objects brought from the four corners of the world as gifts for the Bourbon kings. Joe held the sack with her purchases while Callie spun in slow circles, her phone to her ear, trying to take in the magnificence.

Pleasantly tired after her day of exploring, she relaxed against Joe's side during the taxi ride back to the hotel. She'd enjoyed the afternoon so much that she toyed with the idea of just taking things with Joe as they came, one speed bump at a time. Especially since those little bumps occurred between stretches of such thrilling and intense pleasure.

Like the stretch that began after they crossed the lobby and the elevator doors pinged shut. In a swift move, Joe backed her against the paneled wall. His mouth came down on hers, hard and hungry and demanding the response that flared instantly in her belly.

She didn't even try to temper it. Didn't hold back. *Couldn't* hold back. There was nothing gentle in the kiss. Nothing tame or affectionate. The heat in it ignited an answering flame that she knew burned hot in her face when he raised his head.

"Been waiting to do this since I picked you up at the airport yesterday morning. Damned near killed me when jet lag got to you last night." He dipped his head, took another taste, muttered against her lips, "Tell me the palace didn't wipe you out."

Since his hands were as busy as his mouth, Callie could only gasp an urgent negative. "The palace... didn't...wipe me...out."

The hum that rose from his throat conveyed equal parts relief, satisfaction and a hunger so fierce that every nerve in her body leaped with anticipation. She had time for only a fleeting prayer that the elevator wouldn't stop to let anyone else on before it hit their floor. Then Joe raked both hands into her hair, dislodging the scrunchie, and wedged a knee between hers. His mouth devouring hers once more, he rocked her with a pleasure so intense she almost lost it right there.

The elevator made it to their floor without any stops, thank God, and their suite was only a few doors down the hall. Callie spent those few yards raking a hand through the hair now tumbling around her face and tugging at the hem of her sweater. A useless exercise, since Joe swept her into his arms as soon as he'd keyed the door. Her sweater rucked up again and her hair got caught against his shoulder, but she didn't even wince when the kick he aimed at the door sent it banging into the jamb.

He had to dip to set the security lock and flip on the electronic Do Not Disturb sign. Callie grabbed his

shoulders to keep from being upended and held on as he cut through the sitting room. She was still clinging like a monkey when they hit the bedroom.

Housekeeping had been in, she saw as Joe made straight for the four-poster draped in champagne-colored silk. The gold tassels decorating the bed's richly embroidered comforter marched in a straight line along its hem. A half dozen or more similarly tasseled pillows in varying shapes and sizes sat banked against the carved headboard.

They promptly shot all that neat precision to hell. Joe didn't take time to yank down the spread. Didn't bother shoving the pillows out of the way. He dropped to the bed with Callie still locked against him.

She wasn't sure who attacked whose clothes first. They probably went at it simultaneously. She got his dress shirt off without too much trouble, but Joe was quieter and much quicker. He was feasting on her bare breast while she was still trying to shove his slacks down his lean, muscular flanks. Frustrated, she nipped him on the shoulder. Then nipped again, harder.

That got his attention. His head shot up. Surprise glinted in his eyes.

"You trying to tell me something, tiger?"

"Yes," she panted.

The surprise deepened. "Interesting. Didn't think you were into rough stuff."

"I'm not!" She wiggled under him, fighting the slacks again. "But I could use a little help here."

When he rolled to one side and shucked the rest of his clothes, Callie didn't hesitate. Taking full advantage of having him on his back, she swung a leg over his hip even before his shoes and pants hit the floor. A quick push brought her upright. Another wiggle scooted her

back a few inches. Straddling his thighs, she had full access to his rampant sex.

He was rock hard and slick to her touch. And salty when she scooted back a few more inches and contorted enough to take him in her mouth. She couldn't remember ever doing this before. Couldn't remember wanting to. Yet having Joe at the mercy of *her* hands and thighs and busy, busy lips shot her into a new sexual stratosphere. She'd gone beyond registering anything other than his taste and his scent and his feel when he gave a hoarse grunt that could have signaled pleasure or protest.

"Callie. Sweetheart." He nudged her shoulders. "Let me… Crap!"

Joe being Joe, he insisted on giving her the same pleasure she'd given him. Much to Callie's secret delight, however, it took him a few moments to recoup his strength. Hiding a grin, she wallowed in a trough of feminine superiority right up until the moment he had her digging her nails into the spread and moaning in a long, shuddering, shattering release.

It was a while before they recovered enough to sluice off in the mammoth shower and wrap up from neck to knees in the hotel's plush terry-cloth robes. As Callie walked back into the bedroom busily towel drying her hair, Joe winced at the red scrape on her neck.

"Sorry 'bout that whisker burn."

She looked up from under the towel and smiled. "No complaints on this side. It was worth… Oh!"

She stopped dead. Eyes round, jaw slack, she gaped at the scene outside their floor-to-ceiling windows. Dusk had begun to darken the sky, and a fat, full moon hung just above the stone balustrade of their balcony.

"It's just like in that song," she breathed in delight. "The one about the moon hitting your eye like a big pizza pie."

Whipping back her hair, she wrapped the towel turban-style around the still-damp mass and shoved her feet into the hotel-provided slippers.

"Let's go out on the veranda."

"Go ahead. I'll get some Pellegrino and join you."

While she arrowed straight for the veranda, Joe detoured to the minibar to retrieve two dew-streaked bottles. The chilled water in hand, he took a moment to study the robed and turbaned figure transfixed by her view of the moon-washed bay. She'd turned up the collar on the robe and belted it tighter around her waist against the cooling evening air. Elbows propped on the railing, she leaned forward just far enough to showcase her nice, trim butt.

God, she was gorgeous. She didn't think so. No surprise there. She'd grown up in the shadow of her two friends and tended to retreat into the background whenever Kate or Dawn took center stage. Not because they were smarter or prettier or more accomplished. Because she was so comfortable in her own skin that she felt no need to compete for attention. Which was one of the reasons Joe had known almost immediately Callie Langston was right for him. He admired her quiet presence. Envied her serenity.

He didn't have much of either in his own life. Not that he lived on a razor's edge 24/7. Sometimes he went months between a high-profile client like Carlo di Lorenzo or a seriously vulnerable target like the Naples film festival. Even on the job, Joe had learned to make stress work for him. It kept him and his team alert. Kept them alive. It was those few hours when the adrenaline

rocketed through the roof, those days and nights when sleep wasn't an option, that left him craving a quiet sanctuary to return to after a particularly hairy gig.

He did have a sanctuary or two already. He maintained a house close to his operations base in Houston. Kept a private retreat in the Colorado Rockies. Paid a month-to-month lease on apartment in LA used for strictly business purposes. The places were comfortable. Some might say luxurious. But sterile. Empty. He wanted someone like Callie to fill that emptiness.

Joe's fists tightened on the bottles. No, dammit! He didn't want someone *like* Callie. He wanted *her*.

Looking back, he knew now that he hadn't wanted Nattat this badly. Yeah, he'd lusted for her. Broken every rule in the book for her. Even killed for her. But she'd never stirred this gut-deep need to cherish and protect and…and…

Hell! No point trying to analyze whatever it was Callie stirred in him. Enough to just roll with it. Which he did, at least until she straightened and came inside.

"It's colder than it looks out there," she announced with a little shiver.

He hefted the Pellegrino. "Want something that'll raise more heat than water?"

"No, that's good. Besides, after all that wine we had with our pizza, I need to have a clear head."

"For?"

She gave the ends of the robe's belt a little tug. "I enjoyed today, Joe. This whole weekend. But we need to talk."

Chapter Seven

*W*e need to talk.

Exactly what every man wanted to hear from his woman. Hiding a grimace, Joe arched a brow. "Long talk or short?"

"That depends on you."

His euphoric mood of just a few seconds ago went down in flames. Just your basic crash and burn, he thought sardonically as he gestured to the sitting room.

"Might as well get comfortable."

She curled into one end of the curved-back sofa and tucked her feet under her. Joe took the middle cushion. Not close enough to crowd her, but within reaching distance. Just in case he had to resort to emergency measures. Passing her one of the bottles, he braced for the worst while she unscrewed the cap and took a long swallow.

"I debated whether to have this discussion, Joe. I enjoyed this afternoon so much. This whole weekend. Especially the past few hours," she added with smile.

The smile didn't hack it. "Cut to the chase, Callie. What's this about?"

Unperturbed by the gruff demand, she nodded. "All right. You told me you're not into flowery phrases or stringing together lots of adjectives, so let's keep it simple. If you had to describe what you feel for me in just two or three words, what would they be? And *please* don't say 'a calm port in a storm.'"

Christ! Where'd that come from? He'd thought... been sure...she'd understood it was a compliment. Digging deep, he settled on some lines of Scripture his gran had drilled into him as a kid, accompanied more often than not by the smack of her palm alongside his head.

"Three words? How about 'faith, hope and love. But,'" he added gruffly, "'the greatest of these is love.'"

Her eyes widened in surprise. *Payback*, he thought with a stab of fierce satisfaction, *for the crash and burn*.

"Isn't that from the Bible?"

"First Corinthians, chapter thirteen."

"I didn't know... That is..." She floundered for another moment. "Are you a regular churchgoer?"

"Not according to my grandmother."

"You have a grandmother?" she echoed faintly.

"Most people do," he drawled.

"You've never mentioned her. Or your parents. Are they still alive?"

"Never knew my father. Mom died when I was six. Gran took over then."

"Is she still alive?"

"Alive and kicking. She lives only a few blocks from me in Houston."

It'd taken some persuasion to get the feisty octogenarian to leave the home she'd raised him in. Joe had made sure she was comfortable there, that house had

every modern convenience known to man. But three years ago arthritis all but crippled her and Joe finally convinced her to move to Houston. She was in a wheelchair now and quoting Bible scriptures to the attendants at a luxurious assisted-living center.

"How often do you…?" She stopped, drew a breath. "Never mind. We'll get to that later."

He waited, letting her circle back to whatever had spurred this need for this little talk.

"Why 'faith, hope and love'?" she finally questioned.

Resigned, Joe dug a little deeper. "Faith, because once you give your loyalty, it stays given. Dawn and Kate are living proof of that."

"I guess," she murmured, not quite convinced.

"Hope, because…" He held that deep purple gaze. "For the first time in longer than I can remember, the future holds promise."

Her doubt melted, her voice softened. "And love? Are you in love with me, Joe?"

What the hell? Did she think he went around proposing to every female who looked at him sideways?

"You're the first…the only…woman I've asked to marry me."

"So that's a yes?"

"Didn't I just say that?"

"Not exactly. Say the words. I'd like to hear them."

He opened his mouth, but her too-innocent expression knocked the simple phrase back down his throat. The little witch! She was jacking him. Playing him like a trout on the end of a six-pound line.

"I love you. And now…" Thunking his Pellegrino down on the coffee table, he plucked hers out of her hand and leaned in. "Your turn. What do you feel for me? Three words. Spit 'em out."

She didn't blink, didn't hesitate. "I love you. I didn't realize how much until this moment."

"Right. Okay. Good."

Callie knew better than to smile, but it took some doing. He sounded every bit as flustered as she had a few moments ago. Taking pity on his obvious confusion, she laid a hand on his forearm.

"Will it help if I tell you that you're the first man... the *only* man...whose ring I've worn?"

"It helps," he said, recovering. "It also makes me wonder where this 'we need to talk' sh...stuff came from."

She acknowledged the barb with a nod and took a moment to gather her thoughts. Her religious education had been sporadic at best. One parent was a lapsed Catholic, the other agnostic. They'd both pretty much left her to find her own way. But she'd attended enough weddings to have more than a passing familiarity with the love verse Joe had just quoted.

"Isn't there something in that First Corinthians chapter about love not insisting on having its own way?"

"Verse five. Why? What's your point?"

"Remember what you said this afternoon? When I told you I don't like being on an electronic leash?"

"Hell, Callie. Is that what this is all about? The phone-tracking app?"

"The app's part of it. Mostly it's about establishing and respecting the boundaries I mentioned."

She chewed on the inside of her cheek, needing to get this right. Whatever future they might build together depended on the next few moments.

"You told me you couldn't turn your instincts off and on, Joe. I don't want you to turn them off. Not com-

pletely. Some primitive corner of my psyche thrills to the idea of a strong, protective mate."

He managed to look both vindicated and baffled. "I repeat, what's your point?"

"The point," she said patiently, "is that I want to be a full partner in this relationship, not some pampered pet. I want you to explain up front about any security issues or actions that involve me. Or us. Or you, for that matter."

"The process isn't always that deliberate. There are times…too many times…when I have to go with my gut."

"I get that. I do. And I'd be a fool to tell you to ignore those gut instincts. It's the other times. The ordinary you-and-me times. I need to know you won't just assume you know best for me."

She reached for his hand. Hers was still damp and chilled from the Pellegrino bottle, his warm and sinewy. The contrast wasn't lost on her.

They were so different, she and Joe. They came from disparate backgrounds, apparently. Had followed widely divergent career paths. And they were certainly at the opposite ends of the spectrum when it came to bruising, bare-knuckle experiences.

And yet in many ways they were very much alike. Both self-contained. Both confident of their own abilities. Both, she thought with a warm halo around her heart, seemingly in this for the long haul.

"Promise you won't make unilateral decisions, except in extraordinary circumstances."

He grabbed at the out. "Extraordinary circumstances. Okay, I can live with that."

"I mean it, Joe. Starting here, starting now, we're equal partners in this adventure. Deal?"

He thought about it for a second or two, then raised her hand and dropped a kiss on the back of it. The gesture was so courtly and un-Joe-like that she almost melted into a puddle right there on the hotel's thousand-dollar-plus sofa.

"Deal."

He released her fingers and reached for the belt of her robe instead. It loosened with a single tug. With a satisfied grunt, he curved his palm over her thigh.

"As your full and equal partner, I vote we adjourn to the bed."

"The bed we just left a few moments ago?"

"Yeah." He slid his hand higher. "That one."

A cold, gray drizzle obscured the bay the next morning, but Callie held Joe to his promise to take her to Pompeii before they drove up to Rome. Fortified by the hotel's sumptuous Sunday brunch, they checked out and hit the road.

The nasty weather actually did them a favor by whittling the hordes of tourists down to the hardiest few. Bundled against the chill in her long duster and the paisley scarf looped twice around her neck, European-style, Callie shoved her left hand in her pocket. Joe held onto her right and kept it tucked in the pocket of his leather jacket.

She appreciated his steadying grip as they navigated the cobbled streets. Drifting fingers of fog made the time-worn stones slick and treacherous. They also blanketed the ancient ruin in eerie silence, almost as if the terror of that day in 79 AD had never happened. Yet every excavated dwelling, every scrap of tiled floor or line of decapitated marble columns rising out of the mist gave grim evidence of Vesuvius's destructive power.

"Hard to believe all this lay buried for more than a thousand years," she murmured.

Even harder to believe the hot ash and molten lava had spewed out of the volcano with such speed that Pompeii's citizens had no time or place to run. They had died where they cowered. Or in the case of a noticeably pregnant woman, where she lay. Callie bit her lip as she studied the plaster cast made from the hardened hollow where the woman's body had once been entombed in layers of ash. She'd tried to shield her head with one arm. The other cradled her stomach and unborn babe.

The tragic figure had Callie blinking back tears. She couldn't help thinking of Kate and her emerging baby bump. She hated to miss her friend's exciting time of discovery and impending birth. Hated missing Christmas with Dawn and her new family, too. Her choice, she reminded herself. Her choice. But she made a silent promise to call her friends as soon as she got settled in her new apartment.

That led to a reminder of the job waiting in Rome and the center sheltering desperate female refugees. She stared at the cast of the long-dead woman, thinking that all these years later, death and destruction still rained down from the skies. Man-made now, more often than not, and every bit as devastating. So many tried to escape it. So many needed help.

"I've seen enough," she told Joe. "Let's go."

The dank, heavy mist continued to roll in from the coast as they drove north. Traffic moved at a slow crawl for most of the way. When they finally crested one of Rome's seven fabled hills, angry black clouds had piled up over the city and added to the fast-descending darkness.

The deluge hit moments later. As if navigating the capital's labyrinthine center wasn't enough of a challenge, the torrential downpour turned to slush, then fat, wet snowflakes that gave the SUV's oversize wipers a run for their money. With grim thanks for GPS, Joe followed the system's precise directions to the flat he'd checked out before picking Callie up at the airport three days ago. The parking gods must have been smiling. He squeezed into a space just a few yards from the entrance, unloaded their carryalls and caught Callie's arm for a quick dash through the snow.

The flat wasn't much. One bedroom, one combination kitchen, eating area and living room, with a tiny bath tucked in a corner. But it was on the third floor of a recently renovated building with solid security and located only a few blocks from the women's center where she'd be working. Still, he'd had Emilio, his contact here in Rome, install a fingerprint-activated electronic keypad on her door and new bolts on the windows…which, under the terms of their recently negotiated agreement, he felt obligated to tell her about.

"Was that really necessary?" she asked, eyeing the polished brass hardware that gleamed bright and new against an old but very solid door.

"Probably not. Here, press your palm against the scanner. Fingers flat. Now roll them a little. Right to left. Good."

Feeling a little like a felon being fingerprinted by Rome's *polizia*, she submitted to what she hoped was the last of Joe's electronic gadgets.

"The super has an override code," he said as the door clicked open. "Just in case."

Callie didn't move. "Do you have the code, too?"

"Yeah, I do." He turned and gave her a cool look. "You have a problem with that?"

"Not if you call or text me before you use it."

"Damn." His mouth twisted. "There goes my plan to surprise you when you come home and find me wearing nothing but a smile and big red bow."

It was so deadpan—and so unexpected—that Callie blinked before choking out a laugh. "Trust me. If I walk in and find you in a big red bow, I'll be *extremely* surprised."

"Too late. You ruined it. I'll think up something else." He nudged the door with his carryall. "You want in or not?"

Once inside, Joe flicked on the lights and waited while Callie explored her new home.

It was perfect, she thought in delight. Absolutely perfect. The warm yellow walls dispelled the winter gloom, and the furnishings were an eclectic mix of modern and shabby chic. The kitchen consisted of a two-burner stove with a single-rack oven, a small fridge and cloth-covered cupboards. The eating area held only a narrow drop-leaf table and two chairs that could be turned around to augment seating in the living area. That room's solitary window faced the street and the buildings directly opposite. Roll-down shutters would block the streetlights and traffic noise.

Entranced, she opened a door to the bathroom. A stool, a sink and a shower surrounded by a circular curtain suspended from the ceiling, all squeezed into what she guessed might once have been a closet.

The bedroom just beyond contained only a double bed, a nightstand and a hand-painted wardrobe. But to Callie's great joy, it also boasted a glass-paned door

that opened onto a minuscule balcony that seemed to hang suspended in midair. Snow-dusted buildings stair-stepped down the steep hill below. And in the distance a floodlit dome was just visible through the curtain of snow.

"Is that St. Peter's?" she gasped.

"Looks like."

Thrilled, she twisted the knob and stepped outside for a better look. Skirting a dime-size café table with a single chair, she gripped the wrought-iron railing with gloved hands. Rome had enchanted her during her brief visit with Dawn and Kate a few months ago. Awestruck by the snowy scene spread out before her, she fell completely, irrevocably in love.

More in love, she amended as Joe edged past the rickety little table to join her. Overwhelmed, she turned and framed his face with her gloved hands. The light spilling through the glass-paned door illuminated one side of his face. The scar was lost in shadow. Where it belonged, she thought fiercely. His past had made him the man he was now, but the future belonged to her. To both of them.

"Thank you," she breathed. "For Naples. For Pompeii. For being here with me. This whole day's been perfect."

"You're welcome. It'll be even more perfect," he added with a hopeful waggle of his brows, "if Emilio stocked your kitchen with something quick and easy to fix."

From the sublime to the practical. Laughing, Callie came back to earth.

And now that he'd mentioned it, she was ravenous, too. After that ginormous brunch at the hotel in Naples, she'd vowed to cut out all carbs for the next week. Tour-

ing Pompeii and the long, slow drive back to Rome sent
that vow down the tubes.

"Let's take a look."

They shed their coats and crowded into the tiny
kitchen. Emilio had indeed stocked the fridge and tiny
pantry. Callie inventoried paper-wrapped Parma ham,
a thick wedge of Asiago cheese, garlic cloves, onions,
Roma tomatoes, potatoes, eggs, coffee, creamer, some
canned soup, a bottle of Tuscan red and, of course, sev-
eral variations of pasta.

"How about an omelet?" she suggested. "That's
quick and easy."

"I hit the omelet bar at breakfast."

"Soup?"

"Tell you what. I spotted a trattoria on the corner.
Why don't I just go down and get two takeout orders
of veal scaloppine?"

"Oh, God, that sounds wonderful. But I hate for you
to go back out in the snow."

"Not a problem." He snagged his jacket off the chair
where he'd draped it. "I'll be right back. You open the
wine and get settled."

Before she accomplished either of those tasks, Cal-
lie had a far more important one to attend to. It was just
past six Rome time. A little after noon in DC. Digging
her phone out of her purse, she dropped onto the edge
of the bed and hit Kate's speed-dial number.

"Callie! Travis and I were just talking about you.
How's Rome?"

"Absolutely incredible." Her gaze locked on the win-
dow. "At this precise moment I'm sitting on the side of
the bed in my apartment, looking through the balcony
door, watching snow blanket the dome of St. Peter's."

"Get. Out."

"I kid you not! Hold on while I get Dawn on the line."

Their friend answered on the second ring and shouted over the din in the background. "About time you called."

"What?"

"I said, it's about time you called."

"I can barely hear you. Where are you?"

"Sunday brunch at Paoli's. Where are *you*, and more important, what the heck took you so long to contact your best friends?"

"I've been a little busy."

"That's what I tried to tell her," Kate put in. "She wanted to call you, but I twisted her arm and made her wait until you got your feet on the ground."

"I waited," Dawn groused, "but I didn't like it. So spill it, girl. No! Hold on, I need to go someplace without all these decibels."

Callie heard a thump, a muffled voice, the clash of pots and pans. Then blessed silence.

"Okay," Dawn announced breathlessly. "I'm in the ladies' room. Wait a sec while I put the seat down. There. I'm good. Now talk. How's Rome? What's happening with you and Joe?"

"Rome is clean and bright and dusted with snow from top to bottom. And Joe…"

Callie didn't spin out the pause deliberately. She just needed a couple seconds to sort through everything that had happened in the three tumultuous days since she'd landed in Italy.

"We've been together this whole time. After he picked me up at the airport Friday morning, we drove down to Naples to meet with his prospective client. Then…"

"Wait. Back up. You crawl off a plane after a nine-

hour flight and he takes you to Naples for a business meeting?"

"Actually, we went for a sort of pre-Christmas feast with Signor Audi and his family. At their water buffalo ranch."

Dawn made a "huh" noise but Kate caught the connection immediately.

"Buffalo, as in mozzarella cheese?"

"As in a dozen different varieties of mozzarella, all of them scrumptious."

"And you went to the source of these dozen different varieties?"

"We did! Honestly, it was so interesting. The buffalo get scrubbed, massaged, milked and scrubbed again. All done robotically."

"Sounds fascinating," Dawn commented in a voice that clearly indicated otherwise. "Back to Joe. Three whole days with Mr. If I Tell You I'll Have to Kill You, and you haven't changed your mind?"

"No," Callie said at the same moment the sound of a loud flush came through the phone. "Just the opposite."

"What? I can't hear you."

"I said Joe and I are great. Fantastic. Wonderful."

"Wow," Dawn murmured after a short silence. "Those must have been some three days."

"They were. I'll zip off an email tomorrow with all the juicy details."

"And pictures," Kate insisted. "We want pictures of your apartment and where you work."

"Will do. Say hi to Travis and Brian and Tommy. I love you all and miss you already."

"Give Joe our best. And Carlo, when you see him."

"Will do," Callie promised again. "Ciao for now."

She clicked off and pushed off the bed. Her first

order of business was to uncork the wine and let it breathe. She wasted a few moments hunting for a corkscrew until she realized the cap was a twist-off. Interesting. One of her coworkers back in Boston had been a self-professed and completely unapologetic wine snob. Devin would no doubt have heart palpitations if he had to twist rather than uncork and meticulously decant.

Smiling at the thought, she went ahead and set the table with the silverware and pretty red-and-yellow napkins she'd found in her hunt for a corkscrew. No wine goblets, but the wavy green water glasses would do nicely.

That homey task done, she transferred the carryalls to the bedroom. She left Joe's on the bed but unpacked her toiletries and stuffed the clothes she'd worn over the weekend in the laundry bag she found hanging in the hand-painted wardrobe. Her two suitcases were in the wardrobe, too, left there by the so-efficient Emilio. She pulled one out, but before she could lug it to the bed to unpack, her phone chirped. The succinct text message made her grin.

Coming up. Using the override.

Ha! Who said you couldn't teach an old dog new tricks? Still grinning, Callie went to join Joe for her first meal in her new home.

Chapter Eight

Joe stayed the night, taking up more than his fair share of the double bed, and had to leave early Monday morning.

"I'll be in Zurich until Wednesday," he told Callie as he tucked his shaving kit into his carryall. "Then I have to fly back to the States. You've got Emilio's number. Call him if you need anything before I get back."

"Any idea when that might be?"

"Not sure. I'll try to make it before Christmas, but I have to put together the team I promised Marcello Audi I'd bring in the first week in January. Some top people to beef up electronic surveillance at his venue sites. More to conduct hands-on training for his security staff."

She nodded but suffered another silent qualm about the prospect of spending Christmas on her own in Italy. Her decision, she reminded herself fiercely as Joe zipped his carryall. Her decision.

Besides, if the center was as short-staffed as Carlo had indicated, she wouldn't have time to feel lonely. Or so she thought, right up until she walked Joe to the door of her tiny apartment.

"Have a safe trip home."

"Plan to." He curled a knuckle under her chin and tipped her face to his. "Good luck at the center. You sure you can find it?"

"Two blocks to the north and one to the east? I think so. But if I have any trouble," she promised solemnly, "I'll use the directional finder on my phone."

"Whatever works." He took the hit with a philosophical shrug and made a slow pass over her lower lip with his thumb. "Don't let the heartache you find there get you too down."

Easier said than done, she knew. She still carried painful memories of some of the children's cases she'd worked in her heart.

"I plan to stay too busy to get down."

"After meeting *il Drago*, I can pretty much guarantee you will."

"*Il Drago?* The dragon? I hope that doesn't refer to my new boss."

"Carlo's tag for her, not mine. It fits, though. The woman put us both through the wringer when he told her I wanted to review the center's refugee screening process."

"Wonderful. You pissed off my new boss. Exactly what I needed to hear before my first day on the job."

His mouth curved in one of his rare grins. "My money's on you, Pansy Eyes. Just aim one of your cool, we-need-to-talk looks at her and she'll fold like *washi*. Thin Japanese paper," he said in answer to her

blank look. "They use it make origami and wrap gifts to burn in honor of their ancestors."

This man amazed her. He really did. Bible verses. Japanese origami. Fiery tribal beauties. Hired assassins. She was still trying to fit all these facets of his personality into their respective niches when he dropped a quick kiss on her lips.

"Call me," he ordered as he headed down the narrow S-shaped stairs. "Let me know how today goes."

"I will."

He'd hit the first floor landing before she remembered the Christmas gifts she'd purchased in Naples. She leaned over the railing to call him back, but he was already out the door.

Damn! He could've taken Dawn's and Kate's and Tommy's back to the States with him. Opened his, too, while he was here. She'd have to FedEx the others and keep his until his return to Rome. Hopefully in time for Christmas.

She gave the high-tech palm pad a sideways glance as she wandered back into her new home. Joe's presence had made the two rooms seem cozy. Okay, crowded. Now they felt empty, sucked of their vitality.

All right. Enough of that. She had things to do, places to go, people to see. With a determined roll of her shoulders, Callie shook off her deflated feeling and set to work unpacking the suitcases Emilio had delivered.

Not that she had all that much to unpack. She'd based her wardrobe choices on a study of Rome's average winter temperatures and her preliminary research into the shelter run by International Aid to Displaced Women. The center's residents were older than the children she'd worked with for the past six years. They'd lost their husbands, their families, all ties to their native lands.

Some had survived unimaginable horrors. Callie knew they'd relate more to jeans and a sweater than a tailored black pantsuit.

An hour later she emerged into a city that had come alive after its snowy night. The sun was a bright sphere, the air frosty. Tucking her chin in her scarf and her hands deep in the pockets of her duster, Callie set off for the center.

The Monday morning traffic had churned the streets to slush, but the wrought-iron balconies and green-painted shutters adorning the buildings on both sides of the street still sported downy white eyebrows. School kids with monster book bags clumped by in oversize boots. Housewives bundled up against the cold clutched fishnet shopping bags as they headed to the local butchers and greengrocers. Office workers stood elbow to elbow at espresso bars, munching pastries, scanning folded newspapers and getting the necessary caffeine jolt to jump-start their day.

When a patron exited one of those tiny cafés, the scent of fresh-ground coffee and hot croissants lured Callie inside. She studied the chalkboard menu while waiting in line and managed to order in her few phrases of broken Italian. The white chocolate cream concoction came in a glass with a silver handle and was topped with a frothy heart almost too pretty to slurp. She carried it and a still-warm croissant to a stand-up counter and consumed both while studying the framed black-and-white photos filling every square inch of wall space.

Many were from WWII and depicted US soldiers who must have chosen this little café as a favorite gathering spot. Others looked like they were from the late '40s and early '50s. Callie spotted an extremely well-

endowed Sophia Loren in one, a Jack Kennedy look-alike in another.

Intrigued, she edged closer to examine the scrawled signature. It *was* Kennedy. Young, impossibly hand-some, flashing that famous grin, with his arm hooked over the back of a chair occupied by a pouty blonde Callie didn't recognize. She would've liked to take a closer look at some of the other celebrities, but a quick glance at the clock above the bar sent her back out into the bright, cold morning.

A quick turn brought her to her new place of employment. Identified only by the street number above its door, the three-story building that housed the IADW center blended in with its neighbors. Like them, it was stuccoed, only this was a deeper terra-cotta red than either of its neighbors. Marble pediments decorated the first-floor windows; green shutters framed the others. Callie noted the absence of any security cameras and felt a tingle at the back of her neck as she remembered Joe's comment about terrorists using refugee centers as conduits to the West.

Although he hadn't mentioned it—probably because he hadn't wanted to scare her—she suspected these centers could become targets, too, for extremists at both ends of the spectrum. Ultra-right neo-Nazi types stirred to fury over the influx of "foreigners" might present as much of a threat as leftist revolutionaries seeking to exploit the residents' hopes and fears.

With these—hopefully remote!—possibilities in mind, she pressed the bell centered in a dented and slightly rusted speaker box.

"*Sì?*"

The single syllable came across as clipped and distinctly impatient.

"My name is Callie Langston. I'm…"

"Finally! Come in. I'm in the storeroom. Down the hall, last door on the right."

The locked clicked, and Callie stepped into a foyer tiled in gray marble. A graceful arch led from the foyer to a long hallway. Doors opened off either side of the hall, and at the far end a graceful marble staircase spiraled upward.

She made her way to the last door on the right as instructed while admiring the Murano glass sconces and elaborate ceiling medallions that suggested the center had once been home to a fairly well-to-do family. She was only a few feet from her destination when a thump and a curse sounded from its open door. A quick glance inside showed a cluttered office and a rail-thin woman with short, flyaway white hair. While Callie watched, the woman shoved aside a carton with a logo that depicted what looked like a giant green hand cupping a dark-eyed baby in its palm.

The hearty shove sent the box careening into a stack of similarly marked cartons. They wobbled wildly, precipitating another muttered curse and a quick jump forward from Callie. Between them, the two women managed to keep the tower more or less upright.

The save didn't appear to afford the older woman much satisfaction. Hands on hips, she scowled at the stack, as if daring it to take another wobble. Only after she'd stared it down did she turn a look of unalloyed disgust on Callie.

"I've told this group again and again we need supplies for women and adolescent girls."

Her English was thick and heavily accented.

"Do they listen? No! Do they keep sending diapers and teething rings? Yes! Does my *idiota* intern accept their shipments? Every time!"

Despite her skeletal thinness and dandelion-fine white hair, she looked so fierce Callie half expected her to aim another kick at the precariously stacked boxes. Instead, she drilled the newcomer with a pair of startlingly blue eyes.

"The prince insisted I take you on as my deputy. Your credentials are impressive, I'll give you that. Far better than the one you're replacing. But if you think working with us at the center will convince the prince to offer more than weekends in Monte Carlo or Antibes, you should think again."

"*Excuse* me?"

"Ah! So he didn't tell you? No, of course he would not. He will wait for the right moment."

"Look, Signora Alberti… You are Signora Alberti, aren't you?"

"*Sì.*"

"Look, Signora Alberti. The prince is a friend. A good friend. But if you don't wish to accept me based on my credentials, that's your prerogative."

"*Magari.*"

"I'm sorry," Callie said stiffly. "I don't know that word."

"It means… How do you say in America? *I wish.*"

Callie opened her mouth, but before she could tell the Wicked Witch of the East to take her job and stuff it, the director flapped an impatient hand.

"*Non importa.* I will know soon enough if you're as hopeless as the others. Come along. I'll introduce you to the staff who aren't in session. You'll meet the rest at lunch. The residents, too."

During the next hour, Callie's initial impression of an irate, dandelion-haired virago who waged war with innocent boxes underwent a swift reevaluation.

Despite her abrupt manner, Signora Alberti's staff appeared to adore her. The two mental-health techs, one Italian and one French. The nurse-practitioner from Corinth, Greece. The three translators who between them spoke eleven different languages. The multinational kitchen crew busy cleaning up after breakfast. Even Signora Alberti's *idiota* assistant, who turned out to be an Italian grad student working at the center as part of his hands-on training for a master's in cognitive therapy from La Sapienza, one of the oldest and most prestigious universities in Europe.

Unfortunately, the intern's English was as limited as Callie's Italian. After struggling to communicate using the impatient director as an intermediary, they agreed to compare notes at a later date. Hopefully, when they'd each gained a little more facility with the other's language.

Staff intros over, Alberti gave Callie a tour of the upper stories. The second floor contained an arts and crafts area, a library, a TV room and a series of dormitory-like bedrooms, each two bedrooms linked by a shared bath. The third floor was entirely bedrooms. All but one were occupied.

"We try to match roommates who speak the same language or at least practice the same religion," the director said. "It's not always possible, of course, but we try."

"How long do the residents stay here?"

"We've placed some in jobs and homes within a few weeks. Others…" Her shoulders lifted. "Others stay much longer."

"Can they go out? Get their nails done or go to…"

"Of course they can," Alberti snapped. "This is a shelter, yes? Not a prison."

Properly chastised, Callie was given a tour of the first-floor meeting and counseling rooms, then shown her office. It was directly across from the director's and sparsely appointed. A desk, two chairs, a metal file cabinet. Delicate sconces hinted at the house's former glory, and pale squares marked the walls where pictures or portraits must have once hung.

The director jabbed a finger at the flat-screen computer monitor sitting dead center on the desk. "We update our case files daily. All counseling sessions you have with residents, either one-on-one or in group. No excuses. No delays. Operating procedures require that we change the password once a week. When we remember," she admitted grudgingly. "This week it's Aleppo221."

"Got it."

The director tipped her chin toward a row of black binders perched atop the metal file cabinet. "Those notebooks contain our operating procedures. They're in Italian, but have been translated in English and Arabic. You need to review them along with the case files, also in Italian and English. You've got some time now. We have lunch at noon, yes? There's a group session you should sit in on at two this afternoon. And I've scheduled you to teach the beginning English class at four. It's been on hold waiting for your arrival. Can you handle that?"

"Yes, ma'am."

"Simona," she said with an irritated chop of her hand. "Call me Simona."

With so many new experiences bombarding her, Callie took the precaution of jotting down the password before she forgot it. Years of inbred caution had her re-

versing the digits, however. That done, she logged on and opened the oldest file.

She thought she'd seen the full spectrum of family tragedy. As she worked her way through the computerized case files, she realized she'd barely scratched the surface. Her throat got tighter as she read family histories that included everything from mass murder to honor killings to kidnapping and rape.

A number of the seventy-three women currently residing at the center had lost every living relative to war. Others had suffered pain and humiliation at the hands of vengeful husbands or fathers or brothers. Two girls barely into their teens had been sold into sexual slavery and experienced appalling degradation before escaping their captors by hiding in a dung cart.

Yet when Callie accompanied her boss to lunch, they entered a room filled with lively chatter. The meal was served buffet-style in what must have been the original owners' grand salon. The fare was hearty lamb stew fortified with green peas and couscous, the preferred drink a fragrant apple tea. The women present appeared to be primarily Middle Eastern and African, with a sprinkling of Europeans. They sat at tables of four or eight. The clusters appeared cultural for the most part, with the Muslims in modest robes and hair covered by veils or scarves, the others in more flamboyant dress.

One sat alone. Head down. Shoulders hunched. Head scarf covering her hair, her very pregnant belly evident even under her loose robe. She refused to look up even when Simona stood and called for attention. Pausing at intervals to allow the translators to keep up, the director introduced the newest member of the staff. After a flurry of smiles and welcomes in several different languages, the women got on with their lunch.

Callie waited for a lull in the director's conversation with the woman on her other side to nod discreetly at the solitary diner.

"Who's that?"

Simona followed her glance. "We call her Amal, but we don't know her real name. She washed ashore in Greece a month ago, we think from a boatload of Syrian refugees that sank off the coast. If so, she was the only survivor. She won't…or can't…tell us anything about herself or her life before she arrived here."

"Is she due soon?"

"Nikki Dukakis, our nurse-practitioner, thinks it could be within the next few weeks. We don't have facilities here for a nursery, so she'll move to another center when she leaves the hospital."

How sad, Callie thought, and how frightening it must be to give birth in a strange land surrounded by people you don't know and can't communicate with, only to be shuffled from one facility to another. She couldn't help remembering the plaster cast of the pregnant woman in Pompeii and felt a wrenching hope this mother-to-be would find a safe harbor for herself and her child.

A number of the residents came up after lunch to welcome her, some shyly, some with warm smiles. Callie then sat in on the two o'clock group session conducted by one of the mental-health techs. Despite having to work through an interpreter, the tech did a very credible job getting the women to participate.

At four o'clock Callie walked into the beginning English class feeling nervously inadequate. She soon found she didn't have to worry. The seven women and one teen in the class were eager to learn, and the teaching aids included very basic flash cards, picture books and whiteboards. The youngest class member, named

Sabeen, had a wide gap between her front teeth and seemed to take special delight in repeating sibilants like "sleep" and "snake." With each whistle, she'd giggle, slap her palm over her mouth and set the colored beads at the ends of her hundreds of tiny braids to dancing a merry tune. Having read her case file only a few hours ago, Callie could only marvel at the kidnapping victim's resilience.

Simona had indicated the staff were welcome to eat dinner with the residents, although most preferred a little separation after their long days. Night duty rotated among the paid staff and involved either sleeping at the center or remaining at home, close to a phone.

Since it was Callie's first day on the job, she opted to have dinner at the center. She shared a table with a woman from northern Iraq whose husband and three sons had been beheaded by ISIS last month. A former university professor, she spoke English and kept the conversation focused deliberately and exclusively on Callie. Where she was from. Where she'd gone to school. Why she'd come to Rome. Why the United States had invaded her country, then plunged it into chaos. Well aware she had to earn these women's trust, Callie answered as honestly as she could.

The night air was cold and brisk when she walked back to her apartment, accompanied by dark-haired, dark-eyed Nikki Dukakis. The nurse-practitioner lived only two streets over and invited Callie to have dinner the following evening with her and her husband.

"Simona is coming, too," she said. "And Carlo, if he has returned to Rome. My Dominic is with the Greek Trade Commission. He does business with Carlo, which is how I came to work at the center. But I'll do my best to keep them from talking trade embargoes all night."

She waved a cheerful goodbye at the corner, and Callie climbed the stairs to the third floor. Fumbling off her glove, she activated the scanner and let herself into the two rooms that were already beginning to feel like home. Her first order of business was a hot, steamy shower. Her second, snuggling into warm pj's. Her third and most important, calling Joe.

"Hey," she said when he picked up. "How's Zurich?"

"Cold. Snowing. Traffic pretty much at a standstill. But I got done what I needed to."

"So you're going to fly back to the States tomorrow?"

"If the airport stays open. Your turn. How was your first day?"

"Exhilarating. Exhausting. And really, really humbling. These women have been through so much, Joe. I spent most of the day waffling between a burning desire to help and questioning whether my puny skills are up to the task."

"They are. How'd you get along with *il Drago*?"

"I'm on probation until I prove I'm not just another do-gooder Carlo foisted on her. Which might be kind of tough, since I hope to do good and Carlo *did* foist me on her."

"Like I said this morning, my money's on you. Hang on, I've got another call." He returned a few seconds later. "Sorry, I need to take this. I'll call you back."

"That's okay. I'm pooped. I'll talk to you tomorrow. Good night, Joe."

"Night, Pansy Eyes."

Her voice lingered in Joe's mind as he reconnected with the caller he'd put on hold. "Yo, Frank. What's up?"

His Defense Intelligence Agency buddy didn't waste

time on chitchat. "A report just crossed my desk I think you should know about."

"I'm listening."

"Someone's been making inquiries about the place you had me check out a few days back. Very casual, very innocuous inquiries. They were buried deep in a flurry of other chatter."

"And?"

"And up until these queries surfaced, we were pretty sure we'd taken this particular someone down."

Joe's stomach went tight. "Can you give me details?"

"Not over an open line."

Joe vowed instantly to depart Zurich within the next hour, snow or no snow. If he couldn't fly out, he'd either drive or jump a high-speed train to whatever airport was still open. Once there, he'd charter an executive jet if necessary.

"I'll see you tomorrow."

He cut the connection and stood for a moment, hefting the phone in his palm. The ink had barely dried on the deal he'd cut with Callie. No wrapping her up in cotton wool. No ignoring mutually agreed-to boundaries. No unilateral decisions…except in extraordinary circumstances.

The problem was, he didn't know how extraordinary these circumstances might be. Serious enough for Frank Harden to contact him, certainly. And troubling enough for Joe to pull out all the stops to get back across the pond. Until he was in possession of some cold, hard facts, though, he couldn't see worrying Callie. Besides, this was obviously not something that could or should be discussed over the phone.

Refusing to admit he was rationalizing, he stabbed a speed-dial number and connected with the on-duty

controller at his twenty-four-hour operations center. "I need out of Zurich tonight and into DC tomorrow. Any way you can work it."

"I'm on it, boss."

By the time he'd thrown his toiletries in his shaving kit and stuffed his spare clothes in his carryall, the controller called back to confirm the Zurich airport was still open.

"You're in luck. Flights look iffy for later tonight, but right now they're keeping the runway plowed and the planes deiced. I got you on Lufthansa leaving for New York in two hours and the shuttle from there to DC. You'll have to hustle to make it."

"I'll make it."

Chapter Nine

Callie got up early enough the next morning to make a quick cup of coffee. Just one, though. What she really wanted was one of those sinfully rich white-chocolate espressos at the little café she'd discovered yesterday.

The air was still crisp and cold. Bundled against the chill, she wove through the backpacking school kids and early shoppers. The scent of hot, strong coffee and fresh-baked pastries welcomed her when she ducked inside the café. While she waited for her croissant and espresso in its elegant, silver-handled glass, her gaze roamed the framed black-and-white photos. There was Sophia Loren again, and Jack Kennedy. And a helmeted general in jodhpurs and a low-slung holster.

Patton? Could that really be Patton?

Her glass in one hand and the croissant in the other, she tried to edge past the stand-up counter crowd for a closer look. She was almost there when one of the pa-

trons closed the lid of his computer and turned to leave. She jumped back to avoid a collision but sloshed some foamy white chocolate on his sleeve.

"Oh! *Scusi!*"

The man muttered something that didn't sound too complimentary under his breath and grabbed a napkin to dab at his jacket sleeve.

"I'm sorry," Callie said in English. "I hope it didn't get in your laptop."

He jerked his head up and stared at her with unfriendly eyes. Then he turned on one heel and shouldered his way unceremoniously through the crowd.

"Ohhh…kay," she said to his back, "And no, I didn't splash hot coffee on my hand and burn myself, but thanks for asking."

Shrugging off the incident, she enjoyed the croissant and what was left of her espresso, then headed for the center.

Her second day on the job turned out to be even busier than the first. She sat in on another group therapy session at nine and attended an occupational assessment workshop at eleven. With the aid of a translator, a job placement specialist gently probed a sad-eyed, stoop-shouldered young widow for possible employment choices.

Callie joined a table of three women at lunch. Although English wasn't their native language, all three spoke it with varying degrees of proficiency. One, the victim of a vicious disfigurement by a jealous husband, hid the gaping hole where the tip of her nose had been cut off behind a veil. A native of Bangladesh, Leela had contacted an IADW outreach worker after that same

loving husband had driven her out of their home with a whip.

"Simona says the doctors can fix my face," she murmured in soft, very British English. "She says she will tell Prince di Lorenzo to arrange it."

"Which he will do," one of the other women said with a smile. "He lives in fear of Simona, although he is twice her weight and so much older."

Weight, Callie agreed with. But older? Although she didn't know his for sure, she would guess the prince was somewhere in his mid-to-late thirties.

Her glance shot to the center's director seated at a table across the room. With her snowy hair and lined face, Simona certainly looked to have some years on him.

Leela followed her glance and said quietly, "She has suffered greatly, our Simona. Although she does not speak of it, it's said her hair turned white overnight."

Callie was still digesting that startling revelation when the subject of their discussion pushed away from her table and gestured for the newest member of her staff to join her. Once in the hall, the director posed a curt question.

"Are you qualified to conduct trauma therapy?"

Callie had used a trauma-focused approach with some of the children she'd worked with. Getting them to expose their memories and fears resulting from abuse or other trauma required a delicate touch, however.

"It's been a while…"

The tentative response sent an impatient flicker across the director's face. A younger face, Callie could see now, than her white hair and the deep grooves creasing her cheeks would indicate.

"Is that a yes or no?" she asked curtly.

"Yes."

"*Bene!* I want you to work with Amal. Maybe you can connect with her. God knows none of the rest of us can."

"I'll try my best."

"You do that. You do that."

Callie had to conduct an extensive search for the pregnant woman. She finally found her tucked in a corner of the second-floor arts and crafts room. She was almost completely hidden behind an artificial palm that the center's Christian residents had draped with handmade stars and silver tinsel. The small crèche under the palm reminded Callie of the purchases she'd made in Naples. She would take them out of their wrapping when she got home, she decided, and set up a little bit of Christmas in her apartment. Kate and Dawn and Tommy would just have to wait for their gifts. But first...

"Hello, Amal."

The quiet greeting startled the other woman. She whipped her head around, her dark eyes frightened, and made an instinctive move to shield the clipboard in her lap. Callie caught just a glimpse of a pencil drawing on the top sheet of the paper before the loose sleeve of Amal's robe covered it.

One glimpse was enough. With hardly more than a dozen bold strokes, the woman had masterfully interpreted the clean, fluid lines of Michelangelo's *David*.

"Oh," Callie breathed. "That's beautiful." She gestured in an attempt to overcome their language barrier. "Please, may I see it?"

Amal's arm remained firmly positioned over the sketch. The fear had left her eyes, but there was no

mistaking the message they now conveyed. Ignoring the back-off signal, Callie did a quick scan of the room. The game table held a pencil and small pad for score-keeping. She grabbed both.

"I took a few art classes in school," she confessed as she dragged a chair over and positioned it next to the stone-faced woman. "Mostly art history, although I do like to draw. Unfortunately I'm not very good."

According to Simona, their best guess was that Amal had survived the tragic sinking of a refugee boat from Syria. Callie didn't know a word of Arabic. But she'd used art therapy with children many times in her previous job and knew it could cross generational barriers. She hoped it would cross language barriers, as well.

"This is me." She sketched a fairly decent female figure with longish hair. "This is where I'm from."

She added a quick backdrop of Boston's skyscrapers, although she knew each stroke was a calculated risk. The US and its allies were waging an air war in Syria. Amal's father or brothers or husband might have fought—might *still* be fighting—either with or against rebel forces. Yet everything Callie had been taught, every nugget of experience she'd gained over her years as a counselor, dictated that she lay a foundation of honesty.

"And this is you."

Flipping to a clean page, she stretched the limits of her artistic skills with a quick portrait of a figure wearing a head scarf. Then she held the sketch out to the silent woman at her side.

"Where are you from?"

Callie knew she risked alienation by pushing too hard. Possibly total and irrevocable shutdown. Yet the longer Amal hesitated, the harder Callie's heart ham-

mered. Finally the other woman reached for the pad, but her hand trembled so violently that she snatched it back.

"It's okay," Callie said quietly. "You're safe here."

She knew Amal couldn't understand her. Knew, too, that platitudes meant little to a woman who'd lost everything. She held her breath as Amal retrieved the pad. Then slowly, so slowly, the other woman sketched a backdrop to the solitary figure.

Despite the small size of the canvas she had to work with, the layers came together in stark, minimalistic detail. Bombed buildings. Piles of rubble. Children with eyes too large for their skeletal faces. Just as slowly, she added another rendering of Michelangelo's *David*. Curly haired. Square jawed. With fierce eyes and a lethal-looking semiautomatic held waist high.

"Is this…" Callie had to stop, pull in a breath. "Is this your husband?"

Her question drew no response. The other woman stared down at the sketch for long moments. Then her pencil lashed out. Suddenly. Violently. Slashing from right to left so viciously that the paper shredded and Callie had to grab her wrist to stop the desecration.

"Amal! It's okay! You're safe here. You and your baby. You're both safe."

With a guttural sound, the other woman jerked free and thrust out of her chair. Her own sketch jammed tight against her chest, she whirled and ran out of the room.

Callie didn't go after her. She wanted to. Ached to. But training and experience kept her riveted in place. The next move—if there was one!—had to come from Amal.

Still, doubts stung like an angry swarm of wasps as she went downstairs to her office and powered up her computer. Simona's instructions had been specific. Case

files were to be updated daily. No excuses, no delays. Any counseling sessions with residents, either one-on-one or in group, went in their file.

Callie curved her fingers over the keyboard while she organized her thoughts. Then entered the password, pulled up Amal's case file and battled the excruciatingly slow system to detail her failed attempt to bridge the communication gap. The entry complete, she grimaced at the flickering screen. So much for proving to Simona Alberti that she wasn't just another of Carlo's do-gooders. She logged out, wondering how long it would take before the director jumped down her throat.

Simona pigeonholed her that same evening, not long after Callie arrived at Nikki Dukakis's spacious flat.

Nikki's husband answered the door. The Greek was seriously gorgeous and wreathed in the same hot, spicy aroma that wafted from the rear of the apartment.

"I'm Dominic Dukakis," he said as he took her coat, hanging both it and her shoulder bag on an antique clothes tree in the hall. "And you must be Carlo's American."

Not quite sure how to respond to that one, she merely smiled and held out her hand. "Callie Langston."

"Come in, come in. Nicola's in the kitchen. I'll tell her you're here and fetch you a glass of wine. Or would you prefer ouzo?"

"Wine, please. Red, if you have it."

"Of course."

"Simona's here, too," he said as he gestured to a wide archway that opened onto a high-ceilinged room. "If you care to join her, I'll bring your wine."

"'Carlo's American,'" Simona echoed sardonically

when Callie joined her. "I've no doubt you'll wear that label until his next 'friend' takes your place."

"I've worn worse."

The calm reply earned a sharp look from the director, followed by a reluctant nod. "I don't doubt you have. I read your update in Amal's file," she added in a quick change of direction.

Callie braced herself, but to her surprise, the snowy-haired Simona gave her an unexpected stroke.

"You accomplished what none of us have been able to do. You connected with her."

"Only for a few moments."

"You connected," Simona repeated.

Encouraged by the unexpected praise, Callie shared her thoughts. "Amal whipped a detailed background sketch out so quickly, with such bold, sure strokes. I'm sure she's had formal training. She's that good."

"What are you thinking? That she might be an established artist?"

"Very possibly. I'm going to surf the net and see what I turn up. In the meantime, I'll try to connect with her via art again. Perhaps use it as a springboard for trauma therapy, as you recommended, or adult cognitive behavioral therapy."

Simona cocked her head, her blue eyes piercing. "You're trained in adult CBT?"

"I worked primarily with children in my last job, but I volunteered one weekend a month at the Boston VA hospital. We found CBT to be a very useful tool when working with patients suffering from post-traumatic stress."

The director glanced away. "*Sì*," she murmured. "It can be."

Whatever she was seeing, it wasn't the impressionistic rendition of Mykonos's famous windmills that oc-

cupied a good portion of the far wall. Callie knew better than to probe. Not that she would anyway in a social setting. Instead she stood quietly until the Italian shook off her memories and deliberately changed the subject.

"We don't make Christmas a big celebration at the center, you understand."

"I would guess not, since so many of the residents are of different faiths."

"We try to accommodate those who are Christians, however. So if you have no plans for…"

"Here you are." The interruption came from Dominic, who returned with a bowl-shaped glass. "This is from the vineyard of Katogi and Strofilia, in northern Greece. Although Carlo would never agree, I think you'll find it as good—or better!—than any Italian red. And speaking of our xenophobic prince," he said as the doorbell jangled, "that will be him."

Callie could never quite pin down what it was about Carlo di Lorenzo that seemed to expand whatever room he entered. It certainly wasn't his appearance. The man was a fireplug, as wide at the middle as he was through the shoulders. What's more, his shiny bald spot had crept forward another inch or two since Callie had last seen him at Dawn and Brian's wedding. But his dark eyes danced above his luxuriant handlebar mustache, and no woman alive could remain immune to his obvious delight as he crossed the room, his hands outstretched.

"Calissa, *cara mia*!"

"Ciao, Carlo."

He took her hands in both of his and raised them to his lips with a dramatic flourish that had her smiling, Dominic grinning and Simona rolling her eyes.

"You grow more beautiful every day, Calissa. But

this…" He dropped his gaze to her ring and twisted his lips in exaggerated sorrow. "I couldn't believe it when Joe told me that you were engaged. Surely you cannot mean to marry that block of wood. Not when I have offered to show you the delights of Marrakech and Bali."

"Her," Simona said with a small snort, "and a hundred other women."

"Ah, yes." With a spectacularly unsuccessful attempt to hide a grimace, the prince released Callie's hands and turned to face his nemesis. "Dominic told me you would be here, *il Drago*."

Callie stiffened, expecting fireworks, but Simona Alberti seemed to take the label as a tribute.

"And you still came. How very brave of you," she drawled, the sarcasm as sharp as dagger points.

He drew himself up to his full height, which put him almost at eye level with the director. He looked, Callie thought, like a mastiff going nose to nose with a whip-thin greyhound. Simona didn't appear the least intimidated, but before either of them went for the throat, Nikki strolled in from the kitchen.

"Sorry, everyone. I must confess I'm a better nurse than cook. Dominic, my darling, get Carlo a drink. And check the dolmades."

Sending her husband on his way with an airy wave, Nikki kissed Callie on both cheeks and received one of Carlo's flamboyant greetings.

"Ciao, Nicola. You're far too beautiful for that lump of Greek clay you're married to. Since I can't convince Callie to run away with me, perhaps I can talk you into abandoning Dominic and allowing me to show you the wonders of—"

"Yes, yes, we know," Simona interrupted with unconcealed irritation. "Marrakech or Bali or the South

Pole. Now, for pity's sake, may we stop this nonsense and discuss something actually important?"

"By all means," Carlo returned with soft, silky menace. "Please tell me, Madam Director, what's so important that we must dispense with civility?"

Whoa! Callie had only ever seen the prince at his most charming. This combination of haughty aristocrat and ice-edged commander made her blink and Nikki step in hastily to defuse the situation.

"It's the computers, Carlo. Simona and I were talking about them before you arrived. They're old and slow."

Callie couldn't help recalling her frustrating session just a few hours ago. "Not just the computers. The wireless router, too. The signal's so weak it takes forever to get online."

"When we can get on at all," Nikki put in.

"If I'm to submit the ridiculously detailed reports you and the board require," Simona said tartly, "I must have the tools to do it."

"*Madre di Dio!*" Palms up, Carlo surrendered with a return of his urbane smile. "How can I withstand the onslaught of three such determined women? I'll get you what you need."

The promise won delighted thank-yous from Callie and Nicola and a curt nod from Simona.

"See that you do." The brusque order wiped the smile off Carlo's face. If the director noticed his sudden scowl, however, she ignored it. "Nikki, I think I smell something burning. Shall we go help Dominic in the kitchen?"

"*Ochi!*"

Their hurried departure left Callie standing beside an obviously irate Carlo. A growl rolled up from deep

in his chest as he shot narrow-eyed darts at their re-
treating backs.

"She never allows me the last word, that one. Never!"

Callie had no trouble guessing which she he referred to.

"If she were one of my troops, I would have her up on
charges of insubordination," he steamed. "But does she
care that she shows me little respect? Does she worry
that the entire board quakes every time she comes be-
fore them? No, damn her, no. Instead, she makes me
burn to kiss that condescending smirk off her face every
time I'm with her!"

Callie jaw went slack. Mouth open, she gaped at the
furious prince and fumbled for a response. *Any* kind
of a response. Thankfully, she was saved by the bell.

The loud jangle brought Dominic's head popping out
of the kitchen door. With it came a cloud of gray smoke.

"Carlo, *aprire la porta, per favore.*"

The prince balked, obviously torn between answering
"*la porta*" and making a quick call to the fire depart-
ment. He threw out a spate of urgent Italian and Dominic
returned what Callie sincerely hoped were hearty reas-
surances. Still, she decided to retrieve her phone from
the purse she'd left hanging in the hall and keep it close
at hand. Just in case. She'd taken only a few steps, how-
ever, when she got her second shock in as many minutes.

"Ciao, Giuseppe."

With a mix of surprise, confusion and pure joy, she
watched the prince greet the former chief of his special
security detail with a hearty thump on the shoulder.

"I thought you'd left Rome," di Lorenzo commented.

"I flew home last night and did a quick turnaround."

"That was indeed quick. But why would you…"

He broke off as Joe's glance shot past him and fixed
on Callie.

"Of course." The prince's mustache lifted in a wicked grin. "I would not leave her alone too long, either, were I you."

"Yeah," Joe drawled. "That was pretty much my thinking."

Callie had recovered enough to take exception to that bit of blatant chauvinism. Which she would certainly have done, if Joe hadn't sniffed the air and suddenly stiffened.

"Jesus! Is this place on fire?"

"I'm not sure," Carlo admitted. "I'll go see."

Joe took advantage of his departure to cross to where Callie stood and brush his mouth over hers. As light as the kiss was, she felt the scrape of the bristles darkening his cheeks and chin. She also took note of the red rimming his eyelids and the deep creases bracketing his mouth.

"What's happened, Joe? Why did you turn right around and fly back in Rome?"

"Not here," he said with a small shake of his head.

She didn't bother to ask how he'd known where to find her. She did, however, want to know why he hadn't held to his end of the bargain they'd negotiated a few days ago.

"How come you didn't let me know you were coming right back?"

"Check your phone."

Frowning, she dug it out of her shoulder bag and discovered it was in silent mode. She'd set it on vibrate before the therapy session she'd sat in on this morning, she now remembered, and had forgotten to take it off. She also discovered two voice mails, both from Joe, and four texts, two from him and one each from Kate and Dawn.

"You need to leave the ringer on, Callie."

"I don't want it going off during therapy sessions."

"Then keep it in your pocket, not your purse. So you'll feel it vibrate."

"Why?" she asked again. "What's going on?"

"We'll talk about it at your place. Right now we'd better…"

A wild clanging shrieked through the air. Callie winced and clapped her hands over her ears, thunking herself with the phone in the process.

"Smoke detector," Joe shouted over the din. "Open the door and some windows. I'll see what the hell's happening in the kitchen."

Stuffed grape leaves. That's what was happening. Tight little rolls filled with ground lamb, rice, chopped onion, minced garlic and fragrant spices.

Once they extinguished the fire, Nikki and Dominic and their guests discovered that one of the dolmades had somehow tipped out of the baking pan and fallen unnoticed to the back of the oven. It toasted to a blackened crisp before igniting and setting the remaining appetizers and a pan of souvlaki ablaze.

The cleanup didn't actually take all that long. Dominic drenched the charred remains in the sink, then carried both pans out to the balcony while Nikki assured anxious neighbors their homes weren't about to go up in flames. In the meantime Carlo, Joe, Simona and Callie waved dish towels to dispel the acrid smoke.

Dominic joined their effort after his trip to the balcony. Flapping a towel vigorously, he threw Joe a curious look. "Have we met?"

"Name's Russo. Joe Russo. I came to find Callie."

"Oh. Well, thanks for helping out here, Joe."

"No problem."

* * *

Fifteen minutes later their collective efforts had replaced most of the smoke with cold night air, and Nikki had been introduced to her uninvited guest. Like Dominic, she thanked Joe for coming to the rescue, then suggested they all repair to a nearby restaurant.

"We promised you dinner," she insisted. "It'll take a while yet for the apartment to totally air out, and I don't intend to turn the stove on again tonight. Maybe ever. I did mention, didn't I, that I'm a much better nurse than cook?"

"You are," Simona confirmed before adding a tart, "thank goodness."

Laughing, her husband retrieved their guests' coats and shepherded them out into the night. Still puzzled by Joe's unexpected return, Callie tucked her arm in his and asked quietly whether they should beg off dinner.

"No, this'll work. I need to talk to Carlo. I'll get him aside for a few minutes at the restaurant."

His discussion with the prince took place in a quiet corner of the bar. Callie watched them from the table in the noisier eating area, Joe's head bent close to Carlo's, the prince listening with a frown.

Both men wore neutral expressions when they rejoined the group, and Callie was forced to bridle her unease until she and Joe returned to her apartment some two hours later. She waited until they'd shed their coats and gloves and scarves, dumped some grounds in the coffeemaker and pointed to the kitchen chairs.

"Now," she demanded when they faced each other across the tiny table. "Why are you here? What's going on?"

"Someone's been making inquires about the center. Someone my contact at the Defense Intelligence Agency thought had been taken out."

"Taken out? As in...?"

"Made dead," Joe said flatly. "Bastard was driving a vehicle that took a direct hit from a drone five months ago. My contact thinks now the driver might've been someone who looked so much like the target that whoever called in the strike got it wrong."

"And this...this target is interested in the center? Why?"

"We're not sure. Best guess is because he knows one of the current residents."

That might be their best guess, but there were others. Callie knew Joe well enough now to sense he was holding back. Shielding her. Trying to protect her from the big, bad, ugly world.

"What are the other possibilities?"

"They're a stretch, Callie. Not credible threats."

"Tell me."

He didn't want to frighten her. She could see it in his eyes.

"Tell me."

He answered reluctantly. "One scenario says the women at the center have forsaken their honor by fleeing their homelands and adopting the decadent ways of the West."

"So they should be punished. As if they haven't already been punished enough," she added savagely. "What else?"

"It's the other side of the same coin. You people at the center are working a hidden agenda. In the guise of helping refugees, you're forcing them to deny their heritage, their religion."

"So *we* should be punished."

"Like I said, these scenarios are out there. Not credible."

"Credible enough for you to jump on a plane and come straight back to Rome," she pointed out.

He couldn't argue with that, and Callie couldn't believe they were actually sitting here talking about drone strikes and retaliating against helpless women who'd already suffered so much.

This was Joe's world, she thought with a fist-size knot in her throat. And now hers.

"How much did you tell Carlo?" she asked after a futile attempt to swallow the lump.

"Enough. He's going to advise the other members of the board."

"What about Simona? You have to tell her, too."

"Carlo and I plan to brief her tomorrow."

"She's not going to like this."

"Got that impression." Joe's gray eyes flickered with something she might have mistaken for amusement under other circumstances. "Funny, I've never known di Lorenzo to go six shades of pale at the mere mention of a woman's name. Your boss must put him and the rest of the board through the wringer."

Callie didn't comment. She still hadn't quite processed the prince's earlier outburst, wasn't even sure now that she'd heard him correctly.

"I thought I'd camp out here for a few days," Joe said casually. Too casually. "Or we could move to a hotel. It would give us a little more space."

She glanced around the tiny apartment with its bright yellow walls and incredible view. She hadn't put much of a personal stamp on it yet. Just angled the kitchen table so she could drink in the sight of St. Peter's dome with her morning coffee and set out the nativity figures she'd bought in Naples. They rubbed shoulders on her postage stamp of an end table. Dawn's flame-

haired angel, Tommy's Disney figure, Kate's despised political candidate and the traditionally robed Joseph.

Her gaze shifted from the Virgin Mary's protector to her own. With a sense of inevitability, Callie accepted that her Joe wasn't going anywhere any time soon.

"Let's stay here."

Chapter Ten

Joe had agreed to meet Carlo at the center at eight thirty. Their plan was to beard the director in her den before the problems and events of the day distracted her or fired her temper.

He woke at his usual five o'clock and lay in the shuttered stillness, trying to shift his focus from the warm butt nested against his groin to the sparse data Frank Harden had shared.

The known aliases of the terrorist supposedly taken out by the drone strike. A list of atrocities attributed to the man as verified through human, signal, geopolitical and open-source intelligence. A blurred photo taken from a half mile away. The date, time and coordinates of the airstrike that had—supposedly—taken him out. There was nothing to suggest the bastard had survived the hit. Nothing, that was, except the recent queries about the center operated by IADW.

The probes themselves were innocuous enough.

None would've triggered an alert if not for the fact they'd been made on the same laptop previously owned by the target of the strike. A laptop that went off-line at the precise instant the drone hit. A laptop that had come back online only two days ago.

US cyberspooks had pinpointed the source of the transmissions. By triangulating cell towers and satellite systems, they'd zoomed in on a squalid, teeming tenement in Palermo, on the island of Sicily. A door-to-door search by Italian security forces hadn't yielded the laptop, however, or any indication of who might have powered it up.

Joe had his own people working the problem—his cybersecurity folks at home, Emilio Mancera here in Italy. The affable Roman had met him at the airport last night, gotten a quick briefing and put one of his own men on a flight to Palermo an hour later.

If the residents of that squalid tenement had withheld any information from the police, Emilio's man would squeeze it out of them. He knew the island, knew the inner workings of the criminal element that still flourished there. Knew, too, that the Mafia had shed its skin several times over the decades. They were still heavily into narcotics and protection rackets, of course, but now funneled their profits into legitimate businesses like shopping malls and hotels and apartment complexes...all built by a construction industry that operated on bribes, kickbacks and corruption. Without a single twinge of conscience, Joe had given the green light to apply all three if necessary.

In the meantime, he and Carlo would work the problem from this end. Starting with a thorough scrub of the backgrounds of each and every resident at the center and...

"Nmmg."

The indistinct mumble was accompanied by a twitch that sent Joe's thoughts sliding sideways. He held himself still, his breath stuck in his throat, as Callie wiggled again.

She couldn't seem to find a satisfactory position. With another mumble, she straightened one knee. Bent it again. Canted her hips. Thrust her bottom, and put Joe in an instant sweat.

"Callie. Sweetheart."

He tried to ease back a few inches. She wiggled again and locked onto him with the precision of a laser-guided heat-seeking missile. Smothering a curse, Joe shifted his head on the pillow and threw a glance at the window. His internal clock said it was still predawn. The blackened shutters confirmed that.

Hell! No way he could hold out until six or seven. Not hard and hurting like there was no tomorrow. If he and Callie hadn't ended last night with an extended tussle between the sheets, he might've rolled her over and initiated a repeat performance. But she'd collapsed on his chest, and Joe had barely found enough strength to drag up the covers before they were both out.

He'd let her sleep, he decided, and use this quiet time to contact his cybergeeks. He'd check in with Emilio, too. But not here. Somewhere that served thick, black, vein-opening coffee.

Callie was still dead to the world when he returned with two espressos and a paper sack of fresh-baked pastries. It didn't take long for the seductive aromas to penetrate her consciousness. Especially after Joe held a still-warm *cornetto* mere inches from her nose. She

blinked awake, stared owlishly at the marmalade-filled bun and slicked her tongue over sleep-dry lips.

"Does that taste as good as it smells?"

"Only one way to find out."

An arm snaked out from under the blankets. Fingers latched onto the sticky sweet. Three bites later, a tousled head of mink-brown hair popped up.

"Any more where that came from?"

"On the kitchen table. Espresso, too."

He smiled as she lit up like the gaudy Christmas decorations strung across the streets outside. Rolling out of bed, she dragged a blanket around her like a tent and made for the kitchen.

"I waited for you to wake up to take a shower," he commented. "I'll make it quick."

She was too busy exploring the contents of the bag to do more than flap a distracted hand.

Joe emerged fifteen minutes later showered and shaved. Callie took considerably longer, but the results were definitely worth the wait. The steamy shower had left a delicate blush on her cheeks, and her hair fell in glossy, raisin-dark waves above a sky blue turtleneck sweater. The worry was back, though, shadowing her eyes to a purple so deep they looked almost black.

"What time did you say Carlo is going to meet us at the center?"

"Eight thirty. But it might be better if you stay out of this one."

"Why?"

"Your boss is already torqued at me for asking to review the center's screening process. Even more at Carlo for insisting it happen. No need to get her pissed at you, too."

Callie didn't comment but had to admit she was secretly happy to stay out of the line of fire.

Unfortunately, she didn't stay out of it long.

Bundled in boots, jeans, a warm sweater and her wool duster, she huddled close to Joe's side for the short walk to the center. Carlo was already there and looking none too thrilled with the task ahead.

Callie peeled off with a murmured "good luck" and headed for her office to prepare for the nine o'clock group session. When she came out twenty minutes later, notebook in hand, Simona's door was closed. The thick panel didn't quite block the sound of raised voices, though, or the thump of something banging down on the desk. Simona's palm? Carlo's fist?

She didn't stick around to find out. But when she got to the session room, the news that the mental-health tech who normally conducted this group therapy had called in sick added another wrinkle to the day. Luckily, the group was a small one. Only one translator and four participants: the two teens who'd escaped brutal sexual slavery, the disfigured wife from Bangladesh and the sad-eyed, stoop-shouldered young widow. Hiding her nervousness at being thrust into the role of facilitator as opposed to observer, Callie picked up where they'd left off yesterday.

"We were talking about how we see ourselves, and how what we've experienced colors our self-image."

She waited for the translator, then picked her way carefully over sensitive ground.

"Too often when something bad happens to us, something we can't control, we think it's our own fault. We feel guilty, anxious. Unable to make decisions or relate to others."

The woman from Bangladesh drew her veil tighter across her mutilated face and murmured something Callie couldn't quite catch.

"I'm sorry. What did you say?"

"A leper," Leela said in her soft, British-accented English. "I feel like a leper. I show myself to no one."

The thinner of the two teens spoke next. A single word, muted, reluctant.

"Unclean," the interpreter translated. "After what was done to her, she feels unclean."

Callie nodded and looked to the other two participants. The young widow shrank back against her chair and shook her head, but the second teen, the one named Sabeen, chose to speak out. Usually so happy and giggly, she launched into an angry spate that set the beads at the ends of her braids dancing and the words whistling through the gap in her front teeth.

"She, too, feels dirty," the interpreter related, hurrying to keep. "She bathes two or three times a day but cannot wash the smell of those pigs off her skin, out of her hair."

As if to emphasize her feelings, the girl grabbed a fistful of the braids and shook them angrily.

"Sabeen says she would cut them off. All of them. As she would cut off the thing between the legs of every man who took her."

"Well…"

Callie was treading delicate ground here. For all she knew, those colorful beads denoted rank or marital status in the tribe these girls had been abducted from. They'd chosen not to return to their tribe, however, deciding instead to make a tortuous journey to another country, another way of life.

"Why *not* cut them off?" she asked gently. "The

braids, I mean. Although I think castrating the pigs who hurt her is a pretty good idea, too."

The question was obviously one the girl had debated before. A host of emotions flickered across her face, not least of which was fear of losing the last vestige of her identity in this foreign world.

Callie waged a similar internal debate. She was here to facilitate, not direct. Enable, not lead. Yet she couldn't force herself to remain detached and neutral and merely nurturing. Something drove her to bridge the seeming impossible gulf between these women's world and her own.

"Hang tight," she instructed through the interpreter. "I'll be right back."

She hurried down the hall to her office, throwing a quick glance at Simona's closed door as she went. She didn't hear any raised voices or loud thumps and couldn't decide whether that was a good or bad omen. Joe could be pretty intimidating when he wanted to, she knew. Carlo, too, as she'd discovered last night. Simona would have to be made of kryptonite to stand up to both of them. And after having known the director for all of two days and a few hours, her money was on the director.

Once in her office, Callie riffled through her desk drawer for a pair of scissors. She found them in a bottom drawer, then rooted around in her purse for her handy-dandy little travel mirror. Clutching both objects, she hurried back to the session room.

"I haven't suffered as you have," she told the other women through the translator. "I haven't experienced anything that could even remotely compare to what you've suffered. But, like you, I'm beginning a new

life in a new place. So I think... No, I *know*. I'm ready for a new me."

Brandishing the scissors, she held the mirror at arm's length and tried unsuccessfully to wield the scissors with the other.

"I could use some help here. Will someone please hold the mirror for me?"

The interpreter looked as hesitant as the four residents. When none of them replied, Callie dropped the mirror, grabbed a hank of her hair, and hacked off a good eight inches.

Leela sprang to her feet, half laughing, half scandalized. "Buddha preserve us!"

Her veil slipped, revealing a glimpse of her horrific disfigurement, before she threw the ends over her shoulder again and grabbed the scissors.

"I will do it. But only if you really wish me to."

"Whack away," Callie instructed cheerfully.

Within a remarkable short period of time, hair lay in heaps on the floor. Callie's dark brown. Sabeen's black braids. Leela's hennaed tresses.

Sabeen kept slapping her hand over her mouth to contain her giggles, but her infectious laughter soon drew a half dozen curious residents. Then Nikki. Then an obviously irritated Simona.

"What goes on here?"

"Hair therapy."

Grinning, Callie shook her short, surprisingly curly locks. She felt pounds lighter and thought she looked like a completely different person. Unfortunately, her boss wasn't impressed.

"*Hair* therapy? Is that some new American fad?"

The scorn behind the question cut as sharp and as

deep as the words themselves. Smiles slipped. Expressions turned worried. Sabeen passed a nervous palm over her new buzz cut.

"It's hardly a fad." Callie's response was cool and level. "You might want to read Dr. Elaine Boyer Barrington's *Adaptive Therapies for Female Adolescents.* Her work merely reinforces the basic fact that a teenager's hairstyle is one of the most obvious indicators of her feeling of self-worth. So obvious, in fact, that therapists too often fail to ascribe it the significance they should."

Simona's brows snapped together, but she didn't challenge Callie in front of the others. Instead, she merely glowered and issued a terse command.

"I want to speak with you. In my office."

"Of course. I'll just sweep up the hair and…"

"We'll take care of it," the translator said quickly.

"Thanks."

With a smile and another toss of her short, who-would've-guessed-it curls, Callie followed her boss. Simona marched down the hall, her back stiff and her chin held at a combative angle.

"Adaptive therapies?" she huffed. "Dr. Elaine who-ever Barrington? If I go online and do a search, will I find either?"

"I'd be very surprised."

"So you invented all that nonsense?"

"No, I didn't. I knew Elaine in grad school. She was a very innovative thinker but switched careers after earning her PhD. Last I heard, she and her husband were operating a treetop guest lodge in Tanzania."

Simona stopped with one hand on the doorknob of her office. Blue fire shot from her eyes. "Are you play-

ing with me? If you are, I'll tell you now I'm not in the mood for it."

No kidding. Didn't take a genius to see her meeting with Carlo and Joe hadn't gone well and Callie was about to take the heat for it.

"Well," she said with a calm smile, "the treetop lodge might be in Zimbabwe."

Those blue lasers narrowed dangerously. Callie kept her smile in place but felt the narrowness of her escape when the director whirled and thrust open the door. She stomped in, waited for Callie to follow, then slammed it shut and wasted no time on preliminaries.

"The prince and your fiancé shared some disturbing news."

"Joe told me about it last night."

Simona resorted to the classic Italian gesture. Bringing the fingertips of one hand together, she waved it up and down. Despite her short time in Rome, Callie had seen the gesture often enough to know the most polite interpretation was *What the hell?*

"I cannot not believe this. My center, the target of inquiries by a dead terrorist! It is not to be believed."

Her accent thickened with each word, along with her indignation.

"I think," Callie replied carefully, "that we should trust Joe's instincts."

"The prince most certainly does," her boss huffed. "He informs me—*informs* me, you understand—that your Joe considers our security totally inadequate."

Callie couldn't help thinking of the rusted panel beside the front door. "Well…"

"The prince also informs me," Simona fumed, "that your fiancé sends one of his subordinates to install additional equipment."

Emilio Mancera, Callie guessed, Joe's very efficient head of operations here in Rome.

"I don't see why you would object to a little additional security," she said cautiously.

"Ha! You see no problem?" Bristling from the ends of her superfine white hair to the tip of her indignantly quivering nose, Simona folded her arms across her chest. "Then perhaps you agree that Carlo and your fiancé should have access to our case files."

"What?"

"Ah. So you didn't know?" The director assumed an expression of fake surprise. "Your fiancé didn't tell you that he wants to sit down with us? To go through every case file?"

"No, he did not."

Callie was more indignant than she'd been in longer than she could remember. At Joe, for not discussing this with her before springing it on her boss. At Simona, for thinking she would condone such a breach of ethics.

"And if he *had* discussed it with me," she added icily, "I would've given him the same answer I suspect you did."

Her obvious ire defused some of the director's. Simona's chin lost its pugnacious thrust and a satisfied smirk replaced her fake surprise.

"But, yes! I told him, '*Non lasciatevi la porta si colpisce nel culo sulla via d'uscita.*'"

Callie had picked up enough Italian to string "*porta*" and "*uscita*" together. "I got it. You told him not to let the door hit him in the ass on his way out."

"*Sì!*"

She bit her lip. She wasn't ready to let go of her indignation just yet, but the thought of this tiny sprite of

a woman unceremoniously booting Joe out of her office shaved off some of its sharp edge.

"Well," she admitted after a moment, "I probably wouldn't have given him that exact answer. But close enough."

"Are you sure, Calissa? You really feel this way?"

"For pity's sake, Simona…"

"Do not fire up at me! Carlo and your bedmate have given me enough grief."

"Our intake interviews and case files are privileged information. Carlo must know that. Joe, too."

He had to. He couldn't have been in the security business without smacking up against privacy laws. Although… With an inner grimace, Callie shoved the suspicion that he might've found a way around, over or under a few of those rules and regulations to the back of her mind.

"Carlo does indeed know it," Simona confirmed, "but he says he will take the matter to the board. We will soon be caught in the middle of a fight."

"It won't be my first time."

"Yes?" The director cocked her head. "You've battled with this fiancé of yours before?"

"We've had a few differences," Callie conceded, "but we sat down and discussed them like rational adults. We'll do the same in this instance, too."

"Ha!"

"We will! But…" she said, coming off her haughty stand, "perhaps I'd better take another look at our operating procedures. I read through them my first morning, but I want to be sure I didn't lose anything in translation."

She was thoroughly acquainted with the standards of patient confidentiality as detailed in the American

Psychological Association's code of ethics, of course. She could also quote title and chapter of Massachusetts law that codified those standards. Her initial review of the center's operating procedures had indicated that IADW's policies mirrored APA's. Basically, client information and records of therapy sessions were confidential, with several internationally recognized exceptions.

One of those exceptions involved any reasonable suspicion of child abuse. Callie was intimately familiar with that provision. She'd had to exercise it far too often while acting as an ombudsman for children caught between warring parents or kids seemingly lost in the foster care system.

Belief that a client will harm himself or someone else was another exception to confidentiality laws. Callie had been forced to exercise that option on several occasions, as well.

She hadn't worked as much with the criteria involving lawsuits and court-mandated therapy sessions, however, and would have to dig deeper to make sure she fully understood IADW's position on each of them.

Crossing the hall to her own office, she retrieved one of the dusty black binders from atop the metal file cabinet. She still had her nose buried in the notebook some thirty minutes later when the sound of footsteps outside her door brought her head up. Expecting Simona, she blinked in surprise.

"Joe! I didn't hear the bell. How'd you get in?"

"Please." He gave her a pained look. "Tommy Ellis could pick the lock on the front door blindfolded. The one on the back door's even worse."

"Simona told me you'd decided to beef up our security."

"Just met with Emilio. He'll purchase the equipment and install it himself. What'd you do to your hair?"

She'd forgotten all about her new do. Lifting a hand, she combed her fingers through the curls. "I call it adaptive therapy. Like it?"

"Yeah, I do. Makes your eyes look even bigger. And speaking of therapy…" He wedged into the narrow space in front of her desk and claimed one of the two chairs. "I expect Simona also told you that she stonewalled Carlo and me a while ago."

"She told me you wanted access to our case files. She also said she, quite correctly, refused."

"Correctly?"

"Those files contain privileged information, Joe. You know that."

"They also contain intake interviews that document your residents' nationality and where they entered the refugee aid system. One of those interviews might reveal a link to the drone strike."

"Not every resident's home of origin is documented," Callie countered, thinking of Amal's shrouded past. "And even if that information *is* in the record, it's protected. We couldn't disclose it without the written consent of the individuals involved."

"So get their consent."

He said it so coolly. So matter-of-factly. As though extracting information was a matter of time, patience and technique, not ethics. A little shocked, Callie pressed him to understand.

"Joe, please. Listen to me. Most of these women have been severely traumatized. Simona, Nikki, the professionals here at the center…they've worked with them for weeks and in some cases months. I'm just beginning

to make a few tentative connections. Yesterday, with a sketch pad. Today with this."

Her hand went to her hair again. Raking the shaggy curls. Standing them on end.

"I have to earn their trust, Joe. That won't happen if I ask them to sign a document they may not understand. One that strips them of the little privacy and dignity they have left."

He studied her through eyes that had gone as opaque and as impenetrable as the fog that rolled in across Boston Bay.

"What about our connection?" he asked after a long moment. "Our trust? You don't believe I could protect their privacy and dignity?"

She flinched and searched for a possible compromise, however shaky.

"Let me talk to Simona."

He nodded. Once. A brief dip of his chin. Then he pushed out of the chair. "You do that. And tell her Emilio should be here before noon."

"Wait! Where are you going?"

"I've got some business to take care of. I'll see you later."

Chapter Eleven

Joe labeled it a strategy session. Carlo, still smarting from the wounds he'd received during the morning's firefight with Simona, declared it a war council. Dominic Dukakis thought he'd been invited to the prince's palatial apartment on Via Zanardelli to discuss yet another proposed amendment to the hotly debated Greece-Italy pipeline.

He learned otherwise shortly after the three men gathered around a burled walnut table in the library. Leatherbound first editions lined the shelves that ran the length of two walls. Gilt-framed portraits of Carlo's ancestors covered every square inch of a third. The fourth boasted velvet-draped windows that give an unobstructed view of the Pantheon's colonnaded portico. None of the three men were interested in Emperor Hadrian's architectural gem, however.

When Joe explained the reason for the meeting to

Dominic, the Greek diplomat didn't bother debating the nebulous nature of the threat. Desperate refugees were wading ashore in his county by the thousands. Most carried with them hope for a better life. No small few, Dominic knew, carried a buried—sometimes burning— resentment toward the Western nations that had bombed or strafed in the ceaseless battle against terrorists. That one of those terrorists might have survived a direct strike and was now making inquiries about the center where Nicola Dukakis worked was all her husband needed to know.

He also didn't waste time sympathizing when Carlo related Simona's flat refusal to grant access to the center's computerized case files. His wife was a highly skilled nurse-practitioner, licensed to diagnose and treat in Greece, Macedonia and Italy. Dominic was well aware of the laws governing patient privacy and the confidentiality of medical records. Instead of railing at the system, he wanted to know what had to be done to protect the women who lived and worked at the center, his wife included.

"Emilio's there now," Joe reported. "He's installing new electronic locks with touch pads and putting motion detectors on the ground-floor windows."

Shuffling through a stack of papers, he extracted a schematic detailing all three floors of the center's interior and exterior.

"We're also installing surveillance cameras that feed to our twenty-four-hour monitoring service. Here, here, here and here."

Dominic's brows winged up. "Simona's fiercely protective of the residents' privacy. I'm surprised she consented to cameras, much less to twenty-four-hour monitoring."

"She agreed to exterior surveillance only." Joe shot Carlo a quick look. "But we're adding unobtrusive interior cameras that can be activated with the flick of a remote switch."

"By unobtrusive I assume you mean hidden."

"Correct."

"And you haven't told Simona about them?"

"Not yet."

The Greek blew a soundless whistle. "I sincerely hope I'm not in the line of fire when she discovers what you've done."

"She won't. Not with Emilio doing the installing."

"You live dangerously, my friend."

"Comes with the territory."

"Speaking of your man Emilio," Carlo put in. "Did he hear from *his* man in Palermo?"

"He did," Joe reported grimly. "His guy squeezed every contact, legitimate or otherwise, but got nothing. Whoever powered up that laptop knows how to cover his tracks."

Carlo muttered a curse while Joe shuffled the papers again and slid one across the table.

"This is a copy of the center's daily schedule. Also a list of outings planned for the next two weeks. I'll have someone shadowing each outing."

The list ran the gamut from shopping excursions to a walking tour of streets lit with holiday lights to attendance by three of the center's Christian residents at the pope's traditional Christmas Eve Mass.

"*Christós*," Dominic muttered when his gaze snagged on the last item. "Fifty or sixty thousand people jam into St. Peter's Basilica for that Mass. Another four hundred thousand fill the square outside to watch it on

huge screens. Your men will have a time keeping watch on these three."

"They'll manage."

Carlo picked up from there. "I spoke to a contact at *Questura Centrale*. He agreed to step up patrols by uniformed police in the area around the center. I've also briefed the commander of the ROS."

The *Raggruppamento Operativo Speciale*, or Special Operations Group, was an elite arm of Italy's national military police, specifically established to combat terrorism and organized crime.

Dominic nodded his approval of these measures and voiced a key question. "What can I do?"

"The same thing Joe and I intend to do. Become more involved in center activities. For the next few weeks, at least."

"That may not be easy to pull off," Dominic said slowly. "Some of those women have been severely traumatized by the very men who should have protected them. Nikki understands this. Simona even more so. She allows only three men to work at the center, two cooks and one mental health tech, and Nikki says she personally vetted each of them."

"Which is why it must be the three of us," Carlo responded. "*Il Drago* can hardly object to a casual visit by Nikki's husband or Callie's fiancé. Or," he added with a twist of his lips, "the chairman of the board she supposedly reports to."

Dominic looked skeptical but withheld comment as a phone pinged. All three men instinctively checked their devices, but the text message was for Joe.

"Emilio's almost done," he reported, pushing back his chair. "I'll use checking his work as an excuse for another foray into the dragon's den."

* * *

He activate the override code on the shiny new touch pad Emilio had installed beside the front door but took care to announce his arrival by texting Callie. Her answering text was short and succinct.

I'm in session. Wait in my office.

Another text pinpointed Emilio's location. Joe found his subordinate crouched beside a low sill in a small storage room at the end of the first-floor hall. Its single window was almost obscured by stacked boxes and metal shelves jammed with an assortment of office supplies. Muttering to himself, Emilio scraped at what was probably three or four centuries of paint with a sharp-edged knife.

"These windows," he snarled to Joe in idiomatic Italian, "they're a bitch."

"Need help?"

"No, this is the last. But I could use some mineral water. Or better yet, a stiff shot of grappa."

Joe was more than happy to comply with the first request. It gave him an excuse to conduct a visual surveillance of the kitchen. He'd already studied its floor plan and assessed every possible ingress and egress point. Still, nothing compared to direct eyeballing.

The unmistakable aromas of Italy hit him the moment he pushed through the swinging door. Garlic, olive oil and the sweet, heavy cream of fettuccine Alfredo. Both of the regular cooks on the center's list of employees were present. One was busy grating fresh Romano while his associate stirred several steaming pots. When Joe asked for mineral water, the stirrer merely

stabbed the tip of his spoon in the direction of a stainless steel refrigerator.

Once every nook and cranny was imprinted in his mind, Joe made his way back down the hall. A quick glance in Callie's empty office confirmed she hadn't finished her therapy session. Simona's office across the hall also stood vacant. But when Joe approached the storage room at the end of the hall, Emilio's tense voice stopped him in his tracks.

The Roman tried Italian first. Then French. Then English. Each iteration was more pleading than the last.

"It's okay. It's okay. Please! Don't do anything rash."

Every instinct on red alert, Joe dropped into a crouch. He shifted the water bottle to his left hand and dropped his right to the lightweight Ruger nested in its ankle holster.

"I see what you want," Emilio said. "No! It's okay! It's okay! You do it. Take my knife. Go ahead, take it."

Joe was still in a crouch, still strung wire tight, when he caught the soft thud of footsteps on the stairs at the far end of the hall. He spun around and spotted Callie frozen halfway down the spiral staircase, her eyes wide and questioning.

He put a finger to his lips. She got the message, but only to the extent of creeping down the remaining stairs on tiptoe. Cursing under his breath, Joe signaled for her to stay the hell back.

She froze in place again, her entire body rigid as she, too, caught the faint whisper of what Joe guessed was a naked blade slashing through cardboard. Emilio's voice followed a few second later.

"There. Take as much as you want." A pause, a gentler tone. "When's your baby due?"

Oh, God, Callie thought. That was Amal in there

with Emilio. Amal, who never spoke a word but could sketch like this century's answer to Michelangelo. Amal, who might give birth any day, surrounded by strangers. Callie knew she should intervene. Should let the other woman know she wasn't…

"My name's Emilio."

She held her breath as Joe's associate waited a beat. Two. Three.

"And you?" he said softly. "What's your name?"

The tableau played out in vivid high definition inside Callie's head. The dusty storage room. The impossibly handsome Roman with his buffed-up biceps and bed-room eyes. The pregnant refugee who'd lost everything. She'd just decided to terminate the agonizing inquisition when she caught a whisper so faint she almost missed it.

"They…they call me Amal."

Callie couldn't move, couldn't breathe. Astounded, unbelieving, thrilled, she locked on Joe. He transmitted an unmistakable signal to keep silent as Emilio spun out the tenuous thread.

"Amal? That's a pretty name."

Painful seconds ticked by. Callie had almost given up hope when Amal answered in tortured whisper.

"The name is a mockery."

"Why?"

The reply was low, tortured. "In Arabic it means 'hope.' But I have none."

"Why?" Emilio asked again.

So calm. So unthreatening. Yet the single word pro-voked a fierce response.

"You could not understand!"

"Then tell me. Explain why you're so frightened."

Callie inched closer to Joe. She felt like a world-class voyeur but wasn't about to interrupt this fragile con-

versation. To her intense disappointment, it was terminated a moment later.

Amal burst out of the storage room. Her robe flattening against her distended belly, she flew past Callie and Joe. Emilio emerged almost on her heels. His handsome face contorted into a scowl as he watched her rush up the spiral staircase.

"She shouldn't run like that. She could trip," he worried. "Hurt herself or the baby."

"What was that about?" Joe demanded. "What was she doing in the storage room?"

"I'll show you." Emilio went back into the dusty storage room and returned a moment later with a still-wrapped ream of copy paper.

"Here. This is what she was after." His glance cut to Callie. "She seemed desperate for it. Why don't you take it to her?"

She knew where to look this time. As she'd anticipated, Amal had taken refuge in the corner half-hidden by the potted palm with its mantle of tinsel and silver balls.

Once again Callie signaled her presence with a soft hello. And once again the mother-to-be looked up with wide eyes and refused to return her greeting.

"Emilio...the man downstairs...he said this is what you wanted."

Callie placed the ream on the table beside Amal. Despite the other woman's blank-eyed stare, a dull red crept into her cheeks.

"You know you can have as much paper to draw with as you wish. You've only to ask."

The red deepened.

"I heard you downstairs," Callie continued gently.

"You and Emilio. I'm so glad you speak English. I've been wanting to tell you something."

That produced not much as a flicker of response but she refused to give up.

"I'm completely in awe of your artistic ability," she told the other woman. "Perhaps…perhaps we could visit some of Rome's museums together. The Borghese and the Sistine Chapel top my list."

Amal's lashes swept down, but not before Callie caught the spark that leaped in her dark eyes. Hiding her own excitement, she took that for a yes.

"The Sistine Chapel might be tough to get into this close to Christmas," she said in a deliberately conversational tone. "So many tourists here for the holidays. Why don't I go online and see if I can get us tickets for the Borghese?"

She did a quick mental shuffle of her schedule. "How about tomorrow? I'll talk to Simona and see if I can move the English class to one o'clock instead of four."

She waited a few beats. "Amal? I won't push if you don't want to go. Just tell me yes or no."

The nod was short and excruciatingly slow in coming.

"Great!" Excitement shooting through her, Callie wasn't about to give the other woman time to change her mind. "I'll go downstairs right now and check on tickets."

Joe and Emilio were still in the hall. They were deep in conversation but broke off as she approached.

"Is Amal all right?" the Roman asked with concern stamped across his face.

"She's fine. I can't believe you got her to speak to you. That's the first time she's verbally communicated with anyone."

Callie wanted to kiss him. Almost did.

"You cracked the door, Emilio, and I squeezed through after you. Amal agreed to go to the Borghese with me tomorrow afternoon. I'm going online now to see if I can reserve two tickets."

"Make it three," Joe said. "I'll go with you."

"Four," Emilio put in.

Callie hesitated. "I'm not sure that's a good idea. I barely got her to agree to go with me."

"Reserve four," Joe instructed. "If she balks at an escort, Emilio and I will keep our distance. Neither of you will see us in the crowd."

"And if there is a problem with tickets," his associate added, "my cousin's wife's brother works at the museum. He'll get us in."

Callie didn't have to resort to Emilio's relatives. She reserved four tickets for a 2:30 p.m. entrance time. She also printed out the brochure containing a map and description of the exhibit rooms and took it upstairs.

"We're all set," she told Amal. "I hope you're as excited as I am."

The gleam in the other woman's eyes was answer enough. Callie prayed that including an escort wouldn't kill it.

"Is it okay if my fiancé comes with us?" she asked. "And Emilio, the man you met downstairs. When I told them what we were planning, they both said they'd like to go."

She felt a little guilty withholding the fact that neither man was driven by a burning desire to view the Borghese's art treasures. Not guilty enough to explain the reasons for their presence, however. Primarily because Joe stressed that the precise details of the drone strike were still classified. Secondarily because Simona

had yet to advise Callie on how much or how little to tell the residents.

She saw the reluctance in Amal's face and moved quickly to counter it. "That's okay. They don't have to come with us."

They'd trail along behind instead.

Callie's guilt kicked up another notch. Her professional conscience pinging, she realized she couldn't keep shading the truth like this. She'd destroy her tentative connection with this woman before it even took root.

She'd just decided to cancel the outing, or at least delay it until the security scare was over, when Amal finally communicated verbally.

"The one downstairs," she whispered in a low voice.

"Emilio?"

"He has a kind face."

That wasn't how most women would see it, Callie thought in surprise. With his melting brown eyes, noble nose and sensual mouth, Emilio Mancera was a Roman god come to life. But the fact that Amal had at last deigned to speak with her thrilled Callie so much that she instantly agreed.

"Very kind. So it's all right if he joins us? He and my fiancé?"

Amal nodded.

"Okay!" Feeling as though she'd just scaled a ten-thousand-foot mountain, she shoved the brochure she'd printed at Amal. "Here's a brochure of the museum. You can study the layout before we go tomorrow. And I checked. They have wheelchairs available if you get too tired or the baby starts to weigh you down."

The other woman's hand dropped to her swollen belly. She hesitated for long moments before revealing

the first hint of her past. "We walked for many days, my babe and I. Many nights. We do not need a wheelchair."

Callie couldn't help thinking of Joe's thwarted request to review the residents' intake interviews and case files. She came close, so close, to asking Amal where she'd walked *from*. And who she'd left behind.

She resisted the urge. First, because anything Amal shared with her would still be considered privileged information. Second, because Callie's instincts warned her not to push too hard, too fast.

"Okay," she said instead, "no wheelchair. We'd better take a taxi to the museum, though. You and the baby may be able to walk that far. I can't."

Once back downstairs she confirmed arrangements with Joe and Emilio and left them to finish whatever security improvements they had left while she updated Amal's case file. That done, she braced herself to brief Simona on the breakthrough, as tentative as it was.

As she suspected, the director had yet to fully recover from her contentious meeting with Carlo and Joe. When Callie tapped on her door, she snapped out a "Come in," and looked up to give her deputy a decidedly unfriendly glare.

"Have you seen these locks your fiancé's installed?" she fumed. "They read palm prints."

"I know," Callie responded. "He had one installed at my apartment, too."

The pencil Simona was balancing between two fingers seesawed back and forth, hitting the desk repeatedly. Tap. Tap. Tap. Each tap louder and angrier than the last.

"So tell me," she demanded. "What's to stop this 'security expert' you're engaged to from running these prints through various international databases?"

"I asked him about that."

The pencil hit the desk again. Faster. Harder.

"Did you? And what did he say?"

"The same thing he and Carlo told you this morning. Any prints provided voluntarily outside a therapy session aren't protected by client-counselor confidentiality."

"Perhaps not," Simona fired back. "But running these voluntarily provided prints without their owners' consent violates their privacy."

"You'll have to argue that with Carlo. Joe said the prince got a legal opinion on the matter."

"Oh, yes," Simona huffed. "He did. From one of the half dozen judges he has tucked in his back pocket. One who apparently thinks the safety and security of the masses override our residents' rights to privacy."

After almost witnessing the Boston Marathon bombing firsthand, Callie's own feelings were too contradictory to argue the point.

"Actually," she said instead, "I came in to tell you about Amal."

"What about her?"

As she described the incident with the ream of paper and the subsequent proposal to visit the Borghese, the director's angry pencil stilled.

"And she agreed to go with you?" Simona asked incredulously.

"She did." Callie couldn't help grinning. "I booked tickets for two thirty tomorrow afternoon. Assuming you don't mind me moving the English class up to one p.m., that is."

"Of course not."

To her relief, her boss relaxed into a smile. The result was a Simona Alberti that looked years younger.

Young enough, Callie thought with an inner grin, to have snared the reluctant interest of Italy's playboy prince.

"You've gotten more from Amal in a few days than the rest of us have in a month," Simona said.

"I can't claim all the credit. Emilio coaxed her into talking to him. That broke the ice."

"This fellow, Emilio. What do you know about him?"

"Nothing other than the fact that he works for Joe."

"Are you sure it's wise to include both men in this trip to the Borghese?"

"Amal seemed okay with it."

"Don't forget that drawing you told me about. The one she destroyed. The male figure in that sketch may well represent someone she fears."

"Or hates," Callie agreed, remembering how viciously she'd slashed the drawing.

"Whatever the emotion is, it's obviously very close to the surface. Be careful you don't unintentionally trigger it."

Callie took the warning to heart but could only hope an excursion to one of Rome's most famous museums would trigger joy, not hate or fear.

Joe spent the afternoon helping scan the staff and residents' palm prints into the electronic keypads Emilio had installed at the front and back entrances. Per Simona's strict orders, they made sure everyone understood they could use the palm pad or punch in an override code. Since the code consisted of sixteen alpha and numeric digits, neither Joe nor Emilio was surprised every resident went with option A.

Joe disappeared for a while after the key pads were up and running but was waiting in the little café across

the street when Callie left work that evening. He noted with approval that she'd dressed for the December night in her long duster, a warm scarf and gloves. After a quick exchange with the man sharing his table, he dodged the traffic and joined her.

"Who's that?" she asked with a glance at his companion.

"One of Emilio's crew. Are you up for a walk?"

"Sure. Where to?"

"Via Condotti. We've both been cooped up all day. I thought you might like to stretch your legs and see the shops all decked out in lights."

And Joe needed to buy her a Christmas present. With everything else going on the past few days, it had almost slipped his mind.

"Ooh!" She breathed a delighted puff into the frosty air. "I've been dying to see Via Condotti. When Kate researched our trip this fall, she told us it's *the* street for high-end shopping. We couldn't afford to buy anything in those absurdly expensive boutiques, but we'd planned to cruise them anyway."

That sealed it. Her present would most definitely come from Via Condotti.

"And at Christmastime," she related in delight, "the window decorations are supposed to be spectacular."

Not just the window decorations, they soon discovered. The entire street was festooned for the holidays. Monster chandeliers of twinkling white lights illuminated the thoroughfare from the foot of the Spanish Steps to its intersection with Via del Corso. Shops touting names like Prada and Gucci and Valentino all tried to outdo each other with spectacular displays. But Joe and Callie both agreed Fendi took the prize.

A wide band of blue lights belted the Italian de-

signer's four-story building. As if that wasn't eye-catching enough, the Fendi's signature logo sparkled in the white lights that comprised the belt's massive buckle. Like icing on an extravagant cake, the largest tree Joe had ever seen dominated the traffic circle in front of the store.

"Wait!" Callie dragged him to a halt and yanked her cell phone out of her purse, then stretched out her arm. "I have to send a selfie of us to Kate and Dawn."

Joe flinched. Years as a Delta Force operative had conditioned him to shy away from having his picture taken. His instinctive aversion had ramped up since Curaçao. He didn't need a visual reminder of that failed mission. Not when he could see one every time he looked in the mirror.

"I'll take the picture," he told Callie. "You don't need me in it."

"Yes, I do! Dawn and Kate were so bummed we wouldn't be together at Christmas. It's the first time since we were kids." She waved an arm at the glittering display. "I want them to see you and me together, enjoying all this."

"You've shared *every* Christmas since you were kids?"

"It's not all that hard to pull off when you grow up in the same small town," she retorted. "Hold still."

Okay. He could pose for one shot. For Callie. Still, he angled his head to hide the scar as she stiff-armed the phone. Her reach wasn't long enough. She barely caught the two of them in the frame, much less the lights.

"Let me do it."

He cradled her against his chest and framed them against both the tree and the belted building.

"Oh," she enthused. "That's better."

It was. Much better, Joe agreed. He had Callie in his arms and Rome lit like a Christmas tree behind him. Any thought of Curaçao faded. So did the worry that had goaded him like a vicious spur since Frank Harden's call. For the first time, Joe felt the joy of the season seep into his bones.

He took the shot, then Callie twisted in his arms.

"Take another."

She pushed up on her toes. Her arms hooked around his neck. Her mouth went from cool to hot as it molded his. With his arm still extended, Joe could only hope he would hit the right button on the camera app as he hooked his other arm around her waist and tugged her against him.

The applause pulled them apart. That, and a laughing suggestion from some men who'd stopped to watch the show. Luckily, the suggestion was in Italian. When Joe responded with a grin and lowered his arm, Callie grabbed the phone and switched immediately from camera to photo mode.

"Oh, my God! These are great. Look at that tree. And the Fendi belt! Hold on, I have to send the pics to Dawn and Kate."

Her thumbs flew. When she'd finished, he took her elbow and steered her toward the store entrance. Once again she dragged him to a halt.

"Joe! I can't afford anything in there."

"I can."

"We talked about this. Remember? I want to pay my own way."

"Christmas presents aren't part of that agreement."

"Maybe not. But I'm not into designer bags or belts or boots. Tell you what," she said when he started to protest. "You can buy me a print at the Borghese to-

morrow. Something pretty I can frame and hang on my bright yellow walls."

He gave in, but only because he was already considering another gift…which turned out to be a smart move, because they never made it to the Borghese.

Chapter Twelve

The other half of her bed was empty when Callie blinked awake the next morning. She groped for her phone and peered owlishly at the digital display. Ugh! Six fifteen. Her alarm wouldn't go off for another forty-five minutes. She snuggled under the duvet again but couldn't go back to sleep. The stillness in her tiny apartment was too loud.

"Joe?"

No answer. Not that she'd expected one. She stretched lazily and wondered how in the world the man could slide out of bed, shower and/or shave, dress and depart without making normal human sounds.

Giving up the battle after a few more minutes of snooze time, she stuffed her feet into slippers and wrapped the duvet around her like a tent. When she padded into the kitchen area, she found a note propped against a large takeout coffee and a paper sack containing fresh ricotta-filled pastries.

"Bless you," she muttered as she pried the lid off the coffee and scanned the note. Surprise, surprise. Joe had some business to take care of.

She hitched up the duvet and carried the coffee back to the bedroom with her. In what was sure to become a daily habit, she ducked out on the tiny balcony to get her daily fix of the view. Night still shrouded the city, but the sky to the east showed streaks of purple and red. She still couldn't quite believe she was standing here, suspended above the rooftops of Rome and gawking at St. Peter's softly illuminated dome in the distance.

The frosty air drove her back inside. That, and the urge to take another look at last night's selfie. Plunking down on the side of the bed, she traded the coffee for her phone and scrolled through the photos she'd taken in the past week. As much as she missed Kate and Dawn, her Christmas season was turning out to be truly magical. Sharing Saint Lucia's day with the Audis. Mingling with the throng in Naples's street of the crèches. Last night's stroll through Via Condotti with its amazing display of lights.

She lingered over the selfie and had to smile at how Joe had positioned her in the shelter of his arms. Always the protector. Always the guardian.

Good thing they'd established boundaries this early in their relationship. Without those boundaries Callie knew it would be all too easy to succumb to the seductive promise of being petted and pampered. Now if only…

The phone vibrated in her palm. Joe, she thought. Calling to give her whatever details he could about the task that had gotten him up so early. Instead her boss's name came up on the caller ID. Surprised and just a lit-

tle alarmed by the early call, Callie switched instantly from silent to speaker mode.

"Hi, Simona. Is everything okay?"

"No! Everything is *not* okay." Anger, hot and scorching, jumped through the speaker. "I want you at the center in fifteen minutes."

"Why? What's…?"

"Fifteen minutes! Not one minute later. *Capisce?*"

Agitation had stirred the director's accent. It was so thick and heavy Callie struggled to separate the furious words.

"If you take longer," her boss fumed. "If you are not here then, do not bother to come in. Just pack your bags. Go home!"

"Simona! Wait! Tell me—"

Too late. She was talking to dead air. Callie wasted several precious seconds debating whether to call her boss back. It wouldn't do any good, she realized. She needed a face-to-face to sort out whatever had Simona in such a fury. Tossing her phone aside, Callie raced for the bathroom.

She was out the door nine minutes later. Her duster flapped around her ankles as she hurried through streets just coming alive with morning traffic. With each step, she tried to figure out what she'd done to infuriate her boss.

Maybe it was her unconventional hair therapy. Had that backfired? Had one of the teens suffered a traumatic loss of identity after hacking off their long, beaded braids? Or Leela? Was the mutilated wife now mourning the loss of her hair? Could she feel it added to her disfigurement? Think that not even surgery would help her now?

Or was it Amal? Dear God, had she pushed Amal

too hard? Dragged the agreement to visit the Borghese out of her? Precipitated a panic attack? Her stomach clenching, Callie could visualize the pregnant woman springing out of bed, grabbing her pencil and viciously slashing another drawing.

With her thoughts roiling, she rounded the corner and blew out a relieved breath. Whatever had precipitated the director's summons apparently hadn't included a call to outside authorities. No police cars, no fire trucks, no ambulances or flashing strobes of any kind were parked in front of the center. The terra cotta building sat dark and silent, showing only the dim outline of a single lighted window on the ground floor.

Her office. That was her office.

More confused now than apprehensive, Callie slapped her palm against the keypad and yanked the door open. She started down the dimly lit hallway but had taken only a few steps when she caught the back-and-forth of angry voices coming from her office.

Simona. And Carlo. Trading such fast and furious Italian that Callie couldn't catch even a gist of their heated conversation. She was about to call out when something banged against the metal file cabinet and Simona issued what sounded like a sneering taunt. Then, suddenly, the taunt ended on a squawk.

Uh-oh. This was not good. Not good at all.

Like a bright red warning light, the prince's startling revelation that he itched to kiss the condescending smirk off the director's face flashed in Callie's head. She almost turned tail and ran. A sharp crack and a growled curse held her in place. Her imagination running riot, she decided she'd better make her presence known. Like now.

"Simona? Carlo?"

She heard a rattle. A thump that sounded like the legs of her office chair hitting the floor. Her boss's angry acknowledgment.

"In your office!"

The tableau that greeted her confirmed her worst fears. Simona bristled with fury and Carlo's cheek sported a fat red blotch.

"You, uh, wanted to see me?"

"No." Simona's arm whipped out. A rigid index finger stabbed at the flickering screen of Callie's desktop. "I wanted you to see this."

"Why did you boot up my computer?" Callie asked in confusion. "Did yours crash?"

"*I* didn't boot it up. It was on when I got here."

Thoroughly confused, Callie looked from her to Carlo and back again. "Who turned it on, then? Nikki? One of the mental-health techs?"

The prince rubbed his cheek and took it from there. Shooting an angry glance at his nemesis, he answered stiffly.

"None of the other staff members have come in yet. *Il Drago* found the computer on when she arrived. At which point she called me and started ranting about my having another judge on my payroll. One who would authorize access to your case files."

A chill slithered down Callie's spine. "Someone… someone got into my case files?"

"So it appears," Simona threw at her. "Unless you forgot to log out and shut your computer down last night."

"Of course I logged out!"

Carlo aimed another glance at the director and tried to soften what was feeling more and more like an inquisition. "Are you certain, Callie?"

"Yes!"

Or...

Frantically, she searched her memory. Images flashed by like a slide show. She'd talked to Amal. Confirmed the tickets for the Borghese. Gone down to her office. Logged on and updated the case file. Logged out and hurried to brief Simona on the breakthrough.

Another series of images popped into her head. Of Joe helping Emilio scan the staff and residents' palm prints into the new electronic key pads. One after another. With plenty of time in between to take a break. Amble down the hall. Scope out Callie's office.

No! She wouldn't go there! She couldn't!

Despite the fierce self-denial, a sick feeling curled in the pit of her stomach. She'd jotted down the password, she now remembered. Aleppo221. She'd reversed the digits but acknowledged now that wasn't much of a challenge for a determined hacker.

Her office was too small and crowded to get to her desk. The sick feeling spread from her stomach to her lungs as she uttered a bleak request. "Simona, look under the blotter."

"Why?"

"Just do it."

The director took two steps and jerked up the blotter. The violent movement dislodged the sticky. It floated free and drifted down to lie on the desktop like an accusing yellow eye.

"You wrote down the pass code?" Simona breathed fire. "And left it where any *idiota* might find it?"

Callie couldn't answer. Couldn't breathe. But she could visualize the yesterday's scene as if it replayed in high definition.

Joe and her. Standing toe to toe in this same office.

Not every resident's home of origin was documented, she'd informed him. And even if was, the case file containing that information was protected. She couldn't disclose it without the written consent of the individuals involved. And she could hear his answer. As terse and sharp as a hammer striking iron.

So get their consent.

She staggered back a step as another scene spun through in her mind, too vivid to block. Joe and Emilio. So clever. So skilled. Circumventing legal requirements by plugging an absurdly long override code into the keypads at the center's front and back entrances. Then waiting in the hall when Callie dashed upstairs to tell Amal she'd booked museum tickets.

No! Joe wouldn't search her desk. He wouldn't hack into her files.

Would he?

Stabbed through the heart by sudden, crippling uncertainty, Callie spun on her heel. She ignored the director's sharp command to come back. Ignored Carlo's urgent plea to talk this through. She wanted no part of either of them. No part of the pain that clawed at her heart.

Joe was bent over a map of Rome when his phone buzzed. A quick glance at caller ID showed Carlo's photo and phone number. He hit Connect, knowing his friend's face would flash up on the other end.

"Yeah?"

"We need you at the center," the prince barked. "Now!" His pulse kicked. "Why?"

"Simona. She called me. Callie, too."

"Callie's there?"

"She was. She just stormed out."

"On my way."

* * *

Callie wandered aimlessly. She didn't notice the city springing to life around her, had no idea where she was. She couldn't focus enough to identify any landmarks.

Her thoughts centered on Joe. Only Joe.

He'd promised, she thought, her heart twisting. That morning in Naples. Before they'd explored Pompeii. He hadn't liked being pinned to the mat. Still, he'd agreed that theirs had to be a marriage of equals. Reluctantly, she remembered, and only after grabbing the out she'd offered him with both hands.

Extraordinary circumstances. That was the out. Had he used it? Made a unilateral decision to access the files?

Blind to the traffic beginning to churn the streets, Callie turned a corner. Two seconds later she stopped dead. Oh, sweet Jesus! Not the fountain! Not now, with the silly, *stupid* wish she'd made three months ago rising up to mock her.

She turned away. Made it several yards down one of the three streets leading away from the fountain before she surrendered to its inexorable pull. Her feet dragging, she turned and retraced her steps.

Thankfully, it was too early for the usual horde of tourists. Only a hardy few had braved the cold to add their contribution to the more than three thousand euros tossed in the fountain's basin every year. The offerings of these early risers hit with dull thunks. Callie saw why when she threaded through the sparse crowd.

How appropriate! How ironically appropriate! Rome's iconic fountain was bone dry.

With a hiccuping laugh, she sank onto the steps leading down to the basin. Last night she'd wandered Rome's beautifully illuminated streets and marveled

at how magical the city was at Christmas. Now it felt as cold and empty as the fountain and too dreary for words.

Yet… Dammit! She hated to tuck tail and scurry home like a scolded child. Yes, she'd screwed up. Yes, she'd left a barely disguised version of her computer's password where person or persons unknown might find it. But every time she tried to pin Joe's face on that nebulous someone, her heart stuttered.

Shoulders hunched, nose sniffling in the cold, Callie burrowed her chin in her coat collar and stared unseeing at Oceanus and his pawing steeds. Joe hadn't violated her trust. He wouldn't. The certainty seeped into her heart slowly. Steadily. Replacing the doubt with a soul-deep relief.

She had no idea how long she'd been sitting there, lost in thought, when an excited exclamation pierced the cold morning air.

"Oh! Look!"

Callie's glance cut from the wide-eyed coed just a few feet away to the fountain. It came alive right before her eyes. Water trickled into the top basin. The sun had arced high enough now to add a frosty sparkle as the stream filled that marble bowl.

"They've turned on the fountain." The young coed a few feet away threw Callie an excited grin. "Isn't that awesome?"

"Totally."

The trickle gained volume. The top basin spilled into the second. Its overflow emptied into the third. That overflow fanned sideways. Soon the splash into a half dozen marble shells filled the air. Breathlessly, Callie watched as the giant circular basin at the fountain's base began to fill.

* * *

Joe didn't need a GPS lock to know exactly where to look for her. Sure enough, he spotted her huddled against the cold and sitting shoulder to shoulder with a young woman sporting a Stanford University backpack. The two of them were completely absorbed in the spectacle of the Trevi Fountain coming to life.

He hung back, remembering the last time they'd gathered at this same fountain. Him, Carlo, Travis and Kate, Dawn and Brian and Tommy. And Callie, of the pansy eyes and serene smile. He still found it incredible that none of her friends had seen the worry she'd hidden behind that Mona Lisa facade. Even more incredible that he'd pierced her stubborn defense and gotten her to trust him.

That trust now hung by a thread. After Carlo's terse account of the confrontation at the center, Joe knew she had to think he'd betrayed her. Rehearsing and discarding a dozen different approaches, he settled for simply saying her name.

Her hips swiveled. Her head turned. Those soul-stripping eyes locked with his. "Hello, Joe. Tugging on my electronic leash?"

"We need to talk."

She gave a short laugh. "I thought that was my line."

The coed flashed an uncertain look from her to Joe and back again. "Do you want me to hang with you awhile?" she asked Callie.

"No. But thanks for the offer."

"You sure?"

"I'm sure. Go ahead, make a wish."

The twentysomething pushed to her feet, all long-legged grace and unfettered energy. She tipped her

backpack off one shoulder and rooted around in its cavernous depth for several moments.

Joe preempted her and produced a coin. "Here."

She hesitated and threw another glance at Callie. At her nod, the college student accepted the euro with a mumbled, "Thanks."

Joe sank down in the spot she'd just vacated. Hip to hip, he and Callie watched the young woman face away from the fountain. The euro sailed in a clean arc over her shoulder and splashed into the half-full basin. She turned, spotted the ripples, and gave a jaunty thumbs-up before joining several others her own age for a flurry of group shots and selfies.

"I hope she gets her wish," Callie murmured.

Joe didn't answer for the simple reason that he didn't think a reply was required. Beside him, Callie drew up her knees and rested her chin on the flap of her coat.

"Do you remember the last time we were here?" she asked after a moment, her gaze on the glistening water.

"I remember."

"We made a wish then, Dawn and Kate and I. Should I tell you what my wish was?"

Joe wasn't sure he wanted to know. When he made a noncommittal sound, she angled her chin and pinned him with those incredible eyes.

"I wished for a dreamy romantic hero, *à la* Louis Jourdan," she confessed.

"Who?"

"He was one of the stars in the original movie version *Three Coins in the Fountain*."

Right. Nothing like losing out to some '50s-era matinee idol he'd never heard of.

"A dreamy romantic hero, huh? Sorry, sweetheart. Looks like you scored zero for three."

"Actually," she countered, "I think I scored three for three."

He was still digesting that when she scooted around on the step so they were knee to knee. Pulling off her glove, she feathered her fingertips across his cheek.

"I don't want movie star flash and dash, Joe. I want a real hero. One who's earned his stripes the hard way. One who would never lie to me or betray my trust."

He captured her hand and held it against his cheek. "I didn't hack into those files, Callie."

"I know."

"Nor did any of my crew."

"I know." Her mouth twisted in a grimace. "I admit I freaked when Simona confronted me this morning. It was such a shock, coming out of the blue like that. But once I got here, once I took time to think things through, I knew you wouldn't renege on our agreement."

Joe wanted to let this moment spin out. Given a choice, he would've kept the ugliness at bay until their butts froze to the cold marble step. Unfortunately, he didn't have that option. He needed to bring Callie up to speed and get them both back to the center.

"We've verified the breach didn't originate in-house," he told her. "The hacker overrode the password and powered up your computer from a remote device."

"Device?" She glanced quickly from side to side and lowered her voice. "Like a laptop?"

"Yeah."

She took a moment to process that. "You said he overrode the password. So he didn't use the one I scribbled on a note and stuck to the underside of my blotter?"

"No, but remind me to teach you some of the finer points of computer security."

"Oh, Joe! I'm so glad. Well, not *glad*. But I thought…

Simona and I both thought…" She blew out a frosty breath. "Well, let's just say I was getting ready to pack my bags."

Joe could have relieved everyone's mind about that a lot sooner if he'd instructed Emilio to activate the interior cameras he'd installed yesterday. The hidden eyes would've picked up anyone entering or exiting Callie's office.

Well, that hurdle was now cleared. According to Carlo's terse account, he'd informed an outraged Simona that the cameras were in place and were going active until further notice. Di Lorenzo hadn't related her response.

"Have you determined the location of this remote device?" Callie wanted to know.

"Not yet. But we're close."

They damned well should be, with cybergeeks on two continents pulling out all the stops. Joe's people, DIA, NSA, their Italian counterparts, even Brian Ellis, whose skunkworks cadre sat elbow to elbow with the members of the Military Satellite Communications Systems division at Los Angeles Air Force Station.

"We're also close to tagging which files he went into, if any," Joe told her. "Once we have that information, we can talk to the subjects. And hopefully nail down who's so interested in them, and why."

"That's skirting pretty close to the line," Callie worried. "Simona might object."

"Carlo can take that one on. From what he's told me, he and Simona have been duking it out all morning."

"Um. Not quite *all* morning."

Joe cocked his head. "You know something I don't?"

"Maybe. When we get back to the center, you might want to ask Carlo if his cheek still stings."

"Huh?"

"Just ask him. In the meantime…" She got up and brushed off the seat of her coat. "I guess we should head back. I'd like to find out if I still have a job."

"Hold on." Joe unfolded his tall frame. "You say you got your wish. I sure don't see myself as dreamy or romantic or much of a hero, but what the hell. As long as it works for you."

"It works. Believe me, Joe, it works."

"Maybe. But this is what works for me."

Her nose was cold, her lips almost as chilled. They warmed under his, though, and sent a welcome heat rolling through his veins. When he raised his head, the smile in her eyes confirmed that all was right between them.

"Since that seems to have worked out so well," she said, "maybe I should make another wish."

"Sure you want to tempt fate twice?"

"Pretty sure. Do you have another euro?"

He watched as she took the coin and assumed the proper position with her back to the fountain. Eyes closed, she looked as though she was sorting through dozens of possibilities before settling on one. Then she sent the coin sailing to join the others in the basin.

"You going to tell me what you wished for this time, too?"

"Only after it comes true," she laughed.

Joe still had the specter of a supposedly dead terrorist hanging over him. Still had a hinky feeling in his gut that things were about to break. Yet that laugh made him feel a thousand pounds lighter.

The feeling lasted for all of five minutes. Just until he and Callie were weaving through the jumble of tourist stalls beginning to open for business on the Via Delle

Mutate. They were still several blocks from the center when Joe's phone buzzed. One glance at caller ID had him whipping up the phone.

"Russo."

"He's there." Frank Harden's voice stabbed through the instrument. "In Rome."

Chapter Thirteen

With Harden's warning ringing in his head, Joe hit speed dial and called for another war council at the center ASAP. By the time he and Callie got there, Emilio and Dominic were on their way. Carlo hadn't left the center yet. They found him pacing the hall, nursing a cup of coffee and a fierce scowl.

"Where's Simona?" Callie asked. "I need to know if I still have a job."

"Upstairs. One of the residents is ill."

"Oh, no! Is Nikki with her?"

"Not yet. Dominic just texted. She's coming in with him."

"I'd better go up and see if I can help."

She shed her coat and scarf, tossed them in her office, and hurried up the stairs.

That left Joe to relay Harden's terse message. When he had, Carlo cursed and tossed his half-empty cup in a trash can.

"It's not yet eight o'clock and the morning has already become a nightmare. First *il Drago* wakes me from a very pleasant and most interesting dream. Then she drags me down here, only to fling accusations at me about bribing half the judges in Rome. And then, when I try to deny the absurd charge, she snorts and says I probably wouldn't remember who I've bribed, anyway."

Having worked the prince's security for several months, Joe would bet his last dollar that Carlo was more riled over the forgetfulness charge than the bribery. Sure enough, the prince tugged at one end of his mustache and sputtered indignantly.

"She all but called me senile. Me!"

Callie's earlier remark teased at Joe's brain. He wanted to ignore it. And he didn't want to hear any further details in what could turn out to be a very awkward situation. But Carlo's outrage demanded a response.

"So you, uh, offered to prove that you're still young and virile?"

"What? But no! I merely kissed her."

Joe tried, he really tried, to block the image of Carlo laying one on Simona Alberti.

"So," he said when the image wouldn't go away, "she whacked you a good one."

"A *very* good one." His outrage subsiding, Carlo slipped into a rueful grin and rubbed his cheek. "I should recruit her for the Stormo Incursori, no? My commandos could use someone who packs as much firepower in one arm as that one does."

"Better we brief her on Frank Harden's call," Joe suggested, pulling the prince back to the present. "She needs to know whoever hacked into the case files is here, in Rome."

Carlo nodded, but any plans to make the director

aware of the threat took a sharp U-turn when Callie flew halfway down the stairs. Her eyes wide under her cap of curls, she leaned so far over the wrought-iron rail that Joe almost shouted a warning.

"Amal's in labor," she announced excitedly, "and Simona says the baby's crowning! I've already called nine-one-one. We need scissors or a sharp knife and some string."

She whirled and flew back up the stairs, leaving the two men to exchange looks of sheer male panic.

"Do you know anything about delivering a baby?" Carlo asked with a touch of desperation.

"Only what's in the special ops medical handbook. You?"

"The same."

Swallowing a groan, Joe took off at a lope. "I'll hit the kitchen. They'll have a knife. Maybe some string. You check the offices."

Like Carlo, Joe had spent years in clandestine ops. More years prior to that as a military cop. During those years, he'd put his emergency medical training to the test more times than he wanted to count. Most recently, he remembered like a bayonet to the heart, in Curaçao. Cursing, he shoved that bloody scene out of his head. This was here. This was now.

As he raced for the kitchen, he dredged up a mental image of the special ops medical handbook. There was a chapter on obstetrics, he remembered. Not anywhere as detailed as the chapters dealing with treating battle-field injuries, of course. But pretty damned thorough. The subheadings faded in, faded out, jumped into focus.

Stage One: Onset of cervical changes and uterine contractions.

Stage Two: Full dilation and birth.

Stage Three: Delivery of the placenta.

Okay. Okay. Callie said the baby was crowing. That meant Amal had already progressed to stage two.

Images from the memorized manual flashed into Joe's head. Diagrams of the female reproductive organs. Other diagrams showing a fully formed baby in the birth canal. Instructions on assisting a breech birth. How to do a...

What the hell was that incision? Damned if he could remember the medical term for a cut might be necessary to keep the baby from tearing the vaginal wall and ripping into the rectum, causing a bacterial infection that could kill both mother and child.

Christ Almighty!

He slammed into the kitchen and scared the crap out of the two cooks preparing what smelled like spicy breakfast frittatas. Good thing they recognized Joe from his survey of ingress and egress routes or he might have been smacked in the face with a giant frying pan. Still, they tensed and looked ready to let fly when he grabbed a long knife from the preparation counter.

"The director... Signora Alberti...she needs this." Whirling, he plunged the blade into a pot of boiling water. "And string. *Corda.* Do you have *corda*?"

One of the cooks pointed his spatula at a drawer in the counter. Joe pawed through the jumble and found a roll of plastic twine. He was out of the kitchen and halfway to the stairs when he remembered Emilio. Juggling the knife and twine, he got his phone out of his pocket and stabbed a speed-dial number.

"Where the hell are you?"

"I'm just parking."

"You have your med kit with you?"

"In the dash. Why?"

"It's got sterile gloves, right? Gauze? And scissors. We need scissors."

"*Mio Dio!* What's happened?"

"A baby. That's what's happening."

"Amal? Is it Amal?"

"Yeah! Now get your ass in here!"

Callie's only experience with live birth had occurred when she was nine or ten years old. One otherwise uneventful Thursday evening, the gray-and-white cat who'd adopted her some years previously had mewled and pawed a nest in Callie's fluffy pink bedspread. With no further ado, Boots proceeded to deliver seven adorable kittens.

This birth looked to be considerably more nerve-racking for everyone involved. A panting, white-faced Amal half sat, half reclined in her favorite chair in the arts and crafts room. Hidden behind the artificial palm draped with handmade stars and silver tinsel, she'd obviously been sketching when her pains first stabbed into her. Her pencil and a head and shoulders crafted with her signature bold strokes lay at the side of the chair, kicked out of the way by Simona and Leela.

The director now knelt between Amal's knees. The center's emergency medical kit and a stack of folded white towels were close at hand. Leela crouched beside the straining woman, gripping her hand and murmuring encouragement in her precise English. Another woman, one whose name Callie couldn't remember, stood on Amal's other side and dabbed her sweat-streaked face with a cool cloth.

Other residents crowded the hall and corners of the large room. As Callie hurried past them, she thought for a heart-wrenching moment that she could tell those

who'd had—and lost—children by the mix of hope and desolation on their faces. Aching for them, she issued a breathless report.

"Scissors and some string are on the way, Simona."

"Good, because this little one's about to make his or her debut." The director was calm, cool, rock steady. "Push now, Amal. Push. Once more. Ah, there he is. I'm holding his head. One more… Wait. Wait!"

She flashed a look over her shoulder and caught Callie in a relentless stare. "Grab one of those towels. Now kneel beside me and support the baby's head. No, don't elevate it. Just hold it steady."

Still calm, still steady, the director explained what she was doing to the panting mother. "The umbilical cord is wrapped around your baby's neck. That's not uncommon. My second baby came the same way."

Callie barely registered the words. Her entire being was concentrated on the folded towel that cradled the tiny head crowned with wet, matted black hair.

"There," Simona said. "I'm loosening the cord, making the loop bigger. Now the shoulders can slip through. All right. Push."

When the baby slid into Simona's hands, none of the women in the room uttered a single sound. The incredible drama gripped Callie, too. She could hardly breathe as Simona gently turned the baby over and cleared its mouth with a gloved finger. Then the baby's lusty wail broke the spell. Relief and excitement pulsed through the room in palpable waves.

"It's a girl." The director's voice wavered for the briefest instant as she wrapped the baby in a clean towel and placed the bundle in Amal's outstretched arms. "A beautiful little girl."

Joe heard the pronouncement as he angled his way

through the crowd at the door. Carlo was right behind him, and he could hear Emilio thundering up the stairs. He wanted to believe their services weren't needed but knew they weren't in the clear yet. Someone still had to cut the cord...and take care of the afterbirth. He was hoping to hell he could pass the knife and twine to someone more qualified to perform those tasks when he caught the wail of a siren. It was followed almost instantly by Carlo's fervent prayer of thanks.

"Grazie a Dio!"

Nikki arrived on the scene the same time as the EMTs. Only too happy to yield her place to professionals, Callie pushed to her feet. As she edged around the potted palm, she spotted Amal's discarded sketch. She swooped it up to keep it from being trampled by the medical team but was too absorbed in the continuing drama to give the portrait more than a passing glance.

She was still holding it when the EMTs transferred Amal and her baby to a gurney and wheeled them out. Nikki went with them, leaving Simona to share warm hugs with Leela and the woman who'd mopped Amal's sweaty face. She hugged Callie, too, in a rare moment of pure sentiment.

As the crowd of residents slowly dispersed, Simona went into a bathroom to wash off the blood and fluids. When she came downstairs some time later, she was wearing a borrowed skirt so long it dragged the floor and a T-shirt obviously donated by the younger of the two teens. A female rock star Callie didn't recognize flashed a dazzlingly white smile across Simona's breasts.

"Good, you're still here."

She crossed to Callie, standing in the hall with Joe, Carlo, Emilio and Nikki's husband, Dominic.

"I'm sorry I railed at you earlier about the password. After you ran out, Joe told us someone hacked the case files via a remote device."

"No," Callie protested. "You were right to be angry. It was stupid of me to write the password down."

"Well, that's water under the bridge."

"It is?" Carlo asked, feigning amazement. "Am I hearing right? Is *il Drago* tempering her fire?"

"Not when it matters," Simona warned.

"Ah. Then I must assume you won't apologize to me."

"You assume right," Simona huffed. "You deserved to have your face slapped."

"I was not speaking of that." The mocking gleam in his eyes softened. "But since you mention it, *cara*, I must tell you it was worth the pain."

To the surprise and acute discomfort of their audience, a tide of red crawled up Simona's creased cheeks. She countered it with a reply that dripped unadulterated acid.

"Then what *were* you speaking of?"

"Hmm. Let me think." Carlo pretended confusion this time. "I'm trying to remember."

He glanced from Joe to Emilio to Dominic, his expression comical.

"*Santa Maria!* I must be growing senile." He turned a helpless look on Simona. "Did you…? Did you…? Help me, *cara*! Did you accuse me of having judges in my pocket?"

Her reply was a glacial stare.

Callie caught her breath as the light of battle leaped

into the prince's face. Thank God Joe intervened before blood was spilled.

"Why don't we take this to your office, Simona? I need to tell you about the call I got earlier this morning while Callie and I were on our way back to the center. I briefed her and Carlo, but you and Emilio and Dominic need to know the latest."

The director glared at him, obviously reluctant to surrender the field. But concern for her charges won out over her private war with the prince. Hitching up her ridiculously long skirt, she headed for her office.

Carlo didn't try to disguise his disappointment at her capitulation. Joe, Dominic and Emilio, however, shared a glance of profound relief. Callie ignored all four as the director's calm, steady assurances to Amal echoed in her mind.

That's not uncommon.

My second baby came the same way.

She let the others go on ahead. Simona's words kept ringing in her head.

Callie was a trained psychologist. She'd studied at two of the most reputable universities in the United States. If her ego had needed stroking, she could've hung her framed diplomas in her office. Yet every day, every client reinforced how rarely life conformed to textbook case studies.

Simona's past was obviously as complex and tortured as Joe's, yet they'd both defied the odds. Somehow, some way, they'd drawn on inner reserves to emerge stronger and more resilient than anyone would've predicted.

And Amal, or whatever her real name was. She'd given birth surrounded by strangers. No screams. No

tears. Only muffled grunts as she delivered the child she must pray would grow up in a safe, stable world.

Humbled again by Amal's courage, Callie glanced at the portrait she'd scooped off the floor. She'd almost forgotten she held it and swore softly when she saw her nervous fist had crunched the paper. Carefully, she smoothed the folds.

As before, Amal's talent astounded her. The bold, confident strokes. The clean lines. The pride and...

Wait! She knew that face! But how? Where?

She made the connection just seconds later. Amal had sketched the same face a few days ago. So arrogant. So beautiful. Then she'd slashed the sketch, over and over and over, until she'd obliterated it.

Callie had thought then—she *still* thought—the drawing represented some unidentified, unspecified male figure from Amal's past. A masculine amalgam that summarized her deep-seated hate and fear.

Yet the longer Callie stared at this portrait, the more convinced she became it wasn't an abstract rendering. This man had lived and breathed. His face was so real and alive and...

Oh, God! She'd seen him! Just the other morning! She'd spilled white chocolate espresso on his sleeve, then earned a fierce glare when she'd asked if the foam had seeped into his computer. His *laptop* computer.

Barely able to breathe, Callie gripped the sketch in suddenly icy hands. Could this man be the target? The one who'd escaped the drone strike? Had he made those online queries about the center? And hacked into the case files? The possibilities were too real and too frightening to ignore.

Her heart thumping, she hurried down the hall. A few yards from the director's office, she abruptly stopped.

She could hear the conversation inside. Joe. Simona. Joe again. Their low voices competed with the warnings now firing through her mind.

Amal had sketched this portrait here, at the center. A place that promised her sanctuary and every expectation of privacy. Was this drawing covered by client-counselor privilege? Would Callie violate that privilege if she showed it to outsiders?

As soon as the thought occurred, she killed it. If the man in this sketch was who Joe thought he might be, he represented a potential danger to Amal. Possibly everyone at the center. Callie would take full responsibility for showing the portrait to appropriate authorities.

She pushed through the door and thrust the crumpled sketch at Joe. "Amal drew this. I don't know who the man is, but I've seen him. Just a few days ago. At the café around the corner. He was having espresso… and he had a laptop with him."

The others crowded around to study the portrait.

"Anyone recognize him?" Joe asked.

When no one did, he whipped out his phone and snapped several quick shots.

"I'm forwarding these to Harden and my own people," he said, his thumbs working. "To you, too, Carlo, so you can send them to your contacts in the *polizia*. Emilio, I want you to zap a copy to every man on your crew. Have them canvass the neighborhood. Start with the café where Callie spotted this guy. And get someone to the hospital. I want a watch on Amal's room 24/7."

"Do you think she's in danger?" Simona asked sharply. "Her and the baby?"

"I don't know. Let's hope to hell she can answer that. You'd better come with me. You and Callie."

"It might be better if Emilio talks to her," Callie suggested.

Joe's glance sawed into her. "You think I might frighten her?"

The scar. He thought she was worried about the scar. Her chin lifting, she met that absurdity head-on.

"You have to admit you can be pretty intimidating when you want to," she replied calmly. "But I was thinking of yesterday morning. Emilio actually got Amal to talk to him. And she told me that she thought he had a kind face."

Joe snorted, and the others all turned to study the face under discussion. It immediately turned brick red. Thoroughly embarrassed, Emilio said gruffly that he'd be happy to accompany them to the hospital.

The Ospedale San Giovanni Addolorata was a massive complex in the heart of Rome, located right behind the Egyptian obelisk and within sight of the Colosseum. Interactive displays in the hospital's main entrance depicted its long history, while plexiglass cutouts in the tiled floor gave glimpses the long-buried ruins of the home of Emperor Marcus Aurelius's mother.

A call to Nikki confirmed that Amal and the baby had already been transferred from the ER to the maternity ward. Getting to the ward proved quite a challenge. Signs directed Callie and the others to another building, then to two different banks of elevators and, finally, to the wing containing the obstetrical delivery suites, nursery and neonatal intensive care unit. Their small group drew several glances along the way. Particularly Simona in her gaudy borrowed T-shirt, dragging skirt and flyaway dandelion hair. Blithely ignoring

the stares, she marched up to the nurses' station where Nikki was filling out forms.

"How are they?"

"Fine. The doctor has examined them both. The baby's in the nursery, and Amal's getting cleaned up a bit. I'll need some help with this paperwork." Nikki made a helpless gesture at the forms. "She still won't give us her name or any other identifying information."

"I'll talk to her. What room is she in?"

"Three twelve. Second door on the left."

When the director headed for the room, Nikki gave Callie a quick smile. "You did well this morning."

"I didn't do anything. Amal and Simona did all the work."

"Well, the result was worth their effort. The baby's beautiful."

"You said she's in the nursery?"

"She is. There's a viewing window just there, down the hall."

Nikki went back to her paperwork, Emilio went in search of coffee and Callie waited for Joe to finish checking his text messages.

"I wanted to make sure my contacts received the sketch," he told her when he finished. "They have, and they're running facial recognition programs. If he's in the system, we'll ID him."

"I'm going to see the baby. Want to come with me?"

"Sure."

The shades were up, giving an unimpeded view of the plastic bassinets in their stainless steel stands. Most were empty. The babies were probably with their moms, Callie guessed, being nursed or bathed or cuddled. Only three bassinets were occupied.

In one, the baby wore a blue stocking cap. The other

two wore pink. Both still had the scrunched-up red faces of newborns, but the baby on the left had to be Amal's. The silky black hair peeking below her stocking cap was a dead giveaway. That, and the name on the bassinet. Callie had to squint to make out the hand lettering. When she did, she caught her breath.

Simona. Amal had named her baby Simona.

The rightness of it put a smile around Callie's heart. She hoped it would put one around the director's, too.

"Which one is Amal's?" Joe asked.

"The one on the left."

"How can you tell?"

"Look at the name on the bassinet."

Like Callie, he had to squint. Unlike her, though, he wasn't as confident about the rightness of it.

"I don't know much about your boss's past," he said quietly. "Carlo doesn't, either. Only that she was married once and lost her family in some kind of natural disaster. Hard to imagine how someone who's lost so much will feel about having a namesake."

"I think she'll love it," Callie murmured. Her gaze lingered on the pink stocking cap and tufts of black hair. "Cradling that little head in my hands this morning at the moment of her birth was the most amazing thing I've ever experienced."

With a last glance at the baby, she angled away from the window.

"We haven't talked about having kids, Joe. How do you feel about having a namesake?"

"Just say the word." One of his rare smiles tipped his mouth. "Kate and Dawn would probably advise you to take a trip down the aisle first, but I'm ready any time you are."

"I'm ready, too. For both."

It took a moment for that to register. When it did, his smile became a full-fledged grin. "How does a Christmas wedding sound?"

"Oh, I would love that! But I can't fly home, even for a few days, and leave Simona in the lurch."

"So we have the wedding here."

"But…"

"Kate and Dawn. Yeah, I know. Reminds me of that old saying."

Callie arched a brow.

"If a frog had wheels, it wouldn't bump its butt."

Her other brow rose. "What does that mean?"

"Damned if I know. Gran says it all the time, though." Curling a knuckle under her chin, he tipped her face to his. "Let me work the details, Pansy Eyes. All you'll have to do is—"

"Joe! Callie!" Nikki waved to them. "Simona wants us to join her in Amal's room."

Chapter Fourteen

"He is my husband's brother."

Amal didn't look at them. Gripping the hospital blanket with white-knuckled fists, she stared at wall above their heads.

"He was to drive the car. The one that was hit. But he suspected someone had betrayed him. Coward that he is, he sent his brother to die in his place."

She dropped her gaze, glaring at them as her words gained heat and fury.

"My husband was not like him! He was gentle and kind and would have nothing to do with his brother's hate-filled friends! That's why they tricked him into driving the car. Why he followed at a safe distance, sending messages on his computer to others in their cadre, waiting to see if my husband sprang the trap they'd suspected."

Her fists convulsed on the blanket. Her face, her eyes, her body language all conveyed rage.

"He would kill me, too. I knew what he had done. He could not let me live to tell of his shameful cowardice. So I fled. And when the boat sank and I swam ashore, I told no one my name. Told no one where I'd come from."

She stopped, breathing hard and fast as the memories tore at her. Then her fire shaded to fear.

"I thought we were safe, my baby and I. Now Simona says... She says he may be here. In Rome. Is that true?"

Joe didn't pad the truth. "We think so."

"You must find him! Please! Before he finds me and my baby."

"We plan to. Until we do, Emilio will stand guard. He and the *polizia*. They'll protect you and the baby."

"I'm staying, too," Simona announced. "Callie, you'll go with Joe back to the center, won't you?"

"Of course."

"Explain what's happened to the staff and other residents. Show them the sketch and tell them to be especially aware when they go out."

They were in the SUV, just pulling up at the center, when Joe got a call from Carlo. He screeched the vehicle to a halt with a terse explanation.

"One of Emilio's crew spotted him. He's having espresso at the same little café where you bumped into him. The *polizia* are on their way. Wait here at the center."

She knew better than to suggest she should go with him. Joe didn't need to be worrying about keeping her safe. She wanted him to focus on keeping himself safe! Her heart banged against her ribs as he shouldered the door open.

"Be careful!"

"I will."

He tore off the moment she hit the keypad and was safely inside. The café was just around the corner. She would hear the sirens when the police arrived. Only if they hit the sirens, she amended. They might not want to alert him.

She had no idea how long she stayed rooted just inside the door. Her hands shoved in her pockets, she repeated again and again the wish she'd made just a few hours ago at the Trevi Fountain.

And then it was over.

No flash, no bang, no police sirens.

Just Joe pulling up in the black SUV to deliver another quick report. Callie spotted the monster vehicle through a front window and ran outside almost before he'd braked to a halt. The driver's side window whirred down, and Callie hung on the door while he shared the news.

"We got him. Bastard was too busy banging away on his laptop to realize we had him in our sights. He tried to run when the *polizia* arrived." His mouth tipped in a wolfish grin. "Didn't get far."

"Are you sure it's him? Amal's brother-in-law?"

"Almost one hundred percent. Carlo's going to the hospital with one of the police officers. They'll nail down the last one percent."

"Thank God!"

"I'm heading downtown to share what I know with the anti-terror unit." He put the SUV in gear but kept his foot on the brake. "When I get back, we need to finish the discussion we were having at the hospital. The one about namesakes and Christmas weddings."

Callie was so overjoyed that the worry and fear might

finally be over that she would have married him right there, in the street. She settled for leaning through the window and hooking an arm around him to drag him down for a kiss.

"You take care of the bad guy. I'll take care of the wedding."

Naturally, her first call was to Kate and Dawn. She couldn't wait. Still standing in the street, she woke first one, then the other and had to assure both that she hadn't yanked them from sleep because she was hurt or had been in an accident or had dumped Joe.

"Just the opposite. We're getting married."

"When?" Dawn shrieked.

"Where?" Kate yelped.

"That depends on whether Brian's corporate jet's available in the next few days."

"To fly you home?"

"To fly you guys here. I know it's short notice and you've probably got family coming for Christmas. Brian's folks, or yours and Travis's, Kate. But if you can make it, I would—"

"Don't be stupid. Of course we'll make it. Just tell us where you want us when."

"Christmas Eve. Here in Rome. I haven't worked all the details yet. I'll get back to you as soon as I do."

"What about your folks?" Dawn asked. "The jet has plenty of room if they want to come."

"Thanks for the offer. I doubt they'll want to fly over, but I'll call and check."

She gripped the phone, suddenly teary eyed with emotion and drippy nosed from the cold.

"This has been the most amazing morning," she sniffed. "I almost got fired and I helped deliver a baby.

Then Joe and Carlo took down a really, really nasty bad guy. Oh, and I tossed a coin in the Trevi Fountain. The wish is already coming true."

"All that in one morning?"

Kate sounded amazed, but Dawn zeroed in instantly on the most significant of those events.

"Hot damn! The fountain scores again."

Callie gave a watery laugh. "Okay, I'm standing on the sidewalk freezing my ass off. I've got to go inside and make a bunch more calls. I'll get back to you as soon as I firm up the arrangements. Ciao. And thank you!"

Before she could start working her growing mental list of to-dos, she had to brief Leela and Sabeen and the other residents on the visit to the hospital. They greeted the news that both mother and baby were doing fine with happy smiles.

"We will visit her," Leela declared. "And take gifts for the baby."

Callie left them making arrangements and hurried to her office to make her own. It was still too early to contact her folks, so she called Carlo, intending to just leave a voice mail asking him to call her when he could. He picked up halfway through her message.

"Oh, I'm sorry. Are you at the hospital?"

"We're still on the way. I just spoke with Joe. He tells me you're to be married. Congratulations, *mia bella*, although I can't understand why you would wish to tie yourself to such a lout when you could fly with me to—"

"Yes, yes, I know. Casablanca or Antibes or wherever. Why don't you take Simona? You know you want to."

"Ha! She would not consider it for a moment." He hesitated a beat, two. "Would she?"

"You won't know until you ask. In the meantime, I might need a favor."

"You have only to name it."

"I haven't checked yet what kind of license or permit we'll need to get married in Italy on Christmas Eve. If it turns out there's a bureaucratic tangle, do you think you could you get one of your judges to slice through it?"

"Certainly. And may I make a suggestion? My home here in the city boasts a very large salon. It would give me great pleasure if you and Joe would have the ceremony there. With a supper to follow, perhaps?"

Callie's initial thought had been to hold the ceremony here at the center. Having it at the prince's palazzo would make it a treat for the residents and so very, very special for both Joe and her.

"Oh, Carlo, thank you! That would be wonderful!"

"*Bene*! I'll take care of getting the judge to conduct the ceremony, too, if you wish. One of those many in my pay," he added drily.

"Yes, and thank you again!"

She disconnected feeling slightly dazed. In the space of ten short minutes, she'd nailed down the time, the place, the matrons of honor, the judge, the wedding supper. That left a dress…and a ring for Joe.

She knew exactly how to nail those down, too. Yanking open her desk drawer, she searched for the business card she'd brought back from Naples with her. Luckily, she got through to the buffalo ranch and reached the person she wanted on the first try.

"Ciao, Arianna. It's Callie."

"How good to hear from you. How are you enjoying Rome and your new job?"

"I love both."

"We must have lunch when I come up to Rome. Per-

haps next week, yes? I still have a few presents to buy and haven't seen the lights of the Fendi building yet."

"That's why I'm calling. Joe and I strolled down Via Condotti the other night, but those boutiques are way out of my price range. I thought maybe you could recommend a shop where I could get a wedding ring for him and a dress for me."

"But yes! I frequent many excellent shops. When is the wedding?"

"Christmas Eve. I know it's short notice, and I'm sure you have plans to spend that evening with your family, but we would love if any or all of the Audi family could attend."

"But yes!" she exclaimed again. "And I will drive up tomorrow. It's Saturday and all the Christmas shoppers will be out, so we must start early. Can you meet me at Caffè Domiziano, in the Piazza Navona? Shall we say nine o'clock?"

"I'll be there!"

Unbelievably, every hastily contrived plan came off without a hitch.

With Arianna's enthusiastic assistance, Callie found the perfect dress and a simple gold band for Joe. Carlo sent his head chef to consult with her on the menu for the wedding supper and lined up a judge to perform the ceremony. After filling out reams of paper, she and Joe obtained a special license and arranged for a representative from the US consulate to act as a witness.

When Amal and the baby returned from the hospital, the refugee broke down in tears and shared her real identity. As Callie had suspected, Rasha Hadid was a highly regarded artist whose work was on exhibit in museums in Damascus and Cairo and Athens. And now

that she no longer had to fear her brother-in-law, she could accept the position she'd been offered as an adjunct professor at the University of Thessaloniki. But first, she and the baby must attend the wedding of two to whom they owed so much.

As joyous as Rasha's return was, Callie's happiness brimmed over even more on Christmas Eve morning. She and Joe drove separate cars out to Ciampino Airport to pick up Kate and Dawn and their husbands. Joe wheeled the monster SUV. Callie drove a smaller and more manageable Fiat from Emilio's fleet. They parked at the terminal that handled executive jets and were waiting when the sleek Gulfstream with the Ellis Aeronautical Systems logo on its tail swooped in for a landing. To their delight, the first person to exit when the stairs were let down was Tommy. He raced over to them with his usual energy and promptly announced he wasn't worried about Santa finding him in Rome.

"Dad says his radar is better than the one on the Gulfstream even, 'n' he'll leave presents for Buster back at home. Doggy treats 'n' stuff. Grandma and Granddad are taking care of him. They're gonna make sure he doesn't eat poop. Dogs do that sometimes."

"Good to know," Joe said solemnly, then shook hands with Travis and Brian. "Thanks for making the trip on such short notice."

"No way we could miss seeing the last of the Inseparables bite the dust," Travis assured him. He nodded to the three women wrapped in a fierce group hug punctuated by sniffles and tears of joy. "How long has it been since they've seen each other? Three weeks?"

"Closer to two," Brian drawled.

When they finally untangled, Callie gave all four males a quick kiss before sweeping Dawn and Kate

toward the Fiat. "Six o'clock. Carlo's palazzo. See you there."

"Yeah," Joe confirmed, "you will."

Callie steered through Rome's center with maximum concentration and minimal wrong turns. Kate and Dawn twisted to see the Fendi building as they zipped past. The decorations weren't as awesome in daylight as in the photo Callie had texted, but they both vowed to hit the high-end shopping street before they flew back to the States. Fifteen minutes later Callie squeezed into a parking spot and took them up to her apartment.

They oohed over the warm yellow walls and ahhed over the view of St. Peter's from the tiny balcony. Then they shed their coats and got down to the serious business of checking out the contents of the boxes sitting on the bed and the dress bag hanging on the closet door.

Chapter Fifteen

Callie couldn't have imagined a more stunning setting for a wedding than Carlo's palazzo. When she and Kate and Dawn emerged from the limo Joe had sent to pick them up, they had to fight to keep from gawking at the elegant facade and butler who'd been waiting for them. As tall and aristocratic as his employer was short and muscular, the tuxedoed majordomo bowed and ushered them inside.

He must have sent some silent signal to the prince. As Callie and Kate and Dawn were shedding their coats, Carlo descended a flight of marble stairs wide enough to drive a tractor up. Looking astonishingly royal in a dress uniform crossed by a red sash studded with glittering medals and decorations, he greeted Kate and Dawn with kisses to both hands and cheeks.

His greeting to the bride was no less extravagant. "Ah, Clarissa. You look so beautiful. Are you sure you—"

"Yes," she interrupted hastily, cutting him off be-

fore he could make yet another offer to whisk her off to parts unknown. "I'm sure."

But she had to repeat her suggestion of a few days ago. "Why don't you take Simona? You know you want to."

"I did ask her," he answered with a scowl. "Her reply still burns my ears."

Laughing, Callie stooped to drop a kiss on his cheek. "I know you. You're too much like Joe to take no for an answer."

"Perhaps. Perhaps not. But now…" He crooked his arm. "You break my heart, Clarissa, but do me such great honor by asking me to give you away. Shall we go upstairs?"

Her friends led the way. Dawn had brought a gown in her favorite green. Kate wore one of deep crimson. The rich hues formed a glowing complement to the garlands draping the stone balustrade. Callie's heart tripped as she mounted the marble stairs under the watchful eyes of what looked like ten or twelve generations of Carlo's ancestors.

Banks of poinsettias ringed the second-floor landing. As Carlo led her past the glorious color, Callie could hear an unseen baritone singing "Santa Lucia." She'd now adopted the hymn as her own personal anthem. The baritone was good, she acknowledged, but she intended to download Elvis's version the next time she logged into iTunes.

Then the same majordomo who'd met them downstairs opened a set of double doors. Beyond was a salon as long as the nave of a cathedral and almost as high ceilinged. Rows of gilt-edged chairs lined the salon's parquet floor. Callie blinked in surprise when she saw every seat was filled.

As though perfectly timed, the hymn finished and a string quartet launched into Mendelssohn's wedding march. Carlo squeezed Callie's arm and they followed Kate and Dawn down the aisle between the chairs. She

smiled as she recognized the guests. Emilio and his crew. Marcello Audi, his daughter, Arianna, with her husband and kids. Sabeen and Leela and the other residents of the center. Amal and her baby in the second row with Simona.

Callie had to suppress a gasp at the director's altered appearance. Simona had tamed her flyaway hair and actually applied some lip gloss and blush. Even more astonishing, her floor-length skirt and fitted jacket of wine-colored velvet looked as though they might come from one of the boutiques on Via Condotti. Callie felt Carlo's start of surprise and had to hide a grin.

Travis and Brian and Tommy were in the front row. The men smiled and the boy beamed as Callie floated past. They were her family now, as much as Kate and Dawn. Integral threads in the fabric of her life.

But it was the man waiting for her at the end of the aisle who filled her heart. So tall, so awesome in his hand-tailored tux. Her very own Louis Jourdan, Callie thought with a lump in her throat.

"I must ask," the prince murmured, pressing her arm to his side. "Are you *sure* you're sure?"

She gave a helpless laugh. "Oh, Carlo. I've never been surer of anything in my life."

Then she put her hand in Joe's, and her Christmas wish came true.

* * * * *

LET'S TALK

Romance

For exclusive extracts, competitions
and special offers, find us online:

f facebook.com/millsandboon

🐦 @MillsandBoon

📷 @MillsandBoonUK

Get in touch on 01413 063232